Carmichael, Andrew Williams

Practical ship Production

Carmichael, Andrew Williams

Practical ship Production

Inktank publishing, 2018

www.inktank-publishing.com

ISBN/EAN: 9783750142800

PRACTICAL SHIP PRODUCTION

BY

A. W. CARMICHAEL,

LIEUTENANT COMMANDER, CONSTRUCTION CORPS, U. S. NAVY.
MEMBER SOCIETY OF NAVAL ARCHITECTS AND MARINE ENGINEERS.

FIRST EDITION

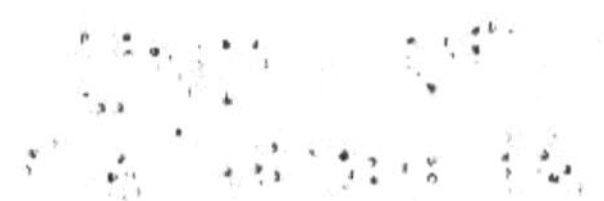

McGRAW-HILL BOOK COMPANY, INC.
239 WEST 39TH STREET. NEW YORK

LONDON: HILL PUBLISHING CO., LTD.
6 & 8 BOUVERIE ST., E. C.
1919

PREFACE

The purpose of this book is to present in convenient form the most important general principles of ship design, with which every naval architect should be familiar, and to describe the various processes in connection with the building of ships. Its nature is intended to be practical rather than theoretical, it being assumed that the principal problem with which the reader is concerned is the quick production of seagoing vessels from plans already in existence rather than the preparation of new plans.

The recent unprecedented increase in shipbuilding in the United States has resulted in a corresponding demand for workmen, draftsmen, and naval architects. It has therefore become necessary for many engineers and technical men, who have never before been confronted with shipbuilding problems, to transfer their activities from the fields of the various other engineering professions to those of the marine engineer and naval architect. These men are familiar with mechanical processes and have the necessary groundwork in theoretical and applied mathematics to fit them for duties in connection with the production of ships, but lack familiarity with those matters that are peculiar to shipbuilding. It is hoped that this book may aid in furnishing, in compact form, some of the more essential parts of this information. It should also be of value to workmen in shipyards who have only such knowledge of the shipbuilding industry as they have gained from practical experience, and who desire to fit themselves for higher positions.

It is manifestly impossible to include in a single volume even a most cursory treatment of all the subjects that are involved in the profession of naval architecture. Since, however, matters of construction are to be considered more fully than matters of design, it has been possible to include enough matter to give a fairly complete general description of the various processes in the production of a modern steel vessel. A certain amount of space has been devoted to matters of a theoretical nature, but only in so far as it has been believed that these would be necessary for a proper understanding of the methods of construction.

Certain diagrams, sketches and illustrations have been inserted where they were considered necessary for a proper understanding of the subject under discussion. Some of the sketches are not accurately proportioned, having been roughly drawn merely for the purpose of showing the principles involved. They should in no sense be considered as working drawings.

The subject matter presented is not new, but has been gleaned from many different sources. This book is in the nature of an introduction to a subject upon which many books have been written and of which a complete knowledge can be gained only by reference to these books, and by extended experience.

CONTENTS

PAGE
PREFACE v

CHAPTER I

REQUIREMENTS OF SHIPS

Introductory 1
Buoyancy 3
Stability 5
Propulsion 11
Steering 20
Strength 22
Endurance 28
Utility 29

CHAPTER II

GENERAL DESCRIPTION OF SHIPS

Form 31
General arrangement 41
Types 50
Tonnage 61
Materials used in construction 63

CHAPTER III

STRUCTURAL MEMBERS OF SHIPS

Transverse and longitudinal framing 77
Stem, stern post, rudder, etc. 91
Shell plating and inner bottom 106
Decks 114
Bulkheads 121
Miscellaneous 124

CHAPTER IV

DESIGN OF SHIPS

Conditions to be fulfilled 130
Choice of principal elements 132
Construction of lines and distribution of weights 133
Principal plans 134
Final calculations 136
Detail plans and specifications 146

CHAPTER V

SHIPYARDS

PAGE
Site for shipyard 147
Building slip and launching ways 156
Yard layout, shops, storehouses, etc. 157
Shipyard machine tools, etc. 163
Personnel of a shipyard 169
Management 178

CHAPTER VI

PRELIMINARY STEPS IN SHIP CONSTRUCTION

Ordering material 180
Molds, templates, patterns, etc. 182
Fabrication of material 185

CHAPTER VII

THE BUILDING OF SHIPS

Erection 195
Bolting-up, drilling and reaming 204
Riveting 209
Chipping, calking and testing 219
Protection against corrosion 224
Welding. 227
Launching. 231
Fitting out 237

INDEX 243

LIST OF ILLUSTRATIONS

Fig. No. — Page

1. Rectangular floating log . . . 1
2. Forces acting on floating log . . . 3
3. Centre of gravity and centre of buoyancy . . . 5
4. Change in position of G caused by load on top of log . . . 6
5. Transverse metacentre . . . 6
6. Pendulum . . . 8
7. Variation of righting arm . . . 9
8. Log hollowed out to form a vessel . . . 11
9. Stream lines . . . 12
10. Developments of ship forms . . . 13
11. "Similar" ships . . . 16
12. Rudder . . . 20
13. Solid and built-up hulls . . . 23
14. Sagging and hogging . . . 25
15. Curves for strength calculation . . . 26
16. "Lines" of a ship . . . 33
17. Parts of a ship . . . 38
18. Inboard profile of cargo steamer . . . 43
19. Types of ships . . . 59
20. Shipbuilding shapes . . . 65
21. Rivets . . . 67
22. Types of keels . . . 77
23. Simple transverse framing . . . 80
24. Transverse framing . . . 81
25. Frame, reverse frame, and floor plate . . . 82
26. Intercostal side keelson . . . 84
27. Side stringer . . . 85
28. Cross section of a ship showing longitudinal framing . . . 86
29. Diagrammatic view of cellular double bottom framing . . . 86
30. Cross section of double bottom . . . 87
31. Cross section of cellular double bottom with intercostal longitudinals . . . 87
32. Longitudinal section of cellular double bottom showing intercostal longitudinal . . . 88
33. Bracket floor . . . 89
34. Watertight floor, cut by continuous longitudinals . . . 89
35. Stern post and stem . . . 92
36. Cross section of lower portion of cast stem . . . 93
37. Solid cast rudder . . . 95
38. Single plate built up rudder . . . 97

FIG. No. PAGE
39. Cast frame of side plate rudder . . . 98
40. Pintle . . . 99
41. Rudder carrier, etc. . . . 100
42. Bossing and stern framing . . . 101
43. Bossing of a twin screw vessel. . . . 103
44. Propeller struts . . . 104
45. Stern tube . . . 105
46. Arrangement of plates in shell plating . . . 108
47. Systems of shell plating. . . . 109
48. Butt lap with tapered liner (seen from outside) . . . 110
49. Butt lap—one plate tapered and chambered (seen from inside) 110
50. Stealer . . . 112
51. Bulkhead liner . . . 113
52. Connections of deck beams to frames. . . . 114
53. Deck beams and carlings . . . 115
54. Connections at sides of watertight decks . . . 116
55. Butt of deck planking over steel deck . . . 117
56. Stanchion. . . . 119
57. Deck girders . . . 120
58. Covers for openings in watertight decks . . . 121
59. Bulkhead. . . . 123
60. Portion of engine foundation . . . 125
61. Boiler saddles . . . 126
62. Hawse pipe . . . 127
63. Bitts and chock . . . 128
64. Rail bulwarks, fenders, docking keel, bilge keels . . . 129
65. Value of *BM* . . . 137
66. Atwood's formula . . . 139
67. Methods of integration. . . . 144
68. Making a shipyard. . . . 149
69. Building slips . . . 151
70. Keel blocks and piling . . . 152
71. Ship on launching ways . . . 153
72. Launching . . . 154
73. Shipyard of the Submarine Boat Corporation . . . 160
74. Operation of shipyard machine tools . . . 164
75. Fabricated parts. . . . 167
76. Shipfitting work. . . . 174
77. Template and mold . . . 184
78. Portion of bending slab, showing frame bending . . . 189
79. Frame beveling . . . 190
80. Flat and centre vertical keel plates in place on blocks . . . 196
81. Drifting . . . 197
82. Erecting double bottom framing. . . . 198
83. Portion of double bottom framing completely erected . . . 198
84. Ship in early stage of construction . . . 199
85. View from stern, showing frames, deck beams, and shaft tunnel. . 201
86. Cross section of building slip . . . 202

Fig. No. Page
87. Wooden ship under construction 203
88. Reaming 206
89. Effect of unfair rivet holes and improper reaming 207
90. Method of using pneumatic drilling machine 208
91. Driving a rivet 210
92. Improperly driven rivets 211
93. Safe and unsafe loading of ropes 212
94. Safe and unsafe loading of riveted joints 213
95. Cutting out rivets 215
96. Tap rivets 217
97. Calking 220
98. Red lead putty gun 223
99. Electric quasi-arc welding 230
100. Forces acting on ships during launching 233
101. Inclining experiment 239

PRACTICAL SHIP PRODUCTION

CHAPTER I

REQUIREMENTS OF SHIPS

INTRODUCTORY

A *ship* may be defined as a large seagoing vessel. In other words, it is a structure that will float and is capable of making ocean voyages. Its purpose is to furnish a means for over-water transportation. It may be considered as an enlarged boat. It is convenient, however,

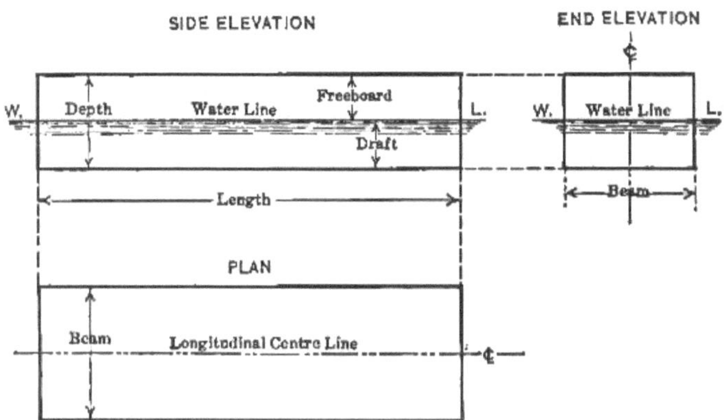

Fig. 1.—Rectangular floating log.

at the start to consider it as a large floating log, as shown in the three views of Fig. 1.

Referring to this figure, the following should be noted: the three principal dimensions are *length, beam,* and *depth.*

The *length* is the greatest dimension and is measured horizontally.

The *beam* is the breadth and is measured horizontally

at right angles to the length, or as it is usually expressed, *athwartships*.

The *depth* is measured vertically or at right angles to the surface of the water.

The form is shown by the three views in the figure: side elevation, end elevation, and plan. (These plans are usually called by other names in the case of a ship, as will be seen later.)

As the plane of the surface of the water is horizontal, the intersections of this plane with the log appear in the side and end elevations as straight horizontal lines. Each of these lines is called the *water line*, and each is usually marked by a "*W*" at one end and "*L*" at the other.

The intersections of a vertical longitudinal plane through the longitudinal axis of the log with the log's form appear as straight lines, the one in the end elevation being vertical and the one in the plan being horizontal. They are usually marked "℄" as shown in the figure, and are called *centre lines*. The *draft* is the vertical distance to which the *log* is immersed. The *freeboard* is the vertical distance that the log projects above the surface of the water.

It is assumed that the log has a uniform rectangular section and that it is homogeneous and lighter than water. It will also be noted that it floats with its wider side horizontal. The reasons for this will be given later.

Such a log represents the simplest form of floating body from which has been gradually developed the modern ship, and in the following pages the various steps in the evolution of such a ship from a simple floating body will be traced and the various requirements of all ships will be discussed. These requirements are as follows:

Buoyancy.
Stability.
Propulsion.
Steering.
Strength.
Endurance.
Utility.

1. BUOYANCY

Consider a log floating in equilibrium in perfectly still water, as shown in Fig. 1. Assume that the specific gravity of the log with respect to the water in which it floats is 0.5. A cross section of the log is shown in Fig. 2. When it is floating thus at rest and in equilibrium, the forces on the log will be balanced as follows:

First.—The forces of the water on the two ends will balance each other.

Second.—The forces of the water on the two sides will balance each other.

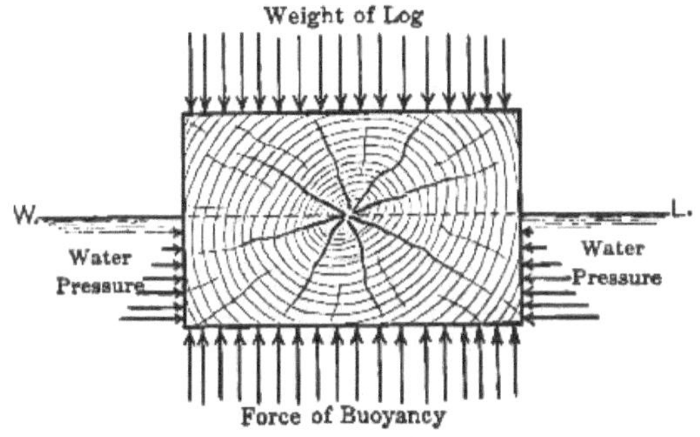

Fig. 2.—Forces acting on floating log.

Third.—The upward pressure of the water uniformly distributed over the bottom of the log will be balanced by the uniformly distributed weight of the log acting vertically downward as shown in the figure.

It is therefore clear that the upward force of the water pressure—which is called the *buoyancy*—is exactly equal to the weight of the log. But if the space occupied by the immersed portion of the log be replaced by water, the condition of equilibrium remains unchanged, and therefore the upward force of the pressure of the water acting on the bottom of the log is exactly equal to the weight of the water displaced by the log, which is, in turn, equal to the weight of the log itself.

This is known as the "Law of Floating Bodies," and the proof given above for the case of a floating body of simple rectangular form may be extended to that of a body of any form by the method of resolution of forces. This law may be briefly stated for all ships as follows:

The weight of any ship floating in water, including all that she carries, must equal the weight of the water that she displaces.

When the draft at which any ship floats is known, it is possible to calculate the volume of the ship that is below the surface of the water. The weight of the ship plus all that she carries can thus be obtained, provided the density of the water in which she floats is known.

In the case of the log referred to above (which has a density of 0.5), it is clear that the log will be half above and half below the water, since the weight of an amount of water of one-half of the volume of the log is equal to the total weight of the log. If the density of the log be increased, the amount of the log immersed increases, and if the density becomes greater than 1.0 the log will sink. Similarly, if the weight of a ship with everything that she carries becomes greater than the weight of the volume of water that she is capable of displacing, she will sink.

The total weight of the log may be considered as acting vertically downward through its centre of gravity, and the equal force of buoyancy as acting vertically upward through the centre of gravity of the displaced water, or the centre of figure of the under water portion of the log. This point is called the *centre of buoyancy.* The centre of gravity of a floating object is usually called G, and the centre of buoyancy, *B*. In the case of the log, *G* is at the centre of the cross section and *B* is halfway between *G* and the bottom of the log. (See Fig. 3.)

Since the force of buoyancy acts vertically upward and the weight of the log acts vertically downward, it is clear that for equilibrium *G* and *B* must be in the same vertical line, for, were this not the case, there would be a couple tending to produce rotation, and equilibrium would no longer exist.

This is another important law of floating bodies, and may be briefly stated: *The centre of gravity and the centre of buoyancy of a ship floating in equilibrium in still water must be in the same vertical line.*

For the two principles just enunciated to be strictly true, it is necessary that the water be entirely displaced by the portion of the floating body that is under water. The "skin" of a ship must therefore be absolutely water-tight. The requirements of buoyancy for all ships and other craft may then be summarized as follows: *The vessel must be so designed and constructed that it will float, in equilibrium, in such a position as to displace by its hull an amount of water equal to its own weight.*

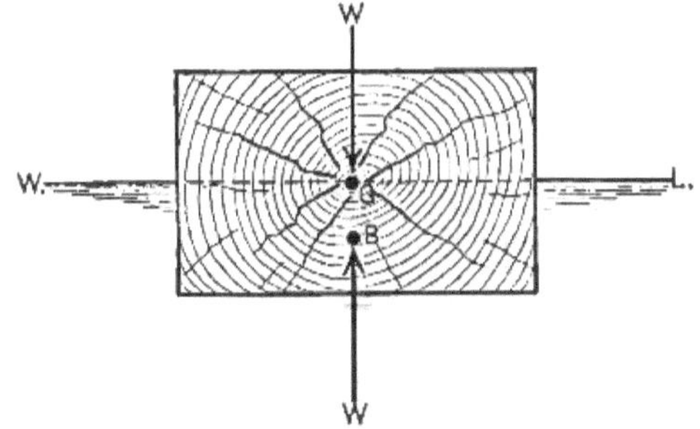

FIG. 3.—Centre of gravity and centre of buoyancy.

A simple rectangular log of the shape shown in the preceding sketches fulfils this requirement, and such a log, if of sufficient size, might be used as a means for transporting merchandise or men over smooth bodies of water. It is probable that the first crude means of over-water transportation were logs. There are, however, certain practical difficulties in the way of this means, the principal of which is lack of *stability*—a quality which will be next discussed.

2. STABILITY

Let it be assumed that the log be loaded so that it sinks to a position as shown in Fig. 4, and let the total weight of the log and its load be W. The centre of buoyancy B will be at the centre of figure of the immersed cross section, (Fig. 4 being assumed to be a transverse section through the middle of the log), but owing to the added weight on the top of the log, the position of the centre of gravity of the

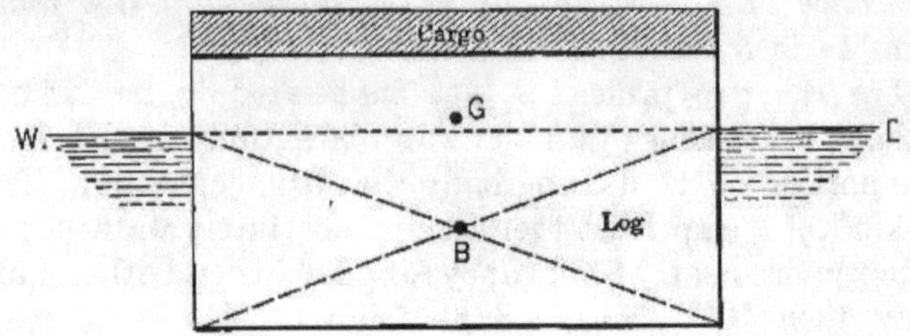

FIG. 4.—Change in position of G caused by load on top of log.

log and load will be higher than that of the log only. Any weight placed on the top of the log will tend to make it "top heavy."

Suppose that the log and load be inclined from the vertical position, by some external force, to the position shown

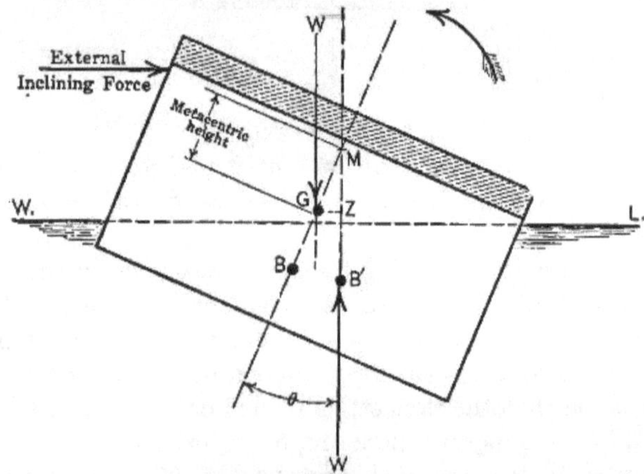

FIG. 5.—Transverse metacentre.

in Fig. 5. The centre of buoyancy, which is the centre of figure of the immersed portion of the log, will move from B, relative to the log, to some position, such as B'. The centre of gravity, G, however, remains unchanged relative to the log. Since the weight of the log and its load W and the force of buoyancy must still be equal, there will be set up a couple, of force W, and arm GZ, GZ being the distance between the vertical lines through G and B'. If the vertical through B' intersects the line BG above G, this couple will tend to produce rotation in the direction shown by the curved arrow and to right the log. If it intersects BG below G it will tend to produce rotation in the opposite direction, and to capsize the log. If it intersects it at G, there will be no couple and no tendency to rotation in either direction.

The first condition (before the external force was applied) is called one of *stable equilibrium;* the second, one of *unstable equilibrium;* and the third, one of *neutral equilibrium.*

The point M at which the vertical through B' intersects the line BG, is called the *transverse metacentre,* or often simply the *metacentre.* The distance GZ is called the *righting arm* and it will be noted that the greater the length GZ the greater will be the couple tending to right the log. Also, if θ be the angle to which the log is inclined GZ equals $GM \sin \theta$, so that for any given inclination the greater the length of the righting arm the greater will be the value of GM. The position of M remains practically constant for small angles of inclination (up to say 10°) and the length GM for such angles is known as the *metacentric height.*

The higher M is above G, the greater will be the value of GM, the metacentric height, and of the righting arm, and consequently the greater will be the tendency of the log to right itself when slightly inclined from the upright position.

It is apparent from the above that the amount of weight that can be carried on top of the log without unduly reducing the value of the metacentric height, and hence the tendency for the log to remain upright, is very limited. This tendency to remain upright is called *initial stability.* Since all weight added to the log *above* its own centre of gravity will result in the location of the combined centre of gravity moving upward, and since M is above G, to start with, the addition of weight on top of the log will reduce the metacentric height, GM.

The metacentric height of any vessel is therefore a very important characteristic, since it is a measure of the vessel's initial stability, or safety against capsizing. The vessel may be considered as a pendulum of which M is the point of support and G the point at which the total mass may be conceived as concentrated. If M be moved down to G the pendulum will pass from a position of stable to one of neutral equilibrium. The instant M passes below G, the equilibrium becomes unstable. (See Fig. 6.)

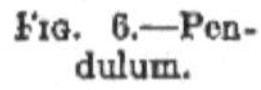

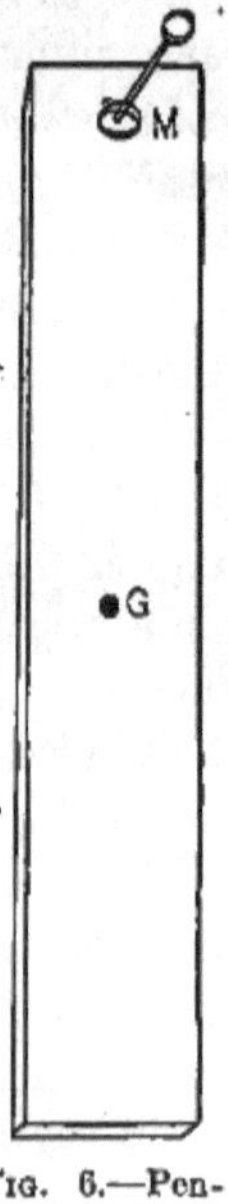

Fig. 6.—Pendulum.

The metacentric height is, however, important only in that it is a measure of the initial righting arm. The righting arm multiplied by the total weight of the floating body gives the value of the moment tending to prevent capsizing. For angles of inclination greater than about 10° the position of the metacentre changes, so that the righting arm itself must be considered.

Let it be assumed that the log be loaded in such a way that its total weight, including the load, be W, and that its centre of gravity be as shown in Fig. 7 (1). Now let it be supposed that the log be inclined by some external horizontal force so that it passes successively through the five positions shown in Fig. 7 (1), (2), (3), (4), and (5). It will be noted that when the log is upright in the water the value of the righting arm GZ is zero, since the forces of the weight and the buoyancy both act in the same vertical line. As the log is first inclined, the length of the righting arm increases at a comparatively rapid rate, as shown in Fig. 7 (2). This is due to the fact that the centre of buoyancy is moving to the right of the figure on account of the increased immersed volume of the log on that side, the centre of buoyancy being the geometrical centre of figure of that immersed volume. It will be noted that after the right hand upper edge of the log is immersed, the movement of B toward the right still continues, but at a diminishing rate, because of the water now above the corner which causes the immersed centre of figure to slow down in its movement to the right. An inclination will finally be reached (as shown in Fig. 7 (3)) at which the righting arm is a maximum, and its rate of increase is zero. Any further inclination will produce a diminution in the righting arm which has already become smaller when the position shown at Fig. 7 (4) has been reached. Finally, at some such inclination as that shown in Fig. 7 (5), the righting arm will again become zero and the stability will vanish.

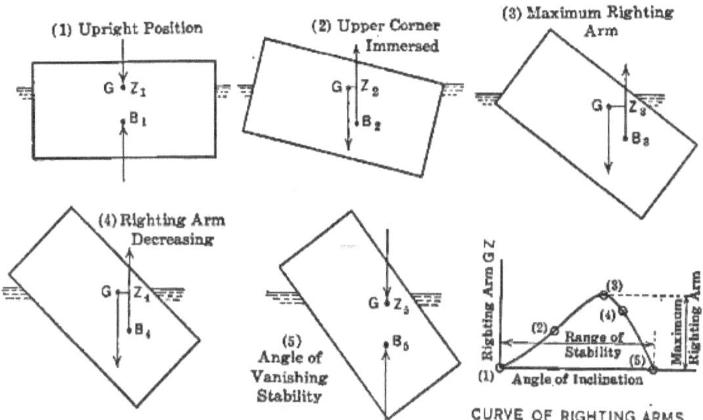

Fig. 7.—Variation of righting arm.

This inclination at which the stability vanishes is called the *angle of vanishing stability* or *range of stability*, and the inclination at which the righting arm is a maximum is called the *angle of maximum stability*. A curve is plotted in Fig. 7 showing how the righting arm increases to a maximum, diminishes, and finally vanishes as the inclination increases from that shown in sketch (1) to that shown in sketch (5). From this curve it will be noted that the maximum righting moment occurs when the log is inclined to an angle of about 35° from its upright position, and that if the log be inclined to an angle much greater than 50° from the upright it will capsize.

These considerations which have been discussed in connection with the simple rectangular log, apply to all floating bodies, but in the case of ships and other vessels of irregular form, the mathematical calculations involved in obtaining values of the righting arms for various angles of heel become much more involved. It should also be noted that as well as being inclined transversely, the vessel may be at the same time inclined longitudinally, thus making the problem still more difficult. For practical purposes, however, in the case of ships it is usually sufficient to consider transverse inclinations only, since the length of ordinary ships is so much greater than their beam that their longitudinal stability is always ample.

The elementary principles of stability enunciated above having been carefully considered it will be noted that the use of a log loaded on its top as a means for over-water transportation is very limited. If the weight be placed on the top, the centre of gravity will be raised and the initial stability consequently reduced. Also, the angle to which the loaded log may be safely inclined depends further upon the proportions of the log. Referring to Fig. 7, it will be noted that the amount of the log above water determines the point (2) at which the rate of increase of the righting arm commences to diminish and thus influences the range of stability (since that is the point at which the upper edge of the log becomes immersed). Furthermore, the width of the log influences the maximum righting arm since the point B_3 will be farther to the right, and the length GZ_3 (in Fig. 7 (3)) greater if the width of the log be greater. Also, the higher the position in the log of G, which is the centre of gravity, the smaller will be the righting arm.

The following points are therefore apparent from the standpoint of stability: first, the width of the log should, as a general rule, be greater than the depth; second, the amount of the log above the water should not be too small; and third, the centre of gravity of the log and all that it carries should be kept as low as possible.

These considerations led to the first step in the evolution

of *vessels* or floating objects *hollowed out*. By these means it becomes possible to carry the same load with the position of the centre of gravity much lower, thus increasing the stability and still retaining practically the same freeboard. (See Fig. 8.)

A hollowed-out log or dug-out, the rude canoe of prehistoric man, was the first boat. As the need for larger craft was felt, it became necessary to use more than one piece of material, and canoes were then fabricated of wood, skins, bark, and other materials. But the object to be attained was still the same—to secure a hollow structure that would keep out the water and permit a larger weight

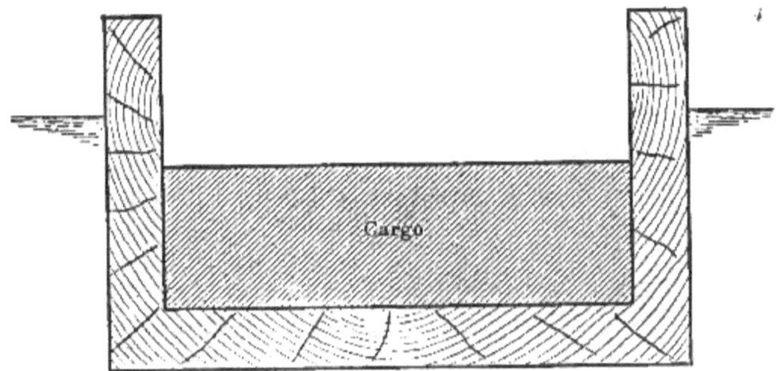

Fig. 8.—Log hollowed out to form a vessel.

to be carried without endangering the buoyancy and stability. Consideration may now pass from the rectangular log to built-up, box-shaped vessels, which have the same external form and possess the first two requirements of a ship, buoyancy and stability. Such vessels can be safely loaded with large and heavy cargoes, but still are of little practical value unless they can be moved from place to place by water.

3. PROPULSION

It is apparent from an inspection of Fig. 1, which may now be considered as representing a large water-tight floating box, that the water would offer considerable resistance in case it were attempted to move such a vessel from place to place. It would, of course, be natural to move the vessel endwise rather than sidewise, but even so, the square ends would offer a great resistance to the water. Figure 9 shows the paths of the particles of water relative to such a vessel moving in the direction indicated by the arrow. These paths of the water particles are known as *stream lines.* The end of the vessel that enters the water is called the *bow,* and the other end, the *stern.* Owing to the sudden change of direction of the stream lines at the bow and stern, considerable energy must be expended in driving

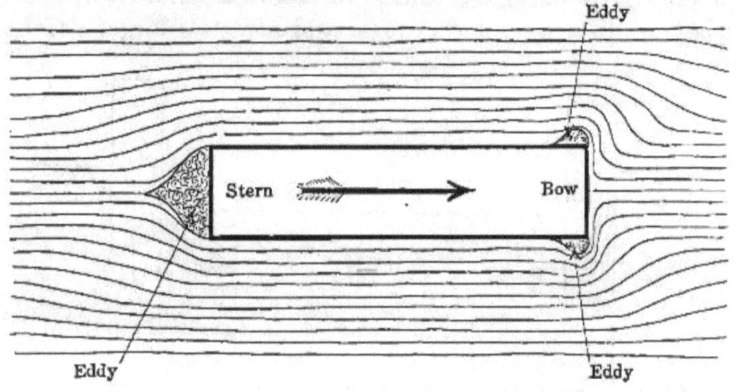

Fig. 9.—Stream lines.

or towing such a vessel through the water. Part of this energy is expended in *wave making,* part in *eddy making,* and part in overcoming the *friction* of the water in contact with the sides, ends, and bottom of the vessel.

In order to reduce these various forms of resistance as much as possible, it is desirable to change the form and reduce the length of the stream lines. This consideration naturally leads to the sharpening of the bow and the tapering of the stern of the vessel, as shown in Fig. 10 (*a*), and a further development is to make the outline a smooth curve, as shown in Fig. 10 (*b*). For similar reasons it is natural to round off the lower edges, or, as they are called, the *bilges* of the vessel, as shown in Fig. 10 (*c*). These changes, and other similar ones made from time to time, have resulted in the present *ship-shape* form of most vessels. The most important of these changes, however, have been made at the ends, and most vessels still retain in their middle portion a form that is practically box shaped. This is particularly true of slow moving vessels, such as tramp steamers, oil tankers, barges, etc.

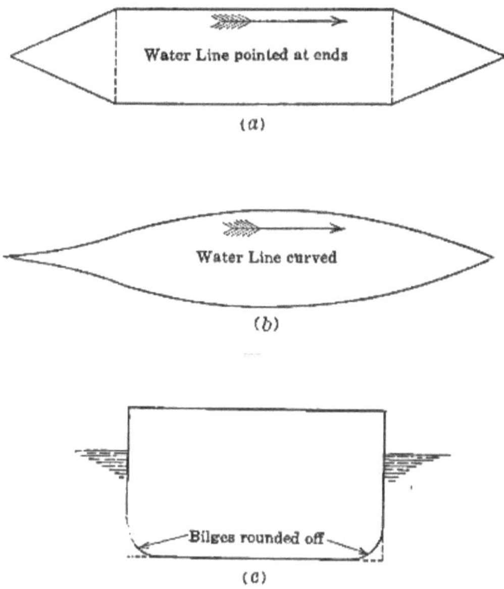

FIG. 10.—Developments of ship forms.

Having given the vessel a ship-shape form, it is now possible to have it move from place to place without such an uneconomical expenditure of energy.

Among the first means of propulsion of boats and other small craft were *poles, paddles,* and *oars,* and finally, *sails.* It is also possible to tow one vessel by a *tow line* from another, or from the banks of a canal. Since the introduction of steam, however, and with the increase in size of vessels, the majority of all but the smallest have been propelled by machinery—at first through the medium of *paddle wheels*, and finally, by the more efficient means of *screw propellers*. (Another means is that of the jet propeller, by which a stream of water is forced outwards from the hull so as to drive the vessel ahead, but this method has never been extensively used).

At the present time practically all self-propelled vessels are driven through the water by means of screw propellers mounted on shafts at their sterns. The shafts may be rotated by means of gasoline, kerosene, oil, or other internal combustion motors, by steam engines of the reciprocating type, by steam turbines with or without reduction gearing, or by electric motors.

The action of the screw propeller may be compared to that of a screw or threaded bolt. Any motion of rotation of the bolt is accompanied by a corresponding motion of translation along its axis. The surfaces of the blades of a screw propeller are simply portions of the surface of a helix or screw, the difference in the action of the propeller from that of a screw in a solid nut being largely due to the *slipping* of the propeller in the surrounding water.

It is possible to determine in advance what will be the effect of a certain propeller in driving a given vessel through the water, provided the amount of power that will be applied to it be known. When a vessel is to be driven by a screw propeller (or by two or more such propellers) it is therefore a great advantage to be able to know in advance how much power will be required to propel the vessel at the desired speed. This is one of the most important considerations in the design of a ship, especially where speed is an important requirement, since the power required will determine the amount of weight and space that must be devoted to engines, boilers, etc. The method in common use for determining the power required for a given ship is known as the *method of comparison*.

For an explanation of this method, a few simple mechanical laws must be considered. *Power* is the rate at which work is done, and *work* is measured by the force acting multiplied by the distance through which it acts. In the case of a ship the force acting must be a force equivalent to the resistance to motion offered by the water through which the ship is driven, the distance being the distance through which the ship moves.

If it is desired to design an engine to hoist a given weight at a certain specified speed, the problem is a simple one, since the power required is simply the product of the speed times the weight or force to be overcome. In the case of a ship, however, the problem is not so simple since the resistance offered to the ship's motion is influenced to a considerable extent by the action of the particles of water through which the ship passes.

A mathematical calculation of the resistance of a ship, even of the simplest form is a very difficult problem, and with the practically infinite number of different forms that it is possible to give to a ship, the problem becomes still further involved. It has therefore been found more desirable to determine the power required to drive a given ship by the practical method of comparison. For instance, if one ship is to be built the exact duplicate, in all respects, of another ship that has already been built and put into service, then the power of the engines required for the contemplated ship, in order to drive her at the same speed as the completed ship under exactly similar conditions, should be the same. This is the simplest case. If the contemplated ship is to have the same form and proportions as the completed ship, but is to be either larger or smaller, it is natural to assume that there must be some law by means of which the two ships can be compared so as to determine in advance the power that will be required for the contemplated ship.

Let it be assumed that it is proposed to build a ship of exactly the same form and proportions as those of another ship already completed and data regarding the performance of which is available, the length of the proposed ship, however, to be different from that of the completed ship. The two ships are shown in Fig. 11, and calling them ships "No. 1" and "No. 2," as indicated, let it be assumed that "No. 2" is n times as long as "No. 1." Then referring to Fig. 11, the lengths, beams, and depths of the two ships are as follows: L, nL, B, nB, D, nD, respectively. The area of the rectangle circumscribing ship "No. 1" is $B \times L$, and ship "No. 2" is $nB \times nL$ or n^2BL. The volume of ship "No. 1" is a certain proportion of $L \times B \times D$, and the volume of ship "No. 2" is the same proportion of $nL \times nB \times nD$, or n^3LBD. In other words, the ratio on ships "Nos. 2" and "1" of corresponding linear measurements is n, of corresponding surface measurements is n^2, and of corresponding volumetric measurements is n^3. The volume of water displaced by ship "No. 2" is thus n^3 times as great as that displaced by "No. 1," and consequently, the weight, or, as it is

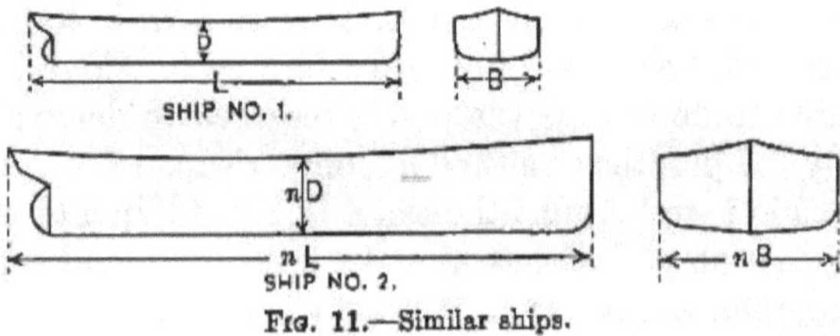

Fig. 11.—Similar ships.

usually called, the *displacement*, of "No. 2" is n^3 times that of "No. 1." Displacement of "No. 1" equals W; displacement of "No. 2" equals n^3W.

The displacement being a weight, is also a force, and therefore should be expressed in the same units as the resistance, which is also a force. Consequently, if R be the resistance of ship "No. 1," the resistance of ship "No. 2" should be n^3R.

Let the speed of ship "No. 1" be V_1 and that of ship "No. 2" be V_2. Speed is the distance through which the vessel moves per unit of time, or if t_1 is the length of time required by ship "No. 1" to travel forward a distance equal to its own length, and t_2 the time required by ship "No. 2" to travel forward a distance equal to its own length, then

$$\frac{V_1}{V_2} = \frac{\frac{L}{t_1}}{\frac{nL}{t_2}} = \frac{t_2}{t_1} \times \frac{1}{n}$$

Let the accelerations of ships "Nos. 1" and "2" be, respectively, $\propto_1$, and $\propto_2$. Acceleration is by definition, *rate of increase of velocity;*

$$\therefore \frac{\propto_1}{\propto_2} = \frac{\frac{V_1}{t_1}}{\frac{V_2}{t_2}} = \frac{V_1}{V_2} \times \frac{t_2}{t_1} = \frac{t_2^2}{nt_1^2}$$

Assuming that gravity is constant, the masses of ships "Nos. 1" and "2" are proportionate to their weights, or M_1 and M_2 are their respective masses, then

$$\frac{M_1}{M_2} = \frac{W}{n^3W} = \frac{1}{n^3}$$

The respective resistances being forces, may be expressed as the products of their respective masses and accelerations; consequently

$$\frac{R}{n^3R} = \frac{M_1 \propto_1}{M_2 \propto_2} = \frac{1}{n^3} \times \frac{t_2^2}{nt_1^2}$$

or

$$\frac{t_2}{t_1} = \sqrt{n}$$

But it has been shown that

$$\frac{V_1}{V_2} = \frac{t_2}{t_1} \times \frac{1}{n}$$

Consequently

$$\frac{V_1}{V_2} = \sqrt{n} \times \frac{1}{n} = \frac{1}{\sqrt{n}}$$

or

$$V_2 = V_1 \sqrt{n}$$

This simple equation represents a fact that is very useful to ship designers. It may be expressed in words as follows:

When comparing one ship with another similar ship, for the

2

purpose of determining the resistance at any given speed, the respective speeds of the two ships must be in the same ratio as the square root of the ratio of the linear dimensions of the two ships.

When speeds are so taken they are known as *corresponding speeds.* By *similar ships* are meant ships having the same geometrical form, all corresponding dimensions having the same ratio, and all weights being similarly distributed and varying as the third power of the linear ratio.

For example, if ship "No. 2" is to be four times as long as ship "No. 1," the speed to be used for ship "No. 1" should be one-half of the speed to be used for ship "No. 2" when making the comparison.

Since power is measured by the rate at which work is done, and since work is measured by the product of the force overcoming the resistance multiplied by the distance through which this force acts, the power required for the proposed ship may be determined as follows: Let P_1 and P_2 be the respective powers of ships "Nos. 1 and 2." The forces of resistance are, respectively, R and n^3R. The distances through which these forces act in a unit of time are respectively V_1 and V_2, and since power is work done per unit of time,

$$\frac{P_1}{P_2} = \frac{R \times V_1}{n^3R \times V_2} = \frac{1}{n^3} \times \frac{1}{\sqrt{n}} = \frac{1}{n^{7/2}}$$

$$P_2 = n^{7/2} P_1$$

which may be expressed in words:

The ratio of the powers at corresponding speeds of two similar ships is equal to the 7⁄2 power of the ratio of their linear dimensions.

This law is very useful for comparing ships that are *similar.* This and the preceding law are merely extensions of the principle of mechanical similitude, the application of which to ships was first demonstrated by Mr. Wm. Froude, who was one of England's most prominent naval architects. They are usually combined and expressed in terms of resistance instead of power, as *Froude's Law of Comparison*, as follows:

If two ships are exactly similar, and n is the ratio of their corresponding linear dimensions, then if they be run at speeds proportional to $\sqrt{n}$, the ratio of the corresponding resistances will be n^3.

This law furnishes a means for comparing one ship with another similar ship provided their sizes do not differ to any great extent. If, however, no ship has ever been built that has the same form as the ship being designed, it becomes necessary to make a *model* of the proposed ship, the resistance of which model can be readily determined, by experiment, in a large long tank called a model tank, by towing the model and measuring its resistance. If it be attempted to apply the law of comparison directly to the results thus obtained by the model experiments it will be found that a serious error is introduced.

The reason for this is that the amount of power required to overcome the resistance caused by friction of the water in contact with the vessel does not follow this law. This is largely due to the fact that the particles of water in contact with the surface of the vessel are dragged along to some extent in the direction of motion so that the friction is relatively less on a long large vessel than on a small short model.

It is possible, however, to calculate the frictional resistance separately, by using the results that have been tabulated from many experiments on surfaces of different characteristics, lengths, and areas. Thus the law of comparison can still be applied by making the proper correction for friction resistance. The method is briefly as follows: First, the model is towed, and its total resistance measured and recorded. Second, the surface or friction resistance of the model is calculated and taken from the total resistance, thus giving what is known as the *residual resistance* of the model. Third, from the residual resistance of the model by means of the law of comparison the corresponding residual resistance of the ship is calculated.

Fourth, the friction resistance of the ship is calculated and added to the residual resistance of the ship, thus giving the total resistance of the ship. Fifth, the power required for the ship is then readily calculated.

After a ship has been given proper buoyancy, stability, and means for propulsion, it is still necessary that means be provided for directing her from place to place.

4. STEERING

A small boat or canoe can be steered after a fashion by a paddle or by oars, and large vessels may be kept on an

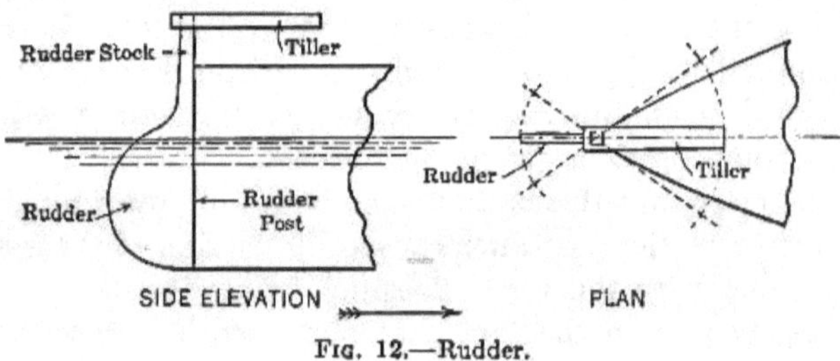

Fig. 12.—Rudder.

approximate course or heading by manipulation of the sails or the propellers (where more than one are provided). In order, however, to keep any moving vessel on a steady course with any degree of accuracy, it is necessary to provide her with a *rudder*. Figure 12 shows a rudder fitted to the stern of a vessel. The rudder is a flat vertical plate, hinged to the stern of the vessel, and capable of being rotated horizontally about its forward edge by means of a lever fitted at its head, called a *tiller*.

As the ship moves ahead, when looking in the direction of her motion, that side of the ship that is to the right hand is called the *starboard* side, and that to the left, the *port* side. When it is desired to change the direction of the ship's motion to starboard, the tiller (or *helm*, as it is sometimes called) is moved to port. The rudder is thus brought to starboard and offers a resistance to the particles of water passing the ship on that side. The resulting pressure throws the ship's stern to port and thus alters her course to starboard. Similarly, if it is desired to change the ship's direction to port, the helm is put to starboard.

The tiller on all but very small vessels, is moved by means of some sort of a mechanism usually actuated by power, known as a *steering gear.* It is customary to fit a wheel, called the *steering wheel,* at some position well forward on the ship, which is connected by suitable ropes, rods, shafting, or other means, to the tiller or to an engine that actuates the tiller. Where a steering engine is attached to the tiller the connections from the steering wheel serve merely to cause the steering engine to function, no power being applied directly to the tiller by the connecting gear. On large ships, several different steering wheels may be fitted at different locations, any one of which may be used for steering the ship.

The vertical post forming the after part of the ship's stern and supporting the forward edge and axis of the rudder, is called the *rudder post.* The rudder swings about *pintles,* which are vertical pins, usually attached to lugs on the rudder, fitting into *gudgeons,* or bearings in lugs which are usually attached to or form a part of the rudder post.

Several different forms of rudders are in common use, the size and shape depending in each case upon the type of ship and her size and speed. War ships are usually fitted with *balanced rudders,* in which a portion of the area is placed forward of the axis, which is extended below the rudder post for that purpose. Rudders of the ordinary type similar to that shown in Fig. 12 are commonly used for merchant vessels. Rudders of both the balanced and unbalanced type may have many different shapes and sizes. For a ship which must turn rapidly, as in the case of most war ships, a much larger rudder is necessary than for merchant vessels.

The principal geometrical requirements of a vessel to make her suitable as a means for over-water transportation have now been considered. The evolution of a simple log of wood hollowed out, shaped and enlarged into a ship, and then provided with means for propulsion and steering, has been traced. Little or no consideration has, however, yet been given to what was inside of the outer hull or skin of the ship, or to the material of which this hull was constructed.

As boats and canoes were increased in size it became necessary to make them *structures* rather than simple hollowed out carved logs. Structural strength had, then, to be considered.

5. STRENGTH

Any floating body is subjected to certain stresses that must be taken care of by the material of which it is constructed. For a floating body to be of practical use in over-water transportation, as has been seen, it must be hollow. The assembled material of which such a floating body is made up is collectively known as the *hull.*

The hull may be considered as performing two functions:

First.—To keep out the water, and

Second.—To withstand the various forces exerted by the pressure of the water and caused by the weight of the structure itself and the other weights that it supports.

If the hull is made in one piece, as in the case of a canoe carved from a single log, its thickness must be comparatively great in order to provide the necessary strength and rigidity. This is shown in Fig. 13 (A), which represents a cross section of such a vessel. If a large enough solid timber could be obtained, even a ship might be considered as so fashioned. Were this hull made of concrete, cast iron, or other such material, the same reasoning would apply, but it can readily be seen that for large vessels the thickness and consequently the weight would be practically prohibitive.

The hull may, however, be made to fulfil the two functions mentioned above by constructing it as a thin skin or membrane supported inside at suitable intervals by framing. In Fig. 13 (B) is shown a cross section of such a vessel. Here the outer skin consists of wood planking, comparatively thin, which is supported against the pressure of the water by transverse frames. Longitudinal strength is given by the planking itself, and also by a timber running along the bottom of the centre line, known as a *keel*. The thicker the planking is made, the nearer will the construction of (B) of Fig. 13 approach that of (A), and consequently the less will be the need for the framing and the smaller and more widely spaced may the frames then be. Conversely, the thinner the planking is made, the greater will be its need for support from the frames.

In rough weather a vessel such as that shown in Fig. 13 is liable to be swamped by waves coming over the top, and

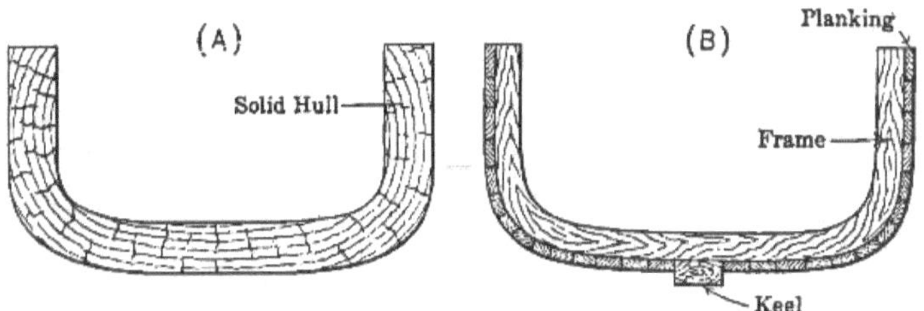

FIG. 13.—Solid and built-up hulls.

therefore this top is commonly covered by a *deck* or planked surface supported by horizontal framing, usually running athwartships, called *deck beams*.

The planking of the deck, sides, and bottom of the vessel may be considered as a continuous membrane stretched over a frame work consisting of the frames and beams. To these is usually added certain *longitudinal framing*, inside of the frames, consisting of *keelsons*, *longitudinals*, *stringers*, *girders*, etc., all of which assist in supporting and reinforcing the planking and furnishing strength and rigidity to the structure as a whole.

The most satisfactory material for use in the construction of ships is steel, and owing to its great strength, much less volume needs to be devoted to the hull itself, thus leaving more space available for cargo, passengers, machinery, fuel, etc. The planking shown in Fig. 13 (B) is replaced by thin steel plating, and instead of the massive wooden frames, comparatively small steel bars of various cross sections are used.

Strength must be provided for a ship in three ways:

1. Strength for the ship as a whole;
2. Local strength;
3. Strength partaking somewhat of the nature of both 1 and 2.

Strength of the Ship as a Whole.—In the first case the ship must be considered as a large girder loaded with various weights, some concentrated and some distributed throughout its length and breadth, and supported by the buoyancy or upward pressure of the water, which may vary at all points in the length on account of the under water form of the ship. This *girder strength* of the ship must be considered both transversely and longitudinally, although for ships as ordinarily constructed, transverse strength is usually greater than longitudinal strength and does not require so much investigation.

In addition to the stresses caused by the loading of the vessel and the forces of buoyancy, it is necessary to consider the stresses that are set up when the ship is passing through large waves. These stresses are caused by forces that are both static and dynamic, the former being due to the form of the waves and the latter being due to the motion of the vessel through the waves.

It is usually customary when designing a ship, to make an investigation of her girder strength by assuming that she is poised either on the crest or in the trough of a wave equal in length to her own length, and on this assumption to calculate the resulting stresses. For ordinary ships the stresses thus obtained will be greater than those that may be expected to be developed in actual service, and the excess thus allowed for in this calculation, which takes account of static forces only, is assumed to be sufficient to offset the stresses caused by dynamic forces. This assumption is based upon the fact that ordinary sized ships seldom, if ever, encounter such large waves.

The upper half of Fig. 14 shows a ship poised in the trough of a wave with a crest at each end. In this case some of the support normally given by the water is taken away from the middle portion of the ship and some is added at each end. The vessel thus has a tendency to droop in the middle. This is called *sagging*. When the crest of the wave comes at the mid-length of the ship, as shown in the lower half of Fig. 14, the reverse is the case, and the ends tend to droop. This is called *hogging*.

Calculations for longitudinal strength may be made both for the condition in still water and with the ship poised on

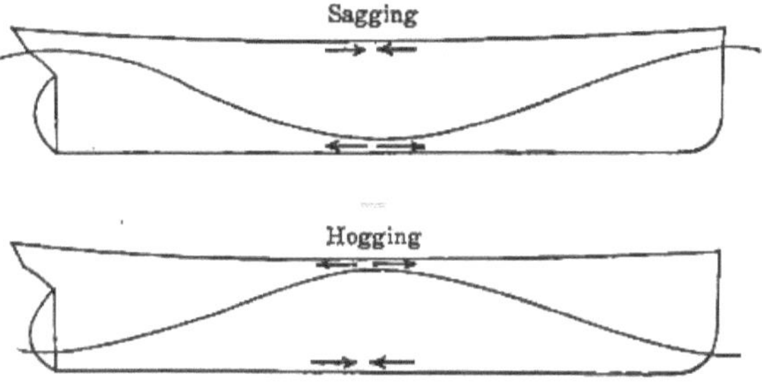

Fig. 14.—Sagging and hogging.

either the crest or the trough of a wave equal in length to its own length. Without going into great detail, the method pursued may be described as follows:

1. From a general consideration of the proportions and form of the ship and the locations of the large important weights, a decision is reached as to whether the most serious strains experienced will be those of hogging or those of sagging, and the case producing the most serious strains is selected.

2. The surface of a trochoidal wave of the same length as the ship and of a height equal to one-twentieth of its length is applied to the plans of the ship, the position of the wave surface being so adjusted that the volume cut by it from

the ship is exactly the same as the immersed volume of the ship when floating in still water.

3. Calculations are then made, by means of which a curve is constructed with the ship's length as a base and with ordinates representing the upward force of buoyancy for each point in the ship's length. These calculations are based upon the principle previously explained, that the upward pressure on a floating body is equal to the weight of the water displaced by that body.

4. On this same base line, from detailed calculations of the weights and locations of the members and various parts that make up the ship and all that she carries, another curve is drawn, each ordinate of which represents

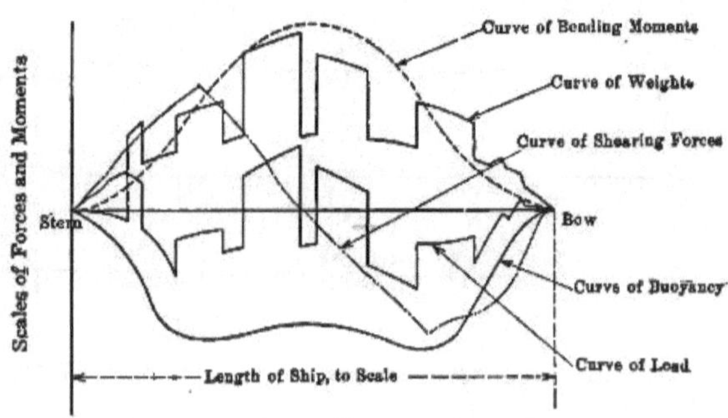

Fig. 15.—Curves for strength calculation.

the weight with which the ship is loaded at the point represented by the corresponding abscissa. These two curves may look something like the curves in Fig. 15, which are marked "curve of buoyancy" and "curve of weights" respectively. These curves are drawn for a ship poised with the centre of its length at the trough of the wave, as will be seen by the general shape of the curve of buoyancy. It will be noted that ordinates representing weights are considered as positive and those representing the forces of buoyancy as negative, since they act in opposite directions.

5. A third curve is obtained by subtracting the ordinates of the buoyancy curve from the corresponding ordinates of the weight curve. This third curve is called the curve

of load, and represents the resultant of the vertical forces of weight and buoyancy at each point. It should be noted that for equilibrium the area of the weight and buoyancy curves must be equal and that the area of the load curve above the horizontal axis must be exactly equal to its area below that axis.

6. By the successive integration of the load curve and its integral curve are obtained the curves of shearing force and bending moment, as shown in the figure.

7. The maximum bending moment and the point at which it occurs are then determined, and calculations for the strength of the ship at this point are made to see that this strength is sufficient. This is done by finding the moment of inertia of this section and calculating the maximum fiber-stress, making use of the ordinary beam formula: $\frac{p}{y} = \frac{M}{I}$. If the stress is found to be excessive, the size of some of the members must be increased in order to reduce it, and a second calculation made to see that a satisfactory maximum stress has been obtained.

A similar method might be pursued in the investigation of the transverse strength of a ship if desired. But this is not usually found to be necessary, as the transverse strength is usually more than ample. In war ships and ships of special type, however, such calculations may have to be made.

Transverse strength may also be investigated where special conditions require this to be done, by means of the "Principle of Least Work."

Local Strength.—Local strength must be provided in special cases to meet special needs. For example, at the bow of the ship there is a tendency for the plating to move in and out when the ship is in a seaway. Such movement, called *panting*, is provided against by means of special stiffening, such as *ram plates, breast hooks, panting stringers,* etc. Other cases where local strength is required are gun and turret foundations, supports for boat cranes and davits, masts, engines, boilers, etc., *i.e.*, heavy concentrated weights or fittings that receive heavy sudden loads or shocks.

Strength, Partly for Ship as Whole and Partly Local.—It is difficult to make an exact distinction between local strength and strength of the ship as a whole in certain cases. For example, the forces of the rudder and propellers must be transmitted to the whole hull. Also if the vessel is towed or is towing, the deck fittings to which the tow-line is attached must transmit practically the entire stress to the whole ship. The same applies to stresses transmitted, in sailing ships, by the masts, and rigging.

In general, it must be remembered that all these stresses must be gradually transmitted from the member receiving the full force, to the remainder of the hull. There should be no sudden break in strength, but as the strength is reduced from its maximum to its minimum, it should be tapered off gradually. Any sudden break in strength causes a point of weakness, and is liable to cause failure in an emergency. This general rule applies to structural design throughout.

6. ENDURANCE

The next quality—which is of great importance only in the case of seagoing vessels—is endurance. If a ship is to be suitable for voyages of any great length she must carry enough coal or other fuel to propel her for the required distances, and, if propelled by steam power, must carry enough fresh water for the boilers, or must be provided with evaporators to convert salt water into fresh water while at sea. She must also have space to carry sufficient food and fresh water for all persons on board during the trip.

The amount of space and weight that must be devoted to fuel and other consumable weights depends upon the service for which the ship is intended. It should always be carefully considered in the design. By far the largest percentage of these weights is that required for fuel. In this connection it is very necessary to know whether the vessel can secure fuel at each of her terminal ports, or ports of call, or whether she can coal (or oil) only at her home port. It is also usually important that she does not carry an unnecessary amount of fuel since this cuts down the space available for cargo, passengers, and other uses, and therefore limits the utility of the ship.

In designing a ship, after the type and size of the engines and boilers have been determined, and the kind of fuel that is to be used has been decided upon, the amount of space that must be assigned to fuel is calculated from data on the fuel consumption that may be expected and the length of the greatest voyage that it is intended the ship shall be capable of making. Data regarding the probable fuel consumption is obtained from the results of past experience in other vessels.

7. UTILITY

Although a vessel may have all the qualifications that have already been described, there is still one more that must be provided. Arrangements must be made to make the vessel suitable for the use to which she is to be put. These arrangements include the following:

1. Living Accommodations for Officers and Crew.—The complement of the ship, which includes the men charged with the care and operation of the engines, boilers, and other auxiliary machinery, the steering and navigating of the ship, her cleanliness, care, and upkeep, and the other duties necessary for her proper maintenance and operation, must be suitably sheltered and fed. This requires sleeping accommodations, eating and toilet facilities, and more or less elaborate systems of lighting, heating, ventilation, plumbing, and refrigeration.

2. Space for Carrying Passengers, or Cargo, or Fuel, or Space Necessary for any Special Service for which the Vessel is to be Used.—Special staterooms, dining saloons, galleys, etc., are necessary for passenger ships in addition to those necessary for a ship's complement, and must also have even more elaborate lighting, heating, ventilating, and similar systems than those provided for the crew.

For vessels designed to carry cargo, large holds and other cargo spaces fitted with special large openings, and derricks and hoisting engines for loading and unloading cargo must be provided. In case the cargo is of a special type, such as oil or other liquids carried in bulk, or fruits, meats, or other perishable goods, special arrangements must be made for stowing and handling it.

In the case of warships, arrangements must be made for turrets, barbettes, guns, torpedoes, mines, armor, magazines, etc., together with the necessary machinery for controlling, operating and supplying the battery.

3. Auxiliary Requirements.—All ships must have means for anchoring and mooring, boats, and means for hoisting and lowering them, gangways, ladders, and other means for ingress and egress, means for signalling or communication with the shore or with other ships, means for pumping water from one compartment to another, protection against fire, sails (to some extent, at least, in case of breakdown of the main engines), special navigational apparatus, various means for interior communication, and many other special arrangements too numerous to mention.

All of these arrangements affecting the utility of the ship vary with her size and the service for which she is designed, but all are very important and must be carefully considered during the course of the design.

Recapitulation

The principal requirements of all ships are:

1. **Buoyancy.**
2. **Stability.**
3. **Propulsion.**
4. **Steering.**
5. **Strength.**
6. **Endurance.**
7. **Utility.**

CHAPTER II

GENERAL DESCRIPTION OF SHIPS

1. FORM

The Lines.—The outer form of a ship is a curved undevelopable surface. It can be represented geometrically by fixing the locations in space of points on this surface. The greater the number of points taken the more accurately will the surface be determined. For convenience it is customary to locate these points by means of co-ordinates or "offsets" measured at right angles to the following three planes:

1. A vertical longitudinal plane dividing the ship into two symmetrical halves. Ordinates perpendicular to this plane are called *half-breadths.*

2. A horizontal plane parallel to the surface of the water and intersecting the first plane in a line called the *base line.* Ordinates measured vertically up from this horizontal plane are called *heights.*

3. A plane at right angles to each of the first two planes, and for convenience often taken at the mid-length of the ship. The intersection of this plane with the ship's surface is called the *midship section* or *dead flat.* Ordinates perpendicular to this plane are thus measured longitudinally and are usually expressed as distances *forward* or *aft* of the midship section, depending upon whether they are measured toward the bow or toward the stern of the ship. (The midship section is usually designated by the symbol ⊃⊗⊂).

If the surface of the ship be considered as cut by planes parallel to each of these three reference planes, then the intersections of the planes will be curved lines which may be projected upon the three reference planes, the projection of any particular intersection appearing as a straight line on two of the planes and as a curved line on the third.

A drawing consisting of such projections is called the *lines* of the ship, and the projections on the first plane make up what is usually called the *sheer* or *profile* plan; on the second plane, the *half-breadth* plan; and on the third, the *body* plan. Such a set of lines is shown in Fig. 16.

Intersections of the ship's surface by planes parallel to the third plane are called *cross sections*. These are marked in Fig. 16 by numbers 2 to 10 inclusive.

Intersections of the surface by planes parallel to the second plane are called *water lines*. These are marked in Fig. 16: W. L. "A", L. W. L., 2 W. L., 3 W. L., 4 W. L. "L. W. L." is the usual abbreviation for *load water line*, which is the intersection of the surface of the ship by the plane of the surface of the water when the ship is floating with her designed load on board and is perfectly upright in the water, or with the base line horizontal.

Intersections of the surface of the ship by planes parallel to the first plane are called *bow and buttock lines* or simply *buttocks*. One buttock only is shown in Fig. 16, but several are usually drawn.

For convenience in drawing the lines it is also customary to take one or more intersections of the ship's surface by a plane or planes perpendicular to the midship section plane but at an angle with each of the other two. Such intersections are called *diagonals*, and appear as straight lines in only one plan and as curves in the other two. A diagonal is usually shown projected in the sheer plan, but *expanded*, or in its true shape, in the half-breadth plan. One diagonal only (the *bilge diagonal*) is shown in Fig. 16.

Certain lines of a ship's form (of which only one—the line of the *deck at side*—is shown in Fig. 16) have curvature in all three dimensions and therefore appear as curves in all three plans.

The drawing of the lines of a ship is simply a problem of descriptive geometry. All offsets must appear in their

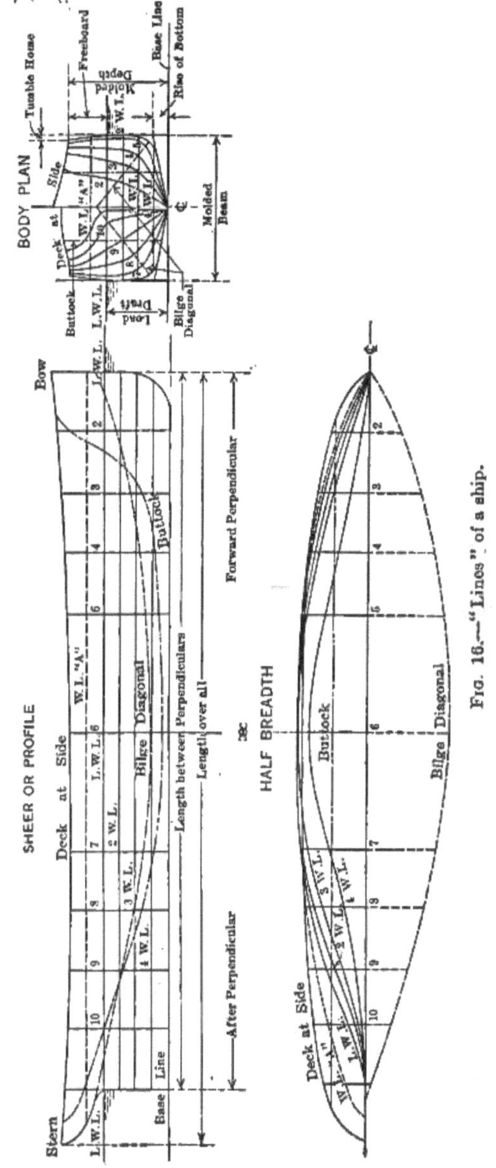

FIG. 16.—"Lines" of a ship.

actual length in two of the three plans. For example, all *breadths* can be measured in both the half-breadth and the body plan. (They appear as points in the sheer plan.) During the process of drawing the lines it is necessary that all such offsets be made to agree, in each case, in the two plans, and at the same time the curves or sections of the ship's form that are determined by these offsets must be regular smooth curves. The process of thus adjusting the various offsets is called *fairing the lines,* and when it has been properly done, all the curves will be smooth and regular and are then said to be *fair.* A surface or curve is thus spoken of as "fair" when it has a smooth curvature—free from humps or hollows.

Definitions Applying to a Ship's Form.—There are certain terms, dimensions, and names of parts that apply to ships' forms in particular. These are used frequently both during the design and construction of ships, and a knowledge of their meaning is essential to all shipbuilders. A few of these have already been explained in the preceding pages and some are indicated in the lines of the ship represented in Fig. 16, but in order to make the subject of *form* complete they will be included in the definitions given below:

1. *Directions on a Ship.*—The end of a ship that cuts the water when a ship moves ahead is called the *bow.* The other end is called the *stern.* The bow and stern form the extremities of the ship's length. Distances measured in the general direction between bow and stern are said to be measured in a *fore* and *aft* direction, or *longitudinally.* Distances measured at right angles to this direction, and horizontally, are said to be measured *athwartships, transversely,* or in an *athwartship* or *transverse* direction. The term *amidships* means at or near the centre of the ship, considered either in the fore and aft or in the athwartship direction. *Inboard* means toward the centre, and *outboard* toward the side of the ship. The terms *fore* and *forward* apply to parts of the ship that are, in general, at, near, or toward the bow, while the terms *aft* and *after* apply to parts, in general, at, near, or toward the stern. For ex-

ample, the *fore-body* of the ship is the portion of her form that is forward of the midship section, or, if the ship has a constant cross section for a portion of her length amidships, that portion forward of this constant cross section. Similarly, the *afterbody* is the portion of the ship's form aft of this parallel middle body, or of the midship section in case no portion of her length is parallel sided. When looking from the stern toward the bow, that side of the ship that is to the right hand is called the *starboard* side and that to the left hand, the *port* side. When steaming at night, ships usually show a green light on the starboard side and a red (*port* colored) light on the port side. Distances measured vertically are spoken of as *heights* or *depths*. When speaking of a part of a ship under any point of reference it is said to be *below*—instead of using the landsman's "down stairs." The term *on deck* usually refers to locations on the highest or upper deck, the decks being nearly (but not quite) horizontal surfaces corresponding to the floors of a building on shore.

2. *Reference Lines and Planes.*—The *keel line* is the line of the fore and aft member running along the centre line of the ship at its lowest part. The *base line* is the intersection of the central longitudinal vertical plane of the ship with a horizontal plane through the top of the keel at the midship section (in some cases the keel line and the base line are the same). The *load water line* (usually marked L. W. L.) is the term applied to the line in the lines of the ship which represents the intersection of the ship's form with the plane of the surface of the water when the ship is floating with her designed load on board. This term is somewhat of a misnomer since it is really applied to the load water *plane* rather than to the load water *line*. It is sometimes applied to the trace of the plane of the water with the central vertical plane, and sometimes to the trace of the water surface plane with the transverse plane at the mid-length of the ship, and also to the projection of the intersection of the water surface with the ship's surface on the horizontal plane. The

forward perpendicular is the vertical line through the intersection of the forward side of the stem with the load water plane. The *after perpendicular* is the vertical line through the intersection of the after side of the stern post with the load water plane. The *midship section* (⨂) is the intersection of the ship's form with a transverse vertical plane midway between the forward and the after perpendiculars.

NOTE.—These above-mentioned lines and planes are shown in Fig. 16, in which they should be carefully noted.

3. *Molded Dimensions.*—The *molded surface* of a ship is the surface passing through the outer edges of all the framing or the inner surface of the planking or plating which forms the outer skin. It is the surface represented by the lines. The length between *perpendiculars* (L. B. P.) is the distance between the forward and the after perpendiculars. The *length over all* (L. O. A.) is the length between the extreme forward and after points of the ship measured parallel to the base line. The *molded breadth* is the maximum transverse breadth of the molded surface at the midship section. The *molded depth* is the vertical distance from the base line to the line of the main deck at side at the midship section. The *draft* is the vertical distance between the bottom of the keel and the water line at which the ship is considered as floating. When measured at the forward end of the ship the draft is called the *draft forward,* and when measured aft, is called the *draft aft.* The arithmetical mean of the draft forward and the draft aft is called the *mean* draft. The difference between the draft forward and the draft aft is called the *trim.* When the draft aft is greater than the draft forward, the vessel is said to *trim by the stern.* When the reverse is the case she is said to *trim by the bow.* When a ship is designed to float normally with a greater draft aft than forward, the difference in the two drafts is called the *drag.* *Load draft* is the draft of the ship when floating at the load water line. *Extreme draft* is the vertical distance of the lowest point of the ship below the surface of

the water. *Freeboard* is the height of the ship above the water's surface, or it is the difference between the moulded depth and the draft. *Rise of bottom,* or *rise of floor,* or *dead rise* are all expressions meaning the amount that the straight portion of the bottom rises in the *half-beam* of the ship. *Tumble home* is the amount that the side of the ship is nearer to the centre line at the top than at the level of greatest width. *Flare* is the opposite of tumble home. (Cross section No. 2 in Fig. 16 has a flare while No. 5 has a tumble home.) *Camber* (also called *crown* or *round up*) is the distance that the centre of the surface of a deck is above its side. Instead of being flat plane surfaces decks usually are curved surfaces of such form that a transverse vertical section will be a curve higher at the centre than at the sides. This transverse curvature is called the camber and is usually expressed as the distance that the arc is above the chord for a given beam. (See Fig. 17.) *Sheer* is the term applied to the fore and aft curvature of a deck. Decks usually have a longitudinal curvature as well as a transverse curvature, but in this case the ends are higher than the centre. (Note sheer of deck at side in Figs. 16 and 17.)

NOTE.—The various terms above described are illustrated in Fig. 16, in which they should be carefully noted.

4. *Terms Referring to Form.*—A few of the most commonly used terms referring to form of ships are illustrated in Fig. 17, and are defined below.

The *entrance* is the forward under water portion of the ship at and near the bow, which enters the water first as the ship moves ahead. The *run* is the portion of the ship's form under water at and near the stern which last leaves the water as the ship moves ahead. The *stem* is the forward edge of the bow which cuts the water when the ship moves ahead. The *stern post* is the vertical post at the after end of the under water portion of the ship. The *bottom* is the flat or nearly flat portion of the ship's surface extending outboard on each side from the keel and usually sloping slightly upward. The term "bottom" is also applied, in a general

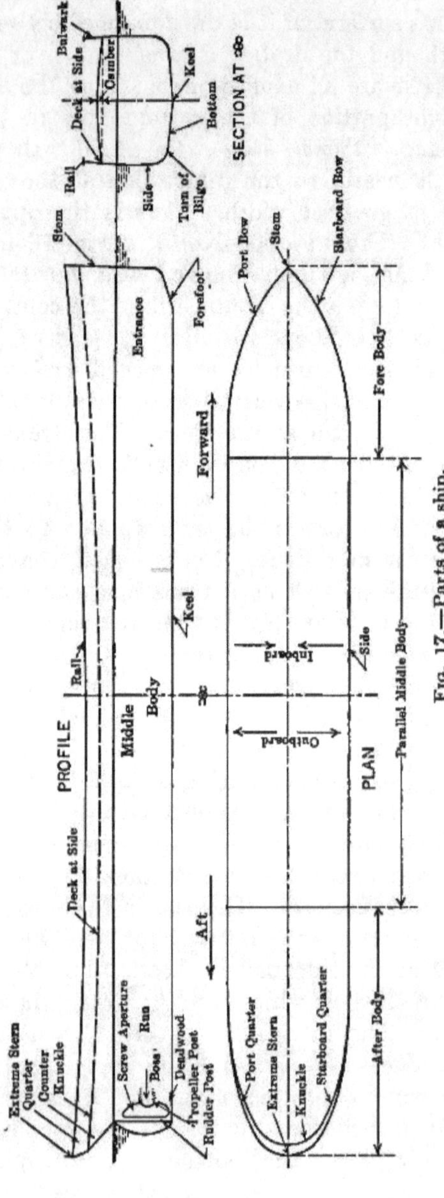

FIG. 17.—Parts of a ship.

sense, to all of the ship's surface below the water line. The *sides* are the vertical or nearly vertical portions of the ship's surface. *Bilge* is the term applied to the curved portion of the ship's surface between bottom and side. This is also sometimes called the *turn of the bilge*. *Fore foot* is the term applied to the after lower end of the stem or the part of the stem that connects with the keel. *Dead wood* is a term applied to the portion of the hull at the junction of the stern and stern post with the keel. The *boss* is the curved swelling portion of the ship's surface around the propeller shaft or shafts. *Knuckle*, in general, is the term applied to any line forming the intersection of two curved surfaces, and in particular, to the intersection of the upper nearly vertical portion of the ship's surface above water at the extreme stern with the lower more sloping portion of the stern. *Quarter* is the curved portion of the ship on either side at the extreme stern. *Bow* (besides meaning the forward end of the ship) is applied to the curved forward portion of the ship on either side of the stem. *Bulwarks* is that portion of the ship's surface between the rail and the highest complete deck, forming an inclosure or railing around the perimeter of that deck. *Rail* is the upper edge of the bulwarks. *Counter* is the term applied to that portion of the ship's surface between the knuckle and the water line near the stern. The *rudder post* is the vertical post at the stern to which is hinged the rudder. In sailing ships or ships with twin or quadruple screw propellers it is also the stern post. *Propeller post* is the vertical post at the stern of a single or triple screw vessel through which passes the shaft of the centre propeller.

5. *Coefficients of Form.*—The form of a ship is determined from a number of considerations. First the volume of the under water form must be sufficient to displace an amount of water equal in weight to the total weight of the ship and all that she carries. Then in order to reduce resistance and to provide a good run of water to the propellers the entrance and run must be tapered. Also, the form must be so proportioned as to give the requisite sta-

bility. In some cases the draft is limited by the depth of the waters through which the ship must pass. These various requirements are usually somewhat conflicting, and the final determination of the form of the ship is more or less in the nature of a compromise. For example, if in an endeavor to reduce resistance, the ship's form be made too narrow and fine or sharp, sufficient stability may not be obtained. In providing sufficient volume to give the desired displacement the lines may be made so full or "bulging" as to give an unduly high resistance.

It will be found that certain classes of vessels have forms that are very nearly the same, and as large numbers of such ships have already been built and put into service it is possible to compare these with contemplated ships. For this purpose it is convenient to refer to certain coefficients and ratios, among the most common of which are the following: block coefficient of fineness, load water-line coefficient, midship section coefficient, longitudinal prismatic coefficient, vertical prismatic coefficient, ratio of length to beam, ratio of beam to draft.

The block coefficient of fineness (usually called simply the *block coefficient*) is the ratio of the under water volume of the ship to the volume of the circumscribing rectangular parallelopiped, or the rectangular solid of the same length as the L. W. L. and with width equal to the ship's beam and depth equal to the ship's draft. *The load water-line coefficient* is the ratio of the area of the load water line to the circumscribing rectangle. The midship section coefficient is the ratio of the area of that portion of the midship section which lies below the load water line to the area of the circumscribing rectangle. *The longitudinal prismatic coefficient* is the ratio of the under water volume of the ship to the volume of a cylinder having for length the length of the L. W. L. and for a base the immersed midship section of the ship. The *vertical prismatic coefficient* is the ratio of the under water volume of the ship to the volume of a cylinder having for height the draft of the ship, and for base the area of the load water line. The terms *ratio of length to beam* and *ratio of beam to draft* are self-explanatory.

A knowledge of these various coefficients gives a general idea of the form and type of the vessel's hull. If the value of the coefficient is high, the lines are said to be full, and if relatively low, the lines are said to be fine. The ratio of length to beam is an index of the fineness of the ship longitudinally, the greater this ratio being, the greater being the fineness and consequently the speed that can be obtained, other things being unchanged. The ratio of beam to draft is, in general, an index of the transverse stability.

As an example of the variation in values of the block coefficient in different classes of ships it may be noted that, roughly, these are:

Slow cargo vessels	.80
Ordinary cargo vessels	.75
Sailing vessels	.70
Older battleships	.65
Later battleships	.60
Mail and passenger steamers	.60
Cruisers	.55
Fast cruisers	.50
Destroyers	.45
Steam yachts	.40

2. GENERAL ARRANGEMENT

The lines of a ship determine her geometrical form or molded surface. The ship is actually built by providing a certain frame work, all the outer points of which lie in this molded surface. Over this frame work and attached to it is then fitted a complete envelope of plating or planking which forms the "skin" of the ship, keeps out the water, and assists in furnishing strength. The inner surface of the plating or planking therefore coincides with the outer surface of the frames, or molded surface.

The framing is, of course, the important part of the ship and furnishes the necessary structural strength. Using the term, in a general sense, the *framing* may be said to consist of all the principal members of the ship except the shell. The framing and shell with their various connections are collectively known as the *hull* of the ship.

The principal parts of the hull of every ship are designed to serve, in general, the same purposes, whether the ship be wood, iron, steel, concrete, or a combination of any or all of these. It will therefore be sufficient, in discussing these parts, to consider only the modern steel ship, which represents by far the most common type at the present time. The corresponding members of ships built of other materials perform similar functions, and can be readily compared with those of the steel ship. The general interior arrangement of a typical steel cargo carrying steamer is shown in Fig. 18, which represents a longitudinal centre line section of such a ship. In order to give a general idea of the interior arrangement of all ships the various subdivisions, parts and fittings of this ship will be briefly described.

Running longitudinally along the centre of the bottom is the *keel*, which is connected at its forward end to the *stem*, a heavy cast or forged steel bar or post bent to the shape shown and extending nearly vertically to the highest point of the bow. At its after end the keel is connected to another heavy steel member, usually a casting, called the *stern-post* or *stern-frame*, which extends up to the counter. This forms the after end of the ship, and to it is secured the stern framing and the after plating of the shell.

The shell plating is supported by *frames* distributed throughout the length of the ship at regular intervals so as to give it sufficient support. At the bow the shell plating is attached to the stem, and at the stern to the stern post. The transverse frames are given support against fore and aft movement by *longitudinal framing* running along their inner edges so that the framing of the ship really consists of a net work of fore and aft and transverse members crossing each other approximately at right angles. All of this framing is in turn further supported by the decks and bulkheads, which are described below.

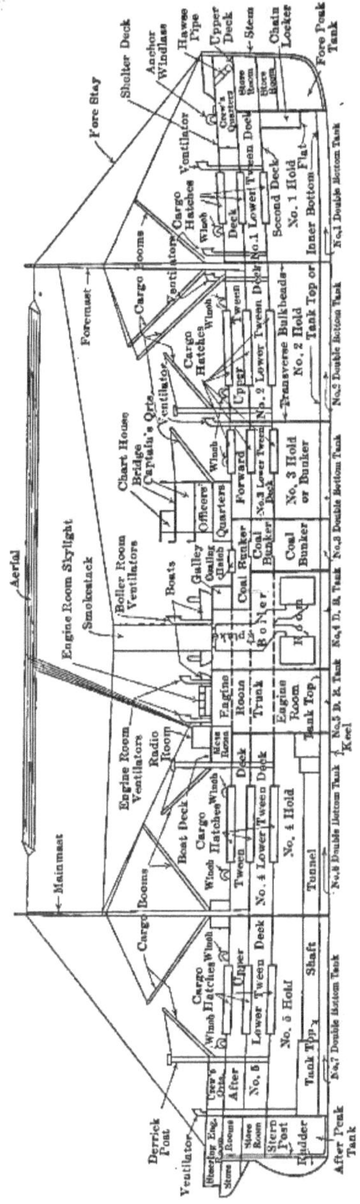

FIG. 18.—Inboard profile of cargo steamer.

The upper portion of the main hull is closed in by a complete deck which, in Fig. 18, is marked *shelter deck*. This is the highest complete exposed deck and is often spoken of as the *weather deck*. As it is usually the principal strength deck, it is often also called the *main deck*. Sometimes it is called the *spar deck*, a term derived from its proximity to the masts and spars. This deck consists of a slightly curved and approximately horizontal surface under which are fitted heavy steel *beams* to the top of which is fastened the *deck plating*.

Below the shelter deck and running parallel to it is another deck called the *upper deck*, and below that and also parallel to it and to the shelter deck is the *second deck*. The space between the shelter and upper decks is called the upper *'tween deck*, and between the upper and second decks the *lower 'tween deck*. Decks are usually fitted with a vertical distance between adjacent decks of from six to eight feet. They are given various names depending upon the type of the ship in which fitted. They correspond to the floors of a building on shore, and serve to subdivide the space in the ship so that it can be conveniently utilized. They also contribute to the strength of the hull by furnishing a certain amount of both longitudinal and transverse stiffness, and also limit the amount of volume that may be flooded in case the shell plating is punctured. In ordinary sized cargo vessels it is not usual to find more than two 'tween decks.

The volume of the hull is further subdivided by means of transverse and longitudinal *bulkheads*, or partitions, which correspond to the walls of a building. These are flat plated surfaces stiffened by means of vertical bars called *bulkhead stiffeners*.

The transverse bulkheads, as well as dividing the volume of the hull up into separate compartments, serve to furnish transverse strength and to transmit the forces set up by the various weights carried in the ship to the lower portion of the hull. In case of damage to the shell plating below the water line, they serve to limit the amount of space in the ship that may be flooded, and are made especially strong for this purpose. It will be noted in Fig. 18 that the transverse bulkheads separate the following compartments: Fore peak tank, No. 1 hold, No. 2 hold, No. 3 hold, coal bunker, boiler room, engine room, No. 4 hold, No. 5 hold, and after peak tank.

Longitudinal bulkheads (which are not indicated in the figure) are fitted mainly for purposes of subdivision, being limited in length so that they contribute very little to the longitudinal strength of the ship.

The *forward and after peak tanks* are large compartments located at the extreme ends of the ship just above the bottom. They are connected by suitable piping so that they can be readily filled or emptied of water. They can thus be used for *trimming* the ship, which is the term applied to the process of raising or lowering one end or the other of the ship. A considerable weight of water can be put into either of these tanks, which, owing to its location at the extreme end of the ship, has a great leverage resulting in deeper immersion of that end. These compartments are also sometimes called the *forward and after trimming tanks*. The bulkhead at the after end of the fore peak tank is sometimes called a *collision bulkhead,* since this bulkhead, in the event of damage caused by the ship's running into another ship or obstacle, would prevent water from entering the remainder of the hull.

The *holds* (Nos. 1, 2, 3, 4 and 5, in Fig. 18) are large spaces used for carrying cargo. They extend completely across the ship to the shell plating on each side and up to the second deck.

In order to load cargo into the holds and 'tween deck spaces there are provided large rectangular openings in the decks called *cargo hatches.* The edges of these openings are fitted with vertical plate boundaries called *coamings,* and covers are provided to fit in these coamings. After a hold has been loaded with cargo the covers are put in place and the loading of the 'tween deck space above can be proceeded with.

The remainder of the main portion of the space in the hull is devoted to the requirements of propulsion, there being provided, as shown in Fig. 18, an *engine room, boiler room*, and *coal bunkers*. In the *engine room* are located the main engines, condensers, pumps, and other auxiliary machinery, the engines being connected to the propellers at the stern of the ship by longitudinal shafts. These shafts pass through *shaft tunnels*, which are long water-tight compartments completely closed in by steel plating so as to be entirely independent of the holds through which they pass. The after end is connected to the weather deck by means of a vertical passage, or *trunk*, which serves both as a ventilator and as a means for escape for the engine room force in case of emergency. A large vertical inclosure, or trunk, extends from the engine room up to the weather deck where it terminates in a large hatch covered by a skylight. This trunk permits large machinery parts to be removed from the engine room and furnishes light and ventilation.

The *boiler room* is located just forward of the engine room and, like the latter, is continued to the weather deck in the form of an enclosure through which passes the *uptake*, a large duct which connects the boilers to the smokestack. In addition to the boilers this compartment usually contains certain pumps and auxiliaries.

The *coal bunkers* are large compartments used for the stowage of sufficient coal for the longest voyages which it is designed the ship shall make. They are fitted with hatches similar to the cargo hatches, by means of which the coal is dumped into them. It will be noted that No. 3 hold, when not desired for cargo, can be utilized as a coal bunker. Coal bunkers are also located outboard abreast the engine and boiler rooms, on both sides, being separated from them by longitudinal bulkheads. (These are not shown in Fig. 18.)

The amount of space devoted in cargo vessels to engines, boilers, and fuel is much smaller than in some other types of ships, since cargo vessels usually cruise at comparatively low speeds, and therefore do not require the power and do not have the high fuel consumption that is necessary for high-speed vessels.

The holds and 'tween decks are usually numbered consecutively from forward to aft, the 'tween deck numbers corresponding to the holds directly underneath them.

The ship shown in Fig. 18 is fitted with an *inner bottom* extending for the full length between the fore and after peak tanks. This inner bottom runs approximately parallel to the outer bottom at a distance of about four feet above it, extending to the turn of the bilge on each side where it curves down and joins the outer bottom thus forming a separate *double bottom* to the ship. This double bottom is divided up into a number of *double bottom tanks* by means of partitions located directly underneath the transverse bulkheads, as shown. These tanks are used for carrying water as ballast when the ship is light or without cargo, and some of them for reserve feed water for the boilers, being suitably connected with piping for filling and emptying. The inner bottom, which forms the upper boundary of these tanks, is often called the *tank top*. When a cargo ship has no cargo on board, the double bottom tanks must be filled in order to give her sufficient stability, and when in this condition she is said to be *in ballast*.

In order that the ship may be anchored when it is not convenient for her to go alongside of a dock she is provided with two or more anchors shackled to the ends of *chain cables*. The chain cables pass from the anchors through large passages through the bows of the ship called *hawse pipes* and over a specially shaped drum of the *anchor windlass* and down through *chain pipes* into a large compartment located just aft of the fore peak tank called the *chain locker*.

The *steering engine* which actuates the tiller is located in a special compartment just above the rudder at the extreme after end of the shelter deck, called the *steering engine room*.

The extreme forward and after portions of the hull above the peak tanks are utilized for *storerooms* and living spaces for the crew (called *crew's quarters*). Quarters for some of the crew are also provided just forward of the steering engine room and also abreast of the engine room and uptake trunks amidships on the shelter deck. The *galley* (kitchen) and *crew's mess room* (dining room) are also located amidships on the weather deck, as shown, all of these compartments being inclosed in a deck house formed by continuing the sides of the ship up for a portion of the length and decking over the top. This deck is called the *boat deck*, since it is utilized for the stowage of the ship's boats. There is also installed on the boat deck the *radio room* which contains the radio instruments and sleeping accommodations for the radio operators.

Just aft of the hatch leading to No. 3 hold is a structure extending up for four deck levels, which consists of officers' staterooms and mess room on two levels, with the captain's quarters above these, and the bridge and chart house on top. The *bridge* is a semi-enclosed platform extending all the way across the ship and so arranged as to give a good view all around the horizon. It is from the bridge that the ship is controlled and steered, there being located there the steering wheel, compass, and various connections to the engine room and other parts of the ship. The *chart house* is a small house located just off the bridge for use in plotting the course of the ship on the chart and doing other work in connection with navigation which must be done in a sheltered position. The captain's quarters are directly under the bridge in order that he may have access thereto with the least possible delay in case of an emergency.

Two masts are installed as shown (the *foremast* and *mainmast*), these serving as supports for the aerial of the radio apparatus, for use in hoisting signals, to provide stations high above the water for lookouts, and as a support for the booms used in loading and unloading cargo. These masts could also be used, in case the machinery should break down, to spread sails. Special *derrick posts* are also installed, as shown, for *cargo booms* serving hatches not located convenient to masts. Steam *winches* are located at various points on the weather deck for furnishing power for the gear of the cargo booms and other hoisting arrangements.

Air is supplied to the various compartments of the ship by means of special *ventilating ducts* fitted at their upper ends with hoods or *cowls* and extending down to the compartments to which they are to supply air. As has been noted, the after ventilating trunk serves also as an escape hatch from the shaft tunnel.

The foregoing brief description will serve to give a general idea of the subdivision and arrangement of the various spaces of this particular type of ship. There is, however, considerable latitude in the arrangement of different types of ships which varies with the purposes for which designed. For example, the amount of space necessary for engines and boilers in a vessel designed to make 25 knots speed would be a very appreciable proportion of her total volume, whereas in a slow tramp steamer it is relatively small. In war ships, with their special requirements of guns, torpedoes, magazines, armor, etc., the interior of the hull is much more cut up than that of the ship shown in Fig. 18. All war ships are much more minutely subdivided in order to limit the damage which may be caused by shell fire or torpedo or mine explosions. Much of the space used for cargo in Fig. 18, would in the case of a passenger vessel be utilized for state rooms, dining saloons, lounges, and other conveniences for the passengers. Vessels designed for carrying fuel oil, gasoline, molasses, or other fluids in bulk have the holds replaced by large tanks, extending to the weather deck and terminated by *expansion trunks* to permit of changes in volume due to variation in temperature.

Many of the features illustrated in Fig. 18 are, however, common to practically all large modern steel ships. These include the double bottom, peak tanks, bulkheads, decks, steering gear, anchor gear, masts, ventilation,

4

bridge, engine and boiler rooms, shaft tunnels, and numerous other parts. The interior arrangement of any ship must be governed both by considerations of convenience (as in the case of a building on shore) and by requirements of buoyancy and stability, which make it necessary to have the weights of the ship so located as to fulfil the conditions that have been discussed in Chapter I.

3. TYPES OF SHIPS

Ships may be classified in several different ways, such as with reference to the material of which constructed, the purpose for which used, the speed, etc.

1. Ships Classified with Reference to Materials of Hulls:

(*a*) Wood.
(*b*) Composite.
(*c*) Iron.
(*d*) Sheathed
(*e*) Steel (bronze, etc.).
(*f*) Concrete.

(a) Wooden Ships.—The first ships of importance were constructed almost entirely of wood, which formed the keels, keelsons, stringers, knees, beams, planking, flooring, ceiling, etc. For many years practically all ships were built of wood, and it was not until well into the nineteenth century that iron appeared as a shipbuilding material. The building of wooden ships thus became more or less of an art, and all skilled shipbuilders were spoken of as *shipwrights*, a term meaning literally "builders of ships," but now applied only to the workmen who fit and install the wood decks and other wooden parts forming integral portions of the hulls. These wooden ships were monuments to the shipwright's skill, and performed excellent service for many years, but as the demand for increase in size appeared, and with the introduction of the use of iron, it was gradually found advisable almost entirely to abandon the use of wood for hull construction.

The reason for this is that it is very difficult to fasten the various parts of a wooden ship together so as to prevent a certain amount of slipping or sliding of each part on its neighbor. These strains becoming accumulative, in a large ship, would cause such a great total distortion as to make the use of wood for ships of such size practically prohibitive. Very few wooden ships have ever been built to lengths of over 300 feet, while the most successful ones have been little over 200 feet long. When it is remembered that ships are now built with lengths approximating 1000 feet, the limitations of wooden ships are readily seen. Nevertheless, for small vessels designed to operate along the coast or in protected waters wood is a very satisfactory material owing to its cheapness and the ease with which it can be worked.

(b) **Composite Ships.**—The difficulties mentioned in connection with wooden ships can be considerably overcome by introducing a certain amount of metal into the construction. In fact, modern wooden ships of any size usually have certain steel strappings and reinforcing members. When the entire framing of a ship is built of iron, steel, or other metal, but the outer skin is still of wood planking, she is known as a composite ship. Such vessels have the advantage of not requiring dry-docking for purposes of cleaning the bottom so frequently.

(c) **Iron Ships.**—Iron came into general use for ships' hulls during the latter part of the first half of the nineteenth century. The principles of iron shipbuilding were, in general, the same as those now applied to steel, the sizes of the various members, however, being necessarily greater for iron on account of its lower strength. Iron is practically never used, however, for shipbuilding at the present time except for certain forgings and for rivets for some merchant ships. Iron has a greater resistance to corrosion than steel, and it is not unusual to find old iron vessels, built perhaps half a century ago, still in an excellent state of preservation.

(d) Sheathed Ships.—In order to protect the under water hull of an iron or steel ship from fouling, due to various marine growths, it is sometimes customary to sheathe it with wood over the iron or steel plating below the water line, and to cover the wood with sheets of copper secured to the wood with copper nails. This necessitates the use of bronze for the stem, stern posts, struts, etc., in order to prevent galvanic action, and great care must be exercised to see that the copper on the outside of the wood sheathing is thoroughly insulated from the steel or iron shell plating inside. Sheathed ships are stronger than composite ships but of more expensive construction. They are used principally in tropical waters where marine growths are excessive, in order to avoid frequent dry-dockings. (Dry-docking consists in landing the vessel in a large basin, or dry-dock, from which the water can be pumped out so as to render the under water portion of the vessel accessible for cleaning and repairs.)

(e) Steel Ships.—The steel ship is the type most commonly built at the present time and has so many advantages over all other types that it is practically universally recognized as the modern ship. Wood and concrete ship construction have recently received a great impetus, but this is admitted to be due rather to the suddenly increased need for overseas transportation, which renders the construction of all types of ships advisable, rather than to any superiority of these ships over steel ships. The principal advantage claimed for wood and concrete ships at the present time is that their construction will supplement rather than replace steel construction, and can be carried on at the same time by utilizing other materials and a different class of labor. It is practically certain that steel ships will be the standard for many years to come and that by far the greatest proportion of ships constructed will have steel hulls. Recent experiments indicate that a great improvement may be made in the methods of steel ship construction by the substitution of electric welding as a means for fastening the various parts together instead of riveting. Yachts and small torpedo vessels are sometimes constructed of bronze instead of steel, but the principles of construction are practically the same as for steel vessels.

(f) **Concrete Ships.**—Reinforced concrete has been considered for a number of years as a material for ships, and a number of small craft, barges, etc., have actually been built on this principle, but it is only comparatively recently that large vessels designed for overseas service have been built of reinforced concrete. However, the recent great demand for ships of all kinds has resulted in a great deal of attention being paid to the construction of reinforced concrete vessels. The principal obstacles in the way of building ships of this material are the relatively great weight and volume of the material required to obtain the necessary strength, the liability of the material to crack when subjected to stress in a seaway, and the deteriorating effect of the action of salt water on the concrete. It is claimed by the advocates of concrete ships that these obstacles can be largely overcome and that they are more than offset by the advantages, the principal ones of which are cheapness and speed of production, and the fact that the labor required for their construction can be obtained without drawing on the supply of labor necessary for building steel ships.

At the present time concrete ships must still be considered as in an experimental stage, and until they have been built in sufficient numbers and operated satisfactorily for continuous and extended periods of time to demonstrate their practicability, the advisability of laying down large numbers of such vessels is open to some question.

2. Ships Classified with Reference to Purpose for Which Used.—

(*a*) **WARSHIPS.**

(I) Battleships.
(II) Cruisers.
(III) Gunboats.
(IV) Torpedo craft.

(V) Mining and mine sweeping vessels.
(VI) Submarines.
(VII) Auxiliary vessels.

(*b*) **MERCHANT SHIPS.**

(I) Passenger vessels.
(II) Cargo vessels.
(III) Combined passenger and cargo vessels.
(IV) Tugs.

(*c*) **SPECIAL TYPES.**

(I) Yachts, house boats, etc.
(II) Salvage and wrecking vessels.
(III) Dredges.
(IV) Fishing vessels.
(V) Surveying vessels.
(VI) Fire and water boats.
(And numerous other miscellaneous types.)

(a) Warships

(I) **Battleships.**—The term battleship is applied, in general, to warships designed to take part in fleet actions. It is a more or less elastic term sometimes including monitors and small coast defense ships, and some vessels that may also be classified as cruisers. The modern battleship represents the standard type of warship, from which other types may be considered as developed. It is the largest, most powerful fighting unit, and far more costly than most other types of warships, so that it is usual to compare the strengths of the various navies of the world in terms of the numbers of first-class modern battleships that they possess. ("Battle cruisers" are also included in this classification.)

Modern battleships are often called "*superdreadnoughts,*" being developments of the all-big-gun type of ship of which the British "Dreadnought" was the forerunner. They are characterized by great size, strong offensive and defensive powers, ability to keep the sea in all kinds of weather for prolonged periods of time, and fairly high speeds. They are especially designed for great strength and safety in case damaged by shell, torpedo, or mine attack, and consequently have numerous water-tight compartments, armored bulkheads, decks, and special under water protection, and their form differs considerably from that of a merchant ship. Great beam must be provided in order to obtain the large displacements required and the necessary stability. The displacements of such ships range between 30,000 and 40,000 tons. The guns carried may be of calibres approximating 16″ with armor of corresponding thickness. Very powerful engines are necessary to drive these great ships at the required speeds, which may be 21 knots or greater.

(II) **Cruisers.**—Vessels of this class are especially characterized by higher speed than battleships. They naturally lack in protection what they gain in speed and usually have a much smaller armament than battleships. They are variously subdivided into different classes, such as *battle cruisers*, *armored cruisers*, *protected cruisers*, and *scout cruisers* or *scouts*. In general, the purpose of cruisers is to serve as auxiliaries to the main battle fleet, doing convoy and scouting duty, protecting commerce, destroying the enemy's commerce, engaging enemy cruisers, etc. *Battle cruisers* are high-speed battleships in which armor and, in some cases, armament are sacrificed to speed. They may have speeds ranging between 25 and 30 knots. In some cases they have guns of the same calibre as contemporary battleships. Owing to their very high speed they may be even larger and longer and may cost more to build than battleships. *Armored cruisers* are less powerful and less speedy than battle cruisers. The distinction between these two classes is not exact since the battle cruiser is a comparatively recent type and may be correctly called an armored cruiser, whereas the old armored cruisers are considerably smaller and slower than battle cruisers. *Protected cruisers* are even smaller and less powerful than armored cruisers, and have little or no side armor, being provided merely with a protective deck near the water line. They are designed more for convoy and raiding service and should not take a direct part in fleet action. *Scouts* are light high-speed vessels designed primarily, as their name implies, for scouting service. They have very little protection, moderate armament, good seaworthiness, and a speed in the neighborhood of 35 knots. The general form of all cruisers resembles that of battleships, the lines, however, being considerably finer.

(III) **Gunboats.**—For special service in shallow waters along coasts or in rivers, small warships known as gunboats are employed. These are usually of special design, depending upon the waters in which they are to operate and may be, or may not be, protected by armor. They usually have displacements of under 1000 tons. Often they are converted yachts.

(IV) **Torpedo Craft.**—Formerly small, fast vessels were built for the purpose of carrying and launching torpedoes. These were called *torpedo boats.* To oppose them larger and faster vessels were built—along similar lines—called *torpedo boat destroyers.* The building of torpedo boats, therefore, was gradually abandoned, the duties formerly performed by them being transferred to the destroyers and also to some extent to *submarines.* Destroyers have been gradually enlarged until they now approach scouts in design and are used somewhat for the same duty. They carry both guns and torpedoes and have no armor, and are given very high speeds, between 30 and 40 knots. Their displacements may be as high as 1000 tons or even more than this. Their principal duties at the present time are to convoy merchant ships and to hunt down and destroy submarines.

(V) **Mining and Mine-destroying Vessels.**—These are specially equipped vessels of small size and light draft used for sowing mines and for sweeping and destroying them.

(VI) **Submarines.**—Submarines are vessels of special construction which enables them either to run on the surface of the sea or to run submerged. Submerged running is accomplished by flooding specially constructed tanks so as to destroy all except a very small amount of the buoyancy, the vessel then being directed downward below the surface of the water by the horizontal thrust of the propellers combined with the action of horizontal rudders or hydroplanes. The hull of a submarine has, in general, a cigar-shaped form and a circular or nearly circular cross section. Propulsion on the surface is usually accomplished by means of internal combustion engines, and when submerged, by means of storage batteries and electric motors. There are two general types of construction—the single hull type and the double hull type. Submarines range in displacements from two or three hundred tons upward—some very large "submarine cruisers" having been recently constructed.

(VII) **Auxiliary Vessels.**—In order to supply and cooperate with the main fleet of a navy certain special types of ships are necessary. Many of these are practically the same as certain types of merchant ships or are readily convertible from them. These include transports, hospital ships, colliers, oil tankers, ammunition ships, supply ships, repair ships, training ships, patrol and dispatch vessels, tugs, and numerous other special types.

The primary purpose of all warships is to make war and they are all designed with that principal object in view, so that questions of secondary importance to that must always give way to such characteristics as offensive power, safety and ability to continue to fight even when damaged in action, ability to keep the sea for long periods of time, etc. For these reasons they must be designed and constructed with much more care than merchant vessels.

(b) Merchant Ships

(I) **Passenger Vessels.**—Passenger vessels usually make voyages on a schedule between the same terminal ports. In other words, they run on the same *lines* and therefore they are usually called *liners*. They are usually of large size and fairly high speed. Almost all ships that carry passengers carry also a considerable amount of cargo, so that the number of strictly passenger vessels is very limited. Examples of these are the large fast vessels of the various trans-Atlantic lines. Some of these approximate 1000 feet in length and have gross tonnages of 50,000 or 60,000 with speeds of about 25 knots.

(II) **Cargo Vessels.**—This class forms the largest of all vessels afloat and handles the world's commerce. For reasons of economy the speed of cargo vessels is usually between eight and twelve knots, even lower speeds being found in the type known as *tramp steamers*. The main objects sought in a cargo vessel are carrying capacity and economy of operation. Consequently, the form is made very full and the amount of space devoted to the complement, engines, boilers, fuel, and water is kept as low as possible. Such vessels are often *parallel sided* or of uniform cross section for a considerable portion of their length. The main portion of the hull is taken up with cargo spaces. Some cargo ships are propelled by sails, sailing ships at the present time being, in fact, practically limited to cargo carriers, fishing vessels and yachts. The greater number of cargo vessels are, however, propelled by steam. A particular class of cargo vessels are those known as *tankers*, which are designed for carrying liquid cargoes in bulk. They are usually constructed on the longitudinal or *Isherwood* system of framing.

(III) **Combined Passenger and Cargo Vessels.**—These comprise vessels having the characteristics of both of the two preceding classes, the amount of space devoted to passengers and cargo varying between wide limits. The passengers are housed in the spaces on the upper decks above the cargo. Among such vessels will usually be found the ships of the various coasting lines. The speed of these ships usually ranges between 10 and 20 knots and their tonnage may be almost any figure from 1000 up to 20,000 or 30,000 tons gross, the design varying to meet the particular needs of the service for which built.

(IV) **Tugs.**—These are comparatively small vessels used principally in harbors and along the coast for towing other vessels or for assisting in handling them about docks and wharves. Seagoing tugs are usually from 150 to 200 feet long. Harbor tugs are considerably smaller. They are given comparatively powerful engines and must be of rugged construction with propellers designed especially for towing.

The form of merchant steamers is, in general, the same in all cases, the lines of the fast ones being, of course, finer,

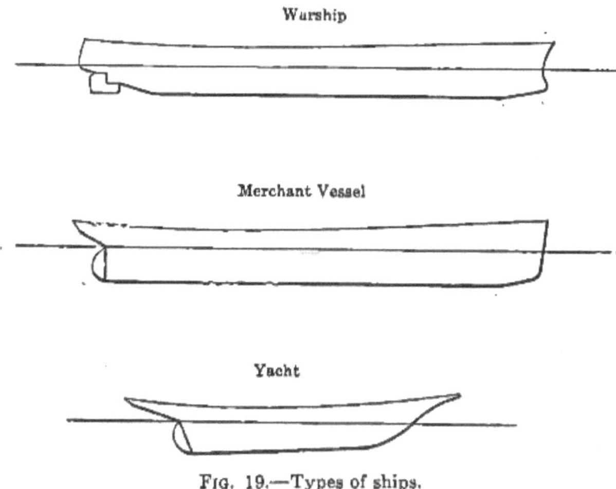

FIG. 19.—Types of ships.

but the general characteristics, such as shape of stem and stern, rudders, etc., being nearly always the same. Fig. 19 shows the general form of the profile of a merchant ship, as compared with that of a war ship, of the battle ship or cruiser type, and a yacht.

(c) Special Types

The various special classes of vessels, such as yachts, dredging, wrecking, and fishing vessels, etc., are too numerous to describe in detail. Each is designed to fulfill a special purpose, and usually varies considerably from the others, even of the same class.

3. Ships Classified with Regard to Speed.—There is no exact classification of ships with regard to speed, but it is worth noting that extremely few ships have a speed as high as 35 knots, and that speeds as low as 6 or 7 knots are often found in the case of tramp steamers, small sailing ships, vessels towing, etc. A rough classification with regard to speeds is given below:

Very high speed (30–35 knots).

Destroyers.
Scouts.

Fast (25–30 knots).

Special mail and passenger steamers.
Battle cruisers.

Moderately high speed (20–25 knots).

Battleships.
Fast passenger steamers.
Slow cruisers.

Good speed (15–20 knots).

Passenger steamers.
Older battleships.
Very fast cargo vessels.
Steam yachts.

Fair speed (10–15 knots).

Faster cargo vessels.
Slower passenger vessels.
Slower steam yachts.
Seagoing tugs (not towing).

Slow speed (under 10 knots).

Slow cargo vessels.
Tramp steamers.
Sailing vessels.

(A *knot* is a speed of 6080 feet per hour).

4. TONNAGE OF SHIPS

As has been stated in Chapter I, the weight of any ship floating in water, including all that she carries, must equal the weight of the water that she displaces. This weight is called the *displacement* of the ship and is usually expressed in tons, of 2240 lbs. each. It will be noted that the displacement is equal to the weight of the ship plus all that she carries, so that the displacement of any ship is variable and depends upon the cargo and other movable weights that she has on board. The displacement of an ordinary cargo vessel, for example, may be three times as much when she is fully laden as when she is light. For this reason a statement of the displacement of a cargo ship, unless the condition of loading is included, gives only an approximate idea of her size. War ships, such as battleships and cruisers, a large percentage of the weight of which is fixed, have comparatively little variation in displacement, and the tonnage of such ships is usually expressed in terms of their normal displacement.

In order to express the size of merchant ships it is usual to refer to their *gross* and *net tonnages*. These are both based upon certain volumetric measurements, 100 cu. ft. being reckoned as one ton. "Tonnage" in this case, then, really means volume. The *gross tonnage* is a measure of the internal capacity of the whole ship. The *net tonnage* is obtained by deducting, from the gross tonnage, allowances made for space occupied by officers and crew and their effects, navigation space, and propelling space. The net tonnage is thus really intended to be a measure of the passenger and cargo carrying, or earning power of the ship. The rules for making these measurements were established by the British Board of Trade and have been adopted by practically all civilized countries.

The net tonnage is always less than the gross tonnage and is usually about 63 per cent. of it, the reasons for this being that the rules allow a deduction of 32 per cent. for machinery spaces in the cases of ships of which that space is between 13 and 20 per cent. of the gross tonnage and that the other deductions usually amount to about 5 per cent. The great majority of all tonnage usually comes within this class.

The *dead weight carrying capacity* is expressed in tons of 2240 lbs., or in the same units as the displacement. It is the difference between the displacement of the ship when *light* and when fully *loaded* to the maximum draft allowed by law. In other words, the total dead weight carrying capacity of any ship may be defined as the weight, in long tons, of cargo, fuel, water, stores, officers, crew, passengers and their effects that can be safely carried by that ship.

There are therefore at least four different tonnages that may be applied to any ship, each expressing in its own way the size and therefore the usefulness of that ship. For ordinary cargo carrying ships the *full load displacement* tonnage is about 1½ times the dead weight carrying capacity, about 2¼ times the gross tonnage and about 3¾ times the net tonnage. The dead weight carrying capacity is about 1½ times the gross tonnage, and the net tonnage is roughly ⅔ of the gross tonnage.

The terms gross and net tonnage and dead weight carrying capacity are not ordinarily used in connection with war ships, which are measured in terms of displacement. The term displacement is seldom used to indicate the size of a merchant ship since it varies, for such ships, through a wide range. Yachts are usually measured in the same manner as merchant ships.

For purposes of insurance there have been established for many years in the principal maritime countries of the world certain *classification societies,* all of which publish ordinarily each year a *Register of Shipping,* which is a large book containing the names of all merchant vessels of the world together with their size, tonnage, ownership, name of builder, date built, and other data. The principal of these societies is Lloyds, the well-known British society. Another British society is known as the *British*

Corporation. In France is the *Bureau Veritas,* and in the United States the *American Bureau of Shipping.*

These Societies issue various rules under which they will insure ships, and they therefore have a very pronounced influence on the trend of ship design and construction. Vessels are *rated* by these various societies in accordance with their design, construction, and the care with which they have been kept up, each ship being periodically inspected by the surveyors of the Society and the rating modified, if necessary, as a result of the inspection.

Merchant vessels are also classified and their tonnage recorded by the government of the nation of which they fly the flag. The methods of determining the tonnages for this purpose are practically the same as those adopted by the various classification societies.

5. MATERIALS USED IN SHIP CONSTRUCTION

The principal material, which is in almost universal use for constructing the hulls of ships, is *steel.* This is found in the form of forgings, castings, plates, shapes, and rivets. Also in warships certain special treatment steel and face hardened steel for armor is used. Other materials used, though nowhere near to the same extent as steel, include *iron, copper, zinc, lead, tin, bronze, brass,* and other *compositions, wood* of all kinds, *canvas, cork, asbestos, linoleum, hemp* and *wire rope, cotton, oakum, rubber, tar, paper, glass, leather,* various *tilings* and *deck coverings, cements, enamels* and *paints.*

Forgings.—Forgings are used for special purposes where great strength is required. Owing to the irregular shapes required for the special large solid parts used in hull construction, the forging of which is more or less complicated, and because of the fact that steel castings possessing sufficient strength for most purposes can now be obtained, there are very few large forgings used in the hulls of ships. Forgings are used principally for machinery parts, such as crank shafts, propeller shafts, connecting rods, and for rudder stocks. Occasionally the stem and stern posts are forgings. Small forgings are used for certain hull fittings and working parts.

Castings.—Steel castings are commonly used for the stern frame, stem, stern tubes, rudder frame, propeller struts, machinery bed plates, anchors, hawse pipes, chain pipes, pipe flanges, gun mounts, and various small hull fittings. Various grades of steel are used for different ones of these castings.

Plates.—Plates are simply rolled sheets of steel of uniform thickness. They range in thickness from about ⅛″ to a trifle over 1″. Plates less than ⅛″ thick are generally spoken of as *sheets*. Very thick plates are used in war ships for protective decks and for armor of sides, turrets, barbettes, conning towers, etc., but these are not classed as ordinary ship plates, being made of specially treated steel by special processes.

Plates are used for the shell, inner bottom, bulkheads, decks, trunks, coamings and other such parts, and for various floors, brackets, girders, and other structural members.

The weight of a cubic foot of steel is approximately 490 pounds, so that a plate 1″ thick will weigh about 40.8 pounds per square foot. Plates are commonly specified by weight per square foot, and thus a "twenty pound plate" means one slightly less than ½″ in thickness. (In the case of wrought iron, which weighs 480 pounds per cubic foot, the weight of a plate, per inch of thickness, is almost exactly 40 pounds per square foot.)

Shapes.—Shapes are rolled steel bars of various special constant cross sections. The shapes most commonly used in ship construction are illustrated in Fig. 20. They are used for various parts of the ship's framing and for connecting different plates and other shapes.

The *angle bar* (*∠ bar*), which is shown in perspective in the upper sketch of Fig. 20, is used for joining two other members that meet at, or nearly at, right angles. The names of the various portions of the angle bar are indicated in the figure. When the angle made by the two legs or flanges is not 90° the angle bar (or *angle*, as it is often called) is said to be *beveled*. If the angle is greater than 90° it is an *open bevel*, and, if less, a *closed bevel*. The same terms apply to the other shapes when so treated.

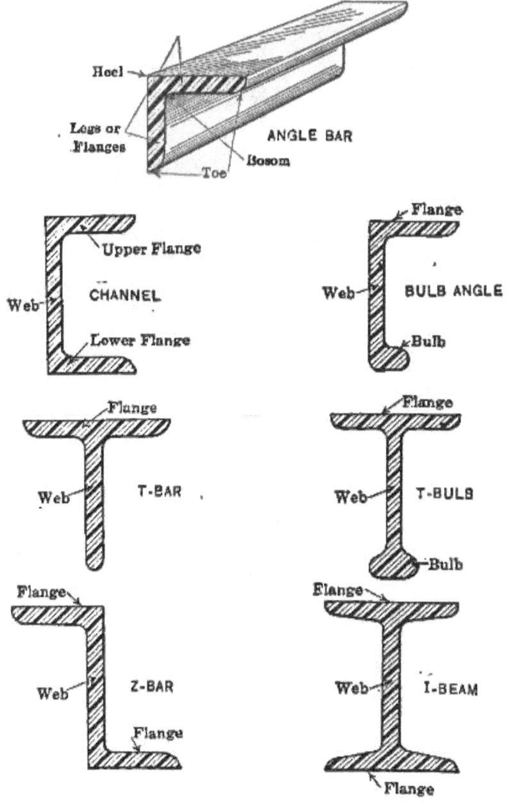

Fig. 20.—Shipbuilding shapes.

Channels, bulb angles and *Z-bars* are developments of the simple angle bar, as shown. They are used in cases where, in addition to connecting other members, they must also furnish more stiffness or girder strength than would be given by simple angles. This stiffness is supplied by the

5

extra "flange" strength. In some cases sufficient stiffness is furnished by *angles with unequal legs* in which case the shorter leg acts as one flange and the longer leg serves as both the web and the other flange.

The *I-beam* has the ideal cross section for girder strength but is not much used in ship construction on account of the difficulty of connecting it to other members.

The *T-bar* and *T-bulb* resemble somewhat the I-beam, and can be more conveniently attached to other members.

Shipbuilding shapes are designated by the dimensions of their legs or webs and flanges and their weight per linear foot—for example, a "3″ × 3″ × 6 lb. angle," a "10″ × 3⅜″ × 3⅜″ × 21.8 lb. channel," etc. These figures are called *scantlings.* These dimensions and other characteristics of the cross sections are given in hand books published by the various steel companies. They differ slightly for shipbuilding shapes (which are rolled specially) from those for ordinary structural steel as used for bridges, buildings, etc.

In addition to the shapes shown in Fig. 20 there are a few others used occasionally in shipbuilding, such as *round, square,* and *flat* bars, *half rounds* (solid and hollow), etc.

Rivets.—Rivets are small malleable metal members or fastenings, used to connect or tie together the various plates, shapes, forgings and castings of the ship's structure. A *rivet* consists of a cylindrical *shank* or *body,* of circular cross section, terminated at one end in an enlarged portion or *head.* The other end is formed, when the rivet is driven, into a *point.*

Fig. 21 shows a rivet before being driven, and also the various forms of rivet heads and points ordinarily used in shipbuilding.

Rivets are usually made of mild steel, although in some merchant work *wrought iron* rivets are used. Where high tensile steel plates and shapes are used the rivets connecting them are also made of high tensile steel. For connecting the plates and shapes of bronze vessels, bronze rivets are used.

A rivet is designated by the diameter of the cylindrical portion, or shank, before being driven. The ordinary sizes are $\frac{1}{4}''$, $\frac{3}{8}''$, $\frac{1}{2}''$, $\frac{5}{8}''$, $\frac{3}{4}''$, $\frac{7}{8}''$, $1''$, $1\frac{1}{8}''$ and $1\frac{1}{4}''$. Larger sizes are rarely needed, and, if so, are ordered specially.

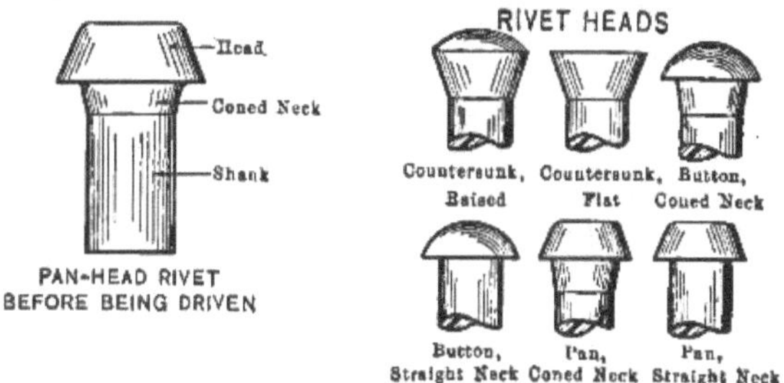

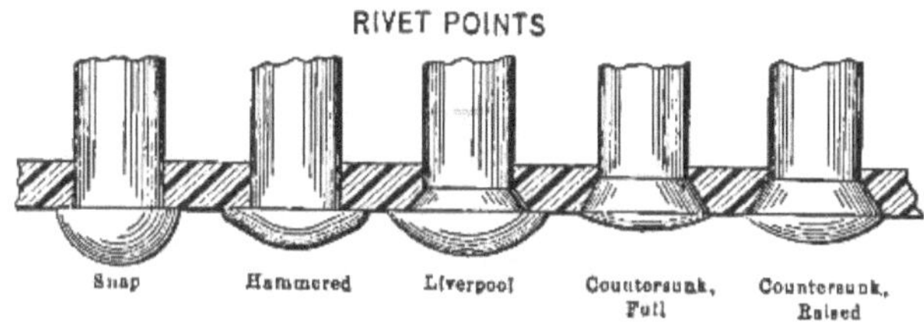

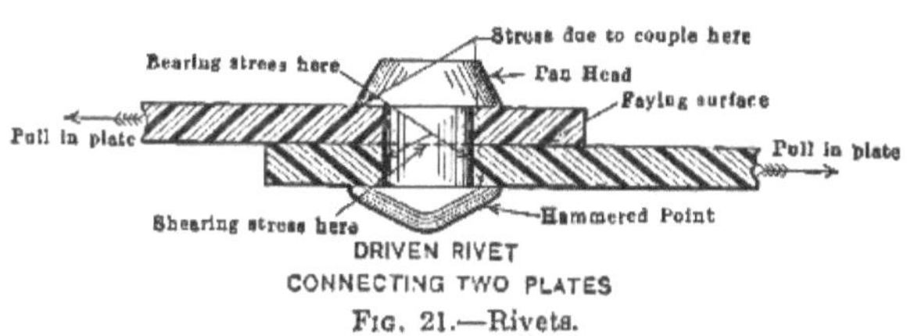

FIG. 21.—Rivets.

The *countersunk head* rivet shown in Fig. 21 is used in places where a flat or flush surface is required, as in the riveting of the shell plating to a bar keel, or in a steel deck to be covered with wood, and in cases where the head must be calked. It reduces the strength of the plate, however, since a larger portion of metal is cut from it. *Pan-head* rivets are used wherever it is possible. *Button-head* rivets are used for appearance. The *raised countersunk head* gives slightly better holding qualities than the flat head. A *coned neck* is for the purpose of causing the rivet to fill completely the space in a punched hole, which is slightly tapered.

Countersunk points, like countersunk heads, are used where a flush surface is required, or where calking the points is necessary. The best example of this is in the under water shell plating where projections would increase the resistance. *Button* points are used for purposes of appearance. *Hammered* points are used wherever possible, being, as a rule, cheapest, and nearly as efficient as any other points. The *Liverpool* point combines some of the advantages both of the countersunk and of the hammered point. The *full* or *raised* countersunk point is somewhat stronger than if perfectly flush. All countersunk points are, in practice, somewhat rounded out, or raised.

The lowest sketch of Fig. 21 shows a rivet, after being driven, connecting two plates that are subjected to a pull, as shown by the arrows. This pull is taken by the rivet in the following ways:

(*a*) There is a tendency for the body or shank of the rivet to be crushed by the bearing pressure on its upper right, and lower left sides. (These bearing pressures are also taken by the plates.)

(*b*) There is a tendency for the rivet to be sheared along the plane that divides the two plates (the *faying surface*).

(*c*) Owing to the fact that the pulls in the two plates do not act in exactly the same straight line there is set up a couple, tending to cause the head of the rivet to move to the left, and the point to move to the right, thus bringing bearing pressures, acting in a vertical direction, onto the right side of the point and the left side of the head, which tend to tear the head and point from the body of the rivet. (These pressures also tend to squeeze in the plates under the edges of the head and point.)

In all steel for ship construction the principal important

qualities required are strength, toughness and elasticity. A ship differs from a permanently fixed structure, like a building, in that there must be a certain amount of elastic flexibility to it. This is due to the forces set up by the motion and vibration of the ship when under way, and the action of the waves when in a heavy sea. It is very important that a strict uniformity of the material be maintained, and all ship steel should be carefully manufactured, inspected, and tested in accordance with properly drawn specifications.

In naval vessels, for which the very highest quality of material is essential, the steel used is purchased under very strict specifications which are published by the Navy Department. Commercial ship steel is of not quite so high a quality but is considered satisfactory for merchant ships. Specifications are published by the various registration societies covering steel for merchant ships.

The shipbuilder should be thoroughly familiar with the various physical and chemical requirements of steel that is suitable for hull construction. Most of this steel is known as *mild steel,* and is made by the open-hearth process. It usually has a tensile strength of about 60,000 pounds per square inch and a shearing strength of about 50,000 pounds per square inch. For special strength combined with lightness (as in destroyers, scouts, etc.) a high tensile steel is used which has a tensile strength varying between 75,000 and 95,000 pounds per square inch. High tensile steel is about ⅓ stronger than mild steel.

Iron.—*Cast iron* is used for certain minor parts where strength is not an essential, although practically never used in the hull proper. Propeller blades of merchant vessels are sometimes made of cast iron.

Wrought iron is used for anchor chains, anchors, steering-gear chains, straps for blocks, etc., miscellaneous blacksmith work, piping, etc. It should have a tensile strength of about 45,000 pounds per square inch and the other physical and chemical qualities necessary for the use to which put.

Iron does not corrode as rapidly as steel but has much less strength.

Non-ferrous Metals.—*Zinc* is used principally to prevent rusting or corrosion of iron or steel parts due to the action of salt water in contact with them. For this purpose the parts may be completely galvanized or small plates of rolled zinc may be attached to various points of the underwater hull where galvanic action is especially apt to occur, such as in the vicinity of propellers, rudder, and openings in the shell plating.

Copper is used for certain piping systems that must stand high pressures, for various kettles and steam tables, in sheets for sheathing wood planking under water and combined with zinc and tin in various bronzes and brasses used for castings.

Manganese bronze is used principally for propeller blades and hubs. It has a very high tensile strength, about 65,000 pounds per square inch, and contains approximately 58 percent of copper, 40 percent zinc and 1 percent manganese with a small amount of tin, aluminum, iron and lead.

Phosphor bronze is used for stem, stern, and rudder frames, shaft struts, etc., of bronze or sheathed vessels. It contains about 90 percent of copper, 9½ percent of tin and ½ percent phosphorus, and has a tensile strength of 30,000 to 35,000 pounds per square inch.

Naval brass contains about 60 percent copper, 37 percent zinc, 1 percent tin, with a small amount of iron, aluminum, and lead. There is less tin as a rule in brass than in bronze. Brass is used for small castings, where great strength is not so important, being much weaker than bronze. These include rail fittings, scuppers, stowage brackets, short rail and ladder stanchions, hatch and hatch cover frames, skylight, door and scuttle fittings, pipe flanges, valves, hand wheels, air port fittings, etc.

The percentages of the materials used in the different copper-zinc-tin alloys vary considerably, slight changes in the quantities of each producing entirely different qualities, to suit different requirements.

Lead is used for lining steel and copper pipe, sheathing in cold storage spaces, plumbing work, storage battery tanks, etc.

Wood.—Nearly all kinds of wood find a certain use in ship construction. Oak and yellow pine are largely used for the hulls of wooden ships, barges, lighters, tugs, etc. In steel ships wood is used for deck planking, partition bulkheads, sheathing in coal bunkers, holds, etc., for masts, spars, derricks, gun- and small machinery foundations, ladders, gangways, hatch covers, gratings, boats, booms, furniture, shelving, lockers, chests, fittings, and for a variety of other minor purposes. For auxiliary purposes, during the building of the hull prior to launching, wood is used to a considerable extent (piles, cross logs, building blocks, launching ways, staging, scaffolding, shoring, wedges, etc.).

Yellow pine is most used for decks, although teak is somewhat used for this purpose. Booms and spars are commonly made of pitch pine, Oregon pine, or spruce. Sheathing may be of white or yellow pine depending upon its location and the amount of wear and tear to which subjected. A considerable variety of woods are in use for furniture, stateroom bulkheads, lockers, etc., etc. Lignum vitæ is used for stern tube bushings. Blocking, shoring and wedges are commonly of yellow pine or oak. Piles are usually pine or fir stems.

Only the best quality of timber should be used for ship work and it should be carefully inspected. The most common defects to be looked out for in lumber are knots, shakes, heart centres, worm and bee holes, crooked grain, sap wood, splits, wane, extreme curvature, etc.

Shakes are fissures or cracks in the wood. The *heart* is the portion of the wood at the centre of the trunk of the tree, and the *sap wood* is that nearest the bark. *Wane* is an inequality in a board or plank caused by its being sawed from a portion of the log too close to the outside.

Flitches are slabs or pieces of timber sawed from the outer part of the log. *Knees* are pieces of timber cut from the part of the tree where the roots join the trunk, so that they have a natural curvature, or bend.

Miscellaneous Materials.—*Canvas* is used for awnings, sails, tarpaulins, hatch hoods, wind-sails and sometimes as a covering over wood decks, and for gaskets and stop-waters. *Cork* is used for sheathing compartments against heat, for life preservers, etc. *Asbestos* is used for lagging or covering certain pipes or bulkheads subjected to high temperatures. *Linoleum* is used as a deck covering. *Rope* is used for tackles, purchases, shrouds, stays, lifts and other rigging parts. *Cotton* and *oakum* are used for making tight the seams between deck planks and outer planking of sheathed or wooden vessels. *Rubber* is used extensively for gaskets of water-tight doors, hatches, manholes, ports, etc. *Tar* and *leather* are used for various purposes in connection with the rigging. Heavy *paper* or *cardboard* is used for making templates and in some cases for gaskets and stop-waters. Tarred paper is used in insulating bulkheads. *Ceramic tiling* and various special compositions are used as deck coverings in bath rooms, wash rooms, galleys, etc.

Paints and Cements.—One of the principal drawbacks to the use of steel for ships is the gradual wasting away of the material caused by rust or corrosion. In order to prevent or minimize this action a great variety of paints and other protective coatings are in more or less general use. The steel bottoms of ships must also be coated so as to reduce, as much as possible, *fouling*, or the attachment to the plating of various marine growths, such as weeds, grass, shells, barnacles, etc.

Ship's Bottom Paints.—The underwater plating of steel ships is painted with *anti-corrosive* and *anti-fouling* paints. The anti-corrosive paint is applied usually as the first two coats, to the underwater plating of the hull and is for the purpose of preventing corrosion or rusting. The anti-fouling paint is applied over the anti-corrosive (usually as one coat) and is for the purpose of preventing fouling, or the attachment of various marine growths. In order to do this two objects are sought: (1) to make the paint poisonous so as to kill or drive off the seaweed, barnacles, etc., and (2) to give it a certain soapiness so that by gradually washing away it will continue to give off the poison. A great many different special ship's bottom paints are on the market—some good and some poor. None is entirely successful in attaining the objects sought. Anti-corrosive paints were formerly almost always oil paints, plain *red lead* being largely used, but certain quick drying paints are now used considerably, these being composed of alcohol, shellac, zinc oxide and other similar materials. Such paints do not, however, adhere well to bare steel, and a new ship should be first painted with red lead, which fills up the pores of the metal and when scraped off gives a good surface for the adherence of the first coat of anti-corrosive. Anti-fouling paints are given their poison quality by the use of copper, arsenic, etc. A typical paint of this sort contains alcohol, shellac, pine tar, turpentine, white zinc oxide, Indian red, and red oxide of mercury.

Oil Paints.—For ordinary steel material exposed to the weather or to moisture the most commonly used protective paint is *red lead* or oxide of lead mixed with raw linseed oil and a small quantity of petroleum spirits and drier. Other paints may contain lead carbonate, iron oxide, metallic zinc, zinc oxide, etc. Red lead is best, however, and is used to a very great extent. It is used as a first coat for practically all steel material, being applied to the dry, clean, bare metal. Other oil paints with suitably colored pigments are used for finishing coats, over the red lead. The vehicle is almost always linseed oil.

Bituminous Compositions.—These are black tar-like compositions which are practically impervious to water, and, when properly applied, adhere well to steel. They are usually in the form of a *solution*, an *enamel*, and a *cement*. They are sold under various trade names and the manufacturers keep their composition more or less secret. However, it is fairly well known that they contain various kinds of asphalt, rosin, Portland cement, slaked lime, petroleum, and similar ingredients. The *solution* is a liquid which is applied cold with a brush and is used as a priming coat for either the enamel or cement. The *enamel* is applied hot over the solution after the latter is nearly dry or set, being poured where possible and otherwise spread over the surfaces. It forms a tacky, sticky mass, which hardens as it cools, but always remains fairly elastic and ductile. The *cement* is also applied hot, but is more difficult to apply than the enamel and can usually be applied only to horizontal surfaces.

Experience with such compositions has not always been satisfactory. It has been noted that they were too thin a coating to give proper protection against coal and other hard lumps rubbing against them, that they are either too brittle and flake and chip off, or that they are too soft and flow at only moderately high temperatures, and that they blister.

Practically all of these objections can, however, be, and are removed by proper care in preparing the materials, and intelligent skill in their application, with the result that a highly efficient protective coating can be thus obtained. Bituminous solution and enamel or cement are therefore used considerably for the following spaces in ships: ballast and trimming tanks, double bottom tanks, chain lockers, reserve feed tanks, fresh water tanks, tank top, coal bunkers, engine and boiler foundations, etc., below floor plates, shaft alleys, and various spaces that are not readily accessible for cleaning and painting.

In applying these compositions great care must be used to see that the metal is dry, bare and absolutely free from rust, dirt, grease, etc., and that wide variations in the temperature of the metal are avoided. Cold weather and conditions liable to cause sweating should be avoided. Artificial ventilation must be provided for the workman, who, even then can work in the fumes for only short periods at a stretch. The success or failure of such coatings depends upon whether or not they are applied properly in the beginning.

Portland Cement.—Portland cement of good quality, mixed with sand (usually about 2 or 2½ parts of sand to 1 part of cement) is used in ships to protect the steel material where it is subject to rubbing of various hard articles, where it is not readily accessible for painting, where also necessary for drainage purposes, and under tiling. Where the thickness must be considerable, as in the pockets between frames near the ends of the ship, it may be lightened by having coke mixed with it. It is not, ordinarily, used in double bottoms. If the cement does not adhere firmly to the metal underneath not only will corrosion not be prevented, but it may go undetected, which is serious. For this reason many persons are opposed to the use of cement. It is also liable to be cracked or crumbled by the action of the vessel in a seaway. On the other hand, if properly applied it should form a good bond with the steel, and has several advantages over coatings that would otherwise be used. The tendency, however, seems to be to use more bituminous compositions and less Portland cement.

Smoke stack paints are designed to withstand the heat to which they are normally subjected. They contain litharge, whiting, lampblack, silica, white lead, white zinc, mineral oil, etc.

Shellacs, varnishes and various other special paints are used for a number of miscellaneous purposes on board ship.

The relative advantages of various paints, compositions, cements, varnishes, etc., are always open to argument, since none are perfect, all are more or less advertised, and results of experience, depending, as they do, upon both material and skill of application, are not always reliable guides.

A knowledge of the values of these different coatings as preventers of corrosion is, however, important to the shipbuilder, and even more so to the ship operator, since if corrosion is not properly prevented the ship will in a few years be wasted away to nothing. Good paints and other coatings, well applied, are economies in the long run.

Weights of Various Materials.—It is necessary frequently to calculate or to estimate the weights of various members, parts or fittings of ships, and for that purpose the unit weights of some of the materials most commonly used should be known. These are given below:

Material	Weight in lbs. per cu. ft.
Ship steel	490
Wrought iron	480
Cast iron	450
Copper	550
Brass (about)	525
Bronze	535–550
Lead	710
Live oak	67
White oak (about)	45
White pine; spruce (about)	30
Teak	45–60
Portland cement and sand (about)	130
Cork (about)	14
Yellow pine (about)	45

CHAPTER III

STRUCTURAL MEMBERS OF SHIPS

1. TRANSVERSE AND LONGITUDINAL FRAMING

In the great majority of ships the framing is of the transverse type—the frames forming the "ribs" which extend out on each side perpendicular to the keel or "back bone." This principle of construction is simply an extension of that shown in Fig. 13 (B). The keel running longitudinally along the centre line of the bottom gives fore and aft strength. Considering the ship as a girder the keel forms a portion of the lower "flange," the main deck similarly forming a portion of the upper "flange."

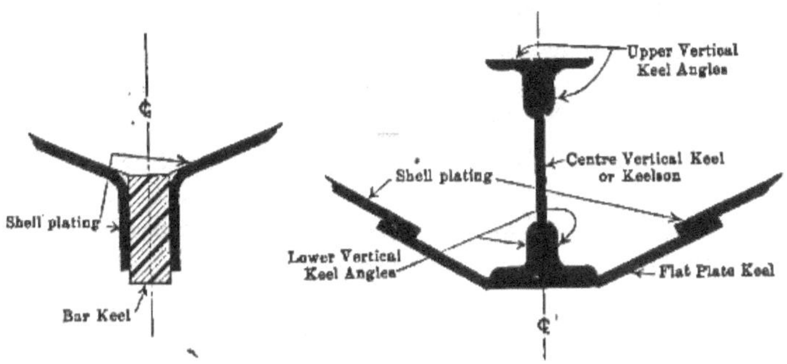

Fig. 22.—Types of keels.

In wooden ships the keel is a heavy solid timber of rectangular cross section, and with the introduction of the use of iron for shipbuilding purposes it was naturally replaced by a heavy wrought iron bar of somewhat similar cross section. Such keels are still used to some extent in steel ships and are called *bar keels*. In the left-hand sketch of Fig. 22 is shown such a keel. The lower plates of the shell plating are *flanged* or bent down as shown so as to fit snugly against the sides of the keel to which they are fastened by means of long through rivets extending through the three thicknesses of plate, keel, and plate. Such a keel, owing to its large cross section, furnishes considerable strength, and, owing to its depth, great vertical stiffness, but it has the disadvantage of increasing the draft of the ship, and it has therefore been replaced in almost all ships by the *flat plate keel.*

The right-hand sketch in Fig. 22 shows a flat-plate keel which is a long course of plating, dished on each side, and connected by lap joints to the lower plates of the shell plating. The keel therefore forms a portion of the shell plating. In this type of construction the flat plate keel is supplemented by a continuous vertical plate, as shown in the figure, called the *centre vertical keel* or *centre keelson.* This is secured to the flat plate keel by an angle bar on each side and is stiffened at its upper edege by another angle bar on each side, as shown. All of these members are continuous so that they serve to form a deep powerful centreline girder. The lower flange of this girder is further strengthened by the shell plating attached to each side of the keel.

The *transverse frames* furnish the direct support for the shell plating against the pressure of the water and also serve to transmit the vertical forces caused by the wieghts carried by the decks down to the bottom of the ship. On account of the shape of the ship they have considerable curvature and constitute one of the features of steel construction in which ships differ from structures of other types.

The transverse frames are located at stations similar to the cross sections 2, 3, 4, 5, etc., in Fig. 16, but are spaced at much shorter intervals. The interval between two successive frames, called the *frame spacing,* varies between about 18″ in small vessels and about four feet in large ones. The frame spacing is normally constant throughout the length of the ship, being reduced only where special local stiffness is required (as under engines, boilers and other heavy weights). At certain of the frame stations the ordinary frames are replaced by transverse bulkheads, which in addition to serving as partitions, may be considered, in this connection, as *solid* frames. The beams of the decks, which run athwartships between the upper portions of the frames, act with them in furnishing transverse stiffness and complete the "ring" of each frame.

The simplest type of frame is a single angle bar, bent to the shape of the section at which it is located. One flange of the angle bar is then flat and lies in a transverse plane throughout its own length, the heel and toe of this flange being curved to the shape of the transverse section of the ship at that frame station. The line of the heel of the bar lies in the molded surface of the ship, and, when viewed from directly forward or aft, has the exact shape of the frame. Due to the form of the ship each frame curve varies slightly from the neighboring ones except in the parallel middle body.

The other, or longitudinal flange is formed to and lies in the molded surface of the ship, so that the inner surface of the shell plating may rest snugly against it. In the parallel middle body the longitudinal flange is everywhere at right angles to the transverse flange, but at all other parts of the molded surface the angles between the flanges are greater than 90°, on account of the transverse curvature of the molded surface. This is due to the fact that the frames are arranged so that the bosoms of those in the forward portion of the ship will "look" aft, and of those in the after portion, forward, thus giving all frames an *open bevel.*

Figure 23 shows a portion of the framing and shell plating of a ship fitted with simple angle frames. The planes *ABC*, *DEF*, and *GHK* are planes of such transverse frames, being drawn square to the keel line of the ship. The distance *AD* or *DG* is the frame spacing. The transverse flanges of the frames lie in these transverse planes, as shown, and the longitudinal flanges lie in the molded surface or against the inner surface of the shell plating. The construction is shown in section in the lower portion of the figure, the necessary bevel of the frame angle, in order for it to fit against the shell plating, being as indicated. The shell plating is fastened to the longitudinal flange by a single row of rivets, which are fairly widely spaced, since their spacing has no effect upon the watertightness of the shell.

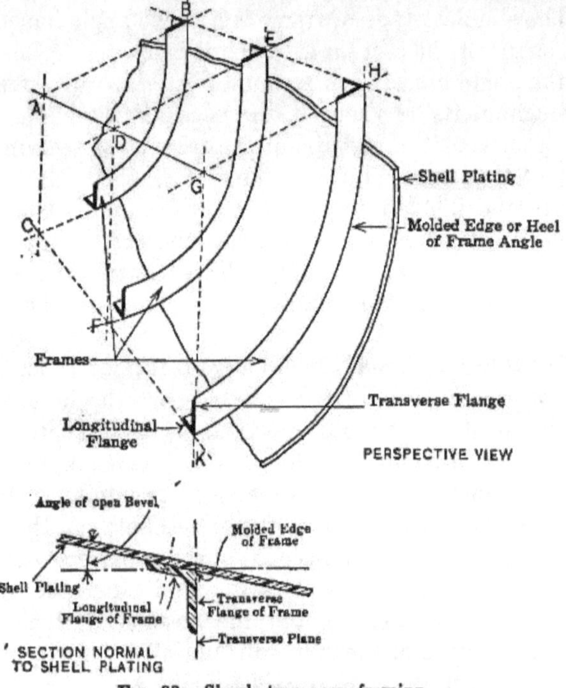

FIG. 23.—Simple transverse framing.

The construction just described might be suitable for a very small vessel, but for larger ones it does not give sufficient stiffness, and therefore it is customary to reinforce the frame angle bar by another angle called a *reverse frame*, or to substitute for the simple angle frame a channel, bulb angle, or *Z*-bar as shown in Fig. 24. The reverse frame is riveted to the transverse flange of the frame and the two combined act as a girder in supporting the shell plating, the two transverse flanges forming the web, and the reverse frame furnishing additional flange strength. The use of channels, bulb angles or Z-bars accomplishes a similar result without so much riveting.

For even greater strength a plate may be introduced between the frame and reverse frame, thus giving a deeper

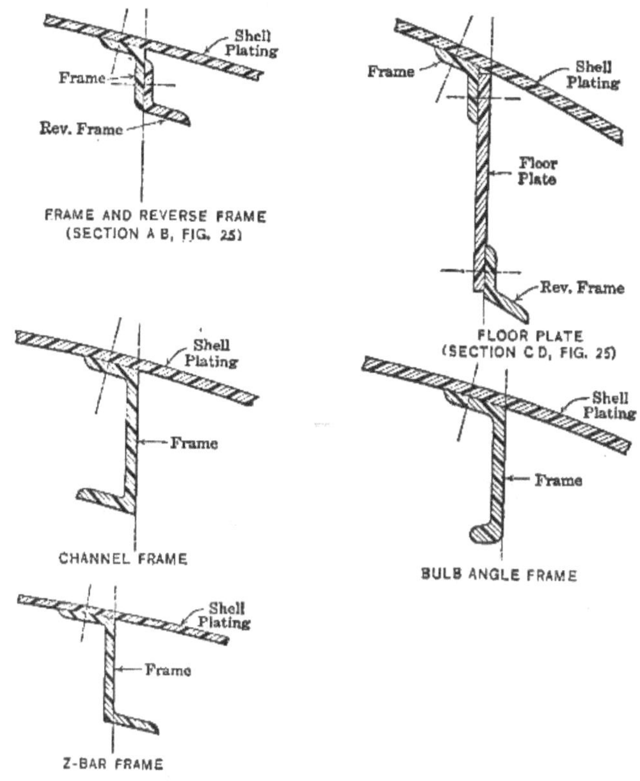

FIG. 24.—Transverse framing.

web and increasing the strength of the whole as a girder. This construction is also illustrated in Fig. 24. Such plates are usually fitted between the frames and reverse frames over the bottom shell plating in order to reinforce and stiffen the bottom of the ship, and are then called *floor plates*. Floor plates have the same depth as the centre vertical

6

keel at the centre line of the ship and are reduced in depth about uniformly from the centre until at or near the turn of the bilge the depth becomes the same as that of the transverse flange of the frame bar, and they are terminated.

A similar construction is found in *web frames* (also called *deep frames* or *belt frames*) in which the full depth of the

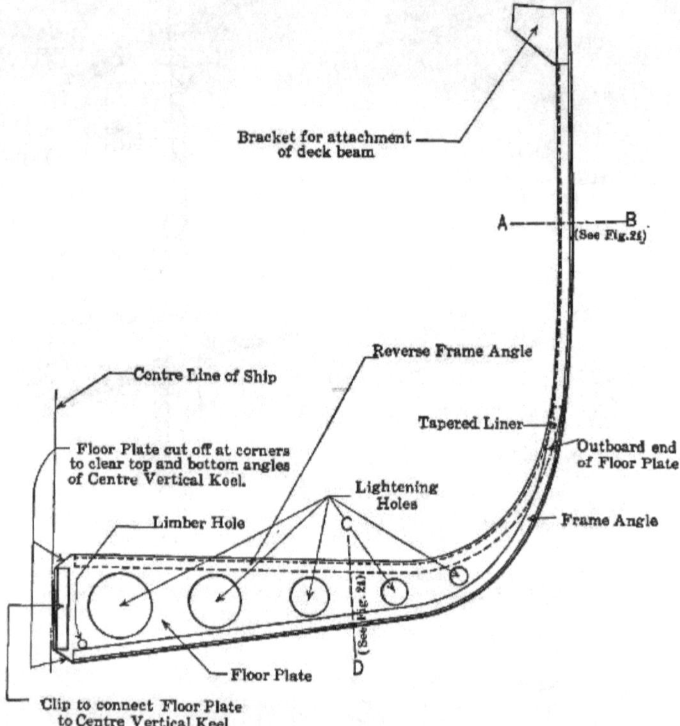

FIG. 25.—Frame, reverse frame, and floor plate.

web plate is maintained throughout the entire girth of the frame. These are special frames fitted to give great transverse strength, and occur at intervals of a number of frame spaces apart. They may be considered as *partial bulkheads*.

In Fig. 25 is shown a transverse frame, reverse frame and floor plate, the section at AB being the same as that of the *frame and reverse frame* shown in Fig. 24, and at *CD* as that of the *floor plate* in Fig. 24. (The *bevel* of the frame and reverse frame angles is not, however, indicated in Fig. 25.) Referring to Fig. 25 the following points will be noted. The outboard or tapered end of the floor plate is bent, in its own plane, to the curvature of the frame and reverse frame angle bars between which it is fitted. It is reduced in weight by means of several large circular *lightening holes* cut or punched in it. At its end is fitted a tapered filling-in piece or *liner* which fills the space between the frame and reverse frame at their junction. Small circular *limber holes* are cut in the lower portions of the floor plates in order to permit water to pass through for drainage. The floor plates are fastened to the centre vertical keel by means of short pieces of angle bar, called *clips* or *lugs*. *Brackets*, or triangular-shaped plates are fitted to give a suitable connection of the beams to the frames. The inboard corners of the floor plates are cut off sufficiently to permit the upper and lower angles of the centre vertical keel to run through continuously.

In order to prevent racking, or fore and aft movement of the frames, reverse frames, and floor plates, and to tie them together and add to the support that they furnish to the shell plating (as well as to add to the longitudinal strength of the ship) certain fore and aft members called *keelsons* and *stringers* are fitted in addition to the keel and centre vertical keel. These consist of angle bars, single or double, running along the inner edges of the reverse bars and connected to the shell plating by flat plates placed normally to the curvature of the molded surface. The number and disposition of these members depends upon the size and type of the ship.

Keelsons run approximately or exactly parallel to the centre vertical keel. Those nearest the keel are called *side keelsons*, and those near the bilges, *bilge* keelsons, the general construction of both being about the same. The surfaces of these members intersect the surfaces of the floor plates approximately at right angles, and therefore the plate portions of them must be made in sections to fit between adjacent floor plates. Such plates are called *intercostal plates,* the term *intercostal* being applied in general to any member which is formed of separate parts fitted between successive continuous members that it intersects. In Fig. 26 is shown a side elevation and cross section of a side keelson and also a separate view of one of its intercostal plates. The intercostal plates fit snugly against the floor plates but are not connected directly to

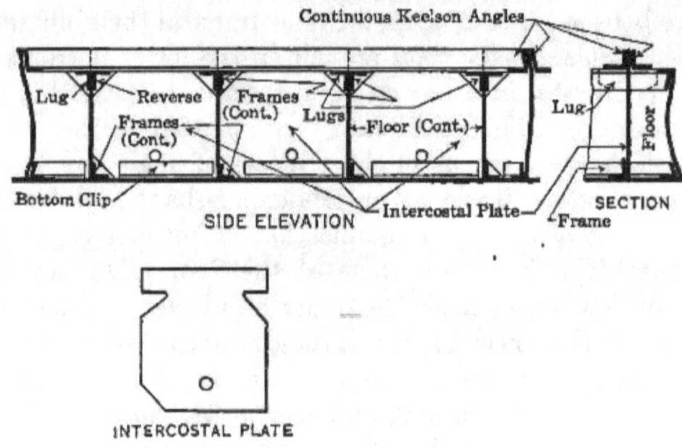

FIG. 26.—Intercostal side keelson.

them. The keelson angles are tied to the shell plating by means of the intercostal plates which are clipped to the shell. Along the line of the keelson angles, which run continuously along the inner edges of the floor plates, are fitted short lugs, riveted to the floor plates on the side opposite the reverse frames, to give a rigid attachment for the keelson angles. The frames and reverse frames are continuous and pass through notches cut in the intercostal plates.

Stringers have a construction very similar to that of keelsons, but being located above the outboard ends of the floor plates (see Fig. 28) the stringer plates do not have to be entirely intercostal and are simply notched out for the frames and reverse frames. The construction of a stringer is shown in Fig. 27, which gives good continuity of longitudinal strength. Stringers located near the bilge are called *bilge stringers*, and those higher up, *side* or *hold stringers*.

In Fig. 28 is shown a cross section of a ship framed on the principles just described, that is, with transverse frames, reverse frames and floor plates, and centre vertical keel. This figure is merely for the purpose of indicating the general construction and the relative dimensions are not strictly accurate. Only one keelson is shown, but in a larger ship several might be fitted between the centre

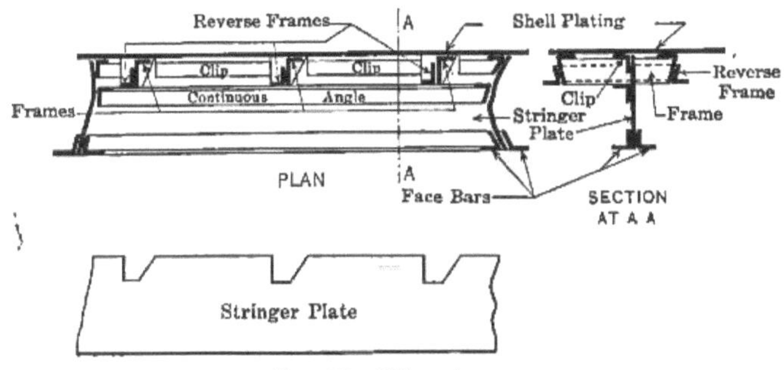

FIG. 27.—Side stringer.

vertical keel and each bilge. It will be noted that the outboard deck plating which is attached directly to the shell also assists in furnishing longitudinal strength. These plates are usually made heavy for this purpose and on account of their function are called deck stringer plates. Girders are also fitted under the decks, as shown in the figure, which, together with the deck stringers and upper portion of the shell plating give longitudinal strength to the upper "flange" of the ship, considered as a girder.

Ships, except very small ones, are usually fitted with *double bottoms* so that the construction of the lower portion is somewhat different from that shown in Fig. 28. The double bottom is formed by fitting plating over the tops of the floor plates and curving it down at the sides to join the shell plating. In this case the depth of the floor plates is maintained nearly constant from bilge to bilge and the inner bottom is usually flat and horizontal. The continuous keelson angles shown in Fig. 26 are omitted and the keelson plates extended only to the tops of the floor plates.

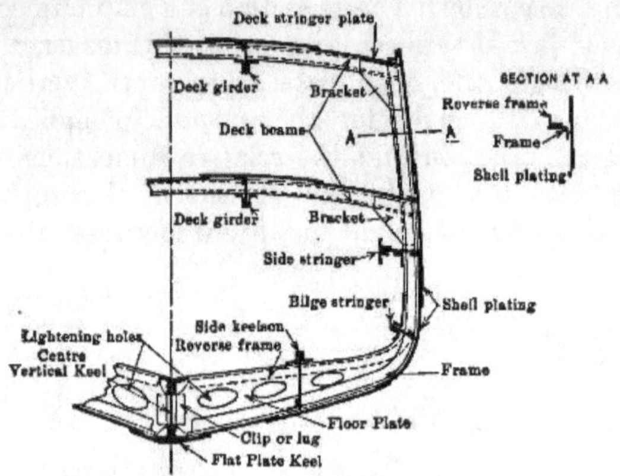

FIG. 28.—Cross section of a ship showing longitudinal framing.

They are given sufficient strength to make up for this reduction by the inner bottom plating to which their upper edges are now attached. Instead of being called keelsons they are then spoken of as *longitudinals.*

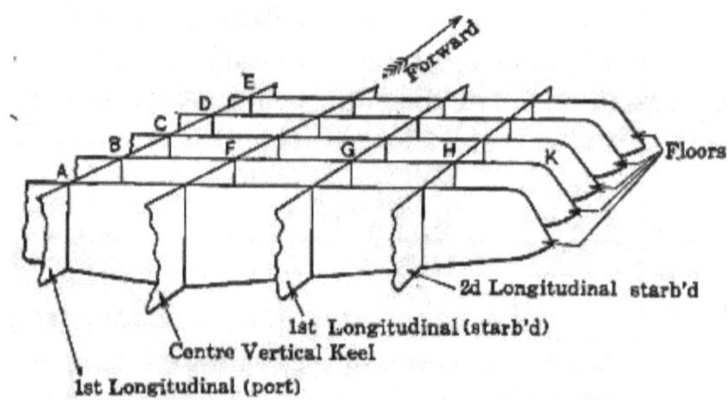

FIG. 29.—Diagrammatic view of cellular double bottom framing.

The floor plates and longitudinals intersecting at right angles form a cellular double bottom composed of a great many rectangular pockets or cells as shown in perspective in Fig. 29. This construction is found in nearly all modern ships of any size. In war ships the double bottom is continued farther up the sides of the ship the longitudinals being then more numerous and being as nearly normal to the inner and outer plating as possible. In large merchant passenger ships a similar construction has been adopted in recent years (since the loss of the "Titanic").

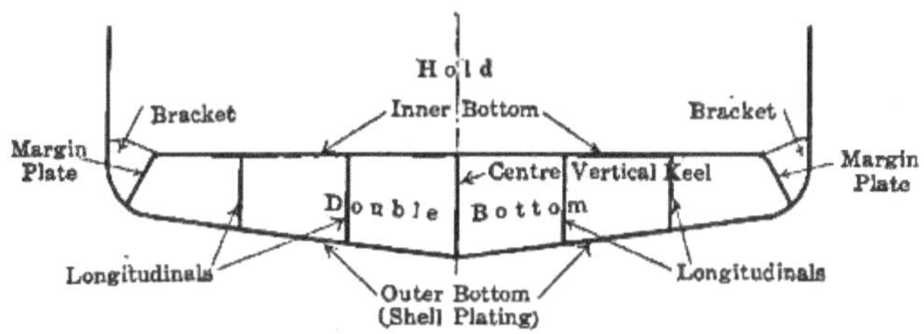

FIG. 30.—Cross section of double bottom.

The ship is thus given two complete under water shells, which greatly increase her safety in the event of collision or grounding.

For ordinary merchant cargo vessels, however, the double bottom is continued only to the bilges, where the inner

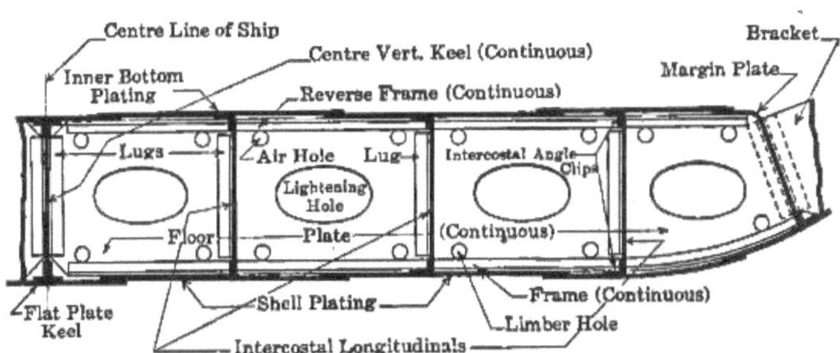

FIG. 31.—Cross section of cellular double bottom with intercostal longitudinals.

bottom is connected to the outer bottom by a *margin* plate placed normal to the shell plating. The arrangement is shown in Fig. 30. Each frame is tied to the floor plate within the inner bottom by means of a bracket as shown.

The details of the construction are shown in Fig. 31 which represents a typical double bottom of a merchant cargo vessel, in cross section. Referring to this figure it will be noted that the floor plates are continuous from centre vertical keel to margin plate while the longitudinal plates and their upper and lower angles are intercostal. In Fig. 29 the line FGHK represents the top of a single continuous floor plate of this type and the longitudinals are composed of a number of short rectangular sections, the tops of which are AB, BC, CD, DE, etc. These short longitudinal plates are attached by clips, or lugs, to the floor plates between which they are fitted, as shown in Figs. 31 and 32. The margin plate is flanged over at its upper edge to form a lap joint with the outer edge of the

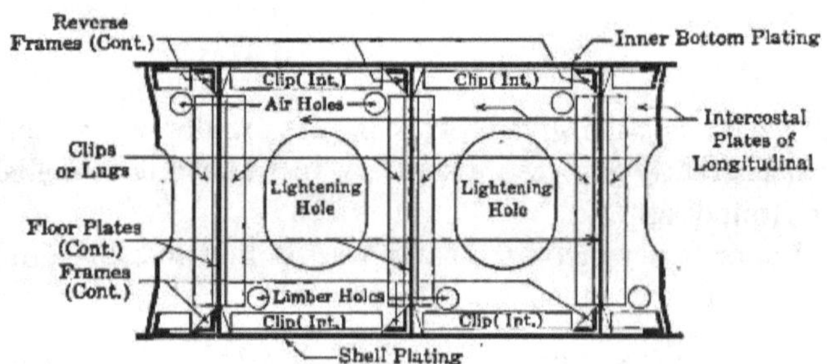

Fig. 32.—Longitudinal section of cellular double bottom showing intercostal longitudinal.

inner bottom plating and is connected on its inboard and outboard sides to the floor plates and brackets, respectively, by angle clips, as shown in Fig. 31.

Fig. 32 is another section through the double bottom, taken fore and aft, or at right angles to the section shown in Fig. 31, and shows how the plates of the longitudinals are cut off at the corners to permit the continuous frame and reverse frame angles to pass through.

The construction shown in Figs. 31 and 32 is used in warships, *with the exception, however,* that the longitudinal plates and their upper angles run continuously and the floor plates are intercostal between them, the frame angles, however, being still kept continuous. Such floor plates (although lightened by large holes) are spoken of as *solid floors.*

It is customary to replace some of the solid floors, both in merchant vessels and in warships, by *bracket floors,* which reduce the weight and still give sufficient strength.

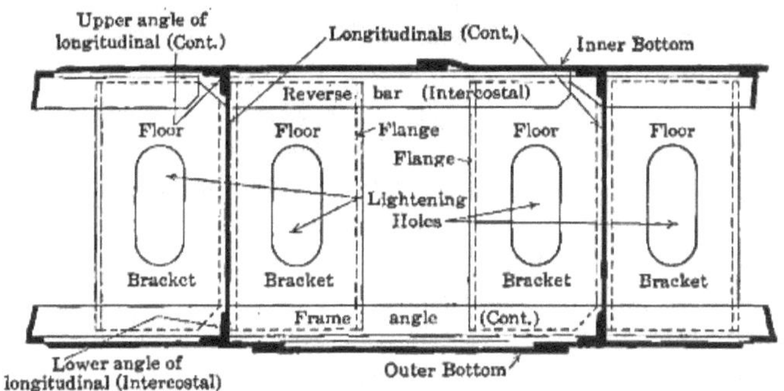

FIG. 33.—Bracket floor.

A bracket floor as fitted in warships is shown in Fig. 33. The continuity of the longitudinal plates and their upper angles and of the frame angles will be noted here, this being typical of warship construction.

At the ends of double bottom tanks (which usually come under athwartship bulkheads) solid water-tight floors

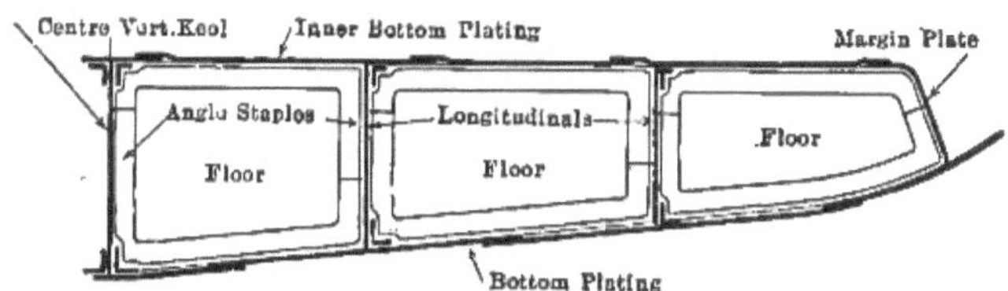

FIG. 34.—Watertight floor, cut by continuous longitudinals.

are fitted. These are nothing but extensions of the bulkheads above, or if there are no bulkheads above may be considered as partial bulkheads themselves. Such a water-tight floor is shown in Fig. 34, in which the special *stapling* of the bounding angle bars, in order to make the connections water-tight, should be noted.

Limber holes, air holes and *drain holes* are cut in longitudinals and floors in order to permit water to be pumped in or out of the double bottom tanks through which they pass. See Figs. 31 and 32. *Limber holes* are usually about 3″ in diameter and located tangent to the upper edge of the frame. *Drain holes* (not shown in the figures) are smaller, about 2″ long × 1″ high, cut through both floor and frame (or longitudinal and its lower angle) just over the bottom flange. *Air holes* are similar to drain holes, only that they should be located as *high*, instead of as *low* as possible. Sometimes larger air holes are also cut resembling limber holes but cut in the *upper* part of the floors or longitudinals.

At the ends of the ship, where longitudinal strength is not so important, the framing is different from that in the middle body. Keelsons, stringers, etc., are often omitted here and the transverse frames are fitted with very deep floor plates which give great stiffness to the shell plating. At the bow special horizontal plates called *breast hooks*, and sometimes vertical *ram plates* are attached to the shell to stiffen it against panting. These usually form the terminations of keelsons or longitudinals. *Panting stringers* are also often fitted. In merchant ships the framing aft of the stern post is usually arranged radially so as to be normal to the plating. Such frames are called *cant* frames.

The preceding description of transverse and longitudinal framing applies to what is commonly known as the *transverse system of framing,* which is the system most often used. Only a few representative constructions have been described and it must be remembered that there is practically no limit to the number of various special designs for framing that may be found in use. Those that have been described will serve to give an idea of the objects to be attained, and of some of the ordinary constructions, from which others may be developed.

Another system of framing that has come into quite considerable use in recent years is the *Isherwood System,* sometimes called the *longitudinal system.* In this the main framing runs fore and aft and the transverse members form the auxiliary framing, being spaced at greater intervals than in the so-called transverse system. As a matter of fact in the Isherwood system the transverse members are heavier, but continuity of all the longitudinal members is attained. A cross-section of an Isherwood-built ship resembles that of a ship with a large number of keelsons, stringers and girders, and deep or web frames. This construction is especially well adapted to oil tankers, for which it is now almost universally used.

2. STEM, STERN POST, RUDDER, ETC.

The lines of a ship at the ends gradually taper off to the "cutwater" at the bow and to the rudder post at the stern. The keel, which is usually straight and horizontal for nearly the complete length of the ship merges, near the bow, into the *stem*, and near the after end, into the *stern post* or *stern frame*. The nature of these members varies with the type of ship. In war ships, which usually have specially shaped bows and sterns (see Fig. 19), they are elaborate steel castings, often made in more than one piece. In merchant ships they are usually of simpler form and may be of wrought iron or steel. In either case they serve to form continuations of the keel, finishing off the ends of the ship and providing a suitable means for the attachment of the shell plating.

Stem.—The stem may be considered as the forward end of the keel, bent up and extended in a vertical or nearly vertical line. In its simplest form it consists of a bar of the same cross section as the keel (when the latter is a bar keel) attached thereto by means of long through rivets, the joint being formed by cutting away a portion of both keel and stem bars so that they may overlap each other without increasing the width of either. Such a joint is called a *scarph*. A stem of this type is shown in the right hand sketch of Fig. 35. If of this simple form it would ordinarily be a forging. The ends of the shell plating are flanged and riveted to it just as to the bar keel.

A bar stem may also be used in conjunction with a flat plate keel, in which case the lower portion is gradually flattened out so as to fit into the last U-shaped plate of the plate keel and is given a vertical fin or web on its upper surface for the attachment of the centre vertical keel. On account of the difficulty of forging this lower portion

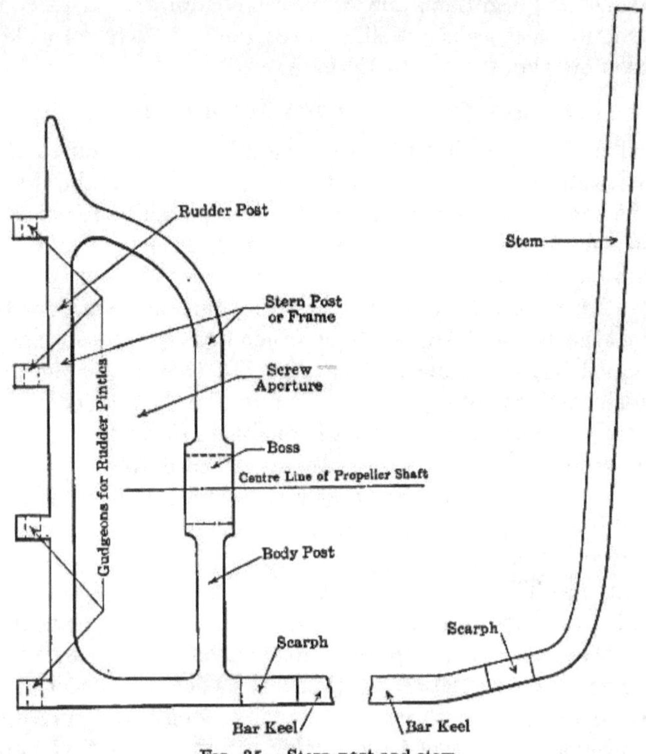

Fig. 35.—Stern post and stem.

such a keel might be made in two parts, the lower one being a steel casting and the upper one, scarphed to the lower, a forging. A cross section, normal to its curvature, of the lower portion of such a keel is shown in Fig. 36. The shell plating is recessed, or *rabbetted,* into the keel, so that its outer surface will be flush with the outer surface of the keel, as shown.

For warships the stem is ordinarily formed of two steel castings scarphed together at a point above the water line and made with webs or lugs for the attachment of decks, longitudinals, floor plates, etc. For extra strength the shell plating is doubled, the outer layer overlapping the inner so that a rabbett of two steps is necessary in the stem casting. Heavy breast hooks and ram plates are also

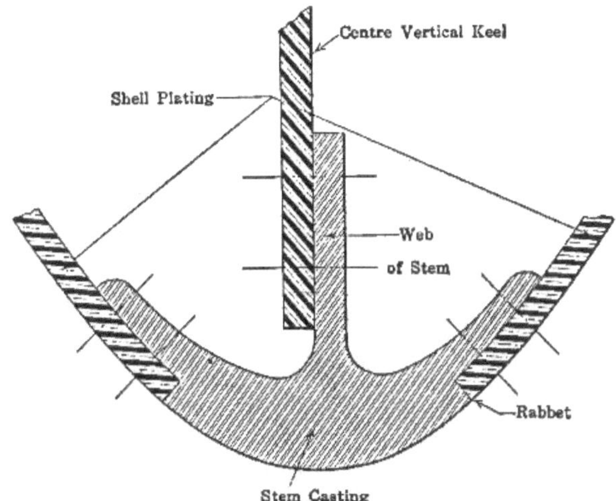

FIG. 36.—Cross section of lower portion of cast stem.

attached to it. Such a stem being of complicated form must be a casting.

The stem of a sheathed vessel is made of manganese or phosphor bronze, so as to prevent galvanic action.

Stern Post.—Like the stem, the stern post may also be considered as an extension of the keel, bent up vertically. It is, however, more complicated on account of the support that it must furnish to the rudder, and, usually, to the propeller. With a bar keel the simplest type may be forged and of a form similar to that shown in Fig. 35. Such a stern post (or stern frame) might also be cast, and with more complicated constructions it is almost invariably so made. As shown in Fig. 35, the stern frame consists of the *rudder post* and *body post* with an opening between for the screw or propeller. The rudder post has projections or lugs, called *gudgeons*, which serve as bearings for vertical pins attached to lugs on the rudder, and called *pintles*. The body post, to which is attached the shell plating, in the same manner as to the stem, serves in single or triple screw ships, as a support for the after end of the propeller shaft, being swelled out and provided with a longitudinal hole or opening for that purpose. It is sometimes also called the *propeller post*, in such cases. In twin or quadruple screw ships the stern post is also the rudder post and there is no screw aperture, the shell plating extending right aft to the rudder post, as a rule. Such a construction is shown in Fig. 18. When fitted in connection with a bar keel the stern frame is scarphed to it, like the stem, as shown in Fig. 35. If fitted with a flat plate keel a casting formed similarly to the stem casting shown in Fig. 36 would ordinarily be used.

For war ships the stern post is usually an elaborate steel casting made in two or more parts made with webs, lugs, rabbetts, etc., in a manner similar to the stem. Its shape is quite different from that ordinarily used for merchant vessels on account of the larger, balanced rudder, and the necessity for keeping the rudder head and steering gear below the water line where they are less liable to be damaged in action.

Recently some merchant vessels have been built with "cruiser sterns," or sterns of the typical war ship form. The various possible combinations and arrangements of rudders and propellers have resulted in a variety of forms of stern posts, all requiring special castings, designed to meet the particular needs. In all cases it is necessary that both the stern post and stem be strongly secured to the shell plating and hull structure in their vicinity, in order properly to transmit to the hull the forces due to steering, propulsion and possible head-on collision or ramming.

Rudders.—A rudder consists of the main flat portion, or *blade*, and the vertical shaft or *stock*. The upper end or continuation of the stock above the blade is called the *rudder head*. Rudders may be of the *simple unbalanced*

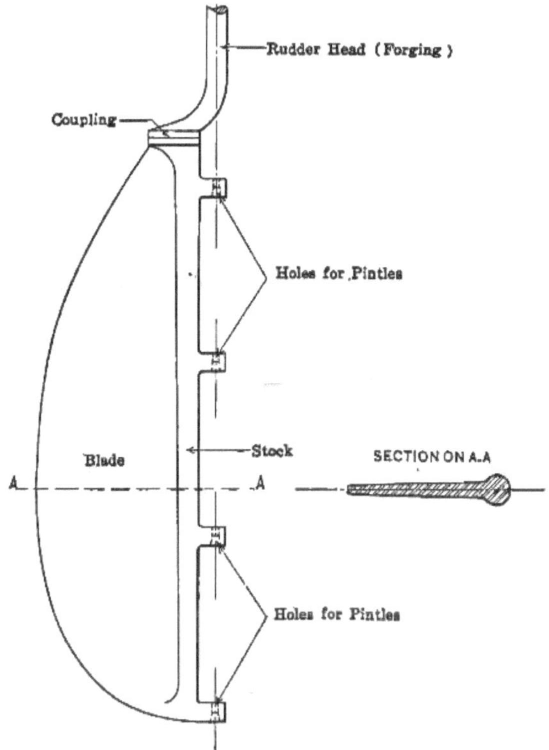

FIG. 37.—Solid cast rudder.

type (as ordinarily fitted to merchant vessels), of the *simple balanced type, balanced type partially underhung* or *balanced type completely underhung*. Balanced rudders are used for war ships almost exclusively, being necessary to give quick turning ability without the use of an exceedingly powerful steering engine. The warship in Fig. 19

has a partially underhung, balanced rudder. The merchant vessel and yacht in the same figure have unbalanced rudders.

As regards construction rudders have a great variety of forms, depending upon the size and type of ship, and the cost of manufacture. The simplest is the solid blade cast in a single piece as shown in Fig. 37. Owing to the difficulty of obtaining such a casting without having it more or less warped rudders of this type are made only in small sizes. The rudder head is always a forging in order to provide the necessary strength to take the torsional stresses. The stresses increase from the bottom of the stock toward the head, and decrease from the stock aft to the after curved edge or bow of the blade. Hence the stock tapers from head to heel and the blade from stock to after edge, as shown. Projections or *snugs* are cast on the forward edge of the stock to take the *pintles,* or pins upon which the rudder hinges.

A development of the simple cast rudder is the *single plate rudder* which consists of a single heavy plate cut to the proper contour and secured to the stock by means of arms on either side to which the plate is riveted. A rudder of this type is shown in Fig. 38. The arms, which are usually forgings (although sometimes they are of cast steel) are made separately and shrunk on to the stock, which is also, as a rule, a forging. The rudder head is bolted to the rudder stock by means of a flat keyed flanged coupling as shown. Notches are cut in the plate to fit around the arms at the stock. The arms are keyed to the stock. In order to limit the angle through which the rudder may be put over *stops* are provided on one of the snugs on each side, as shown, designed to take up against corresponding ones on the stern of the ship.

This type of rudder has the advantages of great strength, ease of construction and accessibility of all parts for cleaning and painting. The arms may also be forged or cast onto the stock.

In warships, and some merchant ships which, on account

of their specially formed sterns, have more complicated rudders, the rudder consists of a *frame*, forged or cast of steel (usually the latter) and covered on each side with light plating. The spaces between the ribs or *arms* of the frame are filled with some light wood, such as fir, spruce, or white pine, embedded in pitch or red lead paste, or with cement, coke, etc. Such a rudder of the simple

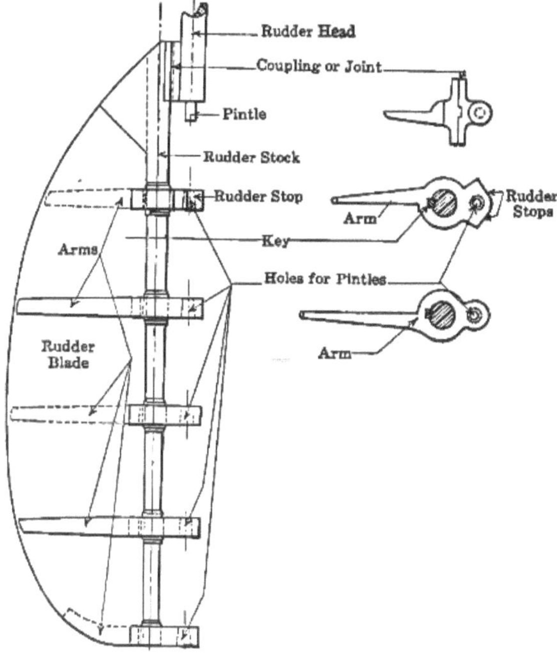

Fig. 38.—Single plate built up rudder.

unbalanced type is shown in Fig. 39. (The general principles of construction of a balanced rudder are much the same.)

The pintles of practically all rudders turn in holes in lugs on the stern or rudder post, called *gudgeons*. In cheaply constructed ships there are no special bushings or sleeves between the iron or steel of the pintles and the gudgeons, but in large well-built ships the construction is

7

similar to that shown in Fig. 40, the pintle being surrounded by a composition bushing in the gudgeon hole, with a conical socket or washer of steel underneath. In very high-class work there are bronze sleeves fitted over the pintles, and bushings in the gudgeons—sometimes fitted with vertical strips of lignum vitæ set in white metal.

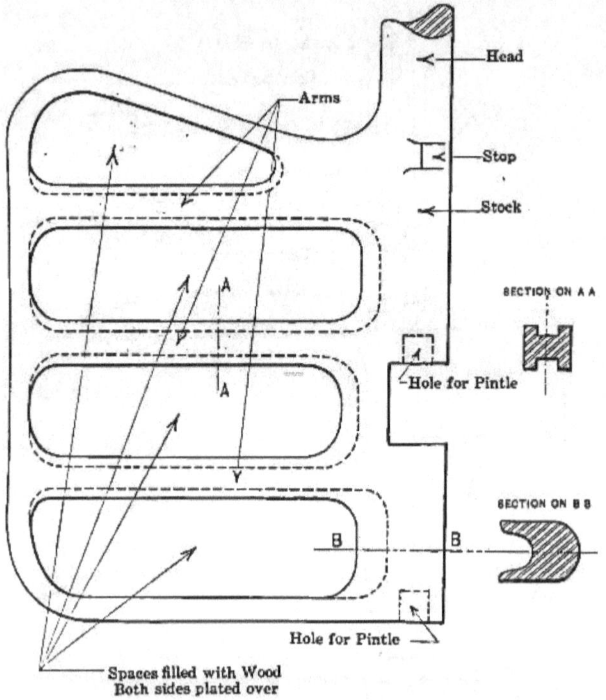

Fig. 39.—Cast frame of side plate rudder.

In merchant vessels the upper portion of the rudder stock, or rudder head, where it passes through the hull is encased in a water tight tube or trunk fitted with a stuffing box either just above the plating of the counter or at the lowest deck above the counter. In some cases no stuffing box is fitted, the trunk being carried all the way up to the weather deck.

The plating of the counter in merchant ships being normally some distance above the water line, watertightness is not so important, but is nevertheless required to prevent water, caused by the splashing of waves or due to excessive trim by the stern, from entering the hull.

In warships the counter is usually below the water line, and in addition to this it is ordinarily necessary to take the weight of the rudder inside of the ship. The construction is therefore considerably different from merchant ships,

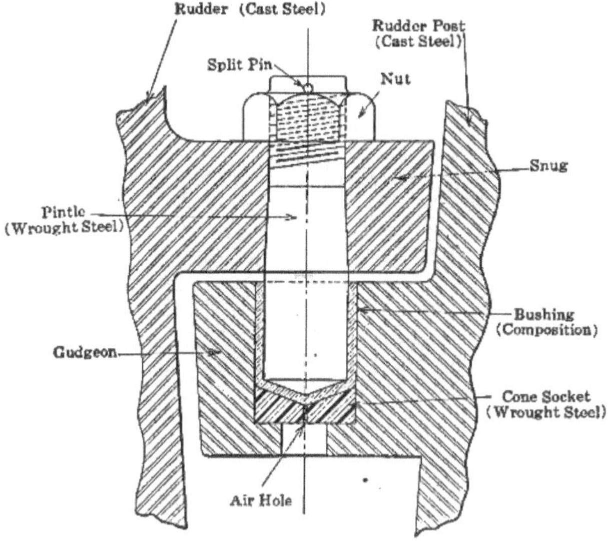

Fig. 40.—Pintle.

an elaborate stuffing box being fitted to the stern casting, combined with a carrier which takes the weight of the rudder. The general arrangement of such a *rudder head stuffing box* and *rudder carrier* is shown in Fig. 41. A portion of the rudder head is covered by a bronze sleeve, shrunk on. Water is kept out by means of a stuffing box and gland, operated, as shown, by means of a nut gearing with a worm. Both gland and nut are made in parts so as to be removable through holes in the side of the carrier casting. Instead of a tiller an athwartship *yoke* is fitted for turning the rudder. An annular key transmits the weight to the carrier.

Stern Tubes, Propeller Struts, Etc.—In ships fitted with propellers special means must be provided to permit the shaft which turns the propeller to pass through the skin of the ship or outer hull in such a manner that it may revolve, and at the same time to prevent water from entering around it into the ship. In order to accomplish this the shaft, where it leaves the ship's main hull, is supported in a specially constructed bearing fitted in a *stern* or *shaft tube*.

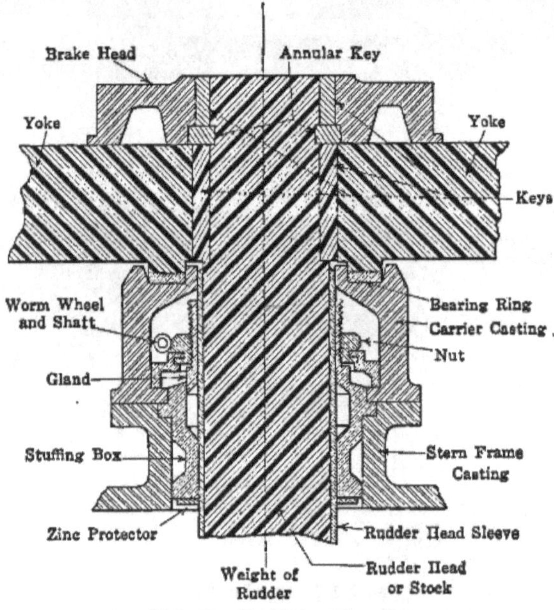

Fig. 41.—Rudder carrier, etc.

Steam propelled vessels usually have one, two, three, or four propellers being designated accordingly as *single, twin, triple,* or *quadruple screw* vessels respectively. If the number of propellers is odd one of the shafts is located along the centre line of the ship and passes through a large cylindrical hole in the stern post which is bossed out to receive it (see Fig. 35). If the number of propellers is more than one, those not located on the centre line are placed symmetrically with respect to the centre line and are called *wing* propellers. The wing shafts usually run nearly

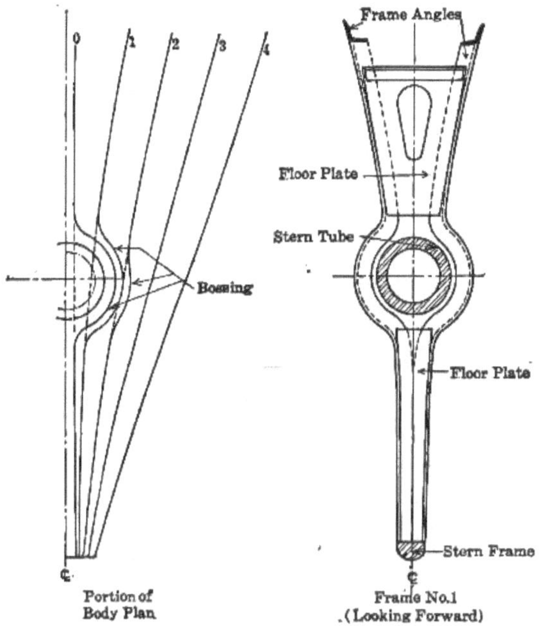

FIG. 42.—Bossing and stern framing.

but not quite parallel to the vertical longitudinal centre line plane of the ship. Whether the shaft is a centre or a wing shaft it usually is inclined slightly to the horizontal, its after end being the lower.

There are in general, then, two types of shafts to consider: (1) centre shafts, and (2) wing shafts.

Centre Shafts.—In order to give sufficient room for the shaft and its tube and bearing the molded form of the ship in the vicinity of the stern post and fine portion of the run must be swelled out or *bossed* as shown in Fig. 42.

This shows the lower after portion of the body plan of a single screw or triple screw ship. The form that the frames would have if they were not bossed is shown by the dotted lines. The shape of a transverse section of the stern frame is marked "O." The general construction of the frames in the fine after portion of the ship is indicated in the right-hand sketch in Fig. 42, which represents the details of frame No. 1 of the left-hand sketch. A very strong transverse construction is necessary in this portion of the ship in order to take the stresses due to the centrifugal force and vibrations set up by the revolution of the propeller. This is provided by means of deep floor plates, as shown, and the shell plating in this vicinity is made extra heavy or is doubled.

The large hole in the stern post is bored out to take the after end of the stern tube, the forward end of which is secured to a heavy transverse water-tight bulkhead (usually the forward bulkhead of the after peak). The stern tube is ordinarily a thick cast steel tube through which the propeller shaft passes. It is described in detail below.

Wing Shafts.—In the case of a shaft passing through the molded surface at some distance out from the centre line the shapes of the frames are somewhat similar to those shown in the upper sketch of Fig. 43, and the shape of the section of the molded surface by the horizontal plane *AB* is similar to that of the full line in the lower sketch. The frames are bent to the shapes shown and are well stiffened by plates arranged somewhat similarly to the floor plates shown in Fig. 42. The shaft tube in this case is fitted at the after end of the bossing.

There are two methods of construction in the case of wing shafts: (1) the bossing may be carried all the way aft to the propeller (as shown in Fig. 43), or (2) the bossing may be terminated considerably further forward and nearer the main portion of the hull.

In the first case the frames extend out to form a sort of fin, terminated by the boss, this fin being about normal to the main curvature of the frames. Such frames, on account of their shape, are often called *spectacle frames.* The shell plating is continued to the after end of this fin and boss as shown in Fig. 43, and is terminated there by a heavy steel casting or *shaft bracket.* This bracket may be made in a variety of different ways but its function is to form a termination of the fin and bossed shell plating and to furnish a strong and rigid support for the shaft tube which is fitted to its outer, swollen end in practically the same manner that the stern tube is fitted in the stern post casting. A cross section of the shaft bracket would have the form

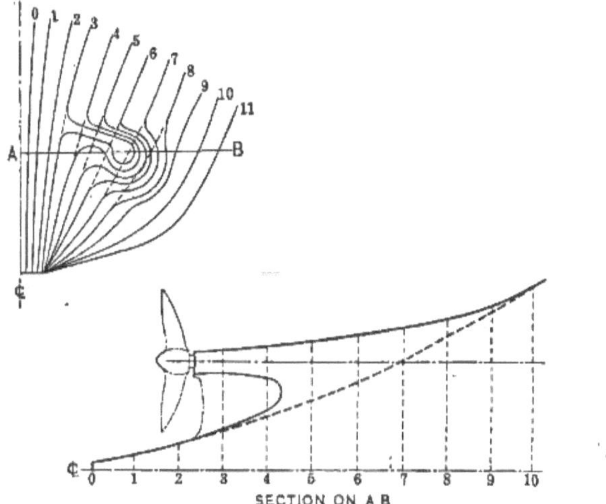

FIG. 43.—Bossing of a twin screw vessel.

shown for frame No. 3 in Fig. 43, but it extends well inside of the hull where it is rigidly secured to the ship's structure by webs and flanges cast on it.

In the second case, or that in which the bossing does not extend much beyond the main hull, the shape of the last bossed frame is similar to frame No. 6 of Fig. 43, and the shaft tube is fitted at the termination of this bossing. The shaft, however, extends for some distance aft of the stern tube and has another bearing just forward of the propeller supported by two *struts.* The struts are heavy steel members cast in one with the bearing of the shaft and suitably attached to the hull. A simple type of strut is shown in Fig. 44. Various developments of such struts are in use, differing principally in the means by which attached to the ship's hull. The bushing fitted inside of the hub is similar to that in the stern tube, *i.e.*, lignum vitæ strips set in composition.

In any case—whether the shaft passes through the stern casting, or, if a wing shaft, whether spectacle frames combined with a shaft bracket, or struts are used—the portion of the hull at which the shaft leaves is fitted with a stern or shaft tube bearing. While the details of this bearing vary somewhat, the principal features are as shown in the sketch of Fig. 45.

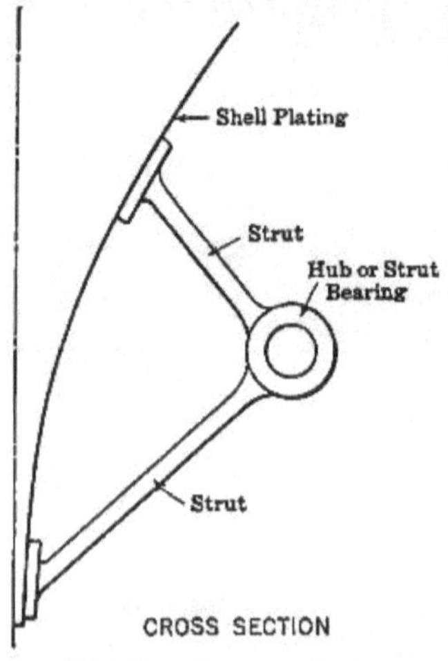

Fig. 44.—Propeller struts.

The shaft itself (solid or hollow forged steel) is covered by a *sleeve* of bronze or similar composition, shrunk on. The shaft and sleeve revolve in the special *stern tube bushing* which consists of strips of lignum vitæ (a very hard wood) imbedded in brass or other composition. The sea water has access to the longitudinal spaces between these lignum vitæ strips and acts as a lubricant for the shaft (see cross section in Fig. 45). This bushing fits into the *stern tube* which is secured to the stern post or shaft bracket by means of a shoulder cast on it and a large nut, as shown. The forward end of the stern tube has a flange which is bolted to a heavy transverse water-tight bulkhead, as shown, and serves as a stuffing box, being provided with packing and a composition lined gland. The other details are shown in the figure. The stuffing box end of the stern tube being

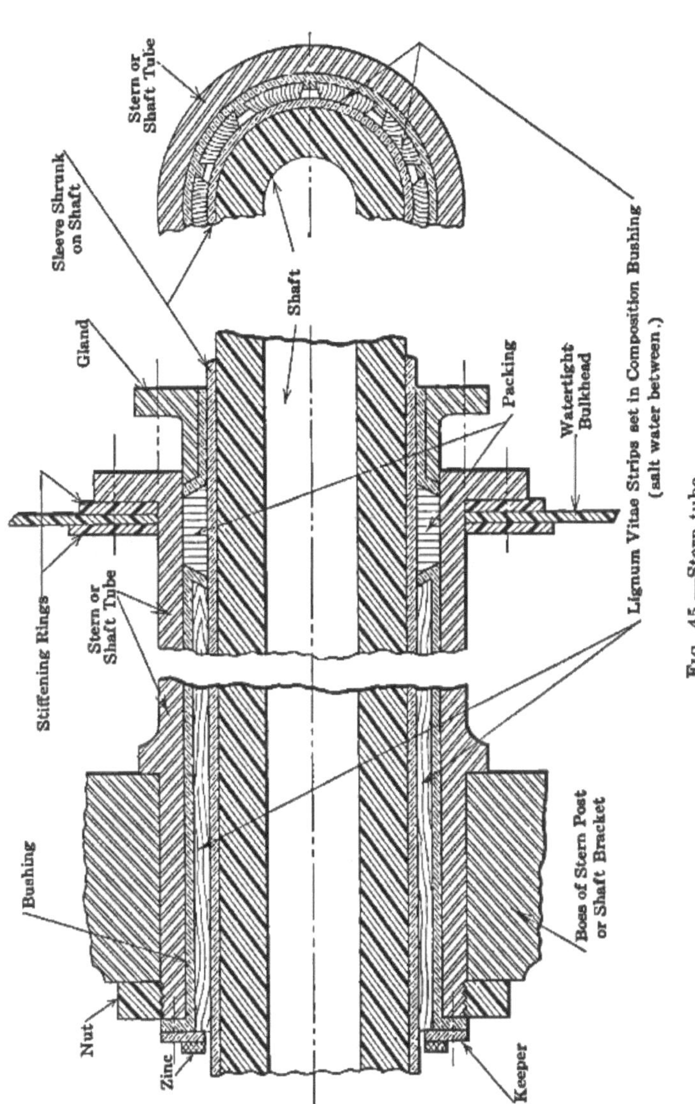

FIG. 45.—Stern tube.

inside the ship can be examined, and the gland set up from time to time as necessary.

In all construction work in connection with stern tubes, struts, brackets, etc., the need for great strength and ability to resist the shocks due to vibration is most important. Rivets must be of sufficient size, proper spacing and of first-class workmanship, and framing and plating must have extra strength. Zinc protectors are fitted in various places to prevent excessive corrosion due to the galvanic action of composition parts placed near steel parts in salt water.

3. SHELL PLATING AND INNER BOTTOM

The main essential of any ship is the shell plating. This forms the outer skin, keeps out the water, assists in furnishing strength and encloses all the other main parts of the hull. Its inner surface—the outer surface of the framing—is the molded surface of the ship.

The shell plating consists of a great many steel plates, of rectangular, or nearly rectangular shape, arranged in longitudinal courses or *strakes*. The thickness of the plates ranges from about ¼″ to about 1″, depending upon the size of the ship and the particular location of the plate considered.

There are in general three classes of plates: (1) flat, (2) rolled, and (3) flanged or furnaced. The first class, which forms, usually, by far the largest portion of the shell, is made up of those plates which have little or no curvature and do not have to be bent. Rolled plates are those having a cylindrical curvature only, and are found principally in the middle body at the turn of the bilge. Flanged and furnaced plates are those having special irregular shapes that require special fashioning—either after having been heated red hot, or in flanging machines. Those that must be heated and fashioned to the proper shape are called *furnaced* plates and usually have curvature in three dimensions.

The strakes run parallel in the middle body and gradually taper toward the ends of the ship. They are commonly designated by the letters *A*, *B*, *C*, *D*, etc., commencing with the strake nearest the keel, which is called the *garboard strake*. The highest complete strake is called the *sheer strake*, since its upper edge has the curvature or *sheer* of the ship. The plates in each strake are given serial numbers, commencing at the bow. Since the ship is symmetrical about its longitudinal central vertical plane the plates of the starboard side are duplicates of those of the port side except that their curvature, in each case, is reversed. Each plate is therefore designated by the letter of the strake, the serial number in that strake and the side of the ship. Example: "D 11 P," means the 11th plate from the bow, in the fourth strake from the keel, on the port side of the ship.

Plates around the propeller shafts are called *bossed plates* and those located where the stern frame joins the counter are called *oxter plates*. *Dished plates* are those of U shaped cross section that form the flat plate keel where it is flanged upward to connect to the garboard plates (See Fig. 22) or to the stem or stern post.

The joints at the edges of the strakes are called *seams*, and at the ends of the individual plates in each strake, *butts* (see Fig. 46). The edges of the plating that are visible from the outside of the ship are called *sight edges*, and the intersections of both inner and outer edges of the plating with the frames over which they pass are called *landing edges* (see Fig. 46).

There are several different systems of arranging the seams of the shell plating. These are illustrated in Fig. 47. The *sunken and raised* system is used in the vast majority of cases on account of its strength, simplicity and because it is less costly than some of the other systems. The edges of the strakes overlap each other. *Parallel liners* are fitted in this system between the fore and aft flange of each frame and all the plates of the outer strakes. The *clinker* system is somewhat similar to the sunken and raised system (the seams being lapped in both) but it requires the use of *tapered liners*, which increases the cost. It is, however, somewhat lighter than the sunken and raised, and has the added advantage that a plate can be more easily removed for repairs. The *flush* system is little used, on account of

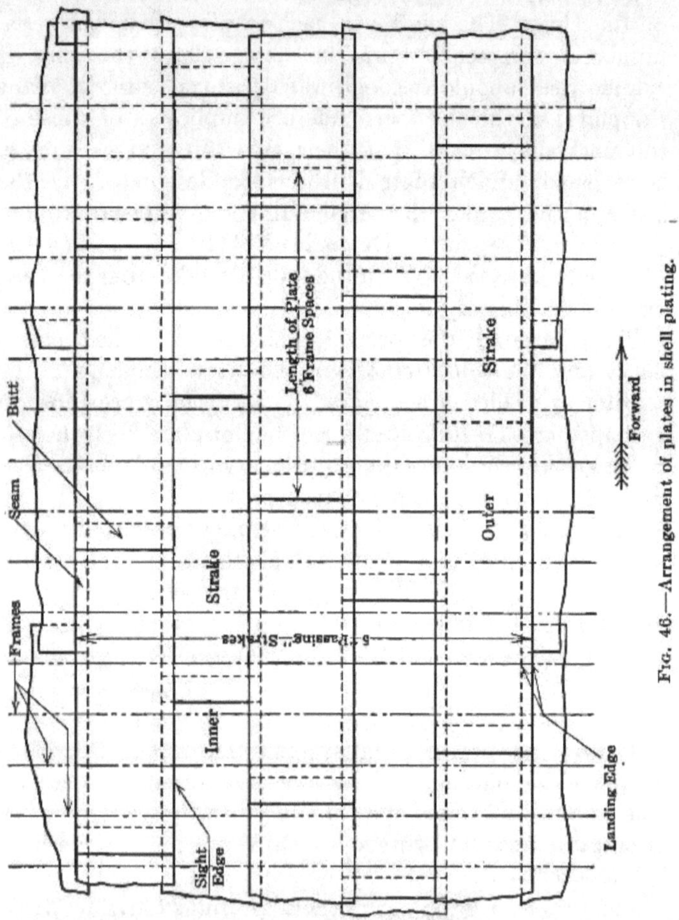

Fig. 46.—Arrangement of plates in shell plating.

the great weight of liners and *seam straps* required. (All strakes must have liners on all frames and the seams are all strapped instead of lapped.) It gives a smooth finished appearance and is therefore much used for yachts. It is also used in cases where a flush surface is necessary for structural reasons, as in the case of plating behind armor. *Joggling,* which is illustrated in the three right-hand sketches of Fig. 47 consists in offsetting one member that fits against another so as to avoid the use of liners. In two of the sketches the edges of the plating is shown as joggled and in the other frame is joggled. This arrangement results in a considerable saving in weight, but this saving is accompanied by a decrease in strength; and it is usually more costly. It is, of course, difficult to apply to plates having irregular curvature. The system ordinarily used is the sunken and raised system, which is here considered.

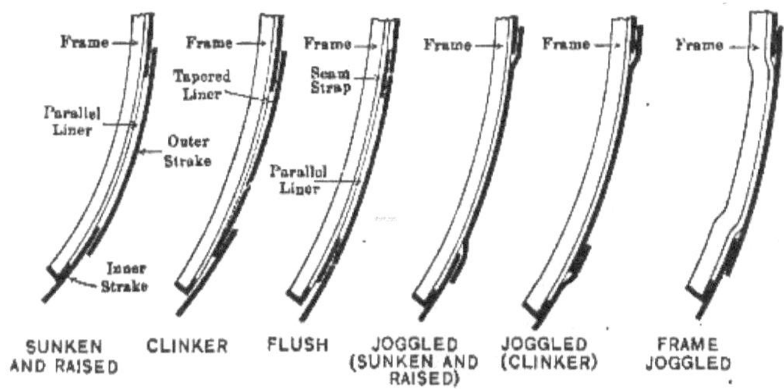

FIG. 47.—Systems of shell plating.

The seams of the shell plating for all but the smallest vessels are double riveted, that is, they contain two rows of rivets. The inner rivet is omitted where it comes at a frame, so as not unduly to weaken the fore and aft flange.

The butts of the plates may be either lapped or butted. When butted they usually have single butt straps fitted on the inside. When lapped, the outer edge of the lap is at the after end of the plate so as to decrease resistance of the water when the ship is moving ahead. A lapped butt takes up less room in a fore and aft direction than a butt-strap and is stronger, but it is more difficult to fit, as will be seen by referring to Figs. 48 and 49. In these figures are shown methods of making the connections between the two plates of one strake that form the butt lap and the plate of the adjacent strake.

The simplest method, and the one most commonly adopted, is that shown in Fig. 48. Here a tapered liner is

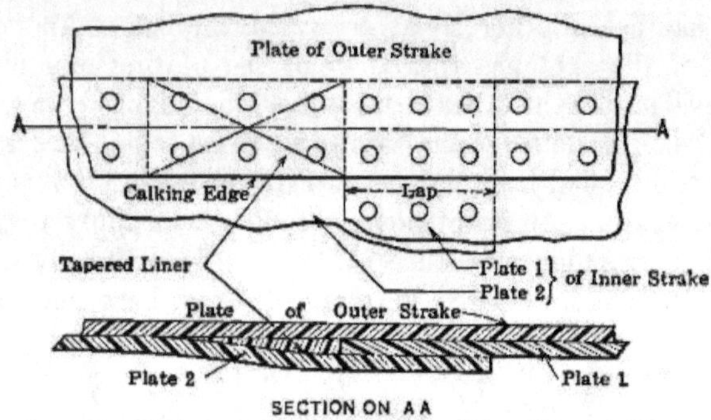

Fig. 48.—Butt lap with tapered liner. (Seen from outside.)

fitted to fill in the triangular space between the plates of the inner and outer strakes caused by the presence of the lap butt.

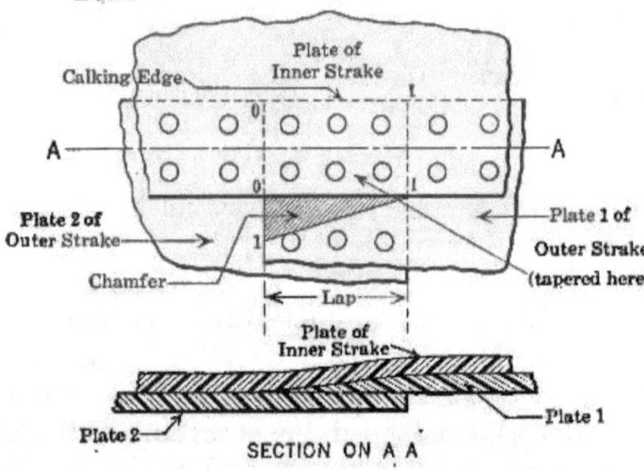

Fig. 49.—Butt lap—one plate tapered and chambered. (Seen from inside).)

A lighter and more compact arrangement, which does away with the need for a liner, is shown in Fig. 49, in which the portion of one plate that is common to both butt and seam laps is tapered off and *chamfered.* The thicknesses are indicated in the figure by "o's" and "1's," "o" meaning no thickness and "1" meaning the full thickness of the plate. This method is not always employed on account of the difficulty of tapering and chamfering the plates, which, if not done by a special machine, must be laboriously done by hand chipping. Furthermore, it is not desirable in the case of plates in inner strakes on account of the difficulty of making such a joint water-tight. (Calking tool cannot be properly inserted in chamfer.)

It will be noted on referring again to Fig. 46 that the butts in the shell plating are so located as to prevent butts in adjacent strakes coming closer together than two frame spaces, and that between any two butts in the same frame space there are five "*passing*" strakes, or strakes having no butt in that particular frame space. This arrangement, or "*shift of butts*," as it is called, is for the purpose of preventing, as much as possible, lines of weakness, since any riveted joint is weaker than the plating itself. In Fig. 46 the shift of butts shown gives five passing strakes and each plate is six frame spaces long. If the plate lengths were different a different shift of butts would have to be made. The lengths of the plates are always exact multiples of the frame spacing (plus, of course, the width of the butt lap, if the butts are lapped) in order to keep the butt joints clear of the frames. Various combinations of plate-lengths and numbers of passing strakes are possible. The plates should be as many frame spaces long as possible in order to obtain a good shift of butts, but the length is of course limited by the capacity of the rolling mills to produce long plates, so that in ordinary sized ships the plates are usually between 20 and 30 feet long.

As the ship becomes fine toward the ends, and the girths of the frames consequently reduced, in order to prevent giving an excessive taper to the strakes it is necessary to drop certain of them. Such strakes, which do not run for the full length from stem to stern or stern post, are called *drop strakes*, or *stealers*. The last plate in such a strake is usually triangular in shape, and one of the adjacent strakes for the remainder of its length to the end of a ship (in the case of lapped seams) becomes both an *inner and outer* or a clinker strake instead of an entirely inner strake, or an entirely outer strake. See sketch of a stealer in Fig. 50.

Where the strakes pass over water-tight bulkheads—which take the places of certain frames and have more closely spaced riveting—*bulkhead liners* are usually fitted to compensate for the excessive weakening caused by the greater number of rivet holes. Figure 51 shows one form of bulkhead liner, the outer strake being reinforced by the

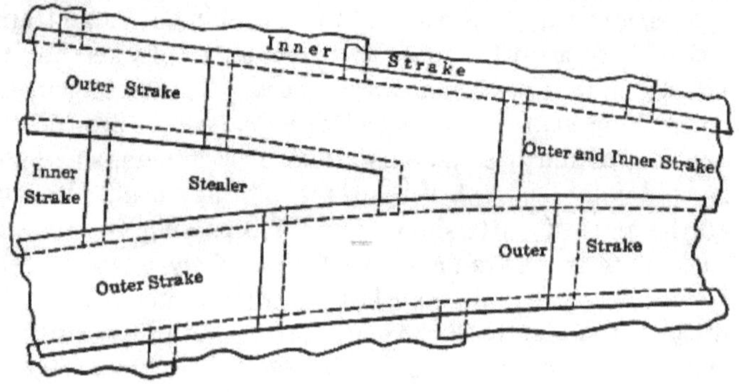

Fig. 50.—Stealer.

diamond shaped doubling of the liner. When a butt occurs between a bulkhead and the adjacent frame on either side of the bulkhead, the bulkhead liner is extended on that side to form a strap for the butt, the two plates then being butted instead of lapped. Longitudinal brackets connecting the outer strakes to the bulkheads are sometimes used instead of bulkheads liners, these being commonly fitted on stringers.

The shell plating terminates, at the ends of the ship, in the stem, the stern post or frame, propeller brackets, etc. It is made especially thick at these places or is doubled and secured by heavy rivets which should be very carefully driven. The plating is also doubled or reinforced at the bows, in the vicinity at which it might be dented in by the anchors or by ice or other floating objects, and also around openings cut in the shell for various fittings, tubes, etc. The garboard and sheer strakes are made of extra thick plating in order to give longitudinal or girder strength to the ship. Usually the bilge strake is also made a trifle heavier than the remainder of the plating. Except for local stiffenings, all strakes have lighter plating near the ends of the ship than amidships.

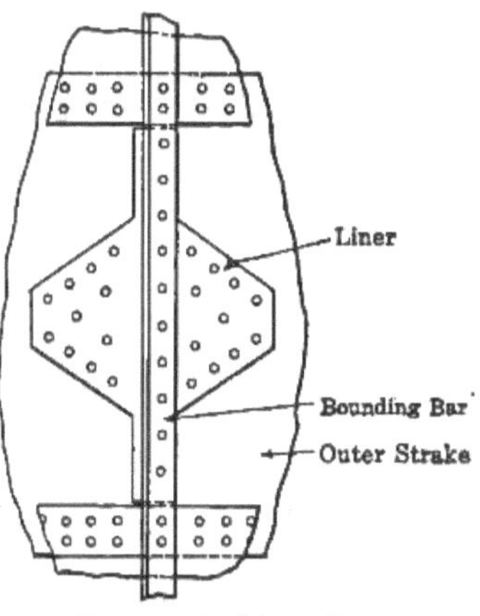

FIG. 51.—Bulkhead liner.

The inner bottom plating is composed of rectangular shaped plates disposed in a manner quite similar to those of the outer shell. The strakes are continuous longitudinally so that the inner bottom furnishes considerable additional girder strength to the ship. The centre strake, attached to the top of the centre vertical keel, is usually made extra heavy and serves in reinforcing the heavy centre line girder over the keel. It is sometimes called the *rider plate.* The lengths of the inner bottom plates are commonly the same as those of the shell and a similar shift of butts is obtained. The thickness of the plates is less than for those of the outer shell. The seams of inner bottom plating are often joggled. Seams are always kept clear of longitudinals.

In merchant vessels the outer flat strake of the inner bottom plating is ordinarily connected to the shell plating by means of a flanged strake set normally to the shell plating, called the *margin* plate. The arrangement of the inner bottom plating is shown in Figs. 31, 32, 33 and 34. In war ships (and some merchant ships) the inner bottom

8

extends completely up to the first deck above the normal water line.

4. DECKS

Decks are ordinarily curved surfaces, having a longitudinal *sheer* and an athwartships *camber*, and are bounded by the sides of the ship and by the edges of trunks, hatches, etc., cut through them. The *deck plating* or *planking* is somewhat similar to the shell plating or planking and is supported at regular intervals by *beams*. The beams are supported at their outboard ends by the frames to which they are attached by *beam knees* or *brackets* and at intermediate points by *pillars, stanchions,* and *bulkheads.*

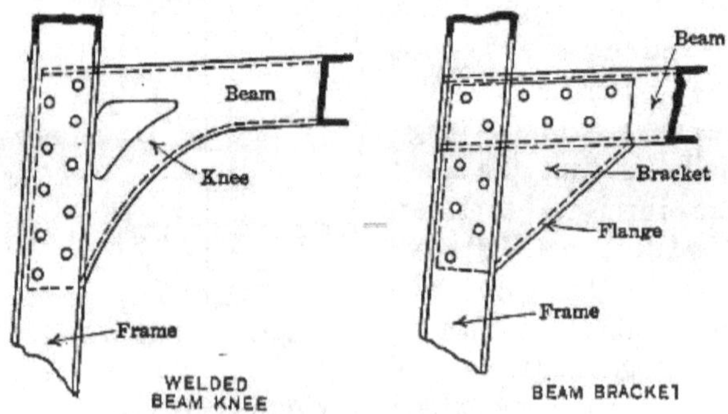

FIG. 52.—Connections of deck beams to frames.

Deck beams are usually deep channels or bulb angles (although other shapes are sometimes employed) and are bent slightly to the proper camber. The methods of attaching the beams to the frames are illustrated in Fig. 52. A *beam knee* is formed by splitting the end of the beam and bending the two parts to the shapes shown, a piece being then welded in to complete the knee. A less expensive construction, but a heavier one is the *bracket,* which is a simple triangular plate fitted between the frame and beam, often flanged on the sloping edge as shown.

Where openings must be cut in decks *carlings* or fore and aft beams are fitted and the beams or "half" beams extend up to and are secured to the carlings. The carlings are terminated at the beams as shown in the lower sketch in Fig. 53, and the general arrangement it shown by the upper sketch in the same figure. Usually a vertical boundary of plating is fitted around the hatch opening called a *coaming.* In this case the coaming plate would replace the right-hand clip shown in Fig. 53.

Deck Plating and Planking.—The upper edges of the deck beams are covered over with plating or planking or both. The upper strength deck or *main* deck is usually completely covered with steel plating, made heavier than

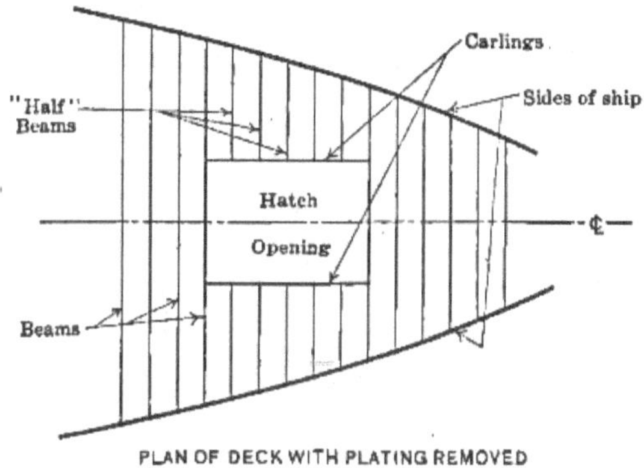

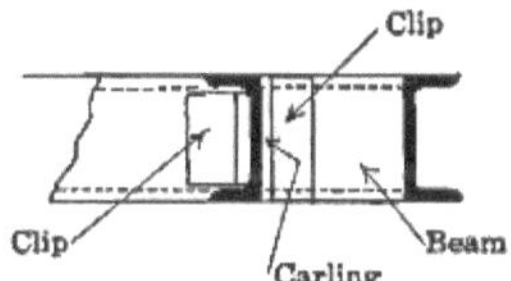

Fig. 53.—Deck beams and carlings.

the other decks for purposes of strength. The outboard strake of this plating which connects with the shell plating is called the *deck stringer plate* and is made especially heavy. It is connected by a heavy angle bar to the sheer strake of the shell plating and acts with it in furnishing upper flange strength to the ship as a girder. The deck stringer is fitted in every case whether the remainder of the deck is to be plated or merely planked. Its inner edge runs approximately parallel to its outer edge.

The remainder of the deck plating is arranged in strakes parallel to the centre line of the ship. The seams are commonly joggled except in cases where the projecting laps would be objectionable, as for a deck to be covered with linoleum or protective deck plating, in which cases the deck plating is worked flush with butt and seam straps underneath.

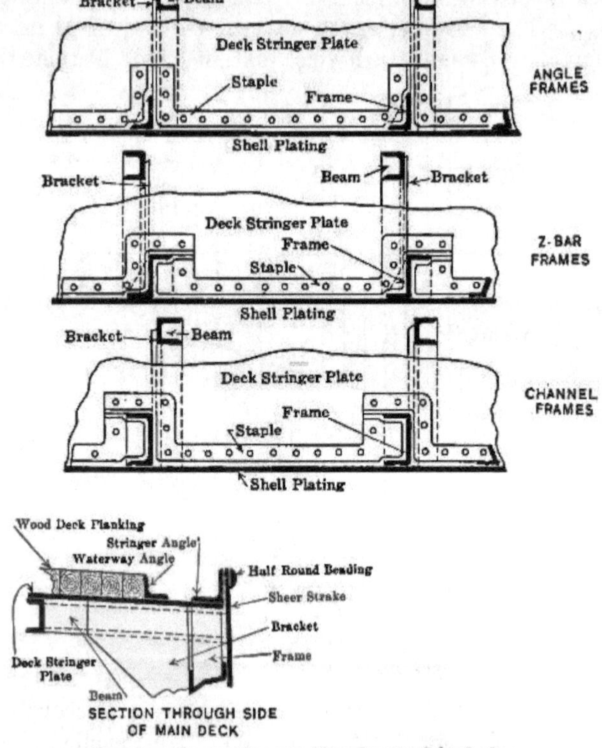

FIG. 54.—Connections at sides of watertight decks.

The boundaries of the deck plating are connected to the intersecting coamings, shell plating or bulkheads by *bounding* or *boundary bars* or simple angles one flange of which is riveted to the deck plating and the other to the coaming, shell plating or bulkhead, as the case may be.

Methods of connecting the deck plating of a water-tight

deck to the shell plating are shown in the three upper sketches of Fig. 54. The stringer plate is notched out around each frame and forged angle *staples* are fitted between and around the frame bars. Typical constructions for angle, Z-bar and channel frames are shown, but numerous other arrangements are possible and will be found used to accomplish the same purpose—which is to furnish a means of making a completely water-tight connection of deck to shell.

In the case of the highest deck of the hull such stapling is not necessary as the frames terminate below the deck. Here the stringer angle bar runs continuously along the inner surface of the top of the sheer strake and outboard

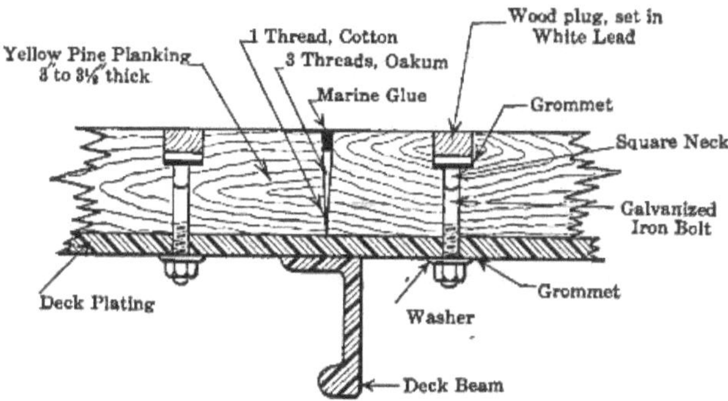

Fig. 55.—Butt of deck planking over steel deck.

upper surface of the deck stringer plate, as shown in the lowest sketch of Fig. 54. Another angle is usually run parallel to the stringer angle to form a waterway along the edge of the deck, and to form the outer boundary of the wood planking, as shown.

The wood for deck planking is ordinarily yellow pine or teak. The planks are generally of square section and about 3″ or 3½″ on a side if of yellow pine, and of nearly the same thickness but 8″ or 10″ wide, if of teak. The planks are commonly run straight and fore and aft except at curved boundaries where specially shaped *margin planks* are fitted, notched to take the ends of the straight planks.

They are secured to the steel plating underneath by means of galvanized iron bolts (usually about ⅝″ in diameter) as shown in Fig. 55. If a complete steel deck is not fitted the bolts are run through the upper flanges of the steel deck beams, or through small steel plates riveted to those flanges. Both the seams and butts of the planking are so formed as to have a section similar to the butt shown in Fig. 55, and are made water-tight by being calked with cotton and oakum driven securely in and covered with about ¾″ of marine glue or pitch. Sometimes, as in the case of yachts, putty is used. Lampwick grommets soaked in white lead are fitted under the heads of the bolts and between the steel deck and washers above the nuts. Round plugs with the grain running the same as that of the planking are driven in to close the holes over the heads of the bolts.

When a complete steel deck is not fitted there are often fitted under the wood planking, and in addition to the stringer plates certain narrow strips of plating running diagonally to help tie the beams together and reinforce the deck. Also there are sometimes one or more inboard strakes of plating at or near the centre line running longitudinally.

In order to reinforce the deck beams and relieve the brackets and side frames of the total load of the deck vertical *stanchions* or *pillars* are usually fitted between decks. These are of various sizes and constructions, some being of simple round section, solid or hollow, and some being built up of various plates and shapes riveted together.

A form often used, the *pipe stanchion,* consists of a wrought steel or iron tube, fitted at its upper end, or *head,* and lower end, or *heel,* with special pieces for securing it in place. Such a stanchion is shown in Fig. 56.

Stanchions should be located in vertical lines, one above the other, between successive decks, so that the forces will be transmitted directly through them to the bottom of the ship. They may be closely or widely spaced, but owing to the room that they take up and the interference that they cause in holds and other compartments it is frequently desirable to have them widely spaced.

When stanchions are widely spaced instead of being attached directly to the beams over them longitudinal *deck girders* are fitted underneath the decks and the stanchions are attached to these girders. The simplest form of girder is a single angle bar running along the lower edge of the deck beams as shown in the left sketch of Fig.

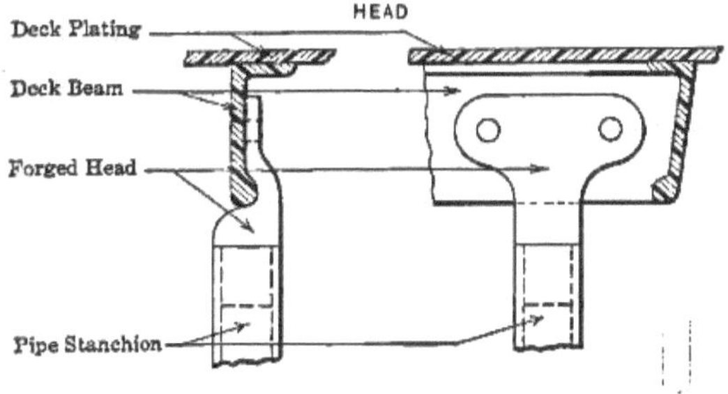

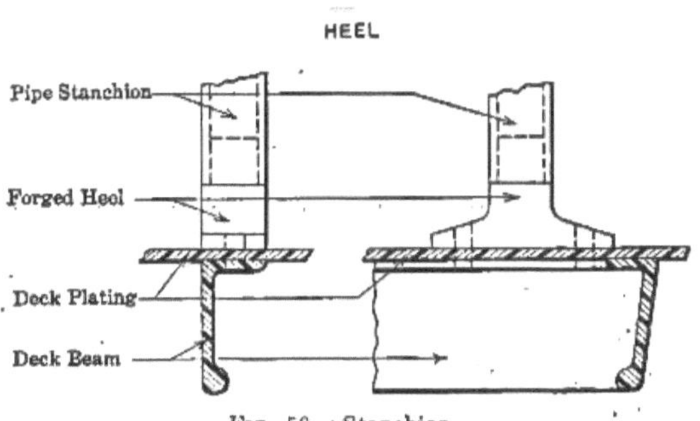

Fig. 56.—Stanchion.

57. If the beam has a lower flange the girder is riveted to this flange. If not, a short clip is fitted on each beam in way of the girder, as shown in the sketch for this purpose. The load of the deck between stanchions is transmitted to the stanchions through the girders.

Many different types of deck girders are in use, some comparatively simple, like the one just described and others of various more or less elaborate construction. Where the number of stanchions must be greatly reduced, or stanchions done away with entirely, very deep girders, built up of plates and angles and reinforced by athwartship brackets similar to the one shown in the right sketch of Fig. 57 are fitted. In this type it will be noted that the girder consists of a continuous deep plate with continuous lower angles and plate below. The construction is similar to that of keelsons, and stringers.

In certain compartments the steel deck plating is covered with linoleum which is secured to it by a special cement. Other spaces have cement and tiling (bath rooms, etc.) over the steel plating, or other special deck coverings.

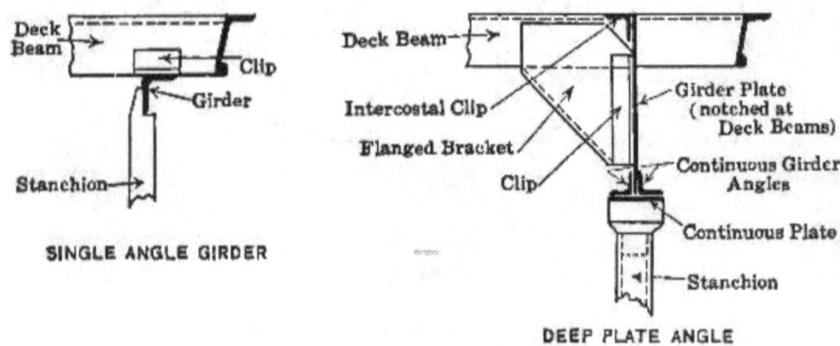

Fig. 57.—Deck girders.

Decks are ordinarily made water-tight in order to increase the danger of loss of buoyancy caused by damage to the shell plating. Therefore as a general rule all openings cut in decks should have means for their being tightly closed. Some of the methods used for this purpose are shown in Fig. 58. The simplest is a flat plate secured by means of stud bolts as shown in the upper sketch. A *gasket* of canvas soaked in red lead or some other suitable material is interposed between the cover and the deck plating. If the joint must be oil-tight canvas soaked in a mixture of pine tar and shellac or card board and varnish is used for the gasket. Another method, used for covers to manholes (small oval holes just big enough to admit a man) is shown in the middle sketch. Here a heavy strong back and a large bolt through the centre of the manhole plate are used. Where perfect water-tightness combined with quick removal is required, some method similar to that shown in the lowest sketch must be used. Here a rubber gasket held by strips is secured around the outer edge of the cover plate, so that when the plate is drawn down, by bolts fitted as shown, the gasket is compressed against the upper

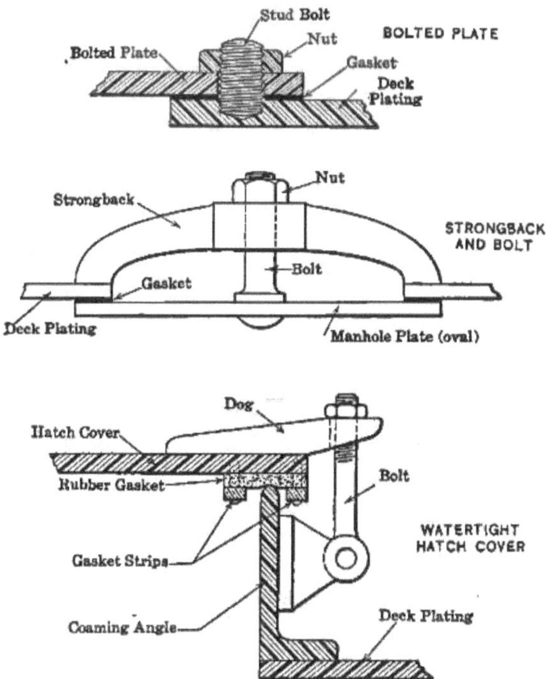

FIG. 58.—Covers for openings in watertight decks.

edge of the coaming. This general method is used considerably for manhole covers, hatch covers, water-tight doors, etc. The circumferences of such openings or of their covers may be reinforced by stiffening rings.

5. BULKHEADS

Bulkheads are vertical diaphragms or partitions of various construction. According to the directions in which they extend they are called *transverse* or *longitudinal.*

Longitudinal bulkheads are not much used in merchant ships, which usually require broad hold spaces, but are important features in warships where they serve to increase the fore and aft strength, and underwater protection.

Transverse bulkheads are important in all types of ships since, as well as furnishing transverse strength by their stiff diaphragm action and the support that they give to stringers, decks, etc., they subdivide the length of the ship into a number of holds or compartments and thus limit the space that may be flooded if the shell plating is punctured. In fact it may be said that the chief function of all such bulkheads, except those not forming an integral portion of the hull structure, is to furnish a means of watertight subdivision.

Bulkheads, like decks, consist of plating and reinforcing bars. In the case of bulkheads the reinforcing bars are called *bulkhead stiffeners.* In some cases the stiffeners are formed by flanging the edges of the bulkhead plates, but the principle is the same. In some cases the stiffeners are fitted in horizontal lines only, sometimes in vertical lines only, and in some cases both horizontal and vertical stiffeners are used on the same bulkhead.

A bulkhead designed to assist in watertight subdivision must be made of heavy enough plating and must be sufficiently stiffened to resist bending or bulging in case of flooding of either of the compartments of which it forms a boundary. If the sightest deflection takes place some of the rivets or seams are almost sure to start leaking. Therefore the stiffeners must be strong, closely spaced, and properly supported at their ends. In very large, deep bulkheads the construction must be much more rugged than in small ones, depending, as it does, upon the head of water to which they may be subjected.

In Fig. 59 is shown a simple construction of a bulkhead. The plating is arranged in horizontal strakes and the stiffeners, in this case bulb-angles, run vertically. The plating is secured to the deck, shell, and tank top plating by means of double angles called *boundary* or *bounding bars.* The lower strakes of plating (which would have to withstand greater pressures) are made heavier, and the lower ends of the stiffeners are given a rigid support by means of plate brackets riveted to their fore and aft flanges and to clips which are in turn riveted to the tank top.

The above described construction is modified and extended in a great many different ways to suit different sizes and types of ships. In some cases single boundary bars are

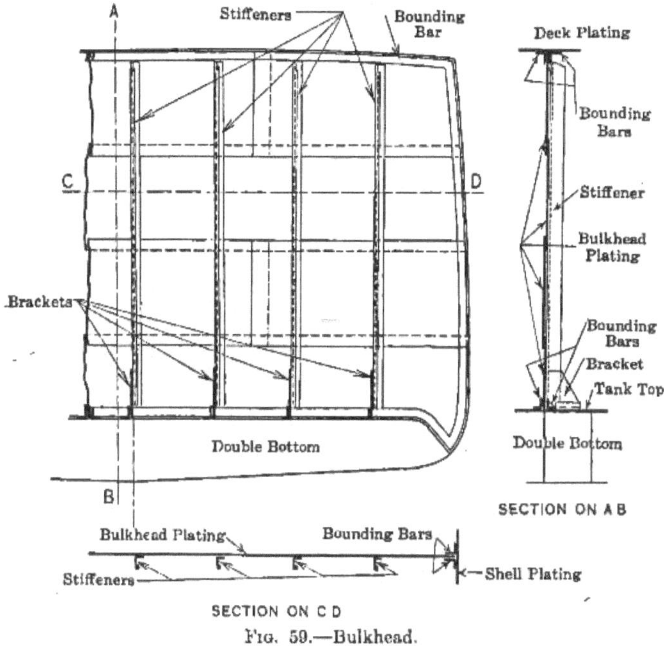

FIG. 59.—Bulkhead.

sufficient. The plating is sometimes arranged in vertical strakes. The seams are frequently joggled. The stiffeners may be simple angle bars, channels, Z-bars, T-bars, I-beams, or may be built up of plates and shapes in the form of heavy girders in which case their heads and heels are reinforced and connected to the decks and inner bottom by large built up brackets with heavy face bars. Ordinarily the plating of the decks is continuous and the bulkhead plating is cut at the decks, although this may not always be the case, especially for longitudinal bulkheads.

Transverse bulkheads designed as watertight diaphragms must be carefully fitted where necessarily pierced by longitudinal members, such as stringers, girders, piping, etc., so as to maintain watertightness. To this end staples and collars made similarly to those shown in Fig. 54 are fitted around the longitudinal members at the bulkheads. The same applies to transverse members piercing longitudinal watertight bulkheads.

Watertight bulkheads are tested by filling the compartments of which they form boundaries with water, and ascertaining if any leaks occur.

Horizontal bulkhead stiffeners are usually arranged so as to connect with side and hold stringers, where such members occur.

Certain *non-watertight* or *partition bulkheads* are found in all ships, being installed for purposes of subdivision of space into staterooms, galleys, pantries, wash rooms, storerooms, etc., etc. These may be of wood, light sheet metal or wire mesh, and furnish little if any strength or watertightness. Longitudinal coal bunker bulkheads in merchant vessels are fairly strong and heavy but are not usually made watertight.

Doors in water-tight bulkheads must be watertight and are usually constructed on the principle shown in the lowest sketch of Fig. 58, the details, of course, being somewhat different.

6. MISCELLANEOUS

The main structural members of ships have been described in the preceding sections of this chapter, but there are, in addition, certain auxiliary structures and fittings which are either built into or securely attached to the hull, and with which the shipbuilder is therefore concerned. Of these there are a great number and their design and construction vary considerably. Among the principal ones may be mentioned engine and boiler foundations, and foundations for shaft bearings, thrust blocks, auxiliary machinery, winches, guns, davits, masts, derricks, etc., hawse pipes, chain pipes, mooring pipes, chocks, bitts, rails and bulwarks, bilge and docking keels, fenders, etc.

Engine foundations must be heavy and strongly built and well supported by the adjacent structure of the ship. Often times the frame spacing is reduced and the floors made deeper under the engines in order to give additional vertical strength. The foundations for the engines are built up on top of the inner bottom usually of plates and angles well

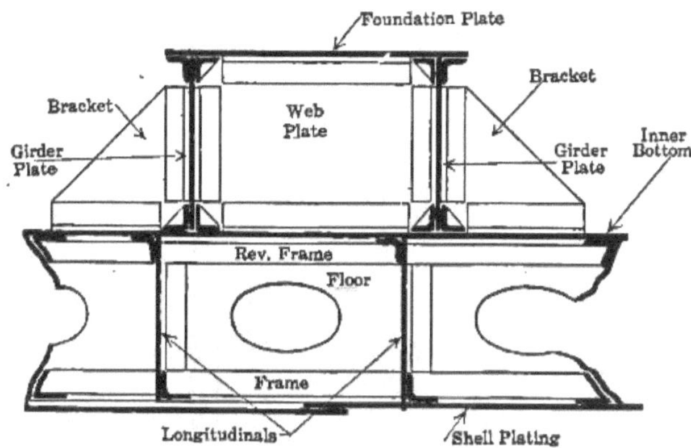

FIG. 60.—Portion of engine foundation.

bracketed and reinforced in all directions. A typical construction is shown in Fig. 60. The girder plates of the foundation should be nearly in line with longitudinals so as to preserve continuity of strength and the athwartship members are ordinarily directly over the floors.

A typical method of *supporting* the *boilers* is shown in Fig. 61. The *saddles* are plates cut to a curved shape to fit against the boiler shell and are reinforced by double angles around their edges as shown, and the successive saddles are connected at their outer sides by longitudinal plates.

Special foundations of a great many different types are installed in other parts of the ship, the principles of con-

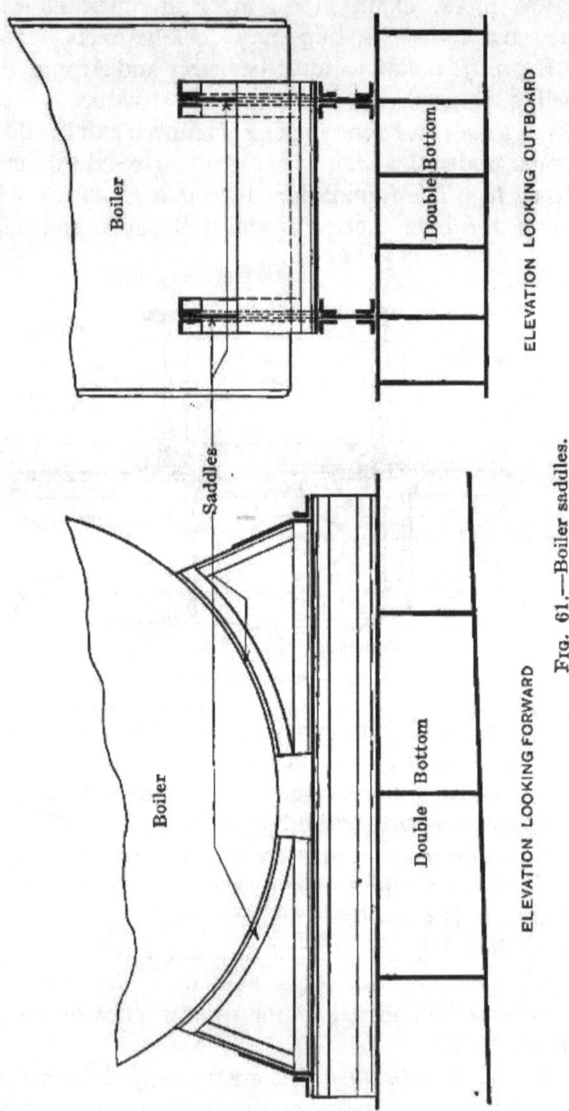

FIG. 61.—Boiler saddles.

struction being in general the same as for engine and boiler foundations.

Hawse pipes are large castings, usually steel, securely built into the bows of the ship, through which the anchor chains may pass (see sketch of hawsepipe in Fig. 62). *Chain pipes* serve a similar purpose but lead entirely inside of the ship and nearly vertically down to the chain locker, as they do not have to have the peculiar terminations of

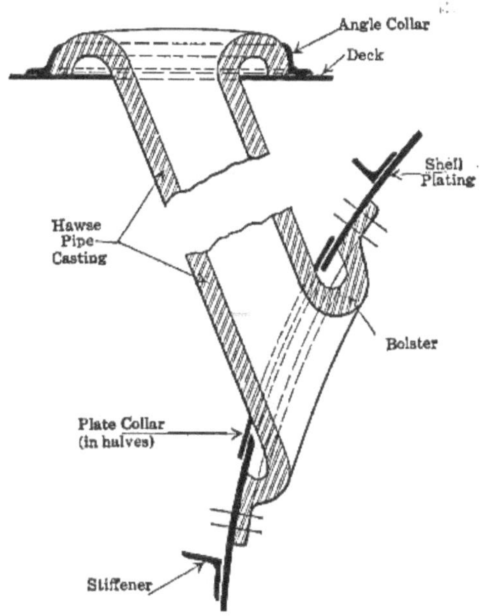

Fig. 62.—Hawse pipe.

hawse pipes. At the ends of either a hawse pipe or chain pipe, where the direction of the chain is sharply changed, the edges must be well rounded off by heavy *bolsters*, as shown in Fig. 62.

For leading and securing hawsers to the ship from a dock or tug *chocks, bitts, cleats,* and similar fittings are securely attached to the decks, especially to the weather deck. Figure 63 shows bitts and a chock and a method of attaching such heavy fittings, which must transmit heavy stresses to the hull.

In Fig. 64 are shown a section of a *rail* and *bulwarks,* two types of *fenders,* a *docking keel* and two types of *bilge keels.* The *rail* and *bulwarks* form a fence or enclosure around the edge of an open deck. The plating is light and should not be considered as furnishing much strength in addition to

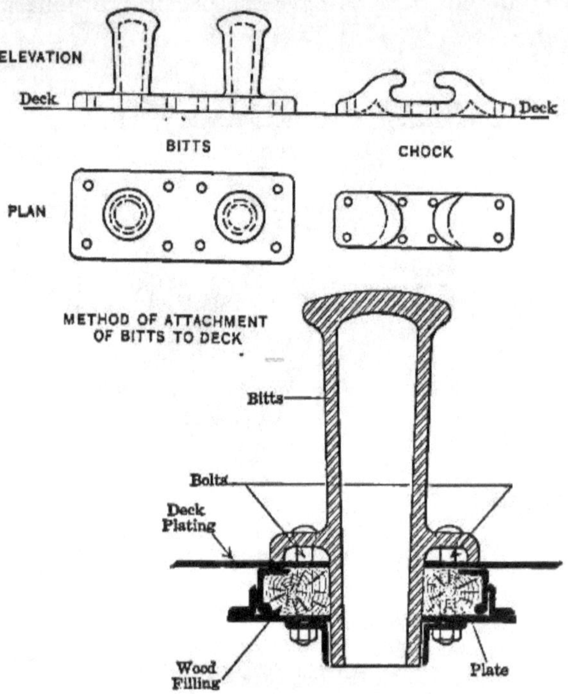

FIG. 63.—Bitts and chock.

that of the sheer strake. In many cases *open* rails are fitted consisting of stanchions and horizontal rods with a wood railing on top. *Fenders* are fitted to prevent damage to the sides of tugs, barges, and similar vessels which frequently bump against other vessels or against docks. They usually run along the sides parallel to the upper deck and a few feet above the water line. *Docking keels* are fitted on battleships and other large heavy vessels to take a portion of the weight when in dry-dock. They run parallel to the centre keel and are usually located roughly at ⅔ of the half-beam of the ship out from the centre line. *Bilge keels* are fitted along the bilges and are designed to prevent or decrease rolling. They are sometimes called *rolling chocks.*

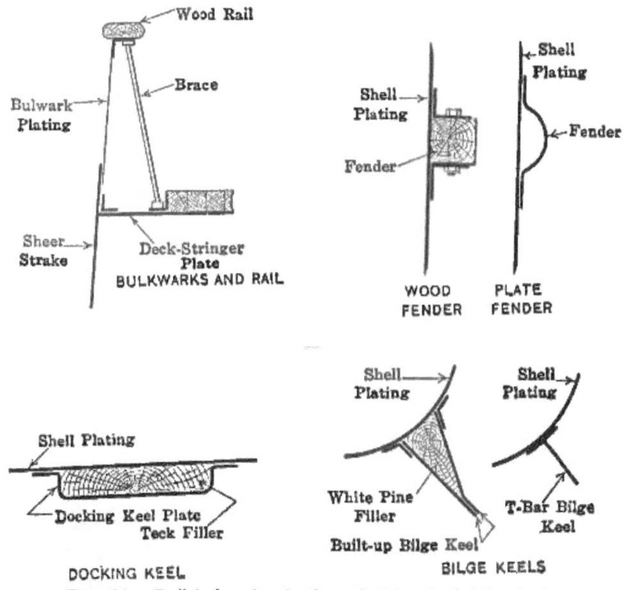

FIG. 64.—Rail bulwarks, fenders, docking keel, bilge keels.

Cofferdams are compartments formed by placing two bulkheads close together, the space between, or cofferdam, being for the purpose of preventing leaks between the two spaces on either side of the cofferdam—as, for example, between the end of an oil tank and an adjacent compartment.

Drainage wells are small pockets placed in the lowermost compartments of the ship (often called, in this connection, the *bilges*) in order to permit water, etc., to collect therein, and thus to be readily pumped out.

9

CHAPTER IV

DESIGN OF SHIPS

1. CONDITIONS TO BE FULFILLED

The design of a ship is the first step in the process of ship production. It should be considered broadly as a question of cause and effect. A ship is needed to fulfil a given purpose. To fulfil this purpose she must meet certain requirements. In meeting these requirements certain obstacles must be overcome. The design of a ship then resolves itself into a problem of fulfilling the requirements sought, while at the same time overcoming the obstacles that are bound to be encountered. The designer is the planner who gives the orders, which must be executed by the shipbuilder. Each must be familiar, to a certain extent, with the problems with which the other is confronted in order that they may work together harmoniously in the process of ship production. Their work is also closely related to the questions of material, tools and labor available. The designer's work is largely theoretical in nature; the shipbuilder's, practical.

If the ship that is desired is to fulfil certain special and unusual requirements, the designer's task becomes more difficult, while, if, on the other hand, the requirements of the ship are practically the same as those of other ships that have already been designed, the designer's work is correspondingly reduced. Many shipyards have developed certain more or less *standard* designs for ships, which they have built over and over again to the same plans. For such ships the designer's task disappears, the problem of producing them being entirely one for the shipbuilder.

At the present time the great need in ship production is *quantity*. Any ship that is capable of carrying cargo or men across the ocean is very valuable, and since there are already available many plans for ships that will fulfil these requirements, the need is now more for shipbuilders than for ship designers.

The space devoted to a discussion of the design of ships will therefore be limited, in order that more consideration may be given to the problems met with in the building of ships. It is, however, desirable that the shipbuilder be conversant, in a general way, with the work of the designer.

The problem which is given to the designer for solution is to produce the plans and specifications for a ship that will have a certain speed, carrying capacity, steaming radius, seaworthiness, etc. These characteristics vary greatly with the type of ship. For example: in fighting ships certain armament and armor must be carried; in passenger ships a certain number of passengers must be fully provided for; in cargo ships a certain amount of cubic space and weight carrying capacity must be provided. The problem is often complicated by the question of cost. A limit in cost naturally causes a limit in size, and certain characteristics can be obtained only by an increase in size. The design of a ship is therefore, in many cases, in the nature of a compromise. Certain qualities must be sacrificed in order to obtain certain others. The ideal case is that in which the designer is simply given the conditions to fulfil, without any limitation as to the size of the ship. Under such conditions he can produce the best results.

Except in very unusual cases, the design of a ship is based upon other ships already built and known to be satisfactory. The process of design consists in adapting data already at hand to suit the needs of the particular ship being designed. For this reason it is very important for the designer to possess as many different plans and as much data of all kinds regarding various ships already built as possible. This statement is based upon the well-known fact that experience is a better guide than theory. Nevertheless, it must not be forgotten that without theory and inventiveness, very little progress could ever be made.

2. CHOICE OF PRINCIPAL ELEMENTS

Having been given the various requirements that are to be fulfilled in the proposed ship, the designer, taking advantage of his knowledge and experience, and of the data that he has available, determines roughly upon the size, or displacement, of the ship. Then, having due regard for the conditions to be met, he selects roughly the principal dimensions and coefficients—such as length, beam, draft, block coefficient of fineness, coefficient of fineness of midship section, and load water line coefficient. This is largely a tentative process, since these elements are more or less inter-related, and is usually determined fairly well by the designer's knowledge of previous ships. If the ship is very similar to another already designed, a number of these elements may be practically fixed in advance. For example the block coefficient of certain types of ships is fairly well known, as are the ordinary ratios of length to beam and beam to draft. Since the displacement is directly dependent upon the product of length times beam times draft times the block coefficient, if the displacement has been decided upon, the other values can be fairly readily determined.

The *earliest rough design* may be divided into two parts:

(1) The determination of the principal elements of form and weight, and

(2) The drawing of the lines and the location of the various weights so as to conform to the elements selected.

The principal elements of form are the length, beam, draft and freeboard and the various coefficients. The principal elements of weight may be roughly expressed as the weight of the hull, fittings, crew, outfit, etc., the weight of the propelling apparatus (engines, boilers, auxiliaries, etc.), and the weights that are consumable or removable. The classifications of these weights are very elastic and depend upon the type of ship. For instance, in war ships the removable weights form a relatively small percentage of the displacement, because of the large amount of weight required to be permanently carried, for military reasons, made up of armor, turrets, barbettes, guns, torpedoes and the mechanism required for the operation of the ship and her weapons of offense, while in most merchant ships a great proportion of the displacement is given over to cargo carrying capacity.

3. CONSTRUCTION OF LINES AND DISTRIBUTION OF WEIGHTS

Having decided tentatively upon the principal elements of form the designer proceeds with the drawing of the lines. After the lines are completed the various "weight groups" are located so as to give a satisfactory arrangement, practically, and at the same time to fulfil the fundamental laws governing the operation of all ships. These "weight groups" consist of the weight of the hull and fittings, weight of engines, boilers and auxiliaries, weight of fuel and water, weight of officers, crew, and their effects, and a number of other weight groups depending both upon the type of ship, and the method of grouping.

Some of the fundamental laws which must be fulfilled are briefly outlined below:

(1) The sum of all the weight groups for the condition of loading assumed in the design must be equal to the weight of water displaced by the ship at the design draft.

(2) The position of the centre of gravity of the combined total of all the weight groups must be in a vertical line with the centre of buoyancy, or centre of figure of the under water volume of the ship.

(3) The vertical position of the centre of gravity of the combined total of all the weight groups must be far enough below the metacentre to give a suitable metacentric height, and sufficient righting arm for all angles of inclination to which the vessel may ever be expected to heel.

Preliminary rough calculations of the positions of the centres of gravity and buoyancy, and of the metacentre, must of course be made for this purpose. A certain amount of adjustment is usually necessary in this process, since so many different conditions must be met that the problem cannot be approached in a strictly mathematical manner. Various locations must be assumed for the centres of gravity of the main weight groups, such as engines, boilers, fuel, cargo, etc., and the amounts of these weights must be estimated on the basis of the speed, endurance, cargo carrying capacity, etc., that it is desired to give to the ship. The methods of making the calculations are described in Section 5, below.

4. PRINCIPAL PLANS

When the weights have finally been located so as to give, roughly, the desired solution of the problem, the next step in the design is the preparation of the *principal plans* which show in detail the locations and weights of the various members, parts, fittings and subdivisions of the ship, and from which exact calculations of all the weights of the ship may be made.

The principal ones of these plans are, usually, the following:

Midship section plan.
Shell expansion.
Stem, sternpost, propeller struts, rudder, etc.
Engines, boilers and auxiliaries, etc.
Inboard profile.
Outboard profile.
Deck, hold and inner bottom plans.
Cross sections.
Bulkhead, deck, and inner bottom plating plans.
Various piping plans.

The *midship section* is a plan showing a transverse section of the ship at the dead flat (similar to Fig. 28) and giving the principal dimensions (or scantlings) of the various shapes entering into the construction of the frames, beams, longitudinal, stringers, etc., and of deck and shell plating, etc.

The *shell expansion* is a plan showing, in detail, the sizes of all the plates forming the shell. It is drawn by laying off along the ship's length as a base, ordinates representing the actual girths of all the frames together with their intersections with the edges of the various shell plates (or the *landing edges*, as they are called). It will be noted that this is an expansion in the transverse direction only, and does not give the true form of the shell plates. A true expansion of the ship's outer form cannot be drawn, since it is an undevelopable surface. In order to obtain the true shapes of the various shell plates a wooden model is made and the plating laid off thereon.

Plans of the *stem*, *sternpost*, *propeller struts*, rudder, etc., are simply working drawings of these various parts.

Plans of the *engines*, *boilers* and *auxiliaries*, etc., represent a large amount of investigation and calculation on account of their intricate nature, and in most establishments are prepared by a set of designers and draftsmen distinct and separate from the hull designers, and forming the *marine engineering department*.

The *inboard profile* is a plan showing a longitudinal vertical section of the ship taken through the centre line (see Fig. 18).

The *outboard profile* is a side elevation of the ship showing the masts, rigging, boats, davits, and other outer fittings.

Deck, *hold* and *inner bottom plans* are views of the various decks, the hold, and inner bottom as seen from above, and show the subdivision of these various spaces.

Cross sections are plans showing transverse sections of the ship at various points along her length. They indicate special features of framing, subdivision, etc., in these localities.

Bulkhead, deck and inner bottom plating plans show the details of plating, riveting, stiffening, etc., of the various bulkheads and decks, and of the inner bottom.

Piping plans show the various systems of drainage, fire protection, flushing, plumbing, fresh water supply, ventilation, etc.

In addition to the above, in the case of war ships, there are drawn plans of the armor, guns, gun foundations, turrets, barbettes, torpedo tubes, etc.

Also there must be plans drawn for special local weights such as boats, davits, windlasses, steering gear, anchors, winches, dynamos, etc., etc., unless, as is often the case, plans for these already exist.

In preparing the principal plans the designer is guided, in the case of merchant vessels, by the published rules of the classification society under which the ship is to be built. These rules provide for certain scantlings to be used for each size of ship, so that the designer, having decided upon the length, beam, depth, and principal coefficients of his ship, can, by referring to the classification society's rules and tables, determine at once the proper sizes for all the principal structural members.

The warship designer is not limited by Lloyd's or any other such rules, and has more freedom in the choice of the scantlings. He is guided principally by his available information regarding other ships of similar type and size already built, and if any radical departure from these is made very careful investigations and extensive calculations are necessary.

5. FINAL CALCULATIONS

Having completed the principal plans the next step of the designer is the *detailed weight calculation*. The principle involved in this process is simple, it being merely the determination of the weight of each part and the exact location of its centre of gravity, and the combining of these in groups, so as eventually to determine the total weight of the entire ship, and the position of its centre of gravity. The work required is, however, very tedious, and involves an enormous amount of calculation, on account of the great number of different parts to be considered and the irregular shapes of many of them. No attempt will be made here to describe in detail the methods by which these calculations are made.

In conjunction with the calculations for weights, calculations must also be made for buoyancy, stability and trim. These also are simple in principle but tedious and involved in practical application. They are based upon the general laws discussed in Chapter I.

The *calculation of the displacement* consists in finding the total volume of the under water portion of the ship in cubic feet. This, divided by 35, is the displacement of the ship in tons—since a ton of sea water occupies 35 cubic feet.

The *calculation of the position of the centre of buoyancy* consists in finding the location of the centre of figure of the under water portion of the ship.

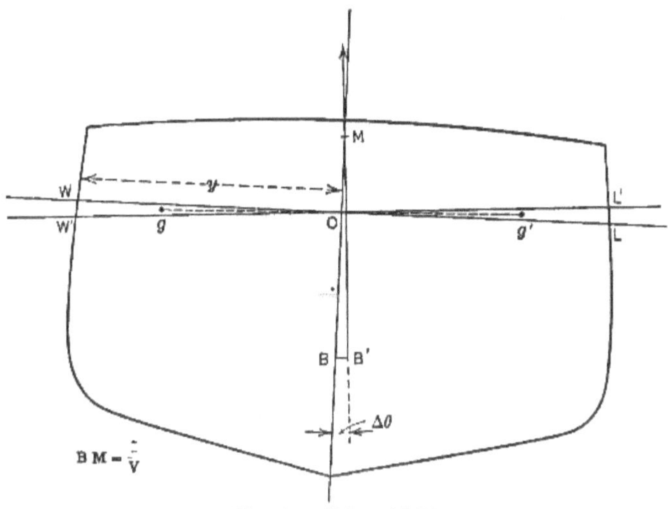

Fig. 65.—Value of *BM*

The *calculation of the metacentric height* is briefly as follows: The value of *BM*, the distance of the metacentre above the centre of buoyancy, calculated after the position of the centre of buoyancy *B* has been calculated, gives the location of the metacentre. This, together with the location of the centre of gravity *G*, calculated as described above, gives a means of finding *GM*, the metacentric height.

The *method of calculating BM* is based upon the following general principle:

Let Fig. 65 represent the cross section of a ship inclined

to a small angle $\Delta\theta$. Let B be the original centre of buoyancy and B' the centre of buoyancy as inclined. Let y be the half-beam of the ship at this section and let longitudinal distances be represented by the variable, x. Let the volume of displacement $= V$.

Since $\Delta\theta$ is small $BB' = BM \cdot \Delta\theta$. Also the moment of the new volume of displacement about the plane passed longitudinally through OB is $\overline{BB'} \cdot V$.

But since this new volume of displacement has been formed by subtracting the wedge, of which WOW' is a section, from the original displacement, and adding thereto the equal wedge, of which LOL' is a section, this moment is also equal to twice the moment of either wedge.

The moment of either wedge is

$$\int \text{area } \triangle WOW' \times \overline{gO} \times dx$$

where $\overline{gO}$ is the distance of the centre of gravity of the triangle from O.

But, again, since $\Delta\theta$ is small,

$$\text{Area } \triangle WOW' = \tfrac{1}{2} y \cdot \Delta\theta \cdot y = \frac{y^2 \cdot \Delta\theta}{2}$$

and

$$\overline{gO} = \tfrac{2}{3} y$$

$$\therefore \overline{BB'} \cdot V = 2 \int \frac{y^2 \cdot \Delta\theta}{2} \times \tfrac{2}{3} y dx = \overline{BM} \cdot \Delta\theta \cdot V$$

or

$$\overline{BM} = \frac{1}{V} \cdot \tfrac{2}{3} \int y^3 dx = \frac{I}{V}$$

(where $\tfrac{2}{3} \int y^3 dx$ is the moment of inertia of the load water plane about its longitudinal axis, which is called "I".)

The calculation of BM therefore involves the calculation of the volume of displacement and the transverse moment of inertia of the load water plane.

The method of calculating the *longitudinal BM* is along similar lines.

Other stability calculations must also be made since the metacentric height is merely an index of the initial stability of the vessel. These calculations are long and involved, although, like the other ship calculations, they are based upon a simple principle. This principle is briefly expressed by an equation known as *Atwood's Formula* which is that the moment of statical stability of a ship when inclined to any angle θ is

$$W\left(\frac{v \times hh'}{V} - \overline{BG}\, sin\, \theta\right) \text{ foot tons}$$

where W = the displacement of the ship in tons
V = the displacement of the ship in cu. ft.
v = the volume of the immersed or emerged wedge in cubic feet
hh' = the horizontal distance between the centres of gravity of the two wedges, in feet, and
BG = the distance between the centre of gravity of the ship and her original centre of buoyancy, in feet.

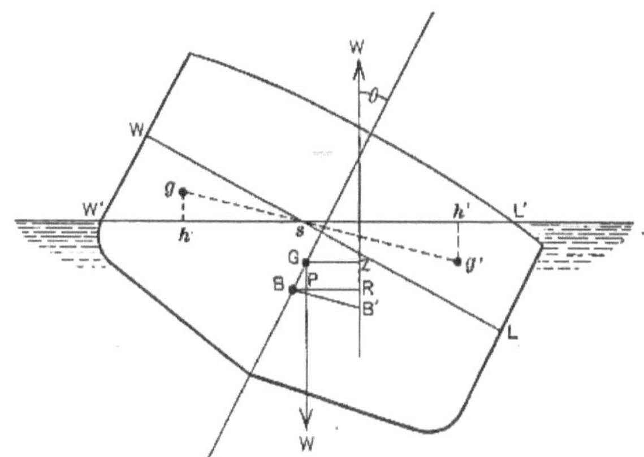

Moment of Statical Stability = $W\left[\frac{v \times hh'}{V} - \overline{BG} \cdot sin\, \theta\right]$.

Fig. 66.—Atwood's formula.

These values are shown in Fig. 66, and, referring to that figure, the proof of Atwood's formula is as follows:

The couple tending to right the ship has a moment $W \times GZ$ which is called the moment of statical stability. But

$$GZ = BR - BP = BR - \overline{BG} \sin \theta$$

But BR represents the horizontal shift of the centre of

figure of the volume of displacement from its old to its new position, and by taking moments:

$$BR \times V = v \times hh'$$

$$\therefore W \times \overline{GZ} = W \left[\frac{v \times hh'}{V} - \overline{BG} \sin \theta \right]$$

By suitable geometrical and arithmetical calculations it is therefore possible to find the moment tending to right the ship when heeled to any angle and when floating at any displacement. By dividing each moment by the value of the displacement the corresponding righting arm may be obtained.

If several different displacements be considered and righting arms calculated for different inclinations, it is possible to plot a series of curves with righting arms as ordinates and displacements as abscissas. Such curves are called *cross curves of stability.* There are a number of different methods in use for making the calculations by which data for plotting these cross curves is obtained. Space does not permit going into detail regarding these methods here. All are based upon the assuming of certain poles about which the ship is considered as inclined, and corrections must be made to obtain the true righting arms because the actual locations of the centre of gravity of the ship are different from those assumed.

By making these corrections it is possible to obtain, from the cross curves, certain curves showing, for various actual displacements and corresponding positions of the centre of gravity, the righting arms for all angles of inclination. Such curves are called *curves of statical stability,* and are similar to the curve shown in Fig. 7.

The *statical stability* at any angle of inclination of the ship is measured by the moment in foot-tons tending to right the ship when she is inclined to that angle. The *dynamical stability* is measured by the amount of *work* that must be done in bringing the ship from the upright position to the position considered. The *curve of dynamical stability* is therefore the integral of the curve of statical stability, or each ordinate of the curve of dynamical stability may be calculated by obtaining the area of the curve of statical stability up to the abscissa corresponding to the angle of inclination considered.

In addition to the calculations already mentioned there are also usually made calculations for: tons per inch immersion, moment to change trim 1″, areas of water lines, longitudinal C.G. of water lines, area of midship section, correction to displacement for 1 ft. trim by stern, area of wetted surface.

The *tons per inch immersion* for any given draft of a ship is the number of tons increase or decrease in displacement that will be caused by the draft being increased or decreased, respectively, by 1 inch. Practically speaking if the ship sinks 1 inch deeper into the water along all of her water line the increase in displacement will be the volume of a slice 1 inch thick and having the area of the water line. (If the sides of the ship were vertical at all points this would be absolutely true). Hence the tons per inch immersion is found by dividing the area of the water line (in square feet) by 12×35. (Thickness of slice is $\frac{1}{12}$ foot and there are 35 cubic feet of salt water to the ton. For fresh water the figure to be used is 36 instead of 35.)

The *moment to change trim 1 inch* is the longitudinal moment, in foot-tons, necessary to cause the ship to change her trim by 1 inch from the water line at which she is considered to be floating. It is equal to $\frac{1}{12}$ of the displacement in tons, multiplied by the longitudinal metacentric height in feet, divided by the length on the water line considered, in feet. The reason for this is that when the ship changes trim 1 inch she is inclined *longitudinally* to an angle with her original position of which the tangent is $\frac{1}{12}$ foot divided by the length of the water line in feet, this inclination also having for its tangent the distance that the ship's centre of gravity may be considered as moving longitudinally divided by the longitudinal metacentric height. (The center of gravity is here considered as moving from G to G' because of the moving of a weight of w tons, longitudinally, through a distance of d feet. The moment causing the change of trim is then $w \times d$ foot-tons.)

Hence, if θ be the angle of longitudinal inclination

$$\theta = \frac{GG'}{GM} = \frac{1/12}{L} \text{ (where } L \text{ is the length in feet).}$$

But $W \times GG' = w \times d$ (where W = displacement in tons).

(Since the ratio of the shifts of the centres of gravity of the ship and the weight moved is the inverse of the ratio of their respective weights).

Hence the moment to change trim 1 inch or

$$w \times d = \frac{1/12 \times GM \times W}{L}$$

The calculations of the *areas of water line*, position of *longitudinal centre of gravity of water line, area of midship section*, and *correction to displacement for* 1 *foot trim by the stern* for any given water line, are made by the methods described below, being simply geometrical calculations. By making calculations of each for several different water lines curves can be plotted giving values for all intermediate points.

The *correction to displacement for* 1 *foot trim by the stern* is the amount that must be added, in order to obtain the true displacement, to the displacement corresponding to a water line drawn parallel to the load water line and at a level corresponding to the *mean draft* at which the ship is floating. When the ship changes trim the shape of the water line changes on account of the difference between the form of the molded surface at the forward and after ends. Since displacements are ordinarily calculated only for water lines corresponding to various drafts *on an even keel* it is necessary to have a means of correcting these to find the displacements when floating out of the designed trim.

The correction is $\frac{12Td}{L}$ tons (additive)

where T is the tons per inch immersion,
L is the length of the water line in feet, and
d is the distance that the centre of gravity of the load water plane is *aft* of amidships, in feet.

(Should the centre of gravity of the water plane be *forward* of amidships the correction will, of course, be subtractive instead of additive.)

The *area of wetted surface* is calculated for use in figuring the frictional resistance of the ship. It cannot be calculated exactly on account of the ship's surface being undevelopable, but for practical purposes, different approximate methods can be used which give sufficient accuracy.

One of these, known as *Kirk's Analysis* consists in calculating the wetted surface by the expression

$$(2LD + \propto LB)$$

where L is the length of the ship, in feet,
D is the draft of the ship, in feet,
B is the beam of the ship, in feet,
$\propto$ is the block coefficient of fineness,
and the resulting value is the total area of the wetted surface in square feet.

Other approximate formulas for the *wetted surface,* in square feet are:

Admiral Taylor's:—

$$15.5\sqrt{WL}$$

where W = displacement, in tons, and
L = length, in feet.

Mr. Denny's:—

$$1.7LD + \frac{V}{D}$$

where L = length, D = draft (feet) and
V = volume of displacement (cubic feet).

A more accurate calculation can be made by finding the area of a curve of *modified girths,* each girth being taken along a frame station and increased by multiplying it by the *average secant* of the angle between the molded surface and a fore and aft line taken at the station considered.

The methods of making the various calculations outlined in the preceding paragraphs are based upon various means

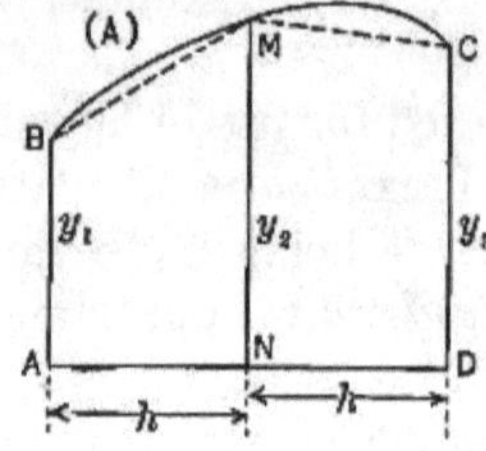

Trapezoidal Rule:—

$$\text{Area } ABCD = \tfrac{1}{2}(y_1 + y_2)h + \tfrac{1}{2}(y_2 + y_3)h = h\left[\frac{y_1}{2} + y_2 + \frac{y_3}{2}\right]$$

Simpson's First Rule:—

$$\text{Area } ABCD = \frac{h}{3}(y_1 + 4y_2 + y_3)$$

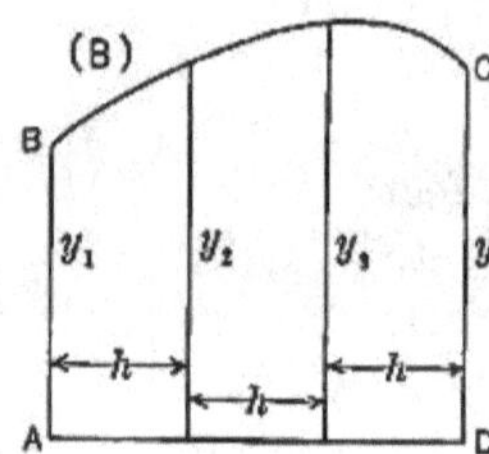

Trapezoidal Rule:—

$$\text{Area } ABCD = h\left[\frac{y_1}{2} + y_2 + y_3 + \frac{y_4}{2}\right]$$

Simpson's Second Rule:—

$$\text{Area } ABCD = \tfrac{3}{8}h(y_1 + 3y_2 + 3y_3 + y_4)$$

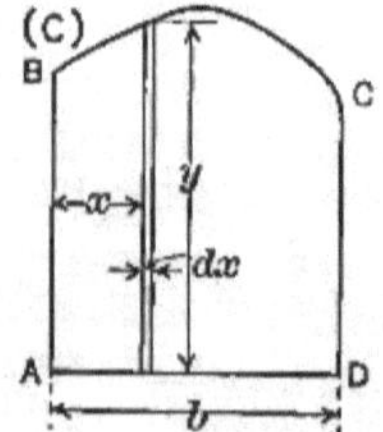

"Five-Eight" Rule:—

$$\text{Area } ABMN \text{ (in diagram (A))} = \tfrac{1}{12}h(5y_1 + 8y_2 - y_3)$$

In General:—

$$\text{Area } ABCD = \int_{x=0}^{x=b} y\,dx$$

Fig. 67.—Methods of integration.

of integration, it being necessary in the case of a ship to obtain certain areas, volumes, moments, and moments of inertia of curvilinear areas and volumes, not susceptible of exact mathematical calculation.

These are most commonly obtained by the *Trapezoidal Rule, Simpson's Rules,* and graphically by means of the planimeter and integrator.

The trapezoidal rule is used when it is assumed that the ordinates are so closely spaced that the curve between any two adjacent ordinates may be considered, for all practical purposes, as a straight line. For a convex curve this gives too small an area (see Fig. 67).

Simpson's Rules are shown in Fig. 67. These may be extended to a large number of intervals, it being noted that the first rule applies when the number of intervals is even; and the second when it is a multiple of three. The *five-eight* rule may be used to find the area between two successive ordinates in cases where the number of intervals is neither even nor a multiple of three.

Both Simpson's and the trapezoidal rules furnish an arithmetical means of finding the value of $\int y dx$ (see Fig. 67). If the value sought were $\int y^2 dx$ the same method might be followed—only that in this case the *square* of each ordinate would be considered—and so in the case of any function of the ordinates.

The detailed methods of making the calculations outlined above form the subject of Theoretical Naval Architecture which is too large a subject to be treated here. The reader is referred, for complete information regarding these matters, to such books as

Attwood's "Text Book of Theoretical Naval Architecture."
Robinson's "Naval Construction."
Biles' "The Design and Construction of Ships."
Peabody's "Naval Architecture."
White's "Manual of Naval Architecture."
Reed's "Stability of Ships."

After the displacement, weight and stability calculations have been made, it may be found that certain shifts of weights, or even changes in the lines will be required in order to give satisfactory conditions of draft, trim, buoyancy, and stability. When these changes have been made the calculations must be made over again—in whole or in part.

When the locations and amounts of weights have been so adjusted, with respect to the lines, as to give satisfactory conditions, the principal plans are completed and the calculations for strength outlined on pages 25 to 27 are made. Such changes in weights, as may be found necessary as a result of these calculations may possibly result in the necessity for further changes in the preceding calculations—although this is not usually the case.

6. DETAIL PLANS AND SPECIFICATIONS

The remainder of the design of the ship consists in the preparation of detail plans for the various minor parts, fittings, installations, etc., not shown in the principal plans, but necessary for the work of the shipbuilders. The number and extent of these plans vary with the size and type of ship and the requirements of the prospective owner.

In addition to the plans specifications are prepared which supplement the plans, and embody instructions to the builders as to the quality and sizes of the various materials to be used in the construction of the ship, and numerous other requirements to be complied with that are not fully shown in the plans.

Based upon the plans and specifications there are also usually prepared, under the direction of the designer, lists of materials that will be required for the building of the ship.

CHAPTER V

SHIPYARDS

1. SITE FOR A SHIPYARD

The site for a shipyard must be, of course, on the edge of some body of water of sufficient depth, and extent, to permit of safe launching of the ships after they have been built. It must also be so chosen as to permit of expeditious delivery of the large and heavy materials required for building the ships, and should, if possible, be located not too far from suitable housing facilities for the workmen who are to be employed. Not only must there be sufficient water for launching the ships but also there must be a channel leading to the sea through which the ships may pass after they are entirely completed and outfitted.

The area of ground necessary for a shipyard depends not only upon the number and size of the ships to be built but also upon their character, and how much of the work of fitting out and equipping the hulls is to be done entirely by the shipbuilder and at the shipyard. Some shipbuilders do practically all of the work, including the manufacture of engines, boilers, large castings, forgings, etc., in their own yards. Others confine their work almost entirely to the hull proper and purchase a large amount of material, ready for installation, from other concerns. In the case of "fabricated ships" even the parts of the hull are made at a distance and shipped to the yard for erection and assembly.

No fixed rule can therefore be given regarding the acreage required for a shipyard, but this can be roughly determined, having due regard for the conditions to be met, by comparison with other established yards.

2. THE BUILDING SLIP AND LAUNCHING WAYS

The first essential in a shipyard is the place in which actually to build the ships. The hull of a modern ship, when ready for launching, weighs a good many hundreds, or perhaps thousands, of tons and this large and relatively concentrated weight must be properly supported.

It is therefore customary, in most cases, to strengthen the ground on which a ship is to be built by means of piling. In some cases—as where the site of the shipyard is over a stratum of rock, or where the ground is very hard—piling is not necessary, but where the ships to be built are large, and except in rare instances, piling is commonly used. Sometimes the piling may be of reinforced concrete, but more often it is of wood.

In addition to the driving of piles it is very often necessary to do considerable excavating and dredging in order to provide proper facilities for the building and launching of ships. Fig. 68 shows, in cross section, the site of a shipyard before and after the dredging, excavating and pile driving have been done.

The space over which a ship is built is called the *building slip*. This ground except where rocky, or very hard, is reinforced by the piles, which are driven deep into the ground until they strike gravel or other firm subsoil. The keel line of the ship, while being built, is usually nearly normal to the line of the water's edge, although, in some cases, where the breadth of the water into which the ship is to be launched is limited, it is necessary to have the building slip inclined to the line of the water's edge (or even *broadside* launching may be necessary. See page 157).

The piles are driven in rows at right angles to the keel line. The spacing of these rows varies with the weight of the ship and hardness of the ground. In most cases it is about four feet although in some cases it may be as great as six feet. For battleships and large, heavy vessels it may be as close as two feet.

There are three lines along the building slip that must be strongly reinforced by piling: the line of the keel, which takes a large part of the weight of the ship during the process of construction, and the two lines, parallel to the keel line on which, later, are laid the *launching ways*, heavy

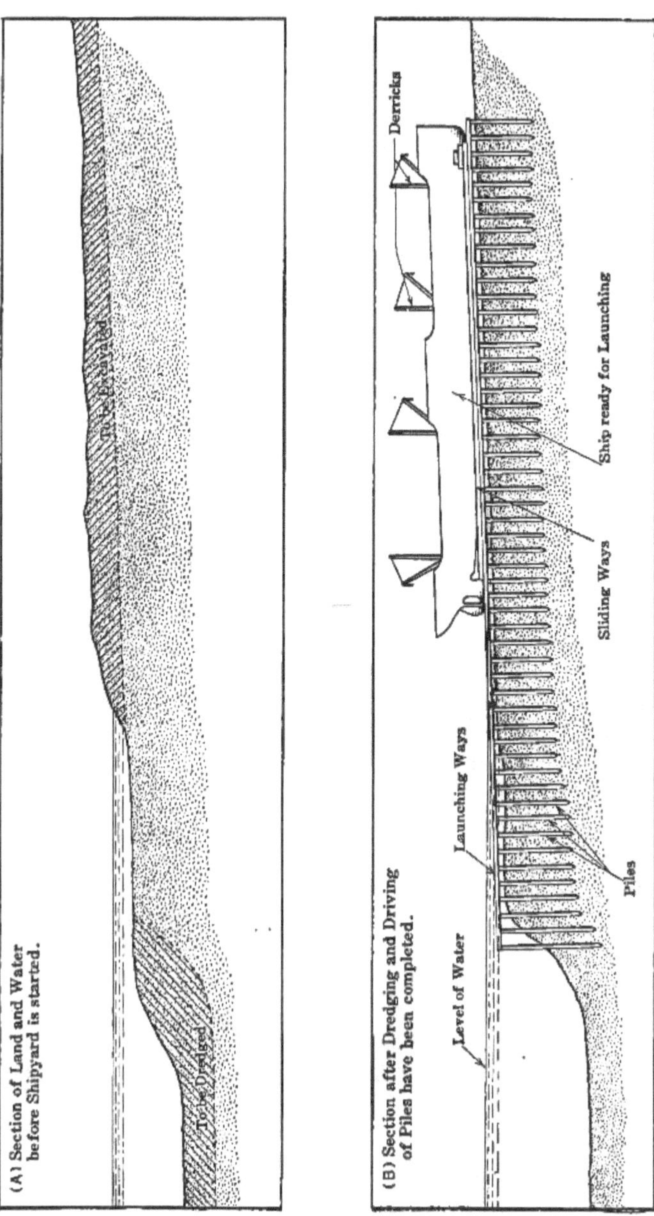

Fig. 68.—Making a shipyard.

timbers, which take the weight of the ship when she is launched. In addition to these lines practically all of the ground under the ship's bottom must have a certain amount of reinforcing to take shores and blocks used to support the bottom and bilges of the ship during her construction.

The piles are usually pine or fir stems about 10″ or 12″ in diameter at the butts and of lengths, dependent upon the nature of the ground, of sometimes as much as 50 feet. The exact number and arrangement of the piles must be decided in each case. It is well, however, in laying out a new building slip to consider the possibility of larger and heavier ships being built subsequently on the same slip.

For a large, heavy ship, such as a modern battleship, it is not unusual to find the piles under the launching ways in groups of six, spaced about 16″ between centres, the groups being four feet apart along the lines of the ways. Under the middle portion of the keel the rows may be two feet apart with eight piles in alternate groups and two piles in the intermediate groups, and under the first docking keels groups of six piles each spaced every four feet. After the piles have been driven their tops are sawed off and on them are placed large cross logs secured with heavy driving bolts. The cross logs may extend across the full width of the ship at eight-foot intervals of the length, the intermediate logs being of shorter lengths. Sometimes the piles are not sawed off at the ground level, but at a considerable distance above it, and a platform of heavy planking is built over them as shown in Fig. 69.

Along the middle of the slip are laid large blocks from 12″ to 18″ square, upon which is laid the keel of the ship. These blocks are placed over the cross logs and are built up to a considerable height above the ground so as to give workmen ready access to the bottom of the ship, and to give sufficient room for launching. A height of at least four feet should be allowed (see Figs. 69 and 70)—and usually a little more—for this purpose. The lower blocks are usually six or seven feet long, the upper ones shorter. The

FIG. 69.—Building slips.

line of the top of the keel blocks is inclined so that the end at the water's edge is lower than the other end. This slope is usually slightly greater than ½″ per foot. In the case of long, light ships it may be as much as 15/16″ per foot. For battleships and cruisers it is generally 9/16″ per foot. The larger the vessel the less the declivity.

The declivity for the launching ways, down which the ship slides into the water after the hull is built, is greater, ordinarily, than that of the keel blocks, being usually 11/16″ or ¾″ to the foot. In some cases the top of the launching ways at the end near the water is given a longitudinal curvature or camber (of from 1/32″ to 1/16″ per

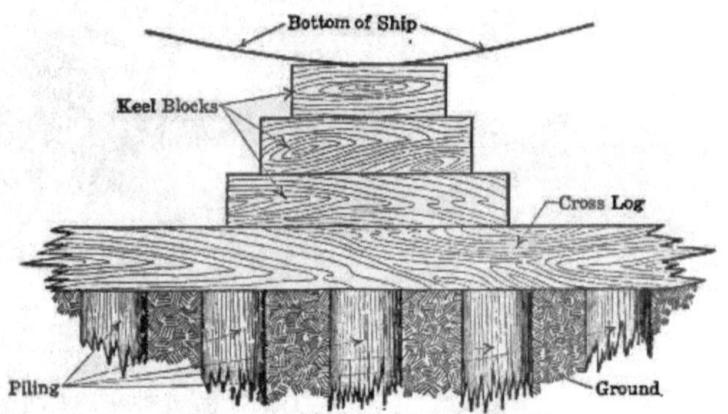

Fig. 70.—Keel blocks and piling.

foot) so as to give an increasing declivity at the lower end. These ways may also have a slight transverse cant inboard (about ½″ per foot).

The launching ways are usually located at about 1/6 of the beam of the ship out from the keel on each side so that their distance apart is about ⅓ of the width of the hull. The size of the launching ways varies from about 15″ breadth by 9″ depth in smaller vessels to as high as 6 feet breadth by 16″ or 18″ depth in the case of very large vessels. The breadth must be so proportioned, with regard to the launching weight of the ship, as to give a bearing pressure of about 2 to 2¼ tons per square foot.

Pressures of $2\frac{1}{2}$ tons per square foot should never be exceeded. The materials commonly used are yellow pine, elm, or oak. A cross section of a ship on the launching ways is shown in Fig. 71.

The launching ways must be extended for some distance beyond the water's edge, together with the necessary supporting piles, so that there will be several feet of water (from 4 or 5 feet for smaller vessels to 10 or 12 for larger ones) over the end of the ways when the ship is launched

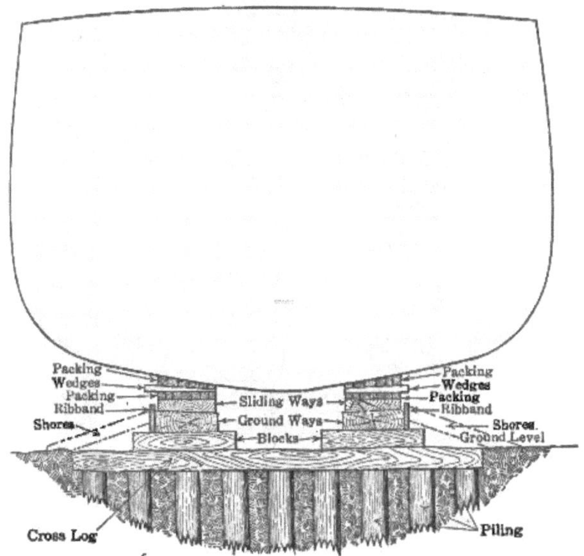

Fig. 71.—Ship on launching ways.

(see Figs. 68, 72 and 73). The rise and fall of the tide must, of course, be considered in this connection.

In designing the building slip, with regard for both the keel blocks and launching ways due consideration must be given to the contour of the ground, and of the bottom of the water, and to the shape, weight and size of the ship to be built and launched. Certain calculations should be made regarding the probable behavior of the ship when launched in order to make certain that the launching ways, especially

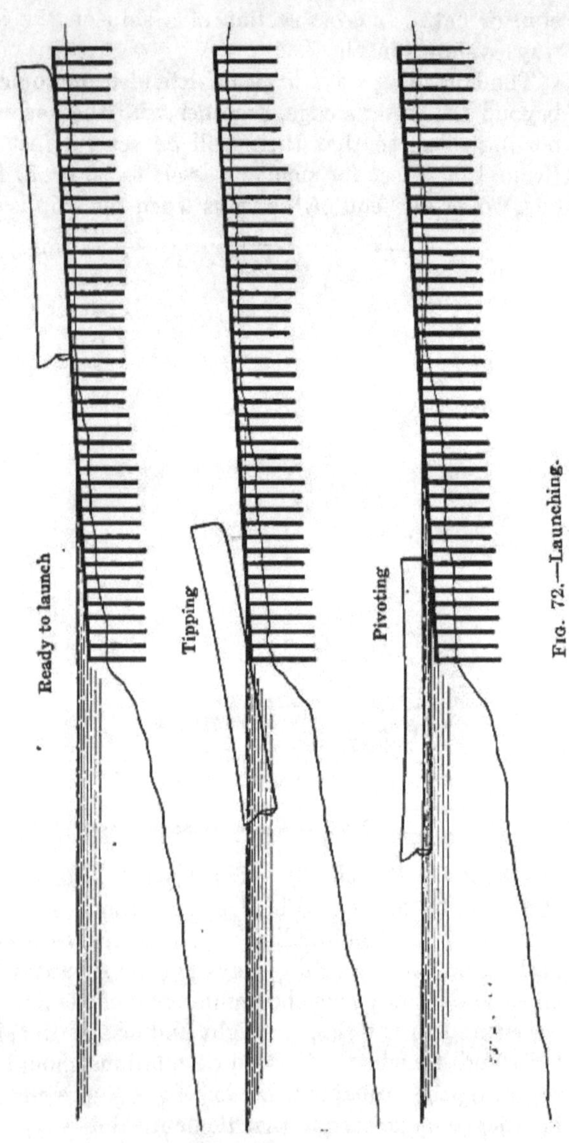

FIG. 72.—Launching.

at their lower end, have been properly designed. These investigations must be made, even before the commencement of the actual building of the ship, since the driving of the piling, the necessary dredging work involved, etc., usually must all be accomplished before the laying of the keel.

In Fig. 72, top view, is shown a sectional profile of the ground and water with piling, launching ways and ship on the ways, ready to be launched. The launching consists in permitting the ship, with supporting cribwork, to slide down the launching ways into the water. As soon as the stern enters the water there is added, to the upward force given by the support of the launching ways, the upward force of buoyancy due to the amount of the hull that is submerged. As the downward motion of the ship continues, the amount of this force of buoyancy increases, but after the stern passes the end of the launching ways it loses the upward support of these ways, and if the force of buoyancy is not great enough the ship may "*tip.*" Such "*tipping*" is shown in the middle diagram of Fig. 72, and should always be avoided, since the ship would very probably be seriously damaged by the great concentrated force thus brought to bear on the portion of the hull directly over the end of the launching ways—if the ways themselves were not crushed in, thus also endangering the hull.

On the other hand if a certain amount of the support of the ship is not soon transferred from the launching ways to the buoyancy of the water beyond the end of the ways, the ship may "*pivot*" about her bow or a point near the bow. Such "pivoting" is shown in the bottom view of Fig. 72. In the case of a very long, light vessel, like a destroyer, *premature* pivoting might cause excessive longitudinal stresses in the hull and result in serious damage. (Pivoting at the proper stage of the launching is not only not dangerous, but is desirable.)

Both tipping and pivoting must therefore be carefully considered and the launching ways must be extended far enough into the water to prevent tipping and not so deeply as to cause premature pivoting. The ways should be so designed, however, that the ship will pivot after a good proportion of her length is in the water.

It is necessary to provide sufficient depth of water to prevent the bow from striking bottom during launching. As will be seen in Figs. 68 and 72, the depth of water just beyond the end of the launching ways should increase quite rapidly.

Summary of Requirements of Building Slip, Launching Ways, Etc.

The most important points to be looked out for in laying out the piling, etc., for a building slip may be summarized as follows:

1. The piles must be so arranged as to give sufficient support for the launching weight of the hull.
2. There must be sufficient breadth of water in the line of the launching ways, produced, to prevent the ship from striking the opposite bank when launched.
3. There must be sufficient depth of water along this line so that the hull will not strike bottom when launched—especially just beyond the end of the launching ways.
4. The distance apart of the launching ways must be such that the weight of the ship will be well transmitted through heavy vertical longitudinal members of the hull, and properly distributed athwartships.
5. The launching ways must not be too far apart, because, owing to the fineness of the ends, a sufficient amount of the length might then not be supported, and too much transverse stress thus be caused.
6. The launching ways must not be too near together—which would cause undue transverse stresses and decreased stability.
7. The launching ways must extend far enough into the water to prevent tipping.
8. The launching ways must not extend too deeply into the water or otherwise pivoting may occur too soon.

9. The height of the keel blocks must be sufficient to permit ready access to the ship's bottom for men working on her construction.

10. The height of the launching ways must be such as to permit an unobstructed slide of the ship down them when launched.

(For additional information on this subject see Chap. VII, Sect. 7.)

In the great majority of shipyards the building slips and launching ways are arranged in the manner just described, but in some yards, notably those on the Great Lakes, ships are launched *broadside on,* being built with their keels parallel to instead of perpendicular to the water front. In such cases instead of two there are laid a number of launching ways usually at 10 or 15 foot intervals along the length of the ship and they are given a much greater declivity than ways for end launchings. One of the advantages of this method is that, due to her striking the water broadside on, the ship is checked quickly, and does not require a broad expanse of water. One of the disadvantages is that a much greater extent of water front is required, which on the seaboard, where water front is usually costly, may be a serious drawback. In the shipyard shown in Fig. 73 about four times as much water front would be required if the 28 ships were all to be built at the same time for broadside launchings instead of as shown.

3. YARD LAY-OUT—SHOPS, BUILDINGS, ETC.

In laying out a shipyard it is important to remember the various processes in the building of a ship, from the time that the raw material is received in the yard until the time when it is secured in place in the vessel. Provision must be made for stowing the material until it is needed, and for "fabricating" it, or fashioning it to the shapes and sizes necessary for its assembly in the ship. The layout of storehouses, stowage spaces, shops, etc., should therefore be so arranged as to require the minimum amount of transporting and handling of both raw and fabricated material. This is not a simple matter, since so many different elements enter into the problem, but certain salient points may always be looked out for.

In general, the route to be followed by the structural steel from the stowage racks should be in a nearly straight line by way of the laying out shed, punching and shearing shed, and fabricating shop to the building slip, with as short distances between each as possible. A similar principle applies to the engine parts which should go from foundry or forge, via machine shop and erecting room to the ship.

Means for transportation between these various points and for handling and placing heavy weights on the ship must also be provided and the more complete the equipment of a yard in this respect, the more efficient will be its operation.

For transporting large quantities of raw materials, or heavy forgings, castings and machinery parts about the yard ordinary railroad standard gauge tracks are usually laid, with suitable spurs, switches and connections, if possible, to the local railroad tracks. The yard should be equipped with a certain number of railway locomotives and freight cars of its own.

For smaller weights narrow gauge tracks are provided on which small flat cars may be pushed by hand. Motor trucks are also often employed. In the different shops various overhead and jib cranes are used for local handling.

A well-equipped yard should also have a number of locomotive cranes capable of lifting, transporting, and handling weights up to from ten to twenty tons. These should run on the standard gauge railway tracks.

Large traveling cranes are also very desirable for ship-yards of any importance. These run on specially constructed tracks of very wide gauge and are capable of negotiating very large weights—of fifty tons or more. These are especially useful in installing engines, boilers, armor, and other heavy weights in large vessels alongside of the fitting out piers, at which the ships are moored after launching and prior to final completion, and with at least one of which every important yard should be supplied.

One large floating derrick or crane capable of handling very heavy weights (100 to 150 tons) is also very desirable, although these are, of course, very costly and not possessed by many shipyards.

For handling and erecting material in place in the ship on the building slip it is necessary that certain other cranes or derricks be provided. Various types are in use but all should be so arranged that a weight may be lowered over any point of the ship's hull for each building slip or berth.

One method is to have a number of fixed masts or derricks each equipped with one or more booms operated by hoisting engines. These derricks must be more or less numerous since each can handle material over only a limited circle (see Fig. 73).

A better, but more expensive, arrangement, is to have high trestles running parallel to the centre line of the building slip for traveling cranes which may be either of the cantilever, overhead, or gantry type.

A birdseye view of the shipyard of the Submarine Boat Corporation is shown in Fig. 73, in which will be seen the building slips, launching ways, fitting out piers, derricks, a large cantilever crane, shops, buildings, railway tracks, etc. This yard, being designed to build "fabricated" ships, does not have the variety of shops found in some yards.

The buildings, etc., necessary for a shipyard usually include the following:

1. Buildings for offices, drafting rooms, etc.
2. Store houses and plate, angle, and other racks.
3. Power house (unless power is furnished by outside plant).
4. Mold loft.
5. Bending slabs.
6. Laying out, punching, and shearing sheds.
7. Fabricating and erecting shops.
8. Smith shop.

FIG. 73.—Shipyard of the Submarine Boat Corporation.

9. Pattern shop.
10. Foundry.
11. Machine shop.
12. Plumbers' and pipefitters' shop.
13. Joiner shop.
14. Shipwrights' and sparmakers' shop.
15. Coppersmiths' shop.
16. Sheet metal shop.
17. Boiler shop.
18. Sail loft.
19. Rigging loft.
20. Electrical shop.
21. Pickling, galvanizing and plating shops.
22. Paint and varnish shop.
23. Boat shop.
24. Upholstery shop.

Among these the following may be noted especially:

Storehouses are necessary in considerable variety and should be located conveniently to the shops requiring the largest quantities of the materials stored in each. *Plate racks* should be provided so that plates may be stowed on edge by various sizes so as to be readily accessible. This is usually accomplished by means of posts or metal bars set in concrete foundations, against which the plates may lean. For angles and other shapes a good arrangement is to have vertical metal posts with horizontal arms extending out on each side at various heights, the upper ones usually being shorter and each successive arm being slightly longer than the one above.

The *mold loft* is a building or shed of great horizontal extent which permits of its having a large continuous floor of sufficient size to have drawn on it the lines of the ship to full scale. The plans of a ship to be built are furnished to the mold loft by the drafting room, and from these plans the workers in the mold loft, called *loftsmen*, lay down and fair up, to full scale, the lines of the ship, and make *templates* for laying out the material for the hull. *Templates* are thin wood or paper patterns which show the size, shape, locations and sizes of rivet holes, and other particulars of the parts to which they apply.

11

The *bending slabs* are heavy rectangular cast iron blocks or slabs, square, or nearly square, and usually five or six feet on a side and from 2 or 3 inches to 5 or 6 inches thick placed together, side to side, and end to end, so as to form a large horizontal flat surface on top of which the frames, reverse frames, and other similar parts of a ship can be bent to their proper shapes. The slabs are usually laid on top of heavy timbers which thus raise them a foot or more above the ground or floor of the shed in which they are located. They have small holes (usually about 1½" square) running vertically through them, so that their upper surface presents a lattice-like appearance as shown in Fig. 78. These holes are used for the insertion of dogs, pins, etc., by means of which the frame bars are clamped down and held to the proper shape while being bent and beveled.

Close to the slabs are located long *furnaces*, of the reverberatory type, usually oil-burning, for heating the frames.

The *laying-out shed* should be located near the mold loft. Templates from the latter are used for laying out the various plates and shapes for fabrication in this shed which often forms a part of the *punching and shearing*, or as it is sometimes called, the *plate and angle shop*. In this latter shop are located the various machine tools used for punching, shearing and planing, etc., the various steel parts of the hull that have been marked in the laying out shed for that purpose.

The *fabricating and erecting shop* may also form a part of the plate and angle shed or it may be in another building close by. Here various small portions of the ship's structure, such as floor plates, hatch coamings and covers, water-tight doors, skylights, trunks, etc., are assembled and riveted up so that they may be taken to the ship ready for installation.

The *smith shop* usually has both small forges and anvlis for hand forgings, and steam hammers and large furnaces for heavy work, and drop forgings. The extent of the forging work varies in different yards, some having many of the larger forgings made by outside concerns.

In the *joiner shop* a great part of the wood work of the ship is done. Furniture, ladders, wooden doors, skylights, chests, lockers, gangways, gratings, and a large number of other miscellaneous wooden articles are made here.

In the *shipwright shop* material for wood decks, foundations, masts, spars and various materials for scaffolding, stagings, blocking, shores, cribbing, wedges, etc., is prepared.

The nature of the work done in the other shops mentioned is indicated by their names. In many of these shops the work done is similar to that done in the same shops in other manufacturing plants, there being in a modern ship much of the same equipment that is found in buildings on shore.

4. SHIPYARD MACHINE TOOLS, ETC.

The principal processes in the fabrication of the steel material that forms the hull proper are as follows:

1. Plate bending and straightening.
2. Shearing.
3. Planing.
4. Punching, drilling, and reaming.
5. Countersinking.
6. Flanging.
7. Sawing.
8. Forging and welding.
9. Punching large holes, notches, etc.
10. Cutting with the oxy-acetylene torch.
11. Joggling.
12. Hydraulic riveting.
13. Frame bending, etc.
14. Furnacing plates.
15. Beam bending.

Plate Bending.—Certain plates of a ship—such as those at the turn of the bilge—have a cylindrical curvature. In order to give such curvature to the flat plate as received in stock from the rolling mill, it is passed through a large machine called the *plate bending rolls*, the essential parts of which are three long heavy rolls as shown in section in Fig. 74. The axis of the larger upper roll can be adjusted vertically so as to give, within reasonable limits, any desired degree of curvature to the plate. The length of the rolls should be sufficient to take the longest plates that it is expected will ever have to be handled. Thirty-six

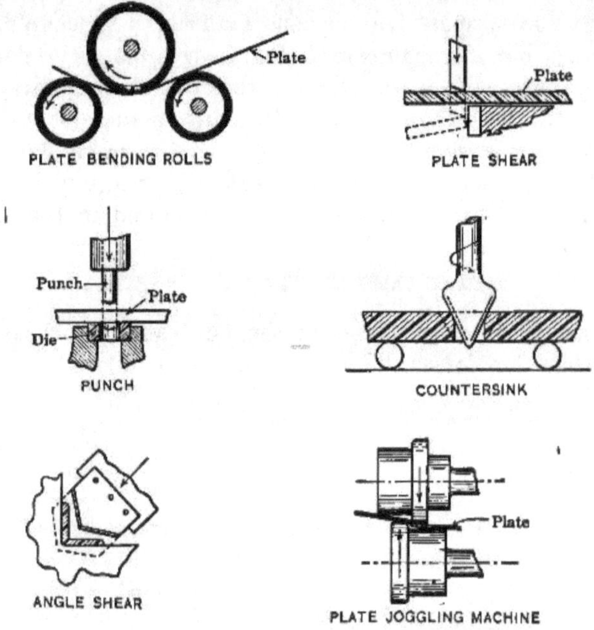

Fig. 74.—Operation of shipyard machine tools.

feet may be considered as a fairly great length, while 26 feet or even less may be sufficient for some yards. The length is, of course, limited by the difficulty of securing rolls of sufficient strength, and the need for great length depends upon the capacity of the rolling mills furnishing the plates.

Plate straightening rolls consist simply of a number of parallel cylindrical rolls through which a plate may be passed to remove any unevennesses and make it perfectly smooth and flat.

Shearing.—This is the process of trimming off the edges of plates, ends of bars, etc. It is accomplished by means of a machine called a *shears* which consists essentially of a large shear or knife that oscillates, as a rule, vertically. Its operation is illustrated in Fig. 74. Each stroke cuts only a limited portion of the plate which must be moved along as the various strokes are taken. For shearing angle bars transversely a special type of machine must be employed (see Fig. 74), and also for channels, Z-bars, etc., although the principle is the same. Shears, especially if slightly dulled, or not properly aligned, have a tendency to tear as well as to shear the material, and as a result the sheared edge usually has a slight burr.

Planing consists in smoothening up the edges of plates, shapes, etc., so as to remove the burr, and give a plane, flush edge for purposes of appearance, calking, etc. This is accomplished by means of a machine called a *plate planer* in which the plate or shape is clamped and trimmed off by means of a traveling cutting tool. The planer should have about the same length as the bending rolls.

Punching is the process of putting holes for rivets, bolts, etc., in various plates and shapes. This is accomplished by machine tools similar in their operation to shears (see Fig. 74). The plate or other piece to be punched is placed upon a die of slightly larger diameter than the punch which, as it moves down with great force, punches out a piece of metal and thus forms a hole. As in the case of shearing a slight burr is formed on the under side of the plate or shape punched and also, on account of the ductility of the material, the hole is slightly conical, instead of being a true cylinder, the larger diameter being at the lower end of the hole. It is to fit such holes that the *coned neck* rivets shown in Fig. 21 are designed. In the lowest sketch in this figure is shown the *faying surface* between two plates riveted together. In order for the rivet properly to fill the rivet hole the plates, if punched, should be punched *from* the faying surface, so that the coned neck of the rivet will fit the cone of the hole caused by the punch.

It is usually considered better practice to have the rivet holes true cylinders (in which case straight neck rivets are used), and with this object in view they are often *drilled.* This is, of course, more expensive and takes much more time than punching and the same result may be accomplished by *reaming* out a hole to the proper size after it has been first punched to a slightly smaller size. A *reamer* is a fluted, revolving spindle tapered at the end, which is inserted into a hole and gradually forced further into it, the revolving flutes cutting away some of the metal as the tool advances.

Reaming has the added advantage of removing the small portion of material just around the hole that has been slightly weakened by the action of the punch.

Countersinking is the process of giving to one end of a rivet hole a conical form, a portion of the metal being removed, as shown in Fig. 74, by a revolving tool with two or more cutting edges. This is done where countersunk rivets are to be driven for watertightness, or to be given a flush surface. The countersinking tool is mounted in a movable arm so that it can be quickly adjusted to any desired location over the plate which is supported on a fixed table by means of ball rollers, so that it also can be quickly adjusted.

Flanging is the process of bending a portion of a plate so as to give it a flange or portion turned to one side. This is often done to brackets, etc., to give them extra stiffness, and to keel plates, garboard plates, etc. (see Fig. 75). It is accomplished by means of a powerful flanging machine consisting essentially of a large roller mounted on heavy swinging supports.

Sawing is necessary for cutting off certain heavy shapes, such as *rounds, half rounds* and other special or heavy shapes that cannot be readily sheared. It is usually accomplished by means of a special *circular saw* designed for cutting metals.

Forging and welding is necessary in fabricating special parts of irregular forms, such as *staples, tapered liners, collars, coaming* and other *boundary bars*, etc., which must be heated and worked by hand (see Fig. 75).

Punching of manholes, etc., may be done by a special powerful hydraulic manhole press which cuts out a large hole in a plate in one operation. A similar operation with a

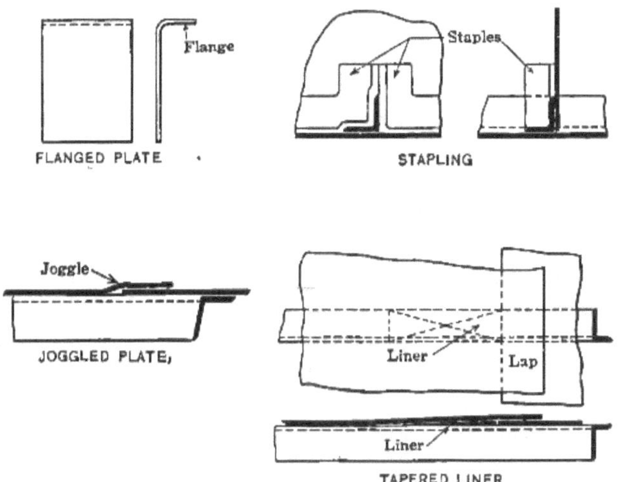

Fig. 75.—Fabricated parts.

specially shaped punch is employed for notches in plates for angle bars, etc., penetrating them at right angles.

Cutting with the oxy-acetylene blow pipe or torch is usually employed instead of hydraulic manhole punching, notch punching, etc. Irregular holes or holes of practically any desired shape can be quickly cut by this method (see Chap. VII, Sect. 5).

Joggling consists in offsetting the edge of a plate or a portion of the length of a shape to avoid the use of liners. In Fig. 75 is shown a joggled plate, and, in Fig. 74, the operation of one type of machine that does the joggling.

Punching and shearing machines are often provided with dies for joggling.

Hydraulic riveting is accomplished by means of a heavily built (and, usually, portable) machine consisting essentially of two massive jaws, hinged so as to be closed together by hydraulic power thus forming and clenching a rivet in one movement.

Frame Bending and Beveling.—This work is done on the bending slabs, previously mentioned. A portion of a bending slab is shown in Fig. 78. From the mould loft is made a template to which a piece of soft iron, known as a *set iron* is bent. This is secured to the bending slab by means of large dogs, as shown. The angle bar to be bent is first heated to a red heat and then bent around the set iron. It is held in place, as bent, by other dogs, not shown in the sketch. A tool called a "*moon bar*" or "*squeezer*" is used to force the bar around where the curvature is greatest. While the frame bar is still hot it is *beveled* by having the angle between its two flanges opened or closed to the proper amount at each point of its length. This is done by means of a special tool (a beveling lever) with a wrench-like jaw that can be fitted over the vertical flange, or by a few light blows of the sledge hammer (see Fig. 79). The other flange, during this operation is secured fast to the bending slab by dogs.

Furnacing of Plates.—Certain plates of the shell plating are undevelopable, as for example the boss and oxter plates. Special molds have to be made for these, built up of light wood to the actual form of the ship, from which heavy metal beds are made, of plates and angles, in which the plates after having been heated red hot are laid and hammered into shape. Such *furnaced* plates are made slightly thicker than would otherwise be necessary in order to compensate for possible loss in thickness and strength caused by the furnacing and shaping.

In the preceding paragraphs have been described the more important processes in ship construction that require the use of machine tools, and the tools most commonly used have been mentioned. Some of these tools are absolutely essential to shipbuilding work, while others may be dispensed with and their functions performed, though in a less efficient manner, by the others. The exact equipment necessary for any given shipyard is difficult to determine and varies with the size of the yard, the capital available, the type of ships to be built, etc.

The following may be considered as a proper equipment for a first-class yard of moderate size:

Bending rolls (1 large; 1 or 2 small).
Plate mangles or straighteners (2).
Plate planers (2 or 3).
Punches (6 or 8).
Shears (6 or 8).
Angle and other special shears (3 or 4).
Flanging machine.
Joggling rolls.
Hydraulic press.
Radial drilling and countersinking spindles (6 or 8).
Steam hammers (several).
Hydraulic riveting machines (2 or 3).
Bending slabs.
Plate furnaces (2 or 3).
Angle furnaces (2 or 3).
Beam press.
Scarphing machine.

The above applies only to the larger machine tools used primarily for hull construction and takes no account of a great variety of miscellaneous small portable tools and machines, or of tools in the woodworking-, plumbers-, machine-, smith-, and other auxiliary shops.

5. PERSONNEL OF A SHIPYARD

The organization of a shipyard is commonly based upon a division of the work into two main parts: that pertaining to the *hull*, and that pertaining to the *machinery*. The plans for the hull and its fittings and equipment, when required to be made in the yard, are prepared by a staff of designers and draftsmen entirely separate and distinct from those preparing the plans for the engines, boilers, auxiliaries, etc. Similarly the work of manufacturing, erecting, testing and installing the machinery is largely done by a different force of mechanics from those who build the hull and make and install its fittings.

Considering the *shipbuilding* or *hull* end, there will be found in a well-equipped shipyard, workers in the following occupations and trades: designers and draftsmen, loftsmen, layers-out, workers in the plate and angle and fabricating shops, frame benders, anglesmiths, furnacemen, shipfitters, erectors, laborers, bolters-up, etc., drillers, reamers, riveters, holders-on, heaters, passers, chippers and calkers, testers, shipwrights or ship carpenters, joiners, plumbers, pipefitters, shipsmiths, drop forgers, heavy forgers, sailmakers, riggers, sheet-metal workers, machinists, wood calkers, coppersmiths, galvanizers, pattern makers, molders, melters, chippers and other foundry workers, painters, and varnishers, masons, electricians, boat builders, not to mention all of the miscellaneous auxiliary trades, such as janitors, watchmen, laborers, helpers, drivers, teamsters, chauffeurs, crane men, firemen, locomotive engineers, etc.

Workmen of each of the skilled trades all have helpers to assist them and in each of these trades there are one or more foremen or "bosses," and various sub-foremen or supervisors, ranging from the bosses down through assistant-bosses, quartermen, leadingmen, etc., to "snappers" each of whom is in charge of a certain group or unit of mechanics.

Designers and Draftsmen.—These are the men who make the necessary calculations, draw the plans, and prepare the specifications from which the ship is to be built. They should have both practical and theoretical knowledge of naval architecture especially the latter, since upon a correct knowledge of the theoretical principles governing the design of a ship depends the success of the ship. No matter how well she may be built, a poorly designed ship may be of little practical value and may even be a source of great danger.

Loftsmen.—The loftsmen are the men who take the plans of the ship as furnished by the draftsmen, and by laying them down to full scale on the mold loft floor, make templates from which the material that is to form the hull can be marked out and fabricated. Their work requires much of the same knowledge that is essential for draftsmen, and in addition a considerable amount of practical experience with shop and yard practices.

Layers-out.—From the templates furnished by the loftsmen various plates and shapes must be laid out for shearing, planing, punching, bending, flanging, beveling, rolling, etc. This work is done by layers-out who are usually possessed of the same qualifications as shipfitters. Their work, however, is confined to the laying-out shop, whereas shipfitters usually do their work largely on the ship. (See under *Shipfitters*, below.)

Workers in the Plate and Angle Shops.—After the material has been laid out it is sent to the various machine tools where the necessary punching, shearing, planing, countersinking, etc., is done. A considerable variety of workers operate these tools, although usually the work is such that men capable of operating one tool can also operate several others. Among the trades engaged in this work the following are found: manglers or plate straighteners, drillers, jogglers, punch and shear operators, plate rollers, countersinkers, acetylene cutters—although not always called by these names. The operations at most of these machine tools consist in guiding the plates or shapes, supported by various types of cranes and hoists, into position, and then pulling the necessary lever or making the necessary electric contact to cause the machine to perform its function in each case. The quality of work and the speed with which it is done is largely dependent upon the skill of the workman. This skill can be gained only by experience.

Frame Benders, Anglesmiths, Furnacemen, Etc.—These and similar names apply to the workmen who do the working of plates and shapes to special forms that must be done with the material red hot. All of this work partakes of the nature of blacksmith work. The greater part consists in bending and beveling frame and reverse frame bars, making staples, collars, coaming angles, shaping special plates of the shell, etc. It is evident that such work can be done properly only by men of good physique, and skill, that is obtained only as the result of long experience.

Shipfitters.—The shipfitting trade is the one metal worker's trade most closely associated with shipbuilding. The shipfitter, with modern steel vessels, corresponds to the shipwright with the old wooden ships. In general, the duties of a shipfitter are to lay out or fit the various members of the ship's hull.

It will be noted that a large amount of the material that enters into the hull of a steel ship is laid out and fabricated from templates furnished by the mold loft. The laying out of all steel material not so handled is, in general, the province of the shipfitter. It is, of course, possible by following carefully prepared plans, and requiring the most careful and accurate workmanship, to get out, in advance, in the shops, all the parts of a ship. In some shipyards this method is very closely approached, but in practice it is found to be very difficult to fabricate all parts in advance so that they will fit together properly when assembled. Therefore it is usual to fabricate a certain amount of material from templates and plans, but to leave a certain remainder to be made specially from templates prepared by shipfitters to fit other parts after these other parts are in place in the ship. For example, after the frames have been erected certain plates of the shell are usually laid out from templates actually "lifted" or made in place on the portion of the frames that is to be occupied by those particular plates. The edges of the plates and the exact positions and sizes of the rivet holes in each case can thus be transferred directly to the template from the work on which the plate for which the template is made is to fit. Such a template consists of thin strips of soft wood, nailed or tacked together to form a skeleton "pattern" of the plate, on which is marked all information necessary for fabricating the plate.

Occasionally, in the case of lighter members, it is found convenient and advisable to place the steel material itself in position in the ship, mark it off, and send it then to the shop for fabrication. In other cases the steel material may be laid off directly by the shipfitter from a plan—without the use of a template. Some of the men skilled in shipfitting work are usually assigned to duty as "layers-out," marking off the plates and shapes for fabrication from mold loft templates.

The shipfitter's trade is one calling for both skill and intelligence, combined with a certain amount of practical mathematical knowledge and an ability to "read" plans. Shipfitters are more or less concerned with the production of practically all the main structural members of the hull. Some of the simpler parts which are usually laid out by the shipfitters (or *fitters-up* as they are sometimes called) are described below, in order to show, concretely, what their duties are, even although some of these parts have been previously referred to. These are illustrated in Fig. 76.

A *bosom piece* is a short section of angle bar used to connect the ends of two other angle bars that butt together. The heel of the bosom piece is planed off to fit into the bosom of the other two bars and the toes of the bosom piece are planed off so as not to project beyond the toes of the bars, as shown.

A *clip* is simply a short piece of angle bar used to connect two other parts at right angles, or nearly so, as shown in the figure.

A *bracket* is a flat plate, usually of triangular shape used to tie together and stiffen two plates or other flat members meeting at an angle. In Fig. 76 is shown a bracket flanged on its edge, for additional stiffness, and having a *lightening hole* in it, to save weight, connecting two plates that are at right angles to each other.

A *butt-strap* (see Fig. 76) is a piece of plate used to connect two plates that butt against each other. The butt-strap makes a *lap-joint* with each plate. Sometimes a butt-strap is fitted on each side of the two plates, in which case the straps are called *double butt-straps.* According to the number of rows of rivets butt-straps are called

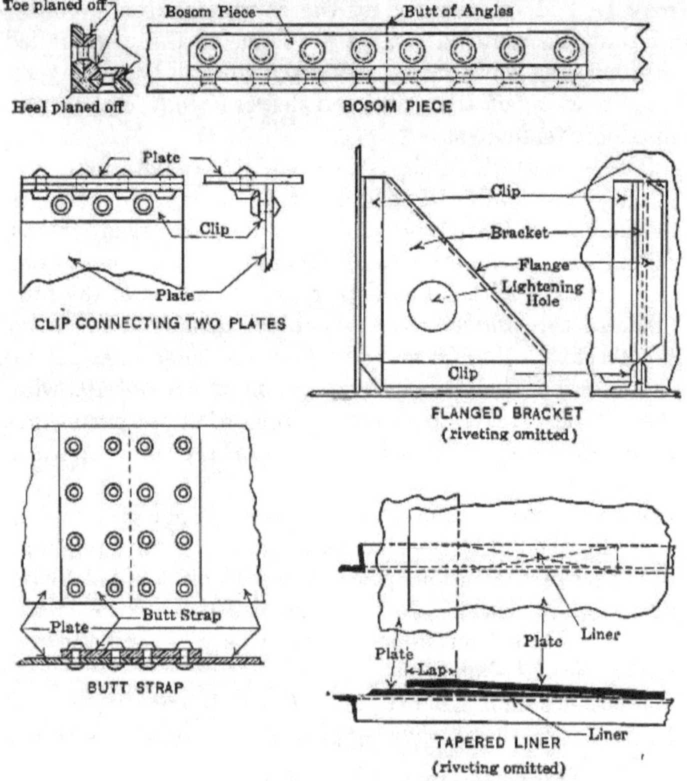

FIG. 76.—Shipfitting work.

single-riveted, double-riveted, treble riveted, etc. The one shown in Fig. 76 is a *single, double-riveted* butt-strap.

Liners are strips of plating fitted between frames, beams, etc., and the plating laid on them to bring the plating flush with other plating over which it laps. Liners may be either *straight* or *tapered.* In Fig. 76 is shown a tapered liner.

The sketches just described will serve to indicate the character of the work done by shipfitters, these being, however, some of the simpler parts laid out by this trade.

Erectors, Laborers, Bolters-up, Riggers, Etc.—After the various members of the ship's hull have been fabricated they are transported to the building slip, hoisted into place by cranes or erected by hand and bolted in place, the bolts being inserted through rivet holes to secure the parts for riveting. Only a portion of the rivet holes need to be so filled, the rest being left empty. The workmen who do this work are variously called riggers, laborers, helpers, bolters-up, regulators, erectors, etc. In order to make the various parts fit it is sometimes necessary to draw them together so that the rivet holes overlap exactly, or are *fair.* This is done by means of a small tapered pin, called a *drift pin* which is driven into the rivet holes until they are in line (see Fig. 81). Excessive use of the drift pin is an evidence of poor workmanship and should not be tolerated.

The bolts are saved after they have served their purpose and used over and over again, and, as the lengths vary, it is customary to have on hand a large number of washers, made by punching holes in small rectangular pieces of plate, for use with these bolts to save labor in screwing up the nuts.

Drillers and Reamers.—After the hull members have been bolted up in place it is usually necessary to drill certain rivet holes that it is not practicable to have punched before erection, and to ream out the holes that have been punched, in order to give smooth, fair holes suitable for the riveting. This work is done by the drillers and reamers. Drillers also are employed to tap certain holes designed for bolts or tap-rivets.

Riveters, Holders-on, Heaters, Passers.—The drillers and reamers are followed by the *riveters,* who drive the rivets that form the fastenings of the various members. Riveting may be done either by hand or by pneumatic hammers, the use of the latter now being the most common practice. A riveter works in a *gang*, which consists, besides himself, of a *holder-on*, *heater-boy*, and one or more *rivet-passers*. The heater boy places the cold rivets in a small portable forge in which they are heated to a cherry red. They are removed from the forge as needed, and taken by the passer (or passers) to the holder-on who inserts each rivet in the proper hole, after removing a bolt, if necessary, from the opposite end to that at which the riveter stands. The holder-on then shoves the rivet into the hole until the head takes up well against the plate or shape and holds it there with a heavy *holding-on hammer or dolly-bar*. The riveter then drives the point of the rivet against the other side of the members to be connected, flattening it out and clinching it so as completely to fill the rivet hole. This work must be done while the rivet is hot. Riveting requires considerable skill and great strength and endurance.

Calkers, Chippers, and Testers.—All plated surfaces that form boundaries of compartments into, or from which water, oil, etc., must not leak, require calking. This consists in tightly closing the joints between the connecting parts through which leakage might occur. As in the case of riveting, calking may be done either by hand or pneumatic tools—the tools in the case of calking, however, being chisels instead of hammers. These tools are used to force the steel material of one part against the surface of the adjoining part. This work is done by the *calkers* who also are employed at times to do *chipping* which consists in the use of chisels, to trim edges, cut holes, etc., the same pneumatic hammer being used as for calking, but with a different tool. These workmen are therefore often called *chippers and calkers*. After the calking is completed the tightness of the joints is tested by filling the compartment with water or compressed air, and any leaks thus discovered are made good. This testing is also usually done by the chippers and calkers, who are therefore sometimes called *testers*.

The draftsmen, loftsmen, layers out, fabricating shop workers, shipfitters, erectors, drillers, riveters and calkers comprise those workers who are intimately connected with the building of the hull proper of a steel ship. The following trades, however, also have considerable to do with shipbuilding:

Shipwrights (or Ship Carpenters).—Who prepare keel blocks, wedges, shores, staging, launching ways, scaffolding, ribbands, etc.—the *auxiliary* wood work in connection with building the ship—and make and install wood decks, masts, spars, foundations, etc.

Joiners—who make and install the lighter wooden parts of the ship, such as wooden doors, partitions, windows, stairways, lockers, cold storage compartments, shelving, bulletin boards, furniture, etc.

Plumbers and pipe fitters—who do work on the various plumbing and piping systems of the ship.

Shipsmiths and heavy, and drop-forgers—who fashion the various fittings and other parts required to be heated and hammered in the smith shop.

Sailmakers—who manufacture the sails, awnings, etc.

Riggers—who make and fit the necessary rigging for the masts, spars, etc. (Not the same as the riggers who assist in erecting the parts of the hull).

Sheet metal workers—who manufacture ventilation ducts, metal lockers, wire mesh partitions, sheet metal, sheathing, etc.

Hull machinists—who do the necessary fitting and installing of steering gears, hull valves and zincs, operating gears, etc., etc.—as distinguished from the machinists who are employed on the main engines and auxiliaries.

Wood calkers—who calk the seams of wood decks and planking.

Coppersmiths—who make copper pipes, kettles and other fittings.

Galvanizers—who galvanize or coat with zinc the outside surfaces of various steel and iron parts exposed to the weather.

12

Pattern makers—who make wooden patterns from which castings can be made.

Molders, melters and other workers in the foundry, where the castings are made.

Painters and varnishers—who have considerable work to do both on the ships and in their shop. The painters usually are the workmen who apply bituminous compositions.

Masons—who install tiling in bath rooms, lavatories, galleys, laundries, etc., and apply portland cement in various out of the way pockets and other inaccessible parts of the hull.

Electricians—who install wiring and electrical equipment.

Boatbuilders—who make the boats that go with the ships.

6. MANAGEMENT

Given a shipyard, with building slips prepared, shops, tools and other yard equipment complete, plans and specifications at hand, in order to produce ships efficiently there must be a *management*, organized for guiding, directing, and controlling the workmen, ordering the necessary materials, co-ordinating the work, etc., etc.

The great factor in the expeditious and economical production of ships (as in all manufacturing enterprises) is management. The function of the management is to do the *thinking* necessary in order that the construction of the ships may proceed smoothly and expeditiously. The building of a ship may be divided into a great many elementary tasks. In the final analysis each of these tasks represents manual work that must be done by some particular workman or group of workmen. If it be assumed that these workmen have the skill, experience and physical condition requisite for the performance of their individual tasks, then the problem of the management becomes one of seeing that each and every one of these workmen is given working conditions that will permit of his work being done quickly and efficiently.

In order that such conditions may exist the following points must be looked out for:

(*a*) *Plans.*—The necessary plans and instructions must be at hand in order that the workman will have no doubt as to just what he is expected to do, and how it should be done.

(*b*) *Material.*—Material required for each task must be ready at the time that it is needed, and it must be of suitable quality and furnished in sufficient quantity.

(*c*) *Tools.*—The workman must be furnished with all necessary tools, and these must be kept at all times in satisfactory operating condition.

(*d*) *Working Conditions.*—In order for the workman to do his work properly he must have good light, ventilation, protection from the weather, etc. If he is using tools operated by compressed air suitable connections to the air supply must be provided. If he is working at night special electric lights must be rigged.

The various problems to be solved in seeing that these four points are looked out for are much more difficult than would be thought at first sight, and the manner in which these problems are met will have a very important bearing on the efficiency of the shipyard as a whole.

CHAPTER VI

PRELIMINARY STEPS IN SHIP CONSTRUCTION

From the time that it is decided to build a ship, even from plans already completed, up to the time when the keel is laid, and the work of actually building the hull is commenced, there is always a considerable interval. In many cases a large proportion of the work is done before a single piece is erected on the building slip, the keel-laying being postponed as long as possible, in order that sufficient fabricated material may be on hand to permit the work of erection, when once started, to proceed rapidly. In every case a certain amount of preliminary work must be done before the building of the hull can be commenced.

Few yards carry a stock of materials so large that at least some new stock does not have to be ordered when it is proposed to build a new ship. Unless the new ship is a duplicate of another previously built by the yard, and for which the molds and templates have been saved, a large amount of mold-loft work must first be done. In every case the material must be fabricated or made ready for erection. The preliminary steps in ship construction are therefore:

1. Ordering the material.
2. Making the molds, templates, patterns, etc.
3. Fabrication of the material.

1. ORDERING THE MATERIAL

Assuming that the shipbuilder has been furnished with complete plans and specifications of the ship (or ships) that he is to build, the first step in the production of the ship is the ordering of the material. This usually includes a great many miscellaneous fittings and auxiliaries which are usually delivered complete and ready for installation, and the type and quality of which are covered by the specifications—sometimes exactly and sometimes somewhat loosely—but the principal material to be ordered is the steel for the hull.

In ordering castings and forgings to be made by other concerns, complete working plans must be furnished with the order, showing exactly what is desired.

The plates and shapes present the greatest difficulty since the sizes of each must be so specified as to allow for shaping and cutting to the proper finished size (which usually cannot be foretold with complete accuracy) while at the same time not allowing so much excess as to cause a serious waste of material.

The shell plates, keel, stringers, keelsons, etc., are usually ordered from a wooden model, made to scale, on which these various parts are laid off accurately in ink. This is necessary since a ship's form is an undevelopable surface so that the plates cannot readily be shown in their true form in the plans. A certain margin of material must be ordered to allow for stretching, shrinkage and change of form due to working the plates to the proper form and size. This depends upon the experience of the person making up the order and the general quality of workmanship of the yard.

Frames, reverse frames and other similar parts that have to be bent are *girthed* from the plans—a certain number being thus actually measured and the girths of the intermediate ones being obtained by plotting curves through the points thus obtained. In bending, frames usually stretch slightly at the heel so that little if any allowance in excess of the girthed length has to be made. For deep members to be bent the girth should be taken along the neutral line.

The material is usually ordered direct from the various structural plans, material schedules being prepared by the draftsmen, but if time permits, or if the templates are already at hand as in the case of a number of ships being built from the same plans, a certain saving can be made by making up the material schedule from the full size templates, since the percentage of error is then less. The amount of scrap from hull material—or the difference between the weight as ordered and as worked into the ship—is usually about 10 percent of the total.

Great care must, of course, be exercised in ordering material to see that all parts are considered and nothing overlooked in making up the order. It is also important to consider the times of delivery, and to see that orders are so placed that the various deliveries will be made before they are actually needed. Materials for keel, keelsons, bottom plating, and inner bottom framing will, of course, be needed before frames, deck beams, etc. Little is gained by having anchors arrive before stem and stern castings.

2. MOLDS, TEMPLATES, PATTERNS, ETC.

As soon as the plans of the ship are completed the work of making molds, patterns, etc., may start, even in advance of the receipt of any structural material. Plans for castings are sent to the pattern shop for use in making the necessary patterns, or to the outside concerns from whom the castings may be ordered.

In the mold loft the lines of the ship are drawn on the floor to full size either with chalk or with lead pencil. For this purpose long flexible strips of wood, called *battens*, are used which are held in place by large flat headed nails with very sharp points. The ordinates for the various curves are furnished in the form of tables of *offsets*, each ordinate, or offset, being given in feet, inches and eighths of inches. For example, the offset 19-7-6 means 19 ft. 7¾″. Owing to the difficulty of obtaining exact accuracy in the plans it is usually found necessary to make numerous changes in fairing up the lines on the floor of the loft. After this has been done a revised table of *mold-loft offsets* is made for record and possible future use. In the lines as laid down in the mold loft appears every frame, these being, of course, much more closely spaced than the frame stations used in drawing the lines in the drafting room.

The work of laying down and fairing up the lines on the mold loft floor is the same as that of the draftsman who made the plan of the lines, except that it is done on a large scale. It is, in brief, nothing more nor less than putting into practice the principles of descriptive geometry. The various details of this work form a study in themselves, and for a complete treatment of these matters the reader is referred to text books on the subject—such as, for instance, Watson's "Naval Architecture." Loftsmen acquire their skill only as the result not only of study but also of actual experience in the loft.

After the lines have been faired the *scrieve board* is made. This consists of a special section of wood flooring (often made in sections, and portable) of sufficient size to take the full size body plan of the ship. On this flooring is drawn the complete body plan—showing every frame, together with inner bottom, decks, stringers, keel, keelsons, longitudinals, margin plates, plate laps, lines of ribbands and such other information as is necessary for the fabrication of the various members. All of these lines are cut into the surface of the scrieve board by means of a sharp, V-shaped tool, called a *scrieve-knife.* This is done to prevent their being obliterated by the rough usage to which this board is subjected during the processes of making molds, templates, etc.

The scrieve board is used for making the various *molds* of frames, beams, floor plates, etc., etc. These are usually made of strips of thin soft wood tacked together, and shaped to the form of the particular members that they represent. The terms *mold* and *template* are often used synonymously but the first applies strictly to shape, whereas a template in addition to having the form of the part also has marked upon it certain information, such as locations of rivet holes, edges to be sheared or planed, lightening holes, countersinking, etc. Some templates are made of paper instead of wood, or even in some cases of light metal. Templates that are to be used repeatedly are made more substantially than those that are to be used only once. Molds for furnaced plates that have curvature in three dimensions are built up specially of more substantial wooden pieces.

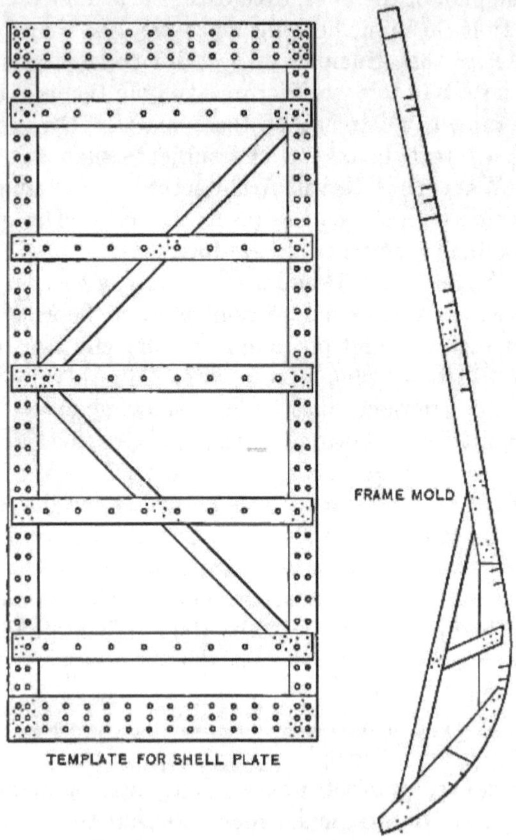

Fig. 77.—Template and mold.

Figure 77 shows a template for a shell plate and (to a smaller scale) a mold for a frame—both made of strips of batten wood tacked together.

The laying off and fairing of the lines on the mold loft floor and the construction of the molds and templates for the hull material that is to be fabricated in advance constitute the principal work of the loftsmen.

In addition to this various *battens* are marked off giving certain dimensions and other information for use by the workmen in the fabricating shops. *Bevel boards* are also made by the loftsmen. These are small strips of batten wood on which are drawn lines which indicate the angle of bevel for each frame at certain fixed points along its girth. The obtaining of these bevels is accomplished by measuring on the scrieve board the distance between adjacent frame curves, taken normal to their curvature, and combining it with the fixed distance fore and aft between frames (or the *frame spacing*) so as to determine the angle of the small right angled triangle thus formed between each pair of adjacent frames. In order to give all frames an open bevel the bosoms of the forward frames *"look"* aft and of the aft frames look forward.

3. FABRICATION OF HULL MATERIAL

Fabrication is the term applied to the various processes by which the raw material as received from the steel mills is laid off and fashioned so that it is formed into the various structural members of the hull, which, when erected, will fit together properly with their neighboring parts. Such parts of the hull as are ordered specially, or made in the yard, as forgings or castings require no special description, as the methods of making ship forgings and castings are no different from those of making such pieces for other purposes. Such finishing of these parts as is required is done after receipt of the rough castings either by machine or by chipping with hand or pneumatic chipping tools. The fabrication of the following parts is more or less peculiar to shipbuilding and will be described below: shell plating, plating of decks, bulkheads, inner bottom, etc., frames and reverse frames, floors, keels and keelsons, etc., deck beams, bulkhead stiffeners, brackets, bounding bars, coamings, etc.

Shell Plating.—The *flat* plates of the shell present little or no difficulty. After being rolled perfectly flat, or mangled, if necessary, these plates are laid off from templates similar to that shown in Fig. 77. The centres of the rivet holes are centre punched on the side of the plate from which to be punched and a small white circle is marked with paint or chalk, to make the position of each more conspicuous. In some cases especial pains are taken to have these small circles exactly concentric with the centre punch marks but this is not absolutely necessary, *provided the centre punch mark is correctly located* in each case. If holes are bored in the template, as shown in Fig. 77, a special tool is used which consists of a short hollow cylinder of just the proper outside diameter to fit the holes in the template, carrying a spiral spring and the punch inside, properly centred. By dipping this tool in white paint both the centre punch mark and the white circle are applied to the plate in one operation. Sometimes simply the centre of each rivet hole is indicated on the template and a small centre punch is driven right through the soft wood of the template against the plate over which it is clamped.

The diameters of the holes to be punched are indicated by figures painted on the plate, and also such holes as are to be countersunk are suitably marked. The symbol "CKOS" denotes "countersink on the other side." Edges to be sheared are marked on the plate by chalk or soapstone lines and are also reinforced by centre punch marks at intervals. The symbol " -ꝏ- ," is often employed to indicate lines to be sheared. In addition to the above, information is also centre punched or painted on the plate regarding any other operations to be performed such as cutting or punching of large holes, or notches, planing, chamfering, joggling, etc., and the strake, side of the ship, and serial number of the plate. If the rivet holes are to be punched small for subsequent reaming care must be taken that the correct sizes of the punches to be used are indicated. After the plate has been laid off it is sent to the plate and angle shed where the necessary shearing, punching, planing, etc., is done as described in the preceding chapter.

When this has been done the *faying surfaces,* or portions of the plate that will rest against the frames, adjacent plates or other members are carefully cleaned and given a coat of red lead. In order to remove mill scale, rust, etc., plates and shapes should be pickled, this being done, of course, before the faying surfaces are red leaded. Pickling consists in placing the plate or shape in a mixture of acid and water (usually about 1 part of hydrochloric acid to 19 parts of water) which eats off the rust and mill scale. The plate or shape is then removed, well washed and brushed, then placed in an alkaline solution, then removed, finally washed with water, and dried.

The *rolled* plates are given their proper curvature in the bending rolls as described in Chapter V. The shearing, punching, planing, countersinking, etc., is ordinarily done before the plate is rolled, but the template must be properly made, to allow for the change in distance between rivet holes, caused by the bending of the plate. Plates are also sometimes given a "twist" when necessary, by being inserted diagonally in the bending rolls.

Furnaced plates present the greatest difficulties. A bed or frame work must be built up of heavy angles and plates to the proper shape so that the plate after being heated can be hammered, in this bed, to the correct shape. The rivet holes are laid off and punched or drilled after the furnacing is completed. The edges are finished by chipping.

Flanged plates may or may not have the punching and countersinking done before they are flanged. They are usually sheared and planed, however, before flanged.

Plating of Decks, Bulkheads, Inner Bottom, Etc.—The plates for decks and bulkheads are practically flat, as are the most of those for the inner bottom. The raw material is marked off from templates in much the same manner as the flat plates of the shell. The fabrication work consists of shearing, planing, punching, countersinking, joggling, cutting, or punching of manholes, notches or irregular-shaped edges, and, in the case of margin plates for the inner bottom, of flanging. The templates are usually made by laying down the part in question to full size on the mold loft floor, and making the templates from these lines.

The manner in which these parts are fabricated varies, of course, in different yards, and with the structural design of the ship. Bulkheads are usually built up complete so that they may be erected, at the same time as the frames, with their bounding bars and stiffeners. Deck plating is often fabricated from templates "lifted" or made from the ship, while she is being built, after the deck beams are in place. Complete detail plans of each bulkhead, of each deck, and of the inner bottom are used in conjunction with the mold loft lines in making the templates.

Frames and Reverse Frames.—The exact shape and size of the heel of each frame is shown in the scrieve board, which is really a full-sized body plan of the ship. A mold is made of the transverse flange of each frame, similar to that shown in Fig. 77. In addition a flexible batten is laid on the scrieve board and on it are marked off the landing edges of the shell plating, edges of deck plating, stringers, etc. At the same time a *bevel board* is made, this being a small strip of template wood on which are marked pencil lines running across it at various angles, each being properly marked. The angles that these lines make with the side of the bevel board are the angles to which the frame should be beveled at the corresponding points of its length.

The mold, batten, and bevel board furnish the necessary data from which the frame can be fabricated. The actual methods of fabrication vary considerably depending upon whether the frame is a simple angle bar or a channel, Z-bar, or bulb angle, whether it is to be fitted in connection with a reverse frame or not, whether it has excessive curvature or not, and upon the general structural design. It is difficult to punch rivet holes in a frame after it has been bent, but on the other hand if the holes are punched first those in the transverse flange are liable to be partially closed during the bending and those in the shell flange stretched. However, the difficulty of punching holes in the transverse flange is not so great as in the case of the shell flange, and therefore, as a general rule, the holes in the transverse flange are left to be punched after the

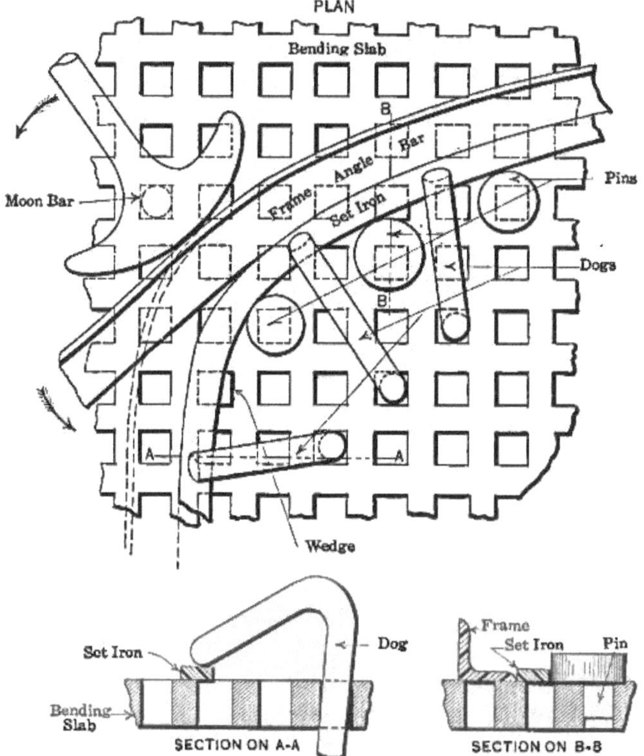

FIG 78.—Portion of bending slab, showing frame bending.

frame has been bent, while those in the shell flange are punched beforehand, a suitable allowance being made in laying them out (based upon experience) for the stretching of this flange during bending. Where the curvature is excessive no holes are punched before bending, those in the shell flange being punched later in a horizontal punch, or drilled.

The method of bending frames, reverse frames, bulkhead boundary bars and other curved shapes is shown in Fig. 78. The shape of the heel of the bar is chalked on the bending slab and another line is laid off parallel to this and inside of it a distance equal to the width of the transverse flange. A soft iron bar, called a *set iron* is then bent to this shape and clamped in place by means of *pins*, *wedges* and *dogs* that fit into the holes of the slabs, as shown in the figure. The frame bar having been heated red hot

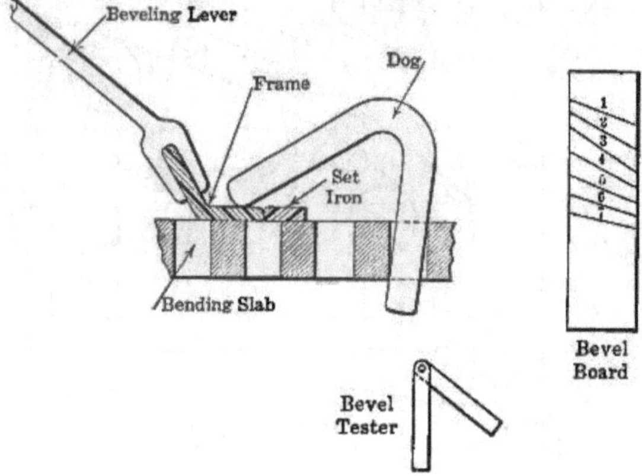

Fig. 79.—Frame beveling.

in the reverberatory furnace is dragged out onto the slabs and one end is placed against the corresponding end of the set iron with the toe of the transverse flange against it, as shown in the lower right-hand sketch of Fig. 78. This end is then secured by dogs in the same manner as the set iron and the frame bar is bent around by means of *moon bars*, or other suitable tools, so that the toe of the transverse flange finally fits against the set iron at all points. As fast as each few inches of the bar have been properly bent they are promptly dogged down against the slabs. (These dogs are not shown in Fig. 78 but one is shown in Fig. 79.)

After the frame has been completely bent to shape, the proper bevels are given to it at all points of its length by means of the bevel board from which the successive bevels are lifted by means of a bevel tester or adjustable square, as shown in Fig. 79. The opening of the flange is accomplished by means of *beveling bars,* or *levers* of which one is shown in the sketch.

Floors.—Templates for the floor plates are made from the scrieve board. In the case of ships fitted with double bottoms (which is generally the case for all but very small ships) the floors together with their upper and lower angles, connecting clips, etc., are made up complete so that they may be erected and bolted to the vertical keel as soon as the latter is in place. Horizontal reference marks are made on the templates of floor, vertical keel angle, margin plate angle, and angles for longitudinals so that the rivet holes will come correct. These same templates are used for transferring the corresponding rivet holes to the templates for the members to which these angles are to be secured. Similar vertical guide lines are marked on the templates of floor and frame and reverse frame angles.

The fabrication of the floor plates consists in shearing, punching and cutting of lightening holes, drain holes, airholes, limber holes, etc.

Keel Plates, Longitudinals, Etc.—The plates for the keel and centre vertical keel are laid off from templates made from the mold loft lines, and plans showing the details of riveting, butts, etc. These templates must be made in conjunction with those for the floor connecting angles and frames and the templates for top and bottom angles for the vertical keel must be made to agree with those for the vertical keel. The plates for the vertical keel are practically all flat and rectangular, so that the fabrication consists in shearing, punching and cutting of lightening or other holes. The flat keel plates are slightly dished as a rule, this being done after they have been punched. Those at the ends, which connect with the stem and stern frame, are considerably dished and usually have to be furnaced. In this case the holes may be drilled after the plates have been shaped. As the keel is the first part of any ship to be erected it must always be made from mold loft templates since at that stage there are no other parts in place from which to "lift" it.

Longitudinals, where continuous, as in warships, are fabricated in much the same way as centre vertical keel plates from mold loft templates. In merchant ships, where they are ordinarily intercostal the longitudinals are made up of a great many short rectangular plates. Sometimes these are flanged at each end for connection to the floor, in order to avoid the use of clips.

Longitudinal members outside of the inner bottom, such as bilge and hold stringers can best be fabricated from templates lifted after the frames are in place, though these are sometimes made in advance.

The fabrication work consists of shearing, punching, and cutting of holes.

Deck beams are fabricated in advance, at the same time as the frames. For this purpose a *beam mold* is made, this being usually of wood about 1" thick, with one edge trimmed to the proper camber, and of length sufficient for the longest beams. The beams are bent cold as a rule in the *beam bending machine* which supports a portion of the beam at two points on one edge while the other edge is subjected to pressure midway between these two points of support. Templates made for the brackets which connect the beam ends to the frame bars must be made in conjunction with the templates for the frames.

Bulkhead stiffeners are ordinarily laid off along with the bulkhead plating and bounding bars, so that all bulkheads may be assembled and riveted up as units which can be erected complete.

Brackets.—In full-lined, parallel sided ships a large number of the brackets are identical and can be laid off from the same template. Sometimes brackets are not fabricated in advance but are lifted from the ship.

Bounding-bars are handled in much the same way as

frames, being laid off and bent and beveled on the bending slabs in a similar manner.

The exact methods of fabricating the various parts of the hull vary so much in accordance with yard practice and the structural design of the particular ship under construction, that little is to be gained by a detailed description of the work in any one case. It is well to note, however, certain general points that apply to all ship construction.

The templates for any two or more members that are to be fastened together must be made in conjunction with each other so that rivet holes in the different parts will be fair when they are erected in their proper positions in the ship.

If templates are to be made in advance in the mold loft the chances for error will be reduced by having plans prepared accurately and in great detail to show all measurements, locations and sizes of rivet holes, butt straps, liners, etc. If these plans are made with sufficient care and in enough detail practically every part of the ship can be completely fabricated before a bit is erected. (This accounts for the rapidity with which it is possible to build ships after the keels have been laid.)

Whether all the members are to be templated in advance of the commencement of building on the ways or not, the flat and vertical keel plates, inner bottom framing, margin plate and usually some of the bottom shell plating must be got out in advance. These parts must be carefully prepared so as to fit fairly, each with its neighbor, when erected.

Where rivet holes are to be punched only and not reamed it is usually necessary to punch some from one side and some from the other of certain plates. Hence in marking them off care must be taken to mark all rivet holes on the correct side or the faying side of these plates so that they may be punched from that side.

Plates and shapes should be pickled to remove all rust and mill scale. After fabrication they should be red leaded well over all faying surfaces, and identification marks carefully painted on them.

For the best class of work rivet holes should be punched small and reamed after the work is in place. This not only makes possible more efficient riveting and increases the strength by cutting away the material around the hole that is weakened by punching but it gives more leeway for reaming unfair holes and thus minimizes the amount of drifting that must be resorted to.

All fabrication work should be carefully done, and templates followed *exactly*. Otherwise the parts will not fit properly in place when erected and filling in pieces, extra liners, and excessive reaming, will be necessary and imperfect calking, and consequent loss in strength and water-tightness will be caused.

CHAPTER VII

THE BUILDING OF SHIPS

1. ERECTION

The first step in the actual building of a ship is the *laying of the keel*, and this being one of the principal events in the process of ship production, is often the occasion of an accompanying ceremony. The time required to build a ship is frequently measured from the date that the keel is laid to the date when the hull is launched. This however does not give a true idea of the time required to produce the ship, unless the length of time spent in fabrication work previous to the laying of the keel, and the length of time necessary to complete the vessel after she is launched are also known.

The amount of preliminary work actually necessary for the laying of the keel is slight, since all that is done in the actual operation is to set in position two or three of the flat keel plates—or a few sections of the bar keel (if that is the type keel used). After this has been done however the work of erection cannot proceed rapidly unless a large amount of fabricated material is on hand, and therefore it is ordinarily the practice to delay the laying of the keel until the getting out of the fabricated material has been under way for several weeks, or perhaps months.

The keel blocks have been described in Chapter V. In order to prepare them for the keel-laying the upper surface of the highest of each group of blocks must be carefully trimmed off so that all are in a straight line having the proper slope (which, as previously stated, commonly ranges between 9⁄16″ and 15⁄16″ per foot) and have their surfaces square to the central longitudinal plane of the ship. The appearance of a set such blocks, ready for the laying of the keel is shown in the foreground of the picture, Fig. 69. A straight line is drawn across the top of each upper block to indicate the exact centre line of the ship.

After the first few keel plates have been carefully lowered into position on top of the blocks (by means of derricks or cranes), so that their centre line coincides exactly with the line drawn on the blocks, and they have been correctly located in a fore and aft direction, the connecting butt straps are bolted in place and the other plates of the flat keel are lowered into place one at a time, carefully set,

Fig. 80.—Flat and centre vertical keel plates in place on blocks.

and similarly secured to their neighbors by their butt straps. On top of the flat keel plates are then placed the plates of the vertical keel, with its two lower connecting angles, which are bolted in place. In Fig. 80 is shown a picture of some of the flat and vertical keel plates with their connecting angles in place on the keel blocks. It will be noted that only a few bolts are necessary to hold them in place, these being inserted through rivet holes. The rivet holes for the connecting angles by means of which the floor plates will be attached to the centre vertical keel, and also those for the top angles of the vertical keel are plainly seen in the picture. The flat plate keel butts in this case are lapped instead of butted.

In order to bring the rivet holes in connecting members into alignment a drift pin is driven into some convenient rivet hole so that its wedge-like action will cause the two members to slide along the faying surface, as shown in Fig. 81, until the rivet holes come fair. If all of the holes are not correctly punched in bringing one hole fair one or more

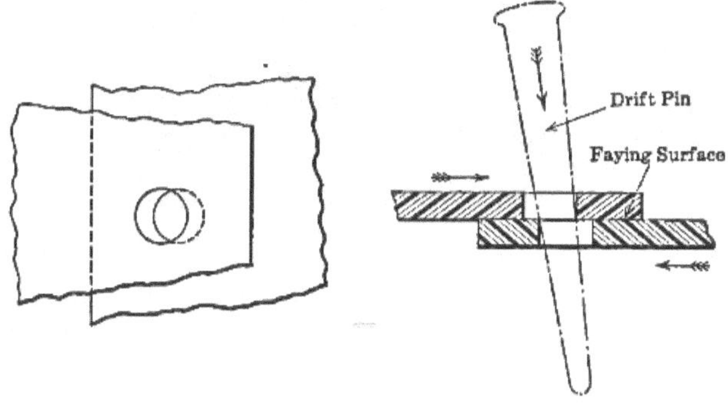

FIG. 81.—Drifting.

other holes may be made unfair. If the unfairness is too great the replacement of one of the members may be necessary—with consequent waste of material and loss of time and labor.

It is usually customary in the case of merchant ships, which have comparatively flat bottoms, to erect the bottom plating soon after the flat and vertical keel plates are in place. In order to support these bottom strakes during this process heavy wooden athwartship timbers are used placed at intervals along the ship's length normal to the keel line, as shown in Figs. 82 and 83. The bottom plating out to and including the first curved bilge strake is usually so handled—as shown in the pictures.

On top of the bottom shell plating is next placed the double bottom framing, which consists of frames, reverse frames, and floor plates with their connecting clips. In the case of the ship shown in Fig. 82 *bracket floors* are used, one of which is shown being lowered into place by the crane.

FIG. 82.—Erecting double bottom framing.

This picture gives a view looking aft along the centre line of the ship over the top of the centre vertical keel, which, not yet having been completely secured, presents a

FIG. 83.—Portion of double bottom framing completely erected.

"wobbly" appearance. A portion of the port top vertical keel angle is shown in place.

A view showing the erection somewhat further advanced is given in the picture in Fig. 83. Here a complete portion

FIG. 84.—Ship in early stage of construction.

of the double bottom framing is erected and the clips for the margin plate and the supports for the tank top plating can be seen. In the lower right-hand portion of the picture will be seen some of the connecting clips by means of which floors are to be attached to the centre vertical keel. The angle at which the top line of the keel blocks is set with the horizontal is also clearly visible.

The next step is the erection and bolting up of tank top plating, margin plates and the brackets for the attachment of frames. Figure 84 is a picture showing the bottom portion of a ship under construction, of which all the inner bottom framing has been completed, and a portion of the tank top plating, margin brackets, shaft alley framing and plating, and after portion of engine room have been erected. Several frames on the starboard side, one on the port side, one deck beam and two plates of a bulkhead just a little aft of these have also been erected. When the construction has advanced this far a certain amount of the riveting in the double bottom should also have been accomplished, since it is much easier for the riveters to do their work in these spaces before the tank top plating is in place.

As the hull is gradually built up shores are placed under the bottom to support the increasing weight of the material in place. Some of these will be noted in Fig. 84, and also the lower portions of the scaffolding on each side of the ship, which will soon have to be built up higher for use of the workmen in erecting the frames, beams, bulkheads, etc.

The erection of the side frames is next proceeded with, together with deck beams, bulkheads, stanchions, girders, stringers, engine and boiler foundations, shaft alleys, etc. Fig. 85 shows a ship under construction with a number of side frames and lower deck beams, stanchions, etc., in place. The coaming for the after cargo hatch in the lower deck can be seen, and also the shaft tunnel, shoring under bottom, derricks and scaffolding used in erecting and bolting up the various members, deck beam brackets, etc.

In order to hold the side frames in their correct positions,

Fig. 85.—View from stern, showing frames, deck beams, and shaft tunnel.

after they have been carefully set at the proper rake with the vertical (to allow for the slope of the keel blocks) by means of a plumb-bob and "*declivity board*," and square to the keel line, longitudinal wooden pieces called *ribbands* are temporarily installed along the shell flanges. These are heavy timbers, which are fitted along the frames in

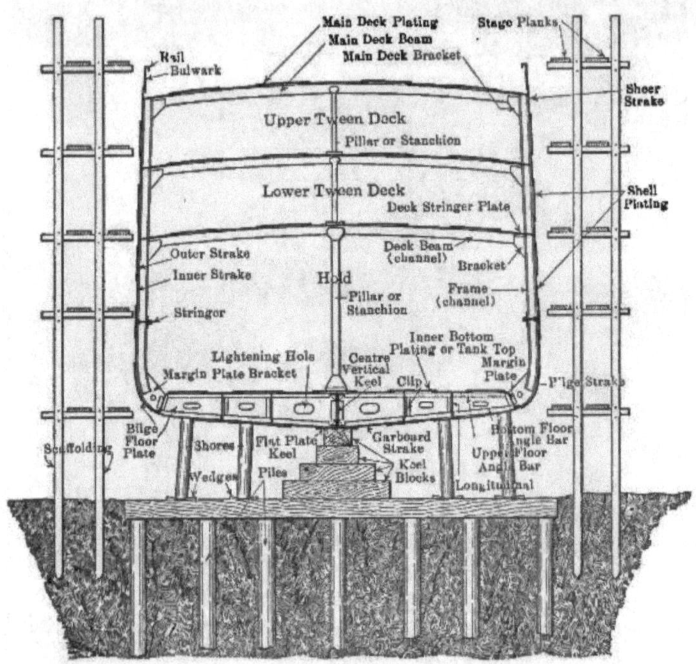

FIG. 86.—Cross section of building slip.

way of *outer* strakes, being clamped to each frame by means of a bolt and small plate washer. As they have only a slight "give" they serve to fair the frames and as they run along the spaces to be subsequently occupied by outer strakes they do not interfere with the bolting up of the plates of the inner strakes. After the inner strakes, and deck stringer plates, hold stringers, etc., have been bolted up, the ribbands are removed and the outer strakes put in place and bolted up. At the ends of the ship, where the curvature is sharp, special timbers have to be used, carefully cut to shape from the mold-loft lines, to perform the same functions in these places that the ribbands perform in the middle body. These timbers are called *harpins.*

The building slips shown in Figs. 84 and 85 are heavy platforms built over the tops of the piling (see also Fig. 69). More often it is the practice to lay the keel blocks on cross logs at the ground level (see Fig. 86).

FIG. 87.—Wooden ship under construction.

After the side frames have been erected the side shell plating is put in place and bolted up, and the erection of deck beams, deck stringer plates, deck plating, coamings, bulkheads, stanchions, and in fact all of the various interior members is proceeded with, certain riveting and calking of the portions of the hull that are now completely erected being taken up concurrently.

The remainder of the erection work is of a miscellaneous character and goes on while the riveting and calking of the lower portion is being done right up to and even after the launching. As the hull rises the scaffolding on each side is extended up (see Figs. 85 and 86) and stage planks are placed on it for use of the bolters up, riveters and calkers.

The order in which the parts are erected in a wooden ship is practically the same as for a steel ship. Figure 87 shows such a ship under construction. (Note the *double* frames.)

2. BOLTING UP, DRILLING AND REAMING

As soon as any part of a ship has been placed in its proper position it is *bolted up*, or secured temporarily, by bolts placed at intervals through the rivet holes, to the adjacent parts to which it is finally to be riveted. At this stage of the construction unsatisfactory workmanship in the fabrication, if such exists, will be made evident. There are two conditions that must be strictly fulfilled, if the construction is to be satisfactory, in the case of each and every structural member of the hull:

1. Each must be in the correct position as called for by the plans, and

2. Each must have all of its rivet holes come fair with those of the adjacent members.

When all the parts have been properly shaped and the rivet holes have all been correctly laid out and punched both of these conditions can be fully met. In practice, however, unless extreme care is used and all the workmen are highly skilled, this will seldom be the case. In bringing one part into its proper position it will often be found that the rivet holes for connecting it to its neighbor will be drawn out of alignment, or conversely in attempting to bring into alignment the rivet holes of a part already in its correct place, that part may be forced out of its proper position.

During the bolting up all such defects should be noted so that they may be remedied before the riveting is started. All parts should be true and fair and free from dents, hollows, unevennesses or other imperfections that would prevent satisfactory riveting and calking (which will be described below).

Members that are not to be riveted until a fairly late stage of the construction, or for which the adjoining parts are to be temporarily omitted for purposes of access, etc., must be especially well bolted up and secured by temporary wooden tie pieces, shores, etc., in order to prevent their shifting out of place.

All sharp and jagged edges, burrs, etc., should be removed.

In certain places, where oil-, or water-tightness is required, *oil stops* or *stopwaters* must be fitted between the adjoining steel members. These consist of canvas, hair felt, lampwick, etc., treated with various paints, etc., and will be described more in detail later. These must be fitted, however, during the process of bolting up.

Reaming.—After the members have been properly aligned, fitted and bolted up the rivet holes must be reamed. This is necessary to remove the slight unfairnesses that are almost inevitable on account of the inaccuracies of laying out and punching the rivet holes, and is also often done to enlarge the holes, which are punched small for this purpose, so as to make a neat fit for the rivets and to remove the portion of metal just outside of the hole, which is weakened by the action of the punch. In addition, in certain cases, reaming is necessary to remove the taper that the holes have as a result of punching (see middle sketch of Fig. 89).

In Fig. 88 is shown a sketch of a reaming tool or reamer which fits in a machine run by compressed air. The end is tapered so that the reamer can be inserted into rivet holes that are unfair. (See third hole from left in bottom sketch of Fig. 88). In reaming holes it is important that the finished hole should be normal to the plate and also that it is not of too great a diameter. In Fig. 88 are shown various types of rivet holes. The one to the left is perfectly fair and will require little or no reaming. The next is only slightly unfair and can be reamed with only a small increase in diameter. The next can be reamed but the diameter of the resulting hole will be considerably greater than would have been necessary had the parts been properly fitted. The right-hand hole, which is half blind, is so unfair that it should not be reamed since the resulting hole would be altogether too large.

Where holes come unfair there is a temptation to avoid increasing the diameter by running the reamer through at an angle. If the angle is very slight, this, though poor workmanship, is sometimes permissible, but if too great will cause a weakening of the joint preventing the rivet

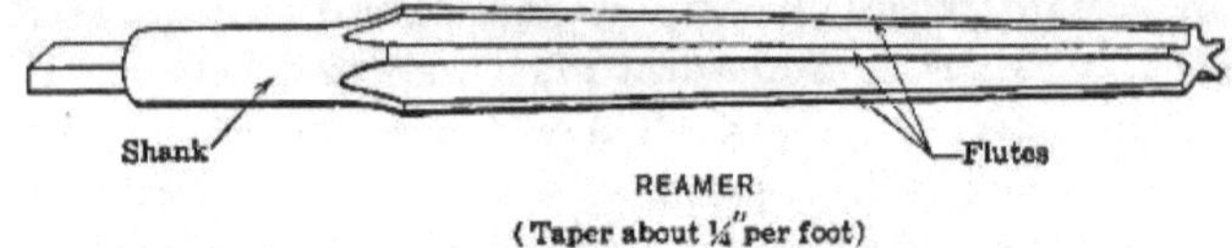

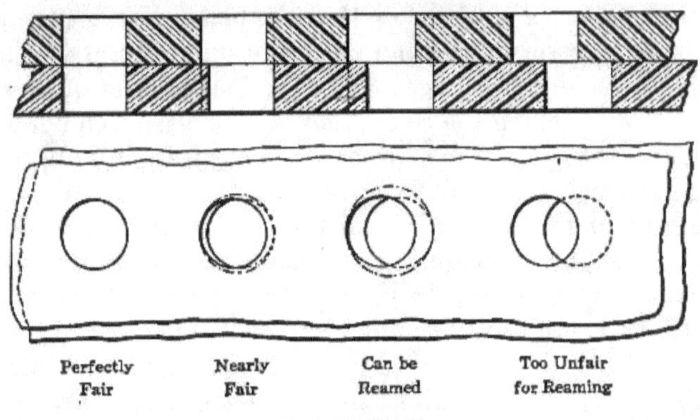

Fig. 88.—Reaming.

from filling the hole completely. Examples of the results of improper fitting and reaming, and of failure to ream at all in the case of "three-ply" riveting are shown in Fig. 89. When the driven rivet is not of the designed diameter, or does not fill the hole completely it loses in efficiency, and the strength of the whole joint is consequently reduced. If many unfair holes occur this will be a serious matter and may endanger the ship.

It is also important to see that the burrs on the edges of rivet holes or shavings, etc., do not prevent the faying surfaces from being drawn tightly together when riveted.

Drilling.—It is not practicable to have all rivet and other holes punched in advance, and it is therefore necessary to have certain drilling (and countersinking) done after the material is in place in the ship. Such holes are those in castings, forgings and furnaced parts that cannot be conveniently punched, holes the exact locations of which

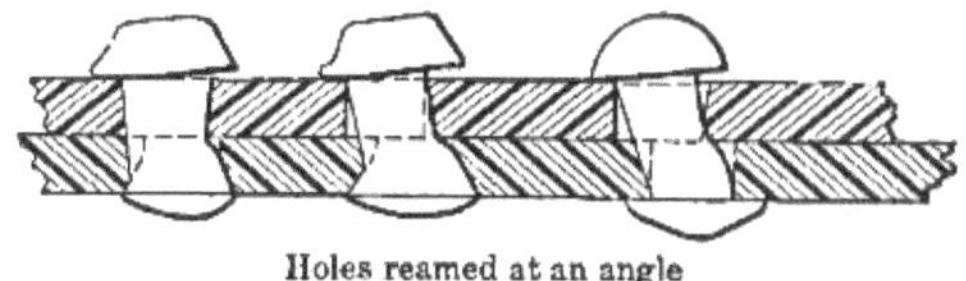

Holes reamed at an angle

Punched holes, in three-ply riveting, not reamed.

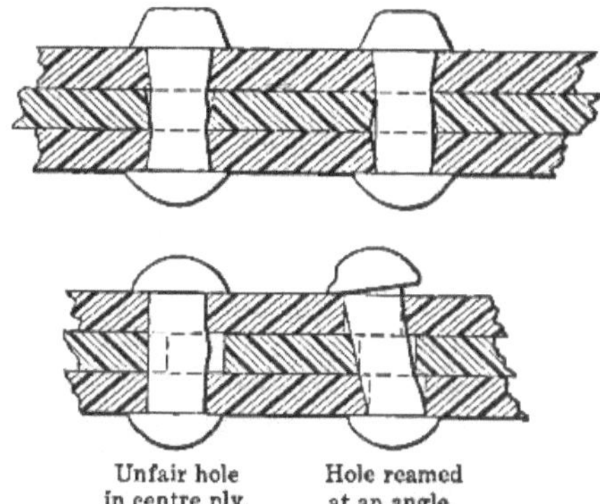

Fig. 89.—Effect of unfair rivet holes and improper reaming.

are not known in advance (such as those for voice tubes, piping systems, electric conduits, etc.) and certain rivet holes for work that requires extreme accuracy, as in the case of oil-tight work, work on submarines, etc.

Drilling may be done by means of electric or pneumatic tools, or by the ordinary hand ratchet drill. The former are much more rapid processes than the latter, but all are very slow compared to the punching and reaming method. On the other hand, absolute accuracy and practically perfect riveting can thus be attained and the material is not weakened thereby, as when punched.

The method of using the pneumatic drilling machine is shown in the sketch in Fig. 90. The upper end of the apparatus is pressed down by some sort of a rig similar to that shown in cases where some rigid bearing for the upper end of the machine is not at hand. When a portion of the ship may be used as a bearing the drill is gradually advancd by screwing up the top spindle by means of the upper handle shown in the sketch. When a wooden stick

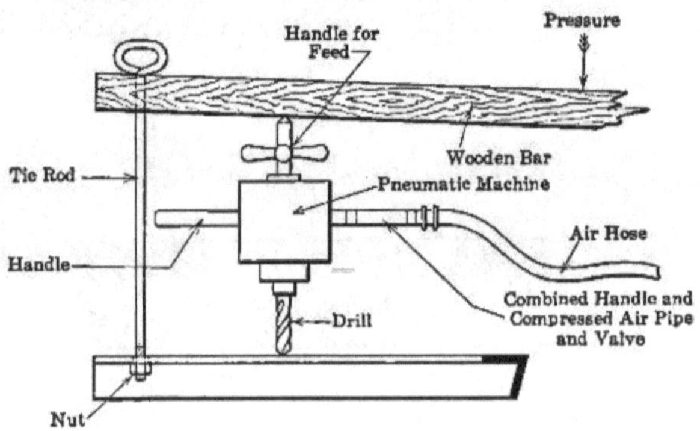

Fig. 90.—Method of using pneumatic drilling machine.

is used, as shown, this is accomplished without the use of this handle by simply keeping pressure on the end of the stick. The two handles on each side of the machine are grasped by the operator in guiding and running it, one of them serving also as a means for starting and stopping the machine. This machine can also be used for reaming and countersinking by replacing the drill by a reamer or countersink. With the ordinary hand ratchet drill a portable arm or support, called an *"old man"* is used.

The speed with which drilling can be accomplished depends upon the diameter of the holes, the thickness and nature of the material to be drilled, the accessibility, condition of tools, air pressure, etc. Similarly with reaming and countersinking, though the latter of course should require much less time, per hole, than drilling. It is not at all difficult, under good conditions, for a workman to ream and countersink 800 or 900 holes in a day.

Drillers are also required to drill and tap holes for bolts and screws (see Section 3, below).

Great care should be exercised and efficient supervision maintained to see that holes are drilled and reamed properly, otherwise defective riveting is bound to result. It is important that all holes should be perfectly cylindrical, normal to the faying surfaces, of the proper diameter, and that burrs, borings, pieces of metal, or other foreign materials do not get between the faying surfaces.

3. RIVETING

As has already been noted riveting is of the greatest importance in shipbuilding. All the structural members of a steel ship (except in the case of *welded* ships which are described below) are tied together by riveting so as to act as a complete unit. If the rivets are not absolutely tight, of the designed size and strength, and located as provided for in the design, the strength of the ship is bound to be impaired. While a factor of safety is, of course, used in designing such a ship, nevertheless a certain amount of careless workmanship may have serious results. It will be readily seen that some of the rivets in Fig. 89 can come nowhere near performing the functions for which they were designed. For example, the upper right-hand rivet, being reduced in sectional area at the faying surface, has its shearing strength reduced, while in the case of bearing pressure it can develop practically no strength.

It is, of course, evident that in many cases defective riveting is not directly the fault of the riveting gang, but rather of the layers-out, or the punch operators, or the drillers or reamers. Nevertheless a certain responsibility must rest with the riveters, for rivets should never be driven in holes that have not first been properly prepared.

14

The operation of driving a rivet is shown in the sketch in Fig. 91. Having removed the bolt, if any, from the rivet hole the holder-on inserts the hot rivet in the hole and drives it well home so that the head rests tightly against the inner plate, around the inner end of the hole, with the holding-on hammer, a large, heavy headed hammer, which he then presses hard against the rivet head. The riveter, on the other side of the plates then proceeds to stave in or drive

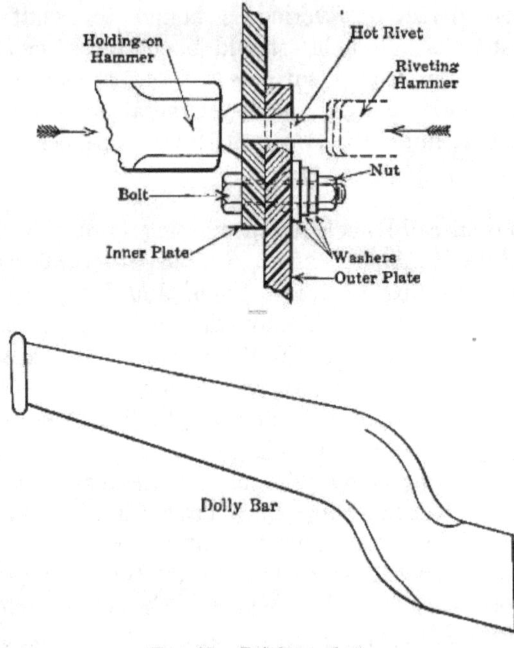

FIG. 91.—Driving a rivet.

the rivet, either by means of a hand or a pneumatic riveting hammer, so as completely to fill the hole. In order to be sure that the rivet has sufficient volume for this purpose it is selected a trifle long, and after it has been well clinched, the excess metal is cut off with a chipping tool by the riveter and the point smoothed up and finished after it has cooled slightly. In order to permit of this cooling it is usual to drive one more rivet and then go back to finish off the rivet driven just previously.

Various methods of holding-on are in use. Sometimes instead of a hand holding-on hammer a pneumatic one may be used, this consisting of a cylinder and piston secured at the end of a stiff brace or rod. In cramped and other inaccessible places a curved or offset holding-on tool is used, commonly known as a "*dolly bar*" (see Fig. 91).

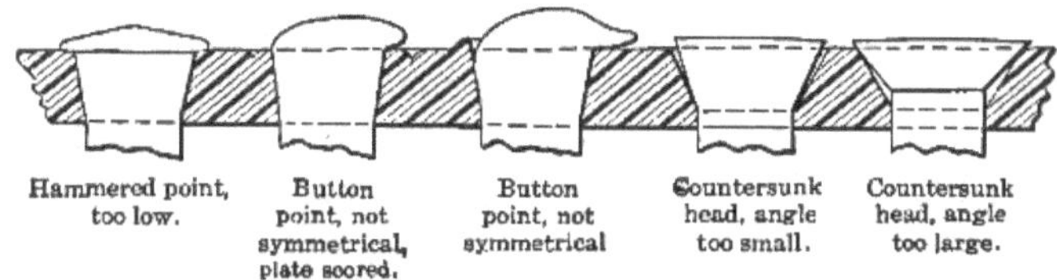

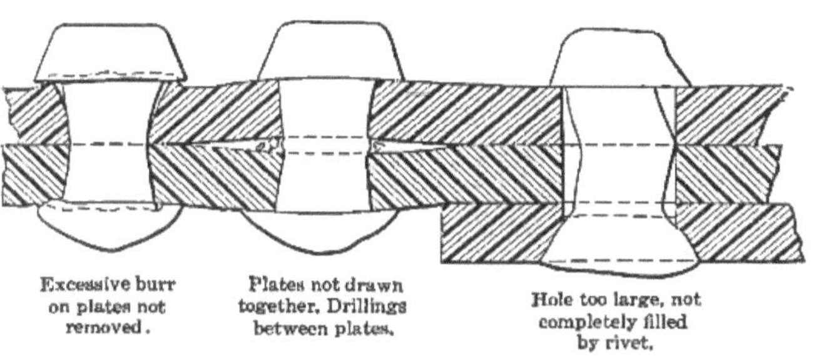

Fig. 92.—Improperly driven rivets.

When properly driven the head and point of a rivet should be symmetrical about the axis of the rivet, the plates around them should not be marred or scored and the two plates should be drawn tightly together. The shrinkage of the rivet in cooling, especially if a long one, has a tendency to accomplish this result. The same applies, of course, to two shapes, or a plate and a shape, riveted together.

In order to test the quality of riveting the heads and points should be inspected visually, and tapped with a hammer—it being possible to tell by the sound and "feel" whether the rivet is tight or loose. With a thin flat knife or "feeler" it is possible to determine whether or not the faying surfaces have been properly drawn together.

In Fig. 92 are shown a few examples of rivets that have not been properly driven. These together with those shown in Fig. 89 represent a few of the kinds of unsatisfactory workmanship in riveted joints that may be met with in practice—all of which should be avoided, since they reduce the structural strength and water-tightness of the ship. It will be noted that defects in riveted work may be due to carelessness or lack of skill of any or all of the following workmen: loftsmen, layers-out, workers in the fabricating shops, bolters-up, drillers, reamers or riveting gangs.

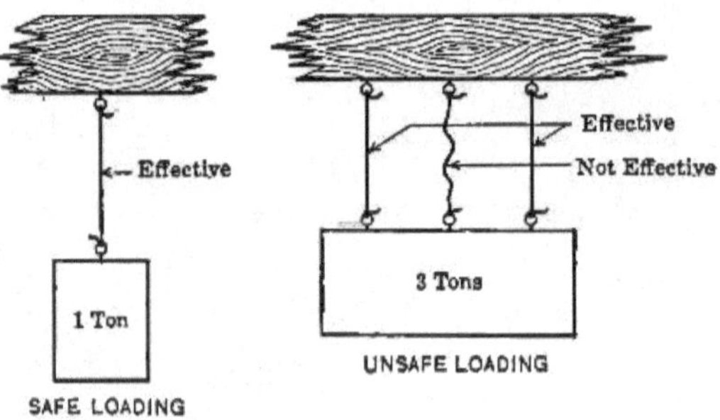

Fig. 93.—Safe and unsafe loading of ropes.

Nevertheless the final blame attaches to any riveter who drives a rivet in a hole that has not been properly prepared to take it, or who does not do his own work properly.

Defective riveting is not only a source of actual danger to a ship, but is the direct cause of added cost in her upkeep, since if the riveting is not properly done leaks, straining of the hull, and excessive corrosion will be continually occurring as the ship is subjected to the various strains incident to her service. Therefore too much emphasis cannot be laid on the importance of requiring good riveting.

The action of rivets in maintaining strength and water-tightness may be illustrated by comparison with the case of a suspended weight. Suppose that a piece of rope is just strong enough to support a weight of one ton. If this weight be suspended by the rope, as shown in the left sketch of Fig. 93, the strength of the rope will be effective, and a condition of safe loading will exist.

Three pieces of this same rope will support a weight of three tons, provided that the strength of each piece is effective. In the right sketch of Fig. 93 one piece of rope is longer than the other two, and consequently its strength is not effective. The other two pieces can support only two tons, the condition of loading is *unsafe,* and the two outer ropes will break if the three-ton weight is given no support other than that of the ropes.

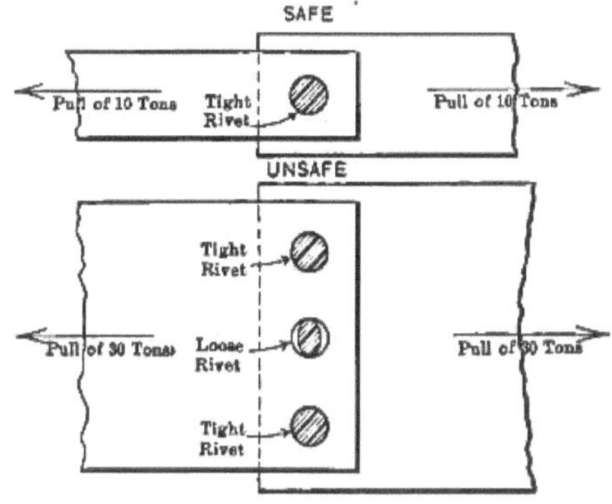

FIG. 94.—Safe and unsafe loading of riveted joints.

In the case of riveted joints a similar principle applies. In the upper sketch of Fig. 94 is shown a safely loaded riveted joint in which is a perfectly driven rivet, large enough to withstand a pull of ten tons. In the lower sketch is shown a joint with three of the same sized rivets, but one of them is defective so that it furnishes no assistance to the other two. The efficiency of this joint is only two-thirds of what it should be, and the joint would fail under a 30-ton pull.

When ships are designed a factor of safety is of course assumed, but this factor of safety is itself based on an assumption, since there is no way of determining accurately the stresses to which a ship may be subjected when at sea in a gale or hurricane. Consequently a sufficient number of defective rivets might cause a ship to be lost at sea. Such cases have actually occurred.

The speed of production of steel ships is necessarily dependent upon the speed with which the riveting is accomplished. Practically all the structural joints of such ships, as usually built, are riveted, and a moderate sized ship will contain over a million rivets. If one gang of riveters drives 400 rivets per day, on an average, it will thus be seen that, to accomplish the riveting of such a ship in three months, over 27 gangs of riveters, working every day of the week would be required. A yard building ten such ships at a time, at this rate, would require nearly 300 gangs of riveters—an unusually large number.

The speed with which rivets can be driven depends upon the size of the rivets, the quality of the reaming and countersinking, the manner in which the bolting-up has been done, whether the holes are "scattered" or not, the accessibility of the work, the air pressure, the condition of the tools, the prevailing weather conditions, etc. Under fair average conditions it may be said that it might easily be possible for a skilled riveting gang to average 50 rivets per hour or 400 in an eight-hour day. As a matter of fact single riveting gangs have actually driven several *thousand* rivets in a day, per gang, but this must be considered as unusual.

A close supervision over all riveting should be maintained during the construction of the ship. All rivets should be carefully tested and those found defective marked. Some may be made good by rehammering, but others will have to be cut out and new rivets driven in their places. The methods of cutting out rivets are illustrated in Fig. 95. Button or hammered points are cut away by the chippers and the rivets then knocked out by means of a backing-out punch and hammer. In the case of a countersunk point a hole of nearly the size of the rivet is drilled so that the remaining ring of metal may be easily torn by the backing out punch, as shown. Sometimes a chipping tool is used, and sometimes the oxy-acetylene blow pipe or cutter, for cutting out such rivets, but both methods must be used with great care, or otherwise the metal around the rivet holes is liable to be damaged.

The diameter of a rivet hole should be about 1/16″ greater than the diameter of the cold rivet. This allows for the insertion of the hot rivet which is slightly enlarged by the heating. The rivets most used in merchant ship building are 5/8″, 3/4″, 7/8″, and 1″. In naval work the smaller sizes (1/2″, 3/8″, and 1/4″) are sometimes used, especially for vessels of light scantlings, like destroyers. Rivets as large as 1 1/8″ or 1 1/4″ are required only for very large

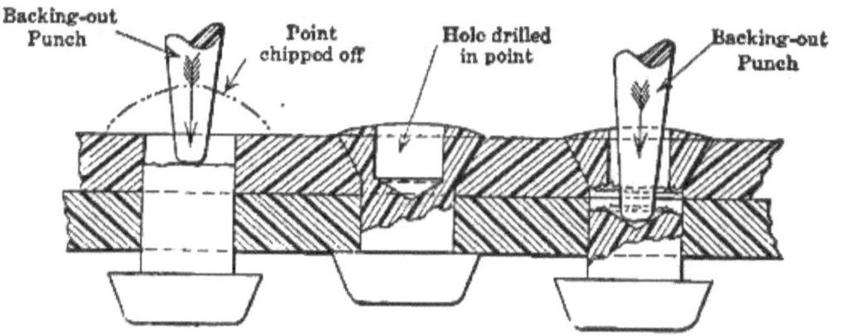

Fig. 95.—Cutting out rivets.

ships or in special cases. The diameters of rivets to be used should be selected to suit the thicknesses of the plates or shapes that they are to connect. The practice varies slightly in merchant and naval work but the following is a rough guide for either class:

10 lb. plate	5/8 in. rivets
15 lb. plate	3/4 in. rivets
20 lb. plate	7/8 in. rivets
25 lb. plate	7/8 in. rivets
30 lb. plate	1 in. rivets
40 lb. plate	1 1/8 in. rivets

Where the two thicknesses to be connected vary slightly the size of rivet should correspond to the greater thickness if strength is more important, and to the lesser thickness if watertightness is more important. If the two thicknesses vary greatly the diameter of the rivet should correspond to the average of the two. The increase in diameter of a punched hole due to subsequent reaming should be about ⅛″.

Hand riveting when done by skilled riveters is superior to machine riveting but is more expensive. There are two riveters in a hand gang, each with a hammer, striking alternate blows on the point of the rivet. One works right handed and the other left handed. Long through rivets such as those through stem, stern post and bar keel are usually driven by hand.

Such rivets are heated only at their points, the main portion of the shank being a driving fit in the hole, since it is practically impossible to drive them tight otherwise, and also since the contraction on cooling of a long rivet might cause it to break. The point must be slightly tapered before it is inserted in the hole on account of its enlargement due to heating. The head may be heated by a torch and well staved up while hot.

Some shipyards that build very large vessels employ portable hydraulic riveting machines. These, on account of the high steady pressure that can thus be applied to the rivets, produce a very high quality of work, and insure the complete filling of the holes by the rivets, a thing that is very difficult to accomplish by hand in the case of large rivets.

Tap rivets are used in places where it is not practicable to drive ordinary or through rivets. A tap rivet is really nothing but a threaded bolt having a head shaped like a rivet head. In Fig. 96 are shown two forms of tap rivets. One has a square head which is cut off after it has been well screwed up. The other has a "*wring-off*" head which is twisted off, by the Stillson wrench with which it is screwed up, as soon as it has drawn the plating up tight and cannot turn further.

Tap rivets generally have to be used to a certain extent for connecting the shell plating to stem, stern frame, and shaft brackets, and in other similar cases where a thin part is connected to a relatively thick one, that does not permit of through riveting. They should not be used in thin plating since the threaded portion is not enough in such cases to give good holding power. The depth of the threaded portion of the hole should be at least equal to the diameter. In places where vibration will occur (as in the case of the propeller boss) a depth of 1½ diameters should be required. The holes must of course be drilled, and both the drilling and tapping must be done very carefully in order that the head may fit the countersunk hole exactly and concentrically in order to draw the two parts tightly together.

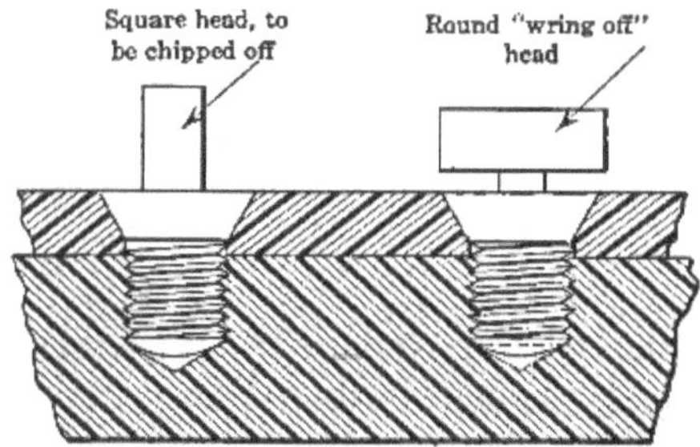

Fig. 96.—Tap rivets.

Sometimes after a tap rivet has been screwed up and trimmed off the head is heated by a torch and driven up by a riveting hammer so as to fill the hole tightly.

Tack rivets are rivets located in the middle portions of doubling plates so as to keep the faying surfaces together at all points.

For oil-tight work an especially high class of riveting is necessary. The rivets are more closely spaced (3 to 3½ diameters between centres, as compared to water-tight spacing which is usually from 3½ to 5 diameters), and should be either drilled or punched small and reamed absolutely fair.

In connecting high tensile steel plates or shapes high tensile rivets should be used. The holes should be drilled.

Before rivets are driven the following points should be looked out for:

1. The holes should be properly located, fair, of the proper size, and reamed if necessary.

2. The plates or shapes to be riveted should be smooth, fair, free from bumps, knuckles, burrs, etc., and securely drawn together with a sufficient number of bolts, well set up. (About every fourth hole for oil-tight work.)

3. There should be no chips, shavings or other foreign matter between the faying surfaces, and these surfaces should be properly coated—usually with red lead, if for a water-tight or nonwater-tight joint, or with a mixture of pine tar and shellac or other suitable coating, if for an oil-tight joint.

4. If for oil-tight work, three-ply work, or work where strength is very important, the holes should be drilled or punched small and reamed fair and normal to the faying surface.

5. All butts and edges should fit tightly together.

6. The joints should be metal-to-metal and filling-in pieces should not be used. (In certain cases, where oil-stops or stop-waters are required, these should be in place.)

During the riveting the following should be looked out for:

1. The rivets to be used should be long enough to allow for the metal required for forming the points.

2. The rivets should be of the proper diameters completely to fill the holes.

3. Care must be used to see that the rivets are not subjected to too great a heat and thus "burned."

4. The rivets must be sufficiently heated (until just before they give off sparks) before being passed to the holder-on.

5. The heads should be well jammed up against the surface by the holder-on before the riveter strikes the points.

6. The hole must be completely filled by driving the hot rivet well home.

7. The excess metal from the point should be cut off while it is a dull red.

8. The point should be properly formed and concentric with the shank of the rivet.

9. In removing bolts care should be taken that the faying surfaces do not spring apart.

10. The plates or shapes around the rivet holes must not be dented or cut during the riveting or chipping off of the excess metal from the points.

11. If a rivet is not driven tightly this should not be concealed by a partial calking of the head or point. All riveting should be carefully and conscientiously done.

In general the effort should be to secure riveted joints that are in strict accordance with the plans, or that will develop the strength and water-tightness that they are intended to develop. All the rivets should be of the proper size, shape, location and tightness, holding the faying surfaces closely together—like the rivets shown in Figs. 21 and 96, and *not* like those in Figs. 89 and 92.

4. CHIPPING, CALKING, ETC.

Chipping consists in cutting or trimming various structural parts by means of a chipping tool or chisel. Like riveting it may be done by hand, or by means of a pneumatic chipping hammer, the action of which is similar to that of the pneumatic riveting hammer. Chipping is often necessary to remove burrs or other unevennesses or to smooth up work in order to obtain a satisfactory fit. Certain large holes are also often cut out by the chippers, especially where neat work is required, and the oxy-acetylene blow-pipe (which is much quicker, but which leaves a rough edge) cannot be used. Chippers are also employed in cutting out defective rivets or other structural parts that have to be removed, although much work of this nature is now done by the oxy-acetylene cutters.

Calking is the process of making joints tight to prevent the leakage of water, oil, air, etc., and, in the case of steel parts, consists in forcing the edges or butts of adjoining members tightly together. It is usually done by the same workmen who do chipping and most frequently is done with pneumatic tools in a manner similar to chipping. Workmen of this trade are often called *chippers and calkers.*

The process of calking is illustrated in Fig. 97. It consists essentially of two operations: first the metal is *split,* or grooved, by means of a splitting tool or *splitter,* and then the portion of the metal between the split and the faying surface or butt is forced tightly against the other

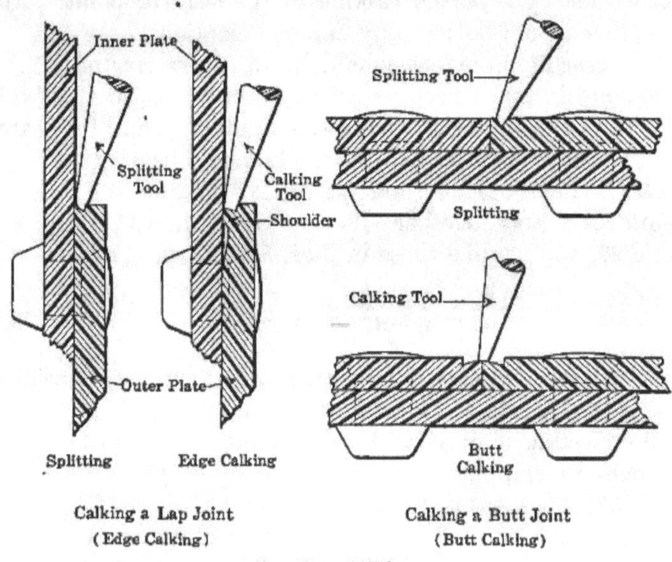

Fig. 97.—Calking.

part, as shown in the sketches, by means of the calking tool, or *finishing* tool. There are two kinds of calking: *edge calking,* and *butt calking,* the nature of each of which will be evident from Fig. 97. In edge calking a slight shoulder is formed, as shown, where the edge of the outer plate overlaps the inner. Countersunk points of rivets should usually be calked, the process being similar to butt calking, but done with a special small ended tool.

Calking is, of course, not done until after the riveting has been completed—the order of the various processes being: (1) bolting up, (2) drilling or reaming (and, if necessary, countersinking), (3) riveting, (4) calking. The edges and butts to be calked should be planed. The row of rivets nearest to the calking edge or butt serves to hold the plates (or parts being riveted) together so that the calking will be effective, the elasticity of the steel resulting in keeping the outer plate pressed tightly against the inner at the calking edge after the calking has been completed. For this reason it will be noted that the line of the rivets, must not be too far from the calking edge, or the calking may open on account of the spring of the plate. On the other hand the rivets must not be too close to the edge of the plate or the strength of the joint will be impaired. Furthermore a certain allowance must be made for corrosion and for repeated calking, as certain seams may have to be re-calked from time to time in the course of repairs and upkeep. Each re-calking reduces the distance between the edge of the plate and the outer row of rivets, which distance may finally become so small as to require renewal of the plate (or shape). For these reasons the distance from the edge of the plate to the line of centres of the nearest row of rivets is usually made equal to 1½ or 1⅝ times the diameter of the rivets. This gives an amount of plate, between rivet and edge, of at least the diameter of the rivet.

Any line of calking must be continuous—that is it must either join another line of calking or form a closed loop. If the calking stops, or is defective at any point, a leak will occur at that point, and the good of the remainder of the calking will be offset by this one point of weakness. The calking of a bulkhead, or other plated surface, forming the boundary of a compartment that is to be filled with water in order to test the calking, should be done on the side away from this compartment in order that such leaks as occur may be located during the testing, and repaired.

Edges and butts that are to be calked should have a tight metal-to-metal fit even before being calked. In some cases, especially around stapling and collars this is very difficult to attain, and in order to secure a proper calking edge the use of metal filling-in pieces or wedges (sometimes called "*dutchmen*") may be permitted. This is, however, a bad practice and should be avoided by insisting upon careful workmanship of the anglesmiths and shipfitters.

Butt calking is more difficult to perform than edge calking since in the latter the inner plate serves as a guide for the calking tool, whereas in the latter there is no guide. In some places calkers have to work "left-handed."

Light plating (less than about $3/16$ inch thick) cannot be calked since there is not sufficient stiffness to the material to hold the calked edges together. Here stopwaters must be used.

Stopwaters (or *oil-stops*) must also be used where an uncalked member passes through a water-, or oil-tight surface, to prevent leakage past the surface through the parts of the uncalked member. *Stopwaters* are pieces of canvas, burlap, felt, etc., soaked in linseed oil and red lead, or coated with some tarry substance or with a mixture of red and white lead. These are placed between the faying surfaces which are drawn tightly against them by the rivets. *Oil-stops* are made of lampwick, canvas, felt, etc., soaked in a mixture of shellac and white or red lead, or of pine tar and shellac, or other suitable substance. Oil-stops are used to prevent the leakage of oil and must therefore be treated with some substance that will not be dissolved by oil. Both oil-stops and stopwaters should be used only where absolutely necessary and they should be freshly coated when the bolting up and riveting is done.

Sometimes leaky joints are made tight by *welding*, which is described in Section 6, below.

In some cases where joints cannot be made tight by calking it is the practice to make use of the *red lead putty gun*. When this has to be done it is always a sign of poor workmanship and its use should be avoided as much as possible. This contrivance is shown in Fig. 98, and consists of a simple hollow cylinder threaded on the inside, which is filled with red lead putty and connected to the part to be gunned as shown in the sketch. As the plug is screwed down the putty is forced into the joint under great pressure and fills all the crevices. When this operation is completed the gun is unscrewed and the hole temporarily made for its attachment is closed by means of a threaded plug, calked in.

Other means of stopping leaks, such as the use of shellac, cement, etc., should not be permitted.

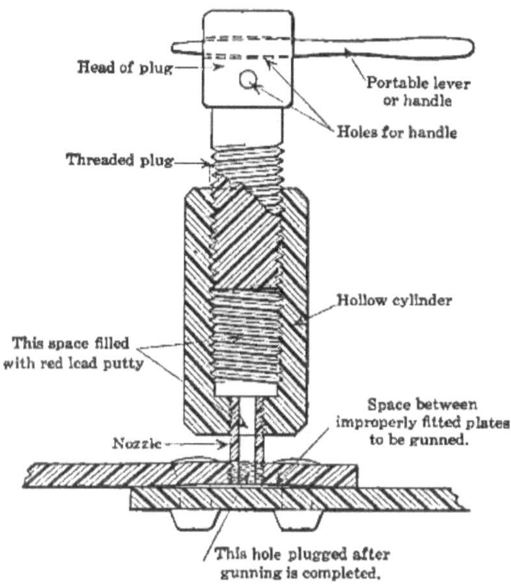

Fig. 98.—Red lead putty gun.

Calking is tested by filling the compartment adjacent, with water (to a head corresponding to that pressure to which the bulkheads or other boundaries may be subjected), or with air under a corresponding pressure—if with water, leaks can be seen directly; if with air, soapy water rubbed along the calking edges will cause bubbles to appear at leaky points. The necessary head for a water-pressure test may be secured by the use of a stand-pipe.

A surface which is properly calked should be equally tight when subjected to pressure from either side, but to be properly calked *all* of the calking should be done on one side, or on both sides.

Calking of oil-tight work is especially important, and should be painstakingly and conscientiously done.

5. PROTECTION AGAINST CORROSION

In order to be able to have a ship carry as great a weight of cargo, fuel, machinery, etc., as possible, the weight of the hull must be kept low. For this reason the thicknesses and sizes of the various structural members should be no greater than is necessary to secure the requisite strength. In almost all ships, however, the thicknesses of the structural plates and shapes are made somewhat greater than necessary for strength alone, in order to provide against the effects of corrosion.

Corrosion is the process of gradually wasting, or being eaten away, of steel or iron. It may occur uniformly, or may be more rapid in certain spots, in which latter case it is sometimes called *pitting*. Steel usually corrodes somewhat faster than iron. Corrosion may be caused either by (1) *rusting* or (2) *galvanic action*, although it is usually due to a combination of both. (Occasionally corrosion is caused by the action of *acids*, as in coal bunkers, or where ashes come in contact with steel.)

Rusting is the oxidation of the iron and steel when in contact with carbon dioxide, or CO_2. Although commonly supposed to be caused by moisture, this is not strictly true, since moisture alone is not sufficient. Iron or steel placed in *pure* water or *pure* air will not rust, but practically speaking water and air both always contain a certain percentage of CO_2, so that some corrosion will always occur unless the surface of the iron or steel is properly protected, by some suitable coating, from the action of CO_2. Corrosion is much more rapid when heat is present.

Galvanic action is the flow of an electric current between two dissimilar metals immersed in an acid and in metallic contact. One of the dissimilar metals will always be electropositive to the other so that current will flow through the acid from the former to the latter, and this flow of current is accompanied by a gradual wasting away of the metal that is electropositive to the other. Sea water, which contains various salts, acts like the acid of an electric cell, and if two different metals, for example copper and steel, are in metallic contact in it, one of them (in this case the steel) will gradually be eaten away. If zinc, which is electropositive to steel be placed near the copper the current will flow from the zinc and it, instead of the steel, will be eaten away. A common method of preventing corrosion of the bottom of a steel ship due to galvanic action is therefore to place slabs or rings of rolled zinc, called *zinc protectors*, or "*zincs*" on the hull at points near propellers, stern tube bushings, gudgeons, valves and other under-water fittings that are made of bronze, brass or similar compositions. Zincs are secured by screws or stud bolts and nuts. Also, where possible, brass or bronze should be insulated or covered with some non-conducting material. (Holes over the heads of brass bolts in composite or sheathed ships are filled in with Portland cement.)

It should be noted that galvanic action, in general, occurs only below the water line, whereas rusting may take place anywhere. As a matter of fact rusting is most rapid along the water-line portion of the shell plating, which is alternately immersed and dried, or is "between wind and water," and also under boilers, where the temperature is high.

Galvanic action may be caused by impurities in steel or by variations in its molecular composition. For example rust which is electronegative to steel will cause the steel to corrode away and the points of rivets which are affected by the hammering given them when driven will corrode away more slowly than the adjacent shell plating.

The various coatings that may be applied to steel to

protect it from the action of CO_2, and consequent rusting, are as follows:

(1) Galvanizing.

(2) Various kinds of paints or varnishes.

(3) Portland cement.

(4) Various bitumastic and other special compositions.

Galvanizing consists in coating the outer surface of steel or iron plates, shapes, castings, or forgings with a thin layer of zinc. This may be done by dipping the parts in a bath of molten zinc or by the electrolytic or deposition process. The former is more generally used. The thin plates of destroyers, where saving of weight and consequent small margin against corrosion are important, are usually galvanized, as are most small iron and steel deck fittings such as rails, stanchions, ventilators, cleats, bitts and other such parts that are exposed to the weather, on all ships.

Paints and varnishes have been discussed in Section 5 of Chapter II. It is very important, in applying any kind of a paint or other coating to iron or steel, that the surface be absolutely clean, dry and free from rust, oil, or any other foreign matter. The object to be achieved is to secure an absolutely perfect adherence of the paint to the pure iron or steel material, and this cannot be accomplished if moisture, grease, rust, etc., are present. If surfaces are properly prepared before paints are applied the results will be much more satisfactory. Owing to the difficulty of so preparing these surfaces, entirely satisfactory painting is seldom secured in practice, but it is very important that it should be, and it should always be aimed at. Rust under paint is often worse than if the surface were left bare, for it thus can go on unobserved.

Portland cement is used to form passage ways for the pumping and drainage of water, oil, etc., and in such places as wash rooms, water closets, etc., being then often used in conjunction with tiling.

Bituminous compositions are used very considerably for the various ballast and trimming tanks, coal bunkers, bilges, etc.

The efficacy of both cement and bitumastics (as of paints) is in great measure dependent upon the care with which the surfaces have been prepared.

During the building of a ship it is especially important that all faying surfaces are properly cleaned and painted before the parts are finally bolted up for riveting. Also the removal of mill scale by pickling or other suitable means and the proper application of a priming coat of red lead on all exposed parts are important.

(In connection with the subject of means taken to prevent corrosion see also Chapter II, Section 5.)

6. WELDING

Although welding up until very recently has been used almost solely for repair work (and for such joining of parts as is incident to the making of forgings) it has during the year 1918 become developed to such an extent that it has actually been used for joining the various parts of a ship together, or, in fact, replacing riveting. A few facts concerning welding should therefore be noted.

Welding, proper, consists in joining, under pressure, two pieces of metal that have been heated to a plastic condition, and as such is exemplified in ordinary blacksmith or forge work. *Soldering* consists in joining metal parts by means of an independent alloy which is *fused*, or melted and applied to them. A solder may thus be called a metallic cement. *Autogenous soldering* is the process of joining two metal parts by the fusing of a portion of some of their *own* material, and the term "welding" is now applied to autogenous soldering as well as to ordinary smith welding.

The heating of the parts to be welded in the case of ordinary pressure welding may be accomplished either in a forge or furnace (in which case the pressure is usually applied by means of hammering) or by the resistance of an alternating electric current (the parts being then joined by being clamped or similarly pressed together). An example of this form of welding is what is known as *spot* welding which gives a finished product somewhat resembling one that has been flush riveted.

The principal forms of fusion welding are by means of the oxy-acetylene or oxy-hydrogen torch, "Thermit" welding and electric welding.

Oxy-acetylene and Oxy-hydrogen Welding.—In this process a blow-pipe or torch, is used to heat the surfaces to be welded to the fusing temperature. Oxygen and some combustible gas (acetylene, hydrogen, coal gas, etc.) are supplied to the blow-pipe from large flasks or cylinders by means of separate lengths of rubber hose fitted with suitable valves for adjusting the pressures. The oxygen and acetylene (or other gas) are combined in a mixing chamber, which is part of the torch, and the mixture is forced out of a small tuyère or nozzle at the end of the torch, and when ignited gives a flame of intense heat. Metal is gradually added to the junction of the parts to be connected and the weld thus built up.

This process of welding is applicable, in general, only to relatively small parts and for the welding of large parts that have been broken, such as stem and stern castings, electric welding is more satisfactory.

A modification of the oxy-acetylene blow-pipe, in the tip of which are several orifices or tuyères, is used for cutting. The central orifice provides passage for a jet of pure oxygen called the cutting oxygen, and the outer orifices carry jets of the mixture of oxygen and combustible gas, called the preheating gas.

Thermit welding consists in placing a mixture of aluminum and oxide of iron (Fe_2O_3) in a crucible over the parts to be welded, which are surrounded by a built up mold of refractory material after having been securely fixed in position. When the mixture is ignited a very high temperature is obtained and the melted iron, being allowed to run into the mold, heats the parts to a fusing temperature and amalgamates with them. This process has some application to the repair of large parts like stem and stern frames, but has not always been entirely satisfactory, electric welding being usually preferred to it.

Electric Welding (Fusion).—It is this form of welding that has recently come into such general use for ship repairing and shipbuilding purposes (as well as many others). The parts to be welded are brought to the highest known temperature by means of an electric current which forms an arc between two electrodes located, one or both, at or near the weld. The work itself usually forms one electrode though this is not always the case. Direct current is used, generally at about 100 volts, and with current varying between 50 and 500 amperes. Sometimes a carbon electrode is used in which case it is the negative one, so as not to carry carbon into the weld. More often the electrode is a slender rod or pencil of a composition similar to the parts to be welded and is carried in an insulated holder which the operator holds in his hand. It then forms the positive electrode and is itself deposited in the weld by the passage of current across the arc, and thus forms and builds up the weld.

Metal electrodes may be bare or coated in various ways. In the *Quasi-Arc* process, used for *ship welding*, the coating is a special composition which melts as the pencil is used up and forms a flux which covers both the end of the pencil and the molten metal deposited in the weld, thus protecting them against oxidation.

In July of 1918 the Technical Committee of Lloyd's Register decided that the application of arc welding to use in connecting the main structural members of ships appeared to be justified, although qualifying this decision by a statement to the effect that "the application should proceed cautiously in view of the unknown factors involved, the most important of which are the need of experience with the details of the welded joints and the necessity for training skilled workmen and supervisors."

Various forms of welds are shown in Fig. 99. The width of the laps varies between 2 inches for 16-lb. plates and 3 inches for 40-lb. plates. The *thickness of throat* of a full weld varies between ½ inch for 40-lb. plates and 0.28 inch for 16-lb. plates. For lighter plates the outer surface of the weld is practically flat and makes an angle of 45° with the plates. The *full weld* is of course the strongest, and next in strength is the *light closing weld.* *Tack welding* is used where strength

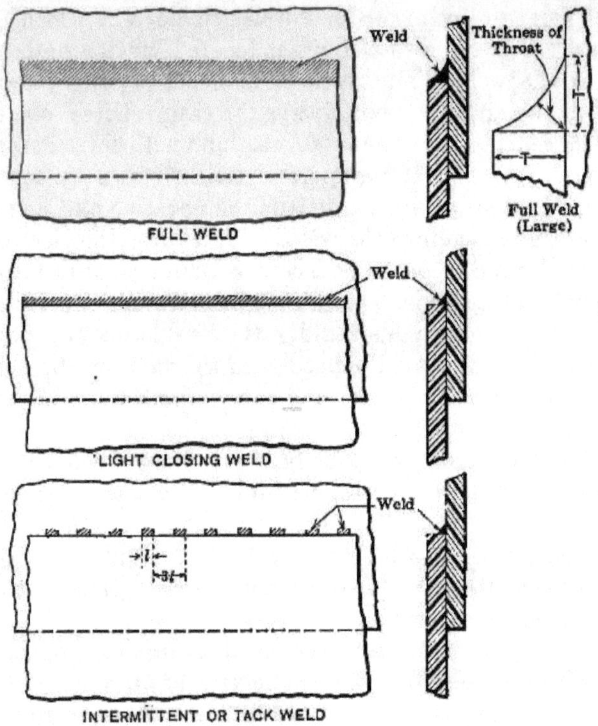

FIG. 99.—Electric quasi-arc welding.

is not so important, only about 33 per cent. of the length of the edge being welded in this case.

For satisfactory work the electrodes must be of uniform quality and the relation of their composition to that of the steel plates and shapes must be such as not unduly to reduce the elasticity of the whole structure.

The size of the electrode and the amperage must be adjusted to vary directly with the thickness of the plate or shape to be welded.

Skilled workmanship is very important and care must be exercised to prevent, in so far as possible, oxidation of the deposited metal. This is accomplished by means of the flux formed by the coating of the electrode.

The faying surfaces must be accurately fitted, and all butt connections must be strapped.

Both edges of plates of butts of shell plating, deck and inner bottom plating, and plating of longitudinals, girders and hatch coamings should be connected by full welds.

A full weld is applied to the outside edge and a light closing weld to the inside edge in the case of edges of shell, deck and inner bottom plating and butts and edges of bulkhead plating.

Frames, beams, stiffeners, etc., have at the heel a light closing weld, and, at the toe, tack welding. All watertight angle bars have continuous welding at each toe with tack welding at the heel.

The great advantages of welded over riveted connections, such as saving in weight, doing away with the need for calking, saving in labor and time, etc., are too evident to require comment, and it only remains to be seen whether this method of building ships will prove as great a step in advance as it now gives promise of doing.

7. LAUNCHING

When the under-water shell plating has been riveted and calked and the progress of construction of the ship otherwise is considered sufficiently advanced she is launched. The amount of work done previous to launching—like the amount done before the laying of the keel—may vary between wide limits. Where a yard is endeavoring to build a number of ships in a short time, so that the keel for one will be laid immediately after another has been launched, it is an advantage to launch as soon as possible. On the other hand, if extreme expedition is not so important, it is usually advantageous to delay the launching until the hull is very nearly, if not entirely completed. When the hull is on the building slip it is practically rigid (and in some yards is entirely roofed over) so that it can be more efficiently worked upon. After the launching the ship may roll or list at times, thus interfering somewhat with work, and furthermore there may be no convenient dock or pier at which to moor her if launched too soon.

In any case before a ship is launched sufficient work must have been done to give her the requisite buoyancy, strength and stability for flotation, and such parts as will be inaccessible for work on them with the vessel in the water must have been completed, unless—as may be sometimes the case for special reasons—she is to be placed in dry-dock prior to final completion. These parts include rudder, struts, propeller shafts and propellers, bilge and docking keels and various other miscellaneous underwater fittings.

During the building of a ship a careful record should be kept of the locations and weights of all parts worked into the hull. With this data calculations are made, shortly before the launching, to determine what will be the exact launching weight of the ship (or her displacement when she takes the water) and what will be the exact location of the centre of gravity of the ship, *as launched*.

Certain calculations are then ordinarily made (unless the ship is a duplicate of another already satisfactorily launched under the same conditions) to see that the ways are properly designed to prevent any accident during launching.

The principal points to be looked out for in designing and preparing the ways are as follows:

1. Bearing pressure on ways.
2. Prevention of tipping.
3. Prevention of premature pivoting.
4. Strength of ways under point about which pivoting will occur.
5. General details of ways, cribbing, shoring, etc., to give sufficient strength at all points.

Some of these points have been discussed in Section 2, of Chapter V, but the following should also be noted here:

Considering the ship at any instant during the launching, after she has moved a certain distance down the ways, the forces acting on her will be, as illustrated in Fig. 100:

1. The weight of the hull, W, acting vertically downward through the centre of gravity;

2. The force of buoyancy, B, acting vertically upward through the centre of buoyancy, or centre of figure of the immersed portion of the ship; and,

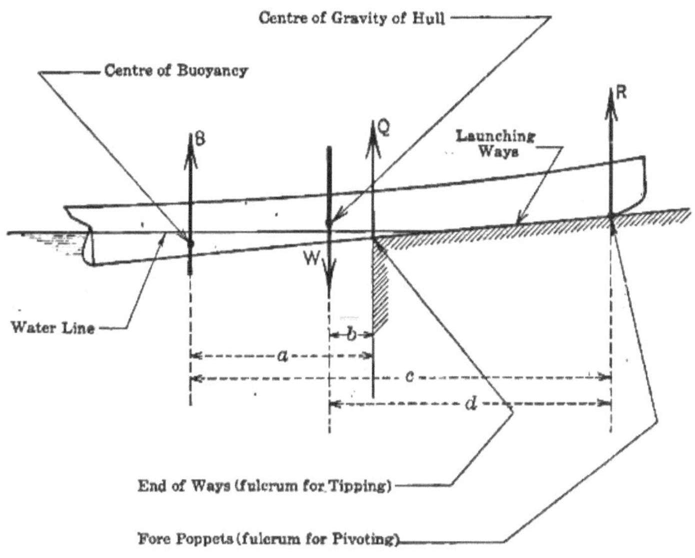

Fig. 100.—Forces acting on ships during launching.

3. The upward vertical support or reaction of the launching ways which may be considered as resolved into two parallel compartments, Q and R, one acting through the end of the ways, and the other through the *fore poppets* which are located at or near the fore foot, and are the points furthest forward at which the hull receives any support from the ways.

Referring again to the figure it will be seen that at the instant represented any one of three things may happen:

(1) If the moment of the force of buoyancy, B about the

end of the ways is equal to the moment of the weight, W about the end of the ways (or if $B \times a = W \times b$), the ship will *tip,* and at that instant all of the support of the ways will be concentrated at their end, or R will vanish, and Q will be equal to $(W-B)$.

(2) If the moment of the force of buoyancy, B about the *fore poppets* is equal to the moment of the weight, W about the fore poppets (or if $B \times c = W \times d$), the ship will *pivot,* and at that instant all of the support of the ways will be concentrated at the fore poppets, or Q will vanish, and R will equal to $(W-B)$.

(3) If neither of the two preceding happens the ship will continue to move down the ways until one or the other of them does happen.

By calculating the values referred to in (1) and (2) for several different assumed positions of the ship, at intervals during her movement down the ways, curves may be plotted, having for abscissas the amounts of travel of the ship from her initial position, and for ordinates the corresponding values of B, $(B \times a)$, $(W \times b)$, $(B \times c)$ and $(W \times d)$. From these curves the point at which tipping will occur (if at all), the point at which pivoting will occur, and the reaction of the ways, in either case, may be found graphically. This information is necessary to check the length of the ways, and their declivity and strength, the necessary strength for the fore poppets, and the point under which the ways should be reinforced to take the pressure of the fore poppets when the stern lifts.

In finding the various values of B, and the locations of the line through which it acts, it is convenient to draw a set of curves called *Bonjean's Curves,* which consist of a curve drawn for each frame station of the lines, the abscissa of which at any height above the base line equals, to scale, the area of that frame station up to that height. These curves, used in conjunction with Simpson's or some similar rule, furnish a convenient means for determining successive values of B and a. (In making these calculations the height of the tide at the hour set for launching must be taken into account.)

The *fore poppets* are portions of the crib work over the forward end of the launching ways, one under each bow of the ship. Ordinarily they consist merely of heavy timbers built up in a manner similar to the rest of the cribbing, but in very large ships they may be made in the form of actual trunnion bearings, constructed of steel and concrete, with trunnions attached to the hull.

The general arrangement of the standing and sliding ways and the cribbing is shown in Fig. 71. Shortly before the date set for launching the standing or *ground* ways are laid in position and properly blocked up, secured and shored to prevent spreading. Their upper surfaces are then coated with some suitable *launching grease* (usually containing tallow, etc.), and the sliding ways, their lower surfaces having been similarly greased, are placed in position and the cribbing which is to transmit the weight of the hull to the sliding ways is installed, *loosely*, wedges between it and the sliding ways being *not* set up.

The above procedure should take place as short a time before the launching as possible in order to prevent the grease from melting or being squeezed out from between the timbers. During this time the hull is supported by the keel blocks and by shores and blocks kept clear of the launching ways.

On the day of the launching a carefully prepared schedule of operations is carried out and all arrangements must be made in advance so that there will be no hitch, and so that the launching will take place with the desired height of tide. A large gang of men must be detailed for the wedging up and other tasks incident to the launching and all must know exactly what to do and at whose order it is to be done. Absolute unity of action is necessary in order to prevent mishaps. The wedging up is done at the word of the official in charge and should be so timed as to have the vessel borne by the ways for *as short an interval as possible* before the launching. This interval must necessarily be the time necessary for *splitting* out or otherwise removing the keel blocks, and removing shores, blocking and other material that would obstruct the launching.

When the word to *wedge-up* is given all the workmen assigned to that duty quickly drive home the wedges so that the weight of the hull is transferred, as much as possible, from the keel blocks and shores to the cribbing and launching ways. The removal of the keel blocks and shores, etc. (which follows the wedging up as rapidly as possible) completes this transfer, so that the entire weight is finally taken by the launching ways as shown in Fig. 71. (To facilitate quick removal of the keel blocks they are sometimes made in the form of metal boxes containing sand, and so constructed that the sand may be allowed to run out and the load thus be removed.)

The launching is accomplished by various forms of releasing devices or triggers, some quite elaborate (such as hydraulic cylinders and pistons) and others very simple (such as two pieces of timber retaining the sliding ways which are sawed off simultaneously.)

Before the launching the ship must be properly shored internally to take any stresses that are anticipated and her stability must be investigated, suitable ballast being added if there is any doubt.

As the ship slides down the ways considerable momentum may be acquired and it is sometimes necessary to provide means for checking her sternway after she strikes the water. Means for doing this vary with the conditions, a common one being to have heavy cables stopped to the ship at intervals, the stops to be broken by the momentum which is thus gradually destroyed. Tugs then transfer the ship other fitting out pier.

The launching of the ship, which is an important event in her production is almost always made the occasion for a suitable ceremony and celebration. As the ship starts to move the lady chosen as her sponsor breaks a bottle of champagne over the bow and christens the ship. For this purpose a large platform is temporarily built up just forward of the bow, supported by heavy scaffolding, and surrounded by a stout railing. On this platform are stationed the sponsor and the launching party. After the ship is in the water a luncheon and celebration is usually given.

8. FITTING OUT

The work done on a ship after she has been launched and before she is finally completed and delivered to the owner consists, in general, in the completion of the structural work of the hull that was not accomplished prior to launching, and the installation of various piping, ventilation, and electrical systems, joiner work, deck fittings, auxiliary machinery, engines and boilers (if not installed before the launching), smoke stacks, ventilators, spars, rigging, bridges, deck houses, etc., and a great variety of other miscellaneous parts and trimmings.

In addition to this, numerous tests must be made to see that everything is in satisfactory working order, the various articles of equipment must be supplied, and the hull cleaned and freed of rubbish and other foreign matter, and all necessary painting done.

The greater portion of this work covers the operations of such trades as those of the plumbers, pipe fitters, joiners, shipwrights, riggers, electricians, machinists, painters, etc., and a full discussion of the various details involved would occupy too much space to be undertaken here. It is really *fitting out*, rather than *building*, a ship; and a large part of it is very similar to work done by the same trades on shore. Certain important points that apply to shipbuilding in particular should, however, be noted.

As is natural, during the latter stages in the construction of a ship, when the time for her delivery to the owners is drawing near, it is important to check up and see if all of the requirements of ships (see Chapter I) have been complied with.

The *buoyancy* is, of course, demonstrated, in general,

by the fact that the vessel floats after launching and that she has been built in accordance with the plans. Any leaks that develop in the shell plating after launching will, of course, be remedied in so far as possible when noted, and if necessary the vessel will be dry-docked and the leaks calked.

There is also to be considered, in connection with the subject of buoyancy, however, the question of *integrity of water-tight subdivision.* A portion of this has probably been demonstrated before the launching by tests of bulkheads and compartments which have been subjected to a sufficient head of water. During the last stages of construction it is very important to see that this integrity is not destroyed by the *cutting of holes* in bulkheads and decks.

It is practically impossible to avoid having some holes in water-tight bulkheads and decks, both for doors, manholes, etc., and for piping and wiring. The former must be of the water-tight type, and wherever a water-tight plated surface is pierced by a pipe or conduit the construction must be so arranged as to prevent the passage of water around that pipe or conduit. This is accomplished by the use of *flanges* or *stuffing boxes,* which must be carefully made and installed and properly packed with suitable gaskets or packing, as the case may be. Means for the attachment of brackets, castings, hangers, etc., to water-tight members must be such as not to destroy or impair their water-tightness. Constant and conscientious supervision is necessary to attain these results.

Stability depends largely upon the correct execution of design, and one very important check on this is the determination of the actual transverse metacentric height of the ship by means of an *inclining experiment,* which should, if possible, be conducted as the ship is nearing completion.

This consists in heeling the ship over to various small inclinations by means of moving heavy weights across the decks and recording the amount of weight moved, the thwartship distance through which it is moved, and the angle of heel, in each case. The displacement is also carefully noted.

The operation is illustrated in Fig. 101, the angle of heel, θ, being measured by means of a plumb bob and graduated scale, as shown. The inclination, θ is in this case produced by the movement of the weight, w a distance, l, transversely. Let W be the total displacement of the ship, and let G' and B' (which must be in the same vertical line)

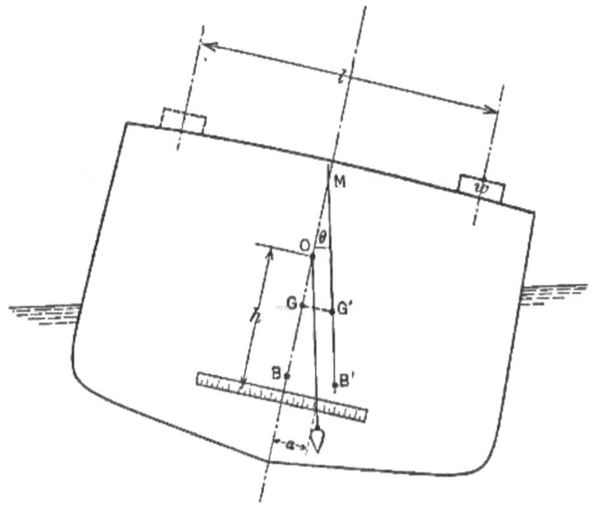

Fig. 101.—Inclining experiment.

be the new centres of gravity and buoyancy. Then, by taking moments,

$$W \times \overline{GG'} = w \times l$$

and

$$GM = \frac{GG'}{\tan\theta} = \frac{w \times l}{W \tan\theta}$$

$$\text{but } \tan\theta = \frac{a}{h} \text{ (which has been recorded)}$$

$$\therefore GM = \frac{w \times l \times h}{a \times W}$$

A number of different "check" readings are taken and if

these all agree the calculated value of the metacentric height, GM, may be assumed to be fairly accurate. During the experiment the ship must be entirely free from the action of any external force or forces, and there must be no "loose" weights on board—such as water in tanks not completely filled.

The longitudinal metacentric height may be found similarly and this is usually done in the case of the submerged inclining experiment of a submarine. (In this connection it should be noted that the metacentre of a submerged body coincides with the centre of buoyancy.)

The *propulsion* of the ship is checked, usually, by *dock trials*, and a *trial trip*, before being accepted by the owners. Similarly the *steering* gear should be very thoroughly tried out before delivery of the vessel. These are, of course, actual operating tests.

Strength must, of course, depend largely upon good workmanship and a strict compliance with the plans and specifications. During the latter stages of construction it is important to see that the strength is not impaired by holes or notches, etc. cut in various structural members, during the installation of piping systems and other fittings, etc. This also requires careful and conscientious supervision. Holes drilled through beams should be near the centre or in the upper half of the web and should be in only one horizontal row. The diameter of such holes should not be over about 20% of the depth of the beam and holes should not be too close together. Whenever alterations are made in the design of a ship during the building great care should be used to see that the strength is not thereby impaired. As has been said before, however, honest, skillful, conscientious workmanship, at all times, is of fundamental importance in securing the necessary strength in a ship.

Endurance is demonstrated by the fuel consumption on the trial trip and a checking up or *calibration* of the bunkers. This consists in taking accurate measurements of coal bunkers or fuel oil tanks and calculating their capacities.

For oil tanks it is done by filling them with water from accurately graduated measuring tanks. The data thus obtained is furnished to the owners with the ship.

The *utility* of the ship depends upon a compliance with the plans and specifications. During the latter stages of construction care should be exercised to see that the multitudinous details, all of which make for utility, are looked out for. This applies also to living spaces and accommodations and similar considerations affecting the health and comfort of the crew and officers.

Throughout the various processes of ship production the objects to be attained should always be kept in mind, for it is only by knowing what is wanted that it can ever be completely obtained. Each and every man connected with the production of ships should realize his responsibilities, and endeavor conscientiously to see that *his* part of the job is properly done.

INDEX.

A

Aft, 34
After peak tank, 45
After perpendicular, 36
Afterbody, 35
Air holes, 90
American Bureau of Shipping, 63
Amidships, 34
Anchor windlass, 47
Anchors, 47
Angle bar, 64
in frames, 79
of maximum stability, 9
of vanishing stability, 9
Anglesmiths, 171
Arc welding, 229
Area of wetted surface, 143
Armored cruisers, 55
Arrangement of a ship, 41
Asbestos used on ships, 72
Athwartships, 2, 34
Atwood's formula, 139
Autogenous soldering, 227
Auxiliary vessels, 57
Average secant, 144

B

Balanced rudders, 21, 95
Ballast, 47
Bar keels, 77
Base line, 31, 35
Battens, 182
Battle cruisers, 55
Battleships, 54
Beam knee, 114
Beam mold, 192
of ship, 2
Beams, deck, 114
Beams, fabrication, 192
Belt frames, 82
Bending frames, 168
moment, curve of, 27
slabs, 162
Bevel boards, 185, 188
of a frame, 79, 83
Beveling bars, 191
frames, 168
Bibliography of naval architecture, 145
Bilge, 39
diagonal, 32
keels, 128, 129
keelsons, 83
stringers, 85
Bilges, 12
Bitts, 127
Bituminous compositions, 73, 226
Block coefficient of fineness, 40, 41
Blow pipe, oxy-acetylene, 167
used in welding, 228
Boat deck, 48
Boatbuilders, 178
Body plan, 32
post, 94
Boiler room, 46
Boilers, supporting, 125
Bolsters, 127
Bolters-up, 175
Bolting up ship frames, 206
Bonjean's curves, 234
Bosom piece, 173
Boss, 39
Bossed frames, 101
plates, 107
Bottom, 37
double, 47, 85
inner, 47, 106
Bounding bars, 122

Bounding, fabrication, 192
of deck plating, 116
Bow, 12, 39
and buttock lines, 32
Bracket floors, 89
Brackets, 83, 114, 173
fabrication, 192
shaft, 103
Brass in ship construction, 70
Breadth, molded, 36
Breast hooks, 27, 90
Bridge, 48
British Corporation, 63
Broadside launching, 157
Bronze in ship construction, 70
Building ships, 195–241
bolting up, 204
calking, 219
chipping, 219
drilling, 207
erection, 195
fitting out, 237
launching, 231
protection against corrosion, 224
reaming, 205
riveting, 209
testing, 237
welding, 227
slip, 147, 148
Buildings in shipyards, 159
Bulb angles, 65
Bulkhead liners, 112
plating, fabrication, 187
stiffeners, 44, 122
fabrication, 192
Bulkheads, 44, 121
water-tight, 124
Bulwarks, 39, 128
Buoyancy, 3, 233, 237
calculation of, 137
centre of, 4
curve of, 26
Bureau Veritas, 63
Butt-strap, 173
Buttock lines, 32
Button-head rivet, 67
points, 68
Butts, 107
calking, 220

C

Calculations in ship design, methods, 136, 146
of strength, 25
Calibration of bunkers, 240
Calkers, 176, 177
Calking, 219
testing, 223
Camber, 37
Cant frames, 90
Canvas, used in ships, 72, 120
Cargo booms, 48, 49
hatches, 45
vessels, 58
Carlings, 114
Carrying capacity, 62
Castings, steel, 64
Cellular double bottom, 86
Cements, 72–74
Centre keelson, 78
lines, 2
of buoyancy, 4
shafts, 101
vertical keel, 78
Chain cables, 47
locker, 47
pipes, 47, 127
Chamfering, 110
Channels, steel, 65
Chart house, 48
Chippers, 176
Chipping, 219
Chocks, 127
Classification societies, 62
Cleats, 127
Clinker strakes, 112
system of plating, 107
Clips, 83, 173
Coal bunkers, 46
Coamings, 45, 114
Coefficients of form, 39
Cofferdams, 129
Collision bulkhead, 45
Comparison, Froude's law of, 19
Composite ships, 51
Concrete ships, 52, 53
Coned neck rivet, 68
Construction of ships, preliminary steps, 180–194

Construction of ships, transverse and longitudinal framing, 78
See also Building ships.
Copper in ship construction, 70
Coppersmiths, 177
Cork, 72
Correction to displacement, 142
Corresponding speeds of ships, 18
Corrosion, protection against, 224
Cotton, 72
Counter, 39, 98, 99
Countersinking rivet holes, 166
Countersunk head rivet, 67
points, 68
Cranes in shipyards, 158
Crew's quarters, 48
Cribbing of ways, 235
Cross curves of stability, 140
sections, 32
Crown, 37
Cruiser sterns, 94
Cruisers, 55
Curve of bending moment, 27
of buoyancy, 26
of dynamical stability, 140
of load, 27
of shearing force, 27
of statical stability, 140
of weight, 26

D

Dead flat, 31
rise, 37
weight, carrying capacity, 62
wood, 39
Deck beams, 23, 114
fabrication, 192
girders, 119
Deck plating, 114, 115
fabrication, 187
wood over, 117
Decks, 44, 114
water tight, 120
Deep frames, 82
Definitions of terms, 2
terms referring to form, 34, 37
Denny's formula for wetted surface, 143
Depth, molded, 36
Depth of ship, defined, 2
Derrick posts, 48
Design of ships, 130–146
Designers in shipyards, 170
Designing the ways, 232
Destroyers, 56
Diagonals, 32
Dimensions, molded, 36
of ships, defined, 1
Directions on a ship, 34
Dished plates, 107
Displacement, 16, 61
calculation of, 137
correction to, 142
Dock trials, 240
Docking keel, 128
Dolly-bar, 211
Double bottom, 47, 85
Draft of a ship, 2, 36
Draftsmen in shipyards, 170
Drag, 36
Drainage wells, 90, 129
Drift pin, 175
Drillers, 175
Drilling machine, pneumatic, 207
rivet holes, 166
ship frames, 207
Drop-forgers, 177
strakes, 111
Dry-docking, 52
Dutchmen, 222

E

Edge calking, 220
Edges of plating, 107
Electric welding, 229
Electricians, 178
Electrodes, 229
Enamel, 74
Endurance of ships, 28
testing, 240
Engine foundations, 125
room, 46
Entrance, 37
Equilibrium defined, 7
Erection of ship frames, 195
Erectors, 175
Expansion trunks, 49
Extreme draft, 36

F

Fabricating and erecting shops, 162
Fairing the lines, 34
Faying surface, 68, 165, 187
Fenders, 128
Fitters-up, 173
Fitting out a ship, 237
Flanges, 238
 transverse and longitudinal, in a frame, 79
Flanging plates, 166, 187
Flare, 37
Flat plate keel, 78
Flitches, 71
Floating bodies, law of, 4, 5
Floor plates, 81
 fabrication, 191
Floors, bracket, 89
 solid, 89
Flush system plating, 108
Fore, 34
Fore-body, 35
Fore foot, 39
 poppets, 233–235
Forgers, 177
Forging steel, 167
Forgings, steel, 63
Form of ships, 31
 coefficients of, 39
 definition of terms, 37
Formula, Atwood's, 139
Formulæ for calculations of weight, etc., 136–146
 for wetted surface, 143
Forward, 34
 peak tank, 45
 perpendicular, 36
Fouling, means of preventing, 72
Foundations, engine, 125
Frame benders, 171
 bending and beveling, 168
 spacing, 78
Frames, bossed, 101
 erecting, 195
 fabrication, 188
 spectacle, 103
Framing of ships, 23, 41, 42, 77
 Isherwood system, 58, 90
 longitudinal system, 90
Framing of ships, transverse system, 77, 90
Freeboard, 2, 37
Froude, William, 18
Froude's law of comparison, 19
Full load displacement tonnage, 62
Furnaced plates, 106, 168, 187
Furnacemen, 171
Furnaces in shipyards, 162
Fusion, 229

G

Galley, 48
Galvanic action on steel, 224
Galvanizers, 177
Galvanizing, 226
Garboard strake, 107
Gasket, 120
Girder strength, 24
Girders, 23
 deck, 120
Girthing frames, 181
Greasing ways, 235
Gross tonnage, 61
Gudgeons, 21, 94, 97
Gunboats, 56

H

Half-breadth plan, 32
Half-breadths, 31
Hammered points of rivets, 68
Hand riveting, 216
Harpins, 203
Hawse pipes, 47, 127
Heart of timber, 71
Heaters, 175, 176
Height, metacentric, 7, 8, 137, 240
Heights, 31
Helm, 20
Hogging, 25
Holders-on, 175, 176
Holding-on, 211
Holds, 45
Hull, 22, 42
 machinists, 177
 material, fabrication of, 185
Hydraulic riveting, 168, 216

I

I-beam, 66
Inboard, 34
profile plan, 135
Inclining experiment, 238
Initial stability, 7
Inner bottom, 47, 106
plating, 113
fabrication, 187
Intercostal plates, 84
Interior arrangement of ships, 42
Iron for ship construction, 69
ships, 51
Isherwood system of framing, 58, 90

J

Joggling, 109, 167
Joiner shop, 163
Joiners, 177

K

Keel line, 35
plates, fabrication, 191
Keels, 23, 42, 77
bilge, 128, 129
docking, 128
laying, 195
Keelsons, 23, 83
Kirk's analysis, 143
Knees, 71
beam, 114
Knuckle, 39

L

Laborers, 175
Landing edges, 107, 135
Lap-joint, 174
Launching ships, 231
broadside, 157
greasing ways, 235
plotting curves for positions of ship, 234
wedging up, 235, 236
forces acting on ship during, 233
Launching ways, 147, 152
designing, 232
Law of comparison, Froude's, 18
of floating bodies, 4, 5
Layers-out, 171
Laying of the keel, 195
-out shed, 162
Layout of shipyard, 157
Lead for ship construction, 71
Length between perpendiculars, 36
over all, 36
Lightening holes, 83, 173
Limber holes, 83, 90
Liners, bulkhead, 112
in a frame, 83
in shell plating, 107, 174
passenger, 57
Lines, fairing, 34
of ships, 31, 32
reference, 35
Linoleum, 72
on decks, 116, 120
Liverpool rivet point, 68
Lloyd's Register, 62, 229
Load, curve of, 27
draft, 36
water line, 32, 35
coefficient, 40
Local strength, 27
Loft, mold, 161
Loftsmen, 171
Longitudinal bulkheads, 45, 122
metacentric height, 240
prismatic coefficient, 40
strength, 24, 25
system of framing, 77, 90
Longitudinals, 23, 86
fabrication, 192
Lugs, 83

M

Machine riveting, 207, 216
tools in shipyards, 163
Machinists, hull, 177
Main deck, 44
Management of a shipyard, 178
Manganese bronze in ship construction, 70
Manholes, punching, 167
Margin planks, 117
plate, 87, 113
Masons, 178

Masts, 48
Materials for ship construction, 63
weights, 76
ordering, 180
Mean draft, 36
Melters, 178
Merchant ships, 57
rudders, 98
Metacentre, 7
Metacentric height, 7, 8
calculations, 137
longitudinal, 240
Method of comparison, to determine power required, 14
Midship section, 31, 36
coefficient, 40
plan, 134
Mild steel, 69
Mining vessels, 56
Modified girths, 143
Mold loft, 161
offsets, 182
Molded dimensions, 36
Molders, 178
Molds, making, 182
Moment to change trim, 141
Moon bars, 168, 190

N

Naval architecture, bibliography, 145
brass, in ship construction, 70
Net tonnage, 61
Neutral equilibrium, 7

O

Oakum, 72
Offsets, 182
Oil stops, 205, 222
Oil-tight riveting, 217
Ordering material for ships, 180
Outboard, 34
profile plan, 135
Oxter plates, 107
Oxy-acetylene blow pipe, 167
welding, 228
Oxy-hydrogen welding, 228

P

Painters, 178
Paints, anti-corrosive, 226
for smoke stacks, 75
for steel ships, 72
Pan-head rivets, 67
Panting, 27
stringers, 27, 90
Passenger vessels, 57
Passers, 175
Passing strakes, 111
Pattern makers, 178
Peak tanks, 45
Personnel of a shipyard, 169
Phosphor bronze, in ship construction, 70
Pickling plates, 187
Piling in shipyards, 148
Pillars, between decks, 118
Pintles, 21, 94, 96
Pipe fitters, 177
Pipe stanchion, 118
Pipes, chain, 127
hawse, 47, 127
Pitting of steel, 224
Pivoting of ship in launching, 155, 234
Plate and angle shop, 162
bending, 163
margin, 113
planer, 165
racks in shipyards, 161
rider, 113
Plates, fabrication of, 186-192
floor, 81, 191
furnaced, 168
intercostal, 84
ram, 90
steel, 64
Planes, reference, 35
Planing plates, 165
Planking, deck, 114, 115
Plans, for ship design, 32, 134
Plating, deck, 114, 115
fabrication, 186
of bulkheads, 122
shell, 42, 106
Plumbers, 177
Pneumatic drilling machine, 207

Port side, 20, 35
Portland cement used in steel ships, 75, 226
Power required for propulsion of ship, 14
Prismatic coefficient, 40
Profile plan, 32, 135
Propeller post, 39, 94
screw, 14
struts, 100
Propulsion of ships, 11
means of, 13
testing, 240
Protected cruisers, 55
Punching and shearing shop, 162
holes, 165, 186
manholes, 167
Putty gun, red lead, 222

Q

Quarter, 39
Quasi-arc process of welding, 229
Rabbetting, 92

R

Radio room, 48
Rail, 39, 128
Ram plates, 27, 90
Range of stability, 9
Rating of ships, 63
Ratio of beam to draft, 40, 41
of length to beam, 40, 41
Reamers, 175
Reaming rivet holes, 166
ship frames, 205
Red lead putty gun, 222
Reference lines, and planes, 35
Register of shipping, Lloyd's, 62, 229
Reinforced concrete ships, 53
Requirements of ships, 2-30
buoyancy, 3
endurance, 28
propulsion, 11
stability, 5
steering, 20
strength, 22
testing for, 237
utility, 29
Residual resistance, 19
Resistance of a ship, 15
Reverse frames, 80
fabrication, 188
Ribbands, 202
Rider plate, 113
Riggers, 175, 177
Righting arm, 7, 8
Rise of bottom or floor, 37
Rivet holes, punching, 165, 186
size, 215
Rivet-passers, 176
Riveters, 175
Riveting, 209
hand, 216
hydraulic, 168, 216
machine, 206, 207
special instructions, 218
speed, 214
Rivets, 66
diameters, 215
tack, 217
tap, 216
Rolling chocks, 129
of plates, 187
Rolls, plate bending, 164
Rope, 72
Round up, 37
Rubber, 72
Rudder post, 21, 39, 94
Rudders, 20, 95
balanced, 21
Run, 37
Rusting of steel, 224

S

Saddles, 125
Sagging, 25
Sawing steel, 166
Scantlings, 66
Scarph, 91
Scouts, 56
Screw propellers, 14
vessels, 100
Scrieve board, 183
Seam straps, 108
Seams, 107
Second deck, 44
Set iron, 168

Shaft bracket, 103
tubes, 100
tunnels, 46
Shafts, wing, 101, 102
Shakes, in wood, 71
Shapes, steel, 64
Shearing force, curve of, 27
plates, etc., 165
Sheathed ships, 52
Sheer, 37
plan, 32
strake, 107
Sheet metal workers, 177
Sheets, steel, 64
Shell expansion plan, 134
Shell plating, 42, 106
fabrication of, 186
inner bottom, 113
seam systems, 107
thickness at ends, 112
Shellac for ships, 75
Shelter deck, 44
Shift of butts, 111
Shipfitters, 172
Ships, building, 195–241
buoyancy, 3
description, general, 31
design, 130–146
dimensions defined, 1
endurance, 28
interior arrangement, 42
law of floating bodies, 4, 5
plans, 32
propulsion, 11
requirements, 2
resistance of, 15
similar, defined, 18
speed of, 60
stability, 5
steering, 20
strength, 22
structural members, 77
tonnage of, 61
types of, 50
Shipsmiths, 177
Shipwright shop, 163
Shipwrights, 50, 177
Shipyards, 147–179
building slip, 147, 148
buildings necessary, 159
Shipyards equipment, 169
launching ways, 147, 152
layout, 157
machine tools, 163
management, 178
on Great Lakes, 157
personnel, 169
piling, 148
site, 147
steel fabricating processes, 163
transporting materials, 158
traveling cranes, 158
Shops, in shipyards, 162
Sight edges, 107
Sides, 39
Similar ships defined, 18
Simpson's rules, 144, 145, 234
Single plate rudder, 96
Slabs, bending, 162
Smith shop, 162
Smoke stack paints, 75
Snugs, 96
Soldering, 227
Solid floors, 89
Solution, to cover steel in ships, 73
Spardeck, 44
Spectacle frames, 103
Speed of production of steel ships, 214
of ships, 60
Speeds, corresponding, 18
Spot welding, 227
Squeezer, 168
Stability, 5
angle of maximum, 9
of vanishing, 9
calculations, 138
cross curves of, 140
dynamical, 140
inclining experiment, 238
initial, 7
range of, 9
statical, 140
Stable equilibrium, 7
Stanchions, between decks, 118
Staples, 117
Starboard, 20, 35
Statical stability, 140
Stealers, 111

Steel for ships, 63
processes of fabrication, 163
protection against corrosion, 224
quality, 69
Steel frames, 23
Steel ships, 52
anti-fouling process, 72
paints for, 72
speed of production, 214
Steering, 20
engine room, 47
Stem, 37, 42, 91
Stern defined, 12
post, or frame, 37, 42, 91, 93
tube, 100, 104
Stiffeners, bulkhead, 44, 122
Stopwaters, 205, 222
Storerooms, 48
Strains in ships, 25
Strakes, 106
clinker, 112
drop, 111
passing, 111
Stream lines, 12
Strength of ships, 22
curves for calculations of, 26
girder, 24
local, 27
longitudinal, 24, 25
Stringers, 23, 83, 84
panting, 90
Structural members of ships, 77
Struts, 103
propeller, 100
Stuffing box, rudder head, 99
Submarine Boat Corporation, 159
Submarines, 56
Sunken and raised system of plating, 107, 109
Superdreadnoughts, 54
Surface, molded, 36

T

T-bar, 66
T-bulb, 66
Tack rivets, 217
welding, 230
Tank top, 47
Tankers, 58
Tanks, double bottom, 47
peak, 45
Tap rivets, 216
Taylor's formula for wetted surface, 143
Templates, 161, 183, 193
Testers, 176
Testing ships, 237
Thermit welding, 228
Tiller, 20
Tipping of ship during launching, 155, 234
Tonnage of ships, 61
Tons per inch immersion, 141
Torpedo craft, 56
Tramp steamers, 58
Transportation of materials in shipyards, 158
Transverse bulkheads, 44, 122, 124
metacentre, 7
system of framing, 77, 90
Trapezoidal rule, 144, 145
Traveling cranes in shipyards, 158
Trim, 36
Trimming ship, 45
Trunk, 46
Tubes, stern, 100
Tugs, 59
Tumble home, 37
Tween decks, 44
Types of ships, 50

U

Unstable equilibrium, 7
Upper deck, 44
Uptake, 46
Utility, 29

V

Varnishers, 178
Varnishes, anti-corrosive, 75, 226
Ventilating ducts, 49
Vertical prismatic coefficient, 40

W

Wane, 71
Warships, 53, 54
construction, 88
rudders, 97
stem, 91, 93
stern post, 94
Water line, 2
lines, 32
Water-tight bulkheads, 124
decks, 120
-tightness, testing, 238
Ways, launching, 147, 152
designing, 232
greasing, 235
Weather deck, 44
Web frames, 82
Wedging up ship on ways, 235, 236
Weight, calculating for launching ship, 234
calculation in ship design, 136
curve of, 26
groups, in ship design, 133
of materials for ship construction, 76
Welding steel, 167, 227
Welding, arc, 229
electric, 229
oxy-acetylene and oxy-hydrogen, 228
tack, 230
thermit, 228
Welds, forms of, 229
Wetted surface, area of, 143
Winches, 49
Wing propellers, 101
shafts, 101, 102
Wood calkers, 177
for deck plating, 117
in ship construction, 71
Wooden ships, 50
Workmen in a shipyard, 169
Wring-off head on rivets, 216

Y

Yoke, 100

Z

Z-bars, 65
Zinc in ship construction, 70
protectors, 225

THIS BOOK IS DUE ON THE LAST DATE STAMPED BELOW

AN INITIAL FINE OF 25 CENTS

WILL BE ASSESSED FOR FAILURE TO RETURN THIS BOOK ON THE DATE DUE. THE PENALTY WILL INCREASE TO 50 CENTS ON THE FOURTH DAY AND TO $1.00 ON THE SEVENTH DAY OVERDUE.

Zeitfracht Medien GmbH
Ferdinand-Jühlke-Straße 7
99095 Erfurt, Deutschland
produktsicherheit@kolibri360.de